THE GIRL WHO DARED TO RISE

THE GIRL WHO DARED TO THINK 4

BELLA FORREST

Copyright © 2017 by Bella Forrest

Nightlight Press

All rights reserved.

No part of this book may be reproduced in any form or by any electronic or mechanical means, including information storage and retrieval systems, without written permission from the author, except for the use of brief quotations in a book review.

1

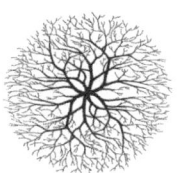

Before the Tower, humanity believed in saviors. Singular individuals who were so charismatic, so persuasive, so hopeful, that those around them became infected by their cause, choosing to see the world as it *could* be, rather than as it was. They'd devote themselves to this person and their newfound cause, risking their lives in the hopes that their self-sacrifice would further the dream of a better world. In turn, their saviors would care for them, support them, and sometimes, if their hearts were true, sacrifice their own lives for them.

Sometimes their causes would bear fruit and bring about a change so great and profound that it sent shockwaves rippling through history. Sometimes the changes were subtler. But never were these changes, these causes, insignificant. And neither were the champions who took up the fight on their behalf.

Before the Tower, humans put faith in those they believed had their best interest at heart. Now, they did the same—only they turned to a being whose longevity was fundamentally tied to the Tower itself: Scipio, the Master AI, created to be our savior, protector, and champion, all rolled into one. He was better than human; he was eternal. He was programmed to protect the people inside the Tower... and they trusted him implicitly.

Because none of them knew the truth: that he was dying.

Then again, it seemed like a lot of people were. First Cali and Roark, then six men who had been in pursuit of Tian, the youngest member of our group, and now Ambrose Klein, the man my friends and I had been blackmailed into protecting. I was surrounded by death, and I had actually been *arrested* for the latest one.

Ambrose. *Oh God.* Ambrose.

My brain fumbled for meaning in the chaos, but all it could settle on was pointing out each of my flaws, and highlighting them in vivid technicolor. The timeline neatly laid out in my mind led directly to me: Quess's call about Tian being chased, followed by my decision not to tell Maddox, for fear this was a trap to lure Ambrose out.

How careless I had been. How blind.

He hadn't been any safer in his own home than he had been inside the Tourney, and I had left both him and Maddox defenseless in order to go after Tian. My stomach churned violently, bile rising to the back of my throat.

And my problems ran much deeper than just the guilt that was eating at me. Keeping Ambrose alive had been part of the deal I had made with Lacey Green, Engineer of the Mechanics Department—or Cogs, as we called them. She and Praetor Strum, the head of Water Treatment, had initially approached me to assassinate Devon Alexander... and then helped me and my friends beat the charges for doing so by manipulating Scipio's memories to corroborate my story.

But there had been a catch. In exchange, Lacey had wanted me to keep her cousin alive so that he could become the next Champion of the Knights. If I did as she asked, she said she would continue to keep us safe. But if I failed...

I *had* failed, and now Lacey could make good on her threat, and turn over (false) evidence that showed that we had tampered with Scipio in order to get away with murder. As soon as she found out that Ambrose was dead, she'd start hunting us down one by one. Hell, she already had access to Zoe and Eric, who were in the condensation room with her at this very moment, trying to track down whatever had killed those men and taken Tian!

You should've called Quess to warn them, an angry voice hissed inside of me. Another failure.

I dragged my gaze over to Leo, who was marching next to me, also cuffed. It was hard looking at him without my heart aching, but that was understandable—considering he was actually an AI that had been implanted into the body of my boyfriend, Grey. Grey had been injured during our fight with Devon, his net overloaded by an electronic charge, his cerebral cortex burnt. The damage had been catastrophic. Grey had been unmoved by my hoarse cries for him to come back to me.

But Leo had bravely downloaded himself into a specialized net developed by Lionel Scipio, the founder of the Tower, and Leo's creator. The net had special healing properties, and Leo had been confident that he could use it to repair the damage to Grey's brain.

Now I'd never know.

After we'd rushed back to the Citadel to find Maddox badly beaten and Ambrose dead, we'd been arrested by Lieutenant Zale, Devon Alexander's second in command. He'd never even given us a chance to explain, but had taken one look and ordered our arrest. Now he was marching us through the halls, no doubt leading us to the cells buried in the bottom of the Citadel. My skin crawled just thinking of that level—the long hall, full of viewing chambers that contained tables with sharp objects and tools jutting out of them. And the rooms the hall led to, which were bisected by a glass pane, so Knights could watch as they gassed those they deemed undesirable.

They called it "expulsion". I called it murder. And it had been learning about those rooms, and the murders, that started me on a path of turning my back on the Tower. Grey had offered a chance of escape and protection, and I had leapt at it.

And then everything had fallen apart, and since then, no matter how many different ways I tried to pick up the pieces and keep them together, everything kept breaking. It left me feeling dejected, depressed, and... hopeless.

And I hated it. I hated the vulnerability it caused in me, and the complete lack of control I was being given over my own life.

But at the end of the day, it also filled me with a cold determination—which helped break through some of the hopelessness that had descended on me like a curtain. I couldn't give up. Not now. Remembering all the ways I had failed only served to remind me of how far I had actually come. There was too much at stake for me to give up.

I could break down later, after I got us out of this. After I figured out how to handle Lacey. After I got Tian back.

First, I had to figure out how to get these cuffs off. I looked down at my hands, which were bound together in front of me, just below the hand that was tightly gripping my forearm, the whiteness of it a stark contrast to the crimson uniform I wore.

The same one *he* wore.

He was a fellow Knight, but that might not mean much. There was every chance that he had been in on the former

CHAPTER 1

Champion's plans. Before I had publicly acknowledged killing him. On Scipio's orders.

Now, the last part wasn't true, but he didn't know that.

What *I* didn't know was how deep Lieutenant Zale's loyalty to Devon ran. Traditionally, the position of the Lieutenant was meant to keep the Champion's power in check. But Devon had been no ordinary Champion. He had been a part of a legacy group—one that had been working to bring Scipio down.

And I suspected that the Lieutenant might have been working with him the entire time, which meant he could still be working with Devon's allies. They knew I had killed Devon, and likely suspected that I was working with another legacy group in opposition to them, given how Lacey and Strum had affected Scipio's memories. That made me a threat, and one that he could now be moving to eliminate, quietly, before anyone could stop him.

I needed to do something to get us out of here. As soon as possible. *Right now*, in fact.

I turned my attention to the Knight holding me, continuing with my train of thought. Zale might be working with Devon, along with several other Knights, but that didn't mean all of them were. If I could produce enough evidence in front of them that proved, definitively, that Leo and I hadn't attacked Maddox and killed Ambrose, he'd have to back off.

Providing not all of these Knights were on his side. It was a gamble, but it was all I had.

Now, to find evidence.

I couldn't use Lacey as an alibi; the moment she found out why I needed one, she would deny everything. Not to mention, the truth would lead them to the site of a violent murder that would lead to an investigation, which would get in the way of any chance we had of finding Tian without getting noticed. No,

I needed something else. Something that would prove without a shadow of a doubt that we hadn't done it.

My eyes shifted back to my bound wrists, my brain boiling as I searched for something—anything I could use. Maybe I could call Zoe and Eric? I could have them act as my alibi and tell them that we were...

No; a quick glance at the indicator on my wrist showed a diagonal red slash across the bright blue ten there. My net permissions had been turned off. I must have missed when the Lieutenant had ordered that.

Crap.

Dejected, I lumbered forward, staring at my indicator, at the number there. A simple line and a circle standing side by side: my ranking inside the Tower. All my life, that stupid number had been held over me as a standard of behavior, a real-time reflection of my usefulness to the Tower. Scipio ranked everyone based on data collected from the nets implanted in our heads. The happier and more dedicated you were to the Tower, the higher your rank.

But the lower your rank... the worse you were for the Tower. And that felt particularly true in my case; even with a ten awarded by Scipio, I failed to make the Tower safe.

Failure after failure after failure. I couldn't make anyone safe. Couldn't keep Ambrose alive. Couldn't warn my friends. Couldn't stop staring at those stupid numbers on my wrist.

Then, quite suddenly, that cold determination snapped me back out of the growing bleakness of my thoughts, carrying with it a simple realization: the ten on my wrist was supposed to keep me *safe* from these sorts of things.

The ranking system had only been implemented in the last one hundred years or so, but had been in place for so long that society had adapted around it, and eventually started using it to determine who was good and safe... and who should not be trusted. That meant anyone with a rank of ten was held in the highest respect, while someone with the ranking of one was likely a dissident and a threat to the Tower.

The nets that were implanted at the base of our skulls used specialized wires to monitor activity on the cerebral cortex, tracking our emotional states throughout the day. And negative emotions that lasted for some time would force a person's rank downward. Anger, depression, envy... all of those would affect the rank. The more severe the emotion, the less time it would take.

I blinked. There were several things about the thought that were relevant, but the most important one was this: murdering another human was not an emotionless act. At least, not normally. A sociopath could have done it without emotion, but sociopaths were singled out and caught early during their development. They couldn't always be treated—though they could live normal lives inside the Tower, with Medica intervention.

Still, only a fraction of the Tower's citizens were diagnosed as true sociopaths. I doubted very much that whoever had killed Ambrose was one. Which meant that whoever had killed him had taken a hit to their ranking—and was now bearing the rank of one.

But I wasn't. Which proved beyond a shadow of a doubt that *I* hadn't done it.

I looked up from my indicator, and blinked when I realized that we'd only made it thirty feet down the hallway. Thank Scipio; I felt like I had been searching for a way out of this for an eternity. If we reached the end of the hall or entered the elevators before I could mount my defense where enough Knights could overhear us, I risked the chance of my argument falling on deaf ears.

Motion at the end of the hall caught my eye, and suddenly a group of Medics was racing toward us, their white uniforms gleaming under the bright light of the hall. Lieutenant Salvatore Zale pushed us to one side, allowing them to pass. I watched them go, heartsick with worry over Maddox, and saw several other Knights standing in the hall in front of Ambrose's door, watching us.

It was now or never.

"Lieutenant Zale, why are we under arrest?" I asked. I frowned. My voice had come out soft and exhausted, while I wanted it to be something cool and authoritative. But I would take what I could get.

Zale turned to me, his bright sapphire gaze spearing me with a contemptuous glance. "You were found with the body, and you are a known murderer."

"If you are referring to Devon Alexander," I said coldly, putting more power into my voice, "then I suggest you take that up with Scipio. As for Ambrose's murder—" My jaw locked around the word, a shot of guilt piercing through the icy cold I had embraced. I swallowed it back, promising to give over to it soon, and focused on clearing my throat and finding a starting point. "—Grey and I were not here. But that isn't even relevant. Do you know what is?"

I could tell that he was already angered by my challenge, but what was worse was that it hadn't been nearly as biting as I'd wanted. That tiny moment of guilt had thrown me off, and now I felt like I was fumbling just to remember what words were, and saying them was like speaking the Divers' tongue, Wetmouth, with cotton stuffed into my cheeks.

I half expected him to just order the Knights to keep shoving us down the hall, ignoring my question completely. But to my surprise, he rolled his eyes and said, "No." The word was drawn out, extended to show his impatience.

I held up my wrists, indicator up. The Knight who had cuffed me had put the metal cuffs above the band, and the ten was still visible, glowing a soft, bright blue that drowned out the red cutting over it. "We couldn't have murdered him without it registering with Scipio," I snapped. "He would have immediately flagged the amount of rage and fear that goes into murder. And he would've dropped our ranks to a one as a result."

I spoke the words clearly, not raising my voice, but it was like a switch being thrown—everyone in the hall suddenly fell silent. I heard the creak and shift of several uniforms behind me, and realized that a few of the Knights had come closer to see why we had stopped. They had heard the tail end, and now, suddenly, they had questions, too.

I had been right—not all of these men were blindly loyal to Zale.

Zale's eyes narrowed a fraction of an inch, one of them twitching slightly, and he pressed his mouth into a thin line. "Be that as it may, you were still there, and we need to confirm your alibi. Protocol dictates—"

"What is going on?" a strong feminine voice demanded, interrupting him. I looked down the hall, past Zale, and to my surprise, saw Lacey Green marching toward us, her dark face holding a thunderous expression.

I froze when I saw her, realizing that this was it. This was where she turned us over to Zale for altering Scipio's memory during Devon Alexander's trial. She must've found out about Ambrose, somehow, and come up here to deliver the so-called evidence. It didn't matter that I hadn't actually altered Scipio's thoughts. Lacey and Strum had. And it wouldn't matter that they had also asked me to kill Devon in the first place. It was their word against mine, and they were council members.

If only I had been able to keep Ambrose safe. If only Tian hadn't been attacked by a group of men. If only I'd spared five minutes to go and get Maddox and Ambrose, instead of racing off with Leo on my own. Would he still be alive? Had this all been a ploy to draw us away from him... and had I stupidly fallen for it?

Lacey stopped in front of Lieutenant Zale and speared him with a look. "What is going on?" she demanded again.

He gave her a considering look, his eyebrows drawing together. "Ambrose Klein has been murdered, and we found Liana Castell and Grey Farmless with the body after the alarm went off."

I frowned. Now that he mentioned it, I realized I hadn't heard the alarm that rang whenever anyone died unexpectedly. It should've been blaring through the entire section... but the halls had been silent when we arrived, and they were still silent.

So then... how had he known that Ambrose was dead?

Lacey picked up on it, too, and lifted a slim black eyebrow into an arched point. "Alarm?" she asked, looking around.

Zale frowned and blinked. "Somebody must have turned off the speakers on the floor," he said. "I'll have the techs look into it. In the meantime—"

"You'll have the techs look into it," Lacey repeated slowly. "This isn't something you'd already thought of? Your investigation must be ongoing, then, if you're still exploring answers to questions like that."

"Yes, our investigation just started, but it seems to me that—"

"Seems?" she cut in, one brow twitching slightly. "I assume that whatever you tell me next will be delivered in the form of cold, hard evidence. Otherwise, I'm going to question your *role* in this investigation."

Lieutenant Zale opened his mouth and then breathed deeply in and out, slowly, as if summoning patience. "Lacey, I do not appreciate—"

"It's *Engineer Green*," she spoke over him smoothly, giving him a faux smile.

I was impressed; she seemed so cool and unaffected, but I was watching her closely, and I saw the tightness around her eyes and lips, her face a touch paler than normal. She was keeping a lid on it... but Lacey struck me as a still-waters-run-deep kind of woman, and I could only imagine how much self-control she was using.

Why was she doing it? She had every reason to let Zale drag me away. I had failed to keep Ambrose alive. I had failed to prevent her cousin's murder. And she had planned for this contingency—had fabricated evidence that I was certain would stick. She'd told me she had. All she had to do was turn it over, and she'd get her revenge.

Maybe that's what she was still planning on doing, after she had an opportunity to gloat. A part of me hoped that was the case; at the very least, I would be able to plead for the lives of my friends.

Oh God, my friends. Zoe and Eric had been with her when I last saw them, and that had only been half an hour ago. They had still been looking for Tian after her panicked net transmission that someone was after her—which had led us to a mess of dead bodies. Leo and I had just made it back in time to discover that Ambrose was dead.

How had Lacey found out and made it up here so fast?

My eyes dropped to her overalls and shirt, and to my surprise, I saw a light dusting of sweat coating her neck and the exposed areas of her chest. The short-sleeved white shirt she wore had clear signs of staining around her armpits. That would have been fine on anyone from the Mechanics Department, but considering I had seen her not too long ago, in an entirely different part of the Tower...

My instincts told me she had run up here. But how had she known to do so?

"Engineer Green," the Lieutenant said woodenly. "I appreciate your interest in this case, but this is a matter for the Knights. You're out of your jurisdiction."

"Correction, Lieutenant," Lacey said smugly. "With the Tourney still going on, the council oversees the day-to-day operations of the Knights. We act as the Champion until a new one can be selected. Now, I assume at this very early stage in your investigation, you have at least gotten Ms. Castell's and Mr. Farmless's alibi. What do you need from me to confirm it? Will a written statement do?"

Zale's frown deepened, and he blinked several times in confusion at her sudden shift in questions. "Confirm... it?"

I was equally baffled, and I looked up at Lacey, wondering where she was going with this. Concern rippled through me at the idea that she was going to reveal our relationship in order to save me. I had been with her before coming back and discovering Ambrose's body. She had been helping me and my friends search for Tian—but that had been as a favor to us, to keep Tian out of the hands of our enemies.

She would risk exposing our relationship by admitting to being my ally, and I honestly couldn't understand why. It was unexpected, really, *really* unexpected considering the circumstances, because it could expose her to her *enemies*. Especially if Lieutenant Zale was what I thought he was: Devon's former ally. She had to have a better idea up her sleeve. She was clever.

CHAPTER 1

And has just lost a family member, a voice inside me whispered, and I realized it was right. Lacey might not be thinking clearly. If she slipped up...

"Indeed. One of the Cog children wandered away from a class tour today, and his net malfunctioned. The child was lost, and I ordered my men and women to start looking for him, before he got hurt. Liana's friend and one of my Cogs, Zoe Elphesian, reached out to her to ask for her help, and she came to do just that."

It was hard not to gape at her. She lied beautifully, giving the information with just the right emotional tick—but not so much that it seemed forced. Almost tired, slightly annoyed, but mainly just matter of fact.

Zale regarded her for a long moment. "There was no report of a missing child."

"Because I thought it more expedient to move quickly, rather than file a report."

"And did you recover him?"

"Yes," Lacey said with a firm nod, not even batting an eye. "He was fine, and should be on his way to the Medica right now for a new children's net. Now, would you like me to provide you with witnesses, or are you willing to admit that Ms. Castell and her friend here are victims of circumstance?"

Zale stared at her, and I held my breath, watching him and trying to get a read on him. If he was disappointed or angry, it could be a sign that he was working with a legacy group—and had failed at his attempt to fix their little "Liana" problem.

Then again, he could just hate me for killing Devon.

Either way, though, he wouldn't fight her—that much was clear from the now-relaxed grip on my arm. The other Knight was still holding it, but barely, and I could have broken free if I wanted to. Lacey and I had together convinced the Knights, so if

Zale pressed, he risked not only revealing his bias against me, but also his standing in the Tourney. Part of the Tourney was a popularity contest, and toward the end, the Knights would be given an opportunity to vote on who they wanted to lead them next.

If he insisted on arresting me, he would lose them. Because they'd realized he was wrong.

But his face never really moved beyond that slow, considering look. "I suppose they are," he said, giving a nod to the Knights flanking Leo and me. Seconds later the cuffs were off, and I was rubbing my wrists. I wanted to give Lacey a grateful look, but knew that she hadn't done it for us.

If Lacey wanted us free, it wasn't because she wanted to be nice to us. It was because she wanted to punish us herself.

And I really couldn't blame her. Ambrose was dead, after she'd gone out of her way to free me, to give me a new life and the mission of keeping him safe in the Tourney.

I had failed. She had every right to be angry.

Lieutenant Zale cleared his throat and gave her an expectant look. "Has the council been notified?"

"I am filling them in as we speak," she replied, her tongue darting over her lips. "Scipio is processing and researching the protocols, but we've already decided that we will have to find someone else to run point on the investigation. You were Devon's Lieutenant, *and* you're a candidate in the Tourney, so the consensus is to hand it over to someone else."

She spoke as if the conversation were really happening, and then I felt like an idiot, because of course it was. At one point in our history, citizens had had implants that allowed them to make net calls without using their vocal cords. But creating them was difficult, and the crystals they had used were hard to cultivate. They'd been slowly phased out over the years. My parents had received them when they became Knight Elites, but now they were only available to the highest positions in each department, and the council members themselves. Which meant that while she had been getting us freed, she had also been holding a completely different conversation with the other councilors. And we hadn't even noticed.

Zale's jaw tightened slightly, but that was it; the rest of his face might as well have been granite. "I understand. LaSalle?"

The Knight next to me took a step forward. "Yes, sir?"

"Please take over the investigation, and pass all findings on to Scipio for the council, until they notify you who will be taking point on the investigation."

LaSalle straightened his back and saluted with a fist over his heart. "It will be done." He spun around and marched back toward Ambrose's apartment, already giving orders on how to properly collect the evidence.

Then he moved to one side, and the Medics emerged, a gurney hovering between the two of them bearing Maddox's form.

They had put a mask over her face, and it was fogging up with her sharp pants. The Medics were leaning over her as the gurney moved forward, talking over each other as they administered aid.

"—Punctured a lung—"

"—Administering adrenaline—"

"—Air in chest cavity—"

"—Need to hurry—"

They raced by, their hands moving over her and opening her suit, and my heart leapt into my throat. Her one good eye was still open, a look of fear and confusion on her face. She kept reaching up toward the mask and gasping in sharp pants, but the male Medic pushed her hand away, keeping her from speaking.

My heart ached, and I realized that she wanted to try to tell us who had done this to her, but they weren't letting her. Which meant they didn't think she was going to make it—not if they didn't get her to the Medica quickly.

And then they were gone, racing down the hallway toward the elevator bank. My feet were already moving of their own accord, the compulsion to follow her, to be there with her so she didn't have to go alone, too strong for me to ignore.

But I didn't make it three steps before Lacey was in front of me, blocking my path. "You are going to tell me what the hell happened to Ambrose," she ground out evenly, her eyes flashing with the promise of a great and terrible anger, the likes of which I had never seen before.

2

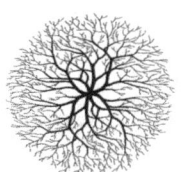

Her voice was like a loud shout in my ears, and I took a quick glance around the corridor, checking to see if anyone else had heard her. Zale had moved a few feet away with the Knight who had been escorting Leo, and the only other people in the hall besides us were the two Knights fiddling with the security panel on Ambrose's door.

I stared at them for a second or two, idly wondering if they would find anything of significance, and then turned back to Lacey. "We shouldn't talk here," I said, my voice coming out more confident than I expected. "C'mon."

In truth, I was terrified. Even as I turned, my knees were beginning to fill with gelatin, making them weak and wobbly. My heart pounded hard in my chest, and I could feel the force of it in all of my extremities, making everything quiver inside.

I summoned up the icy coldness that had helped me stand against Zale, using it to add steel to my spine. I knew I couldn't keep this up for long—cracks were beginning to form in the shell

I had crafted around myself. But I had to keep going. Lacey was another threat, and until I knew what she planned to do with us, I couldn't give in to the pain that was threatening to tear me apart.

Also, she didn't need me breaking down on her. She was already hurting, and had more of a right to be than I did. I needed to keep it together for her sake. And beyond everything else, I owed her an explanation. I owed her an apology—not that there were enough words in the world to make up for the pain my mistakes had brought her.

Besides, I needed to make sure that no matter what she did to me, my friends would get out of this alive. I wasn't sure how I was going to get her to agree to that, but I was going to figure it out.

I opened the door to my apartment and stepped in, sliding my back against the wall in the entryway to let her and Leo through. Leo gave me a concerned look as he stepped past me, and for a second, I wanted nothing more than to stop him and pull him in for a hug.

I squashed the impulse almost immediately, attributing the momentary weakness to my exhaustion and shock. Thinking things like that about Leo was wrong, and I had to remind myself, over and over, that Leo wasn't Grey.

Don't mistake me—I liked Leo. He was a source of calm in the chaos of our world. Watching him unfold and learn to enjoy all the little things that humans did... It made me exquisitely happy for him, even if it came with a touch of sorrow. I had come to rely on the steadfast machine, both as a moral touchstone and as a genuine friend.

Especially given his sacrifice in implanting himself into Grey's body. The terminal that made up his home was now gone —destroyed by a virus that Ezekial Pine had downloaded into it,

CHAPTER 2

in order to kill Leo and keep him from interfering with his plans to kill Scipio. By placing himself inside the net and then inside Grey's head, Leo had left that terminal to its fate, and put his own existence in jeopardy.

Because without a place to sustain him, he would eventually die.

Just like Scipio was doing at this very moment. It seemed Ezekial's plan had paid off, albeit hundreds of years later, because the great AI was now failing. My brother had discovered that massive chunks of data had been ripped away from Scipio, leaving only fragments of his personality to hold everything together.

Of course, Leo wanted to do something to help him, but knew he couldn't do it alone. He had asked me to help him, and, in spite of my desire to leave the Tower for good, I had agreed. It turned out I couldn't leave—not when I knew that everyone inside the Tower would die if something wasn't done.

Suddenly I realized I had been staring at Leo a touch too long, and the concern in his eyes had deepened considerably. He opened his mouth, my name forming on his lips... and something inside warned me that hearing my name in Grey's voice right then would put a crack in the cold armor I had built for myself. I needed the sweet embrace of logic if I was to focus on what was in front of me—and only that. I had no more room for pain, even an old one.

So I turned a cold shoulder to him, ignoring him completely. It was rude of me, and I would apologize later, but for now... it was going to take every scrap of strength I had left to deal with Lacey.

My eyes found her frame in the doorway, but she had paused mid-step over the threshold, her head swiveled around and staring through the open door of the opposite apartment. I shifted my gaze past her, into the apartment, and paled when I saw Knights moving Ambrose's still form, loading him into a body bag.

The sight of them touching him, moving his body, without any protest or argument from him, made my heart seize up in spite of the walls I had crafted around myself. A protest at the clinical way in which they were putting him in the bag half formed in my throat, but I swallowed it down, focusing instead on Lacey. If I was upset, then she was probably devastated—and she definitely didn't need to be seeing that.

On impulse, I reached out and grabbed her wrist, jerking her inside, past me. She was so absorbed in watching Ambrose that I caught her off guard, and she stumbled across the threshold. I hit the panel next to the door and sealed it.

"You don't need to see that," I said roughly, my throat tight.

I turned and faced Lacey. The woman's back was now to me, Leo as still as a statue a few feet from her. She stood motionless for several long heartbeats, and then whirled. It was all I could do not to break down and cry at the look of heartwrenching loss in her dark brown eyes. The edges of the mask that she had maintained in the hall were cracking.

"What. Happened." The words were squeezed out through a tight throat, raw and vulnerable and angry, and Lacey's face told me she wouldn't tolerate any more delays.

And yet, I couldn't make the words form. I kept trying to find a starting point, but couldn't pick a place. I had lost my grip on that ice-cold determination, and was now floundering. I had to get control back. I couldn't break down here.

Luckily, Leo was there to buy me time. "We returned to the Citadel, as you requested," he began formally. "We decided to go talk to Ambrose and Maddox about the challenges for the Tourney tomorrow." He shifted his gaze from Lacey to me,

Grey's warm brown eyes quizzical. I knew what he was asking: he wanted to know if I was going to jump in.

I was. I couldn't be a coward about this. "Whatever we missed, we missed it by mere minutes," I announced softly, somehow managing to summon up that frozen demeanor. "When we entered, the room showed signs of a struggle. I found Maddox first, near the kitchen. She was confused, and tried to fight me. She couldn't give me any details about what happened, but I could see she was badly injured. Then Grey called me from the common room. Ambrose was there, lying on his back. He..." I trailed off, my voice suddenly deserting me.

Lacey's face hardened and she stared at me intently, tears glistening in her eyes. "Say it," she said through clenched teeth.

I sucked in a shuddering breath, trying not to get sick. "He was..." Again, my throat tightened, constricting around the last word. I clenched my teeth together, curling my hands into fists. "He was already dead."

Lacey's face was transfixed, but a tremor ran through her body. Her stiff arms and rigid spine lost their tension as the trembling continued. I watched as the planes of her face morphed from anger to terror, and then despair, the edges of her mouth, her nose, her eyebrows, her cheeks, all pulling inexorably down, reflecting the collision course her heart was undergoing. She hadn't wanted to believe it, not even staring it in the face. But now... now she had to.

A ragged sob escaped her, and she dropped to her hands and knees on the floor, her shoulders quaking. One hand went to her mouth, while the other pushed her back into a kneeling position, her arm wrapping around her. Tears streamed down her cheeks, though she tried to stifle her sobs behind her trembling hand, and she rocked back and forth, seeming to curl further and further into herself.

My own hand went to my mouth, my heart breaking to see such a strong woman so shattered and devastated.

Your fault, a voice inside my head reminded me grimly, and I accepted the blame solemnly. I would take it all on if it meant sparing Lacey some of this pain. If only I could take it all back.

I used it all and channeled it back into the frigid cold, forcing my raucous emotional state down once more. I was getting tired of doing it—soon I wouldn't be able to maintain any semblance of calm—but I managed to find one last reserve of strength, and use it.

I moved over to her, unable to see her on the floor like that without doing anything, and knelt down next to her, my arm going over her back. The intention was to help her up and onto the sofa, but as soon as my hand touched her back, she jerked away from me with a harsh "Don't touch me," one arm shooting away from her and shoving me.

The move caught me by surprise, and she tipped me off balance, causing me to fall onto my rear. I wasn't hurt, just surprised, and I watched her wearily as she clambered to her feet. Leo raced over to me, his hands outstretched to help me up, but I held up a hand and waved him off. I wasn't injured. At least, not physically.

Lacey finally righted herself and towered over me, her fists clenched into tight balls. "You stupid girl!" she spat, her voice warbling with sorrow. "You did this—you got him killed!"

I met her gaze solemnly, trying not to break. "I know."

Lacey made a strangled noise from the recesses of her throat and clenched her eyes shut, tears leaking from them. "I should do it," she said, shuddering. "I should turn you and your friends over to Zale and let him throw you in those awful expulsion chambers."

Her eyes slid open as she spoke, and the look she gave me

was full of hatred and loathing. My heart seized up as her words settled down on me, and I remained locked in place. "Lacey... please don't hurt my friends. I'm their leader, and it's my fault. Please don't punish them. Please."

I was aware that I was begging, but I didn't care. My friends meant everything to me; if Lacey hurt them or got them killed, I'd never be able to forgive myself. I'd die knowing that I had failed them—but with the state of mind Lacey seemed to be in, she'd see that as justice.

She stared at me, and then suddenly turned and walked away, into the kitchen area. I followed her with my eyes, and watched as she put her hands on the edge of the counter and gripped it tightly. She stayed there, not saying anything.

I waited, and then slowly started to pick myself off the ground. I made it to my feet, and still, she didn't say or do anything. She just stood there with her back to us, motionless. Leo and I exchanged glances, and then I took a tentative step forward.

"Lacey?" Her head shifted slightly, but that was all. I took it as a sign to continue. Only, I wasn't entirely sure what to say. What could anyone say, really? My mind searched for the right words, but there was only one thing in my heart I wanted an answer to. "Are my friends safe?"

Lacey shifted her weight. "Do you think I had them killed as soon as Grey's call came in?"

I looked at Leo sharply, and he gave me an apologetic look. "She needed to know," he said simply.

He was right, but netting her had been a risk, and still was—nothing I had said thus far had given her any reason to spare us, and I had little reason to believe that anything we did say would have an effect. Still, I had to try.

I focused on Lacey's back. "Are my friends *safe*?" I asked, stressing the word. Lacey turned around slightly, showing me the profile of her face. "Please, Lacey. I need to know."

She licked her lips. "They're fine," she bit out. "They're still looking for your youngest friend, along with my men."

A breath I didn't even know I had been holding escaped, and I felt a moment of relief. But it quickly faded. Just because they were safe now didn't mean that they would be later. I needed to focus, and find out what Lacey was going to do with us.

"Lacey, I—"

"Just shut up, Liana," she said in an irritated whisper. I let my words die, and waited. She raised a hand to her eyes and began wiping the tears away, trying to compose herself. After several more long, pregnant seconds, she glanced over at us. She didn't quite meet my gaze. "The council is suspending the Tourney for now, while the investigation is ongoing," she mumbled thickly.

She must've gotten the information through her net, though it amazed me that she could still participate in the council while grieving.

She paused, her mouth open, and then closed it, shaking her head. I waited patiently, and eventually she started again. "Stay here. Answer the investigators' questions when they come, and stick to the story. I need..." She faltered again, and swallowed, clearing her throat. "I need some time to think."

A deep fissure cracked through my defenses, and I felt the small amount of control I had over myself slip. The lost sound of Lacey's voice—her confusion and pain—touched a place inside me that made my heart shatter into a thousand pieces for her. I was breaking—I knew it—but I managed to keep it from showing as she made her way to the door, moving at a ponderous pace.

She opened it up with a soft sigh, stepped into the hallway, and then turned around and looked back at us. I could feel the weight of her gaze on me, pinning me in place. Then she was gone, the door shutting between us.

My knees buckled seconds later, and I fell to the floor, my entire body shaking.

3

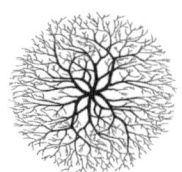

Lacey was going to kill us. And we couldn't run—not without Tian. Plus, we didn't have anywhere to hide. I didn't know what to do.

My chest seized as a deep, fierce agony caught me, and I lost what little strength I had left and began to sob. I had failed. I had killed us all. I was a monster.

Hands gently slid along my back and middle, rolling me onto my side, but too many tears were flowing for me to see who it was—and my heart was too broken to care. I couldn't help anyone. I couldn't save the Tower. I couldn't help Leo.

The hands slid under my knees and back, becoming arms, and the next thing I knew, I was floating, moving. Leo. Leo was carrying me. I couldn't tell where we were going, but I clutched at his uniform, tears running steadily down my cheeks.

I barely noticed when he sat me down on the bed, my body still shaking and trembling, but growing calmer as an icy numbness settled in, bringing with it a dense and thick fog that seemed to encase me in numbness. I stared just past him, at a closet. All of the doors were still open from when I had searched for Tian, and I could see my meager belongings inside. A spare pair of boots, three extra uniforms, a stack of undergarments, some black, some white, and some nondescript clothing.

Something tugged gently at my foot, and I looked down. Leo was kneeling on the floor, his hands carefully pulling off my boots. I watched him numbly, trying to figure out what he was up to.

He took gentle care as he removed first one, then the second, followed by my socks, to reveal my feet one by one. His hands slid over them, squeezing gently, and a curious warmth began to spread up my legs as he rubbed. He looked up from what he was doing, his eyes quizzical, and I met his gaze, but was unable to present anything other than a blank expression.

He let go of the foot he was rubbing, reached up, and stroked my cheek with the back of his fingers, wiping away the tears. Suddenly he stood up and left the room for a second, returning with a square piece of black fabric in his hands. He returned to a kneeling position, and carefully began wiping my face clean.

My eyes burned from the force of the tears, and still felt wet all along the lashes, but I had stopped crying. I sat still as he stroked the cloth gently over my cheeks and nose, cleaning me. Nobody had ever shown me such tenderness before... and it was almost enough to make me start crying again.

Instead, I sat there, trembling from a deep and bitter cold that had pierced my very soul. Leo must've sensed my distress, because he set the cloth next to me and began unzipping the front of my suit. In the back of my mind, I approved; the uniform was tight, and it was doing nothing to warm me. I heard

CHAPTER 3

the high-pitched hiss as it slid open, and then cool air slipped into the open space, making my shivering increase. I was wrong, I thought suddenly. I'd freeze if he exposed any more flesh.

"Cold," I mumbled, my voice roughened to a harsh gasp from the force of the crying.

His eyes flicked up to me, and he nodded solemnly. "I know. I'm going to get you under the blanket just as soon as your uniform is off. It'll help you get warm faster."

Blanket. That sounded warm. His words made sense. I trembled violently, and then gave him a tight nod, giving him permission to proceed.

Ever so gently, he slid his fingers under the edge of my uniform and began easing it over one shoulder, guiding my arm out. The hand controls for my lashes got stuck on the cuff, but Leo slowly worked it free, then moved over to the other side and repeated the procedure, before easing the back of my uniform off the harness that contained my lashes. The lashes were still connected, but Leo didn't seem to care about unthreading them from the suit. Instead, he placed a knee on the bed and swung around behind me.

His hands dipped down over my shoulders, grabbing the first clasp of the harness where it crossed over my chest and carefully unclipping it, taking great pains not to touch me in a disrespectful manner. I acknowledged that dimly, but was too wrapped in the cocoon of bitter cold, which reached deep into the marrow of my bones, to feel anything else.

Then he moved his arms even lower, fiddling with the second clip before releasing it. The gear on my back began to sag, and Leo carefully lifted the straps off of my shoulders and eased the harness off.

The sudden lack of weight on my back felt great, and I

sucked in a slightly deeper breath, hearing the sound come in as a sharp wheeze. My throat was still tight, but it felt good, too. Whatever he was doing, it was helping.

The mattress shifted and then rose, indicating that he had left, and moments later he was helping me to my feet, moving to pull the uniform from my hips and down my legs. He knelt to do it, and I watched him.

His hands were strong and tender, and even though he took care not to touch me, his fingers would occasionally skim over my skin. I stared at the uniform as it started to come off me, and then my mind drifted back into the hallway with Zale. Back to Maddox trying to push the Medic's hand away to remove her mask, her eyes dazed and confused.

They had been opening her suit, too, I realized, trembling inside. They had undressed her like this.

Panic slammed into me, and I moved for the door, stumbling as my foot tangled in the uniform my legs still wore. I caught myself, and then bent over blindly, desperately trying to drag my uniform back up to cover my exposed skin. I imagined Maddox never getting to do it again.

I imagined life without her.

I imagined the last image I would ever have of her being that one in the hall—with her desperately trying to say something to us.

Oh, Scipio. I had let her go alone to the Medica. She was alone there right now! No one knew what was happening! I had to get there... had to be there for her!

I looked at the bed and saw that Leo had left it, closing the distance between us with his hands up, ready to soothe me, and I backed away like a cowed animal, afraid to let him touch me.

"I can't..." I mumbled, my breathing increasing again, rising with the swell of my panic. "Have to go to Maddox. Tell Quess and Zoe what happened. Keep looking for Tian."

I spotted my harness on the bed and went for it automatically, knowing that I would need it to get to the Medica as fast as possible. I managed to pick it up, but moments later it was firmly pulled from me and tossed onto the floor with a loud clang that made me quiver. Leo towered over me, his eyes blazing, and I was surprised to see a muscle in his jaw working.

"You are no good to anyone like this," he said, his voice coming across evenly.

He didn't understand. I was responsible for them, for their lives! I had to get to Maddox; I had to make sure she wasn't alone. This wasn't about me. This was about them!

"Have to help them," I mumbled, my eyes burning.

His eyes softened. "I'm taking care of them," he said, smoothing his hands over my shoulders. "I've been in communication with Zoe, Eric, and Quess. Zoe and Eric are going to continue their search for Tian with Lacey's people, and Quess is on his way to the Medica now."

"It should be me," I moaned softly, hot tears slipping from my eyes. And I didn't mean being there for Maddox. I meant... it should've been me in the apartment with Ambrose. I should've been there—it had been my responsibility.

"This isn't a request," he said firmly, his eyes hardening. Moments later he had grabbed my hand and tugged me over to my bed, where he removed the rest of my uniform so quickly that my head was dizzy with it. My legs and arms were now exposed, but I was wearing a sleeveless black undershirt and a pair of shorts that fell to mid-thigh. The important bits were covered.

Good. I couldn't deal with being any more vulnerable. I'd never felt so raw and exposed before, and so completely out of control. If anything else happened, I'd probably just go to sleep and never wake up. It'd be easier.

It'd be cowardly. More tears streaked out of me at that thought, and I felt the truth of it. I was a coward. A coward and a failure.

But Leo was moving me again, pulling back the heavy cover and guiding me into a lying-down position. I chose to lay on my side, my head resting on the pillow, my knees up to my chest. He held the blanket up, giving me plenty of room to lie down, and then carefully placed the cover over me, taking time to tuck me in.

I shivered under the cover, still cold, my face wet, feeling the soft press of his fingers as he pushed the thick fabric under me. By the time he had finished one side, the shivering had stopped some—though I was left with a deep, icy pit inside, radiating with cold.

Leo gave me a cursory look and then nodded to himself, as if satisfied with his handiwork. "Close your eyes," he said gently. "I'll be right outside."

He turned to go, but another burst of panic shot through me, so intense that I threw back the blanket and grabbed his wrist with both my hands. "Don't go," I said, my voice cracking. "Please."

I was being weak and needy. He had every right in the world to tell me to grow up and get some sleep—but he didn't. Instead, he turned to me, and his warm brown eyes softened, as if his own heart were breaking to see me so devastated. His eyes traced over my face for a second, and then he nodded slowly.

"I can sleep on the floor," he said softly. "I'll grab a pillow and blanket from my room and be right back."

He turned to go again, but I tightened my grip on his wrist, my heart pounding in fear. "No. Stay here. Please. Hold me."

What was I doing? Why had I even asked him that? I wasn't sure, exactly. All I knew was that if he left me alone with these thoughts and feelings... I didn't want to think about what would happen. I needed comfort, even if I didn't deserve it, and I was selfishly asking for it.

And Leo... Leo couldn't deny me. I could see it in his eyes. "All right," he said, reaching out and thumbing away my tears. "Please don't cry. I'm here. I'll take care of you."

I relaxed some, letting go of his arms and lying back down in my bed. Leo stood in front of me for a second or two, awkwardly hesitant about how to proceed, and then slowly reached up and began unzipping his suit. I watched him for a second, and then turned my gaze up to the ceiling. He'd had to look at me when he was undressing me, but I wasn't undressing him.

I heard the sound of him kicking off his boots, followed by the solid *thunk* of his harness hitting the ground. There was a soft whisper of sound as he removed the rest of his uniform, and then he was padding to the side of the bed. I moved over, scooting closer to the wall it was built against, and then pulled the blanket aside for him as much as I could without removing it from myself. He climbed in slowly, and as soon as he was in, I draped the blanket back over him.

He shifted his weight around, the mattress dipping and bouncing a few times as he tried to get comfortable, and then he went still. The only place we were touching was where his shoulder was pressed against my own. I waited, wondering if he had simply forgotten that I had asked him to hold me, and then he broke the silence.

"I'm not sure what to do."

A laugh escaped me—where it came from, I had no idea—and I leaned over, grabbed his arm where it sat on the cover, and pulled it over my waist. "You have to get closer," I said, and seconds later, I felt the hot press of him as he spooned me.

The heat was a relief, and within moments the panicked nervousness that had encased me started to ease. Some, but not completely. Leo lay behind me, his breathing deep and even, but if it weren't for the heat he was radiating, I wouldn't even have known he was there. Everything was silent and still. Just like Ambrose's body... lying on the floor, blood trickling from his nose, ears, and eyes.

Leo's arm tightened around my waist, pulling me against him, and I realized my shivering had increased again. "Tell me what to do," he said.

"Make noise. Tell me a story. I don't know, anything. It's too quiet. I can't get Ambrose out of my head."

"Shhhhh," he breathed soothingly, his thumb starting to move back and forth on my stomach, massaging me gently. He paused for several seconds, and then to my surprise, he began to hum.

The tune was unlike anything I'd ever heard before. I let him get a few bars in before I asked, "What is that?"

The humming died down. "It's a song called 'Danny Boy.' It has words, too, but I think they might be a bit sad for you right now. Maybe I shouldn't have picked this song."

"No, sing it," I pleaded, twisting my head around slightly to look at him. "It sounded so beautiful."

Leo licked his lips and then nodded, clearing his throat. I relaxed back into the pillow. The position I had been in was too painful on my neck to hold. Seconds later, he began to sing. "Oh, Danny boy, the pipes, the pipes are calling. From glen to glen and down the mountainside. The summer's gone, and all the roses falling. 'Tis you, 'tis you must go, and I must bide." His voice was surprisingly good, rich with timbre and warmth, but the song... It was hauntingly beautiful, and exquisitely sad at the same time.

More tears, seemingly drawn from a never-ending reserve, slipped from the corners of my eyes and dripped down onto my pillow. I wanted to interrupt him—I had so many questions about the song—but instead, I just listened, letting the warm cadence of his voice take me away.

4

My eyes slid open, barely a slit, and I sighed. Grey's strong arm was draped possessively over my waist, his body a hard line behind me. It was a simple thing, but one that helped chase away the nightmare I had been having. So many awful things this time, too: Tian disappearing, Maddox injured, Ambrose dead, and Leo somehow winding up inside of Grey.

Thank Scipio it was all a nightmare.

Behind me, Grey shifted slightly, his arm tightening around me, and my sleepy smile grew wider. He inhaled deeply, his nose planted against my neck, and then made a sound of masculine pleasure.

"Liana."

I turned toward the familiar voice, moving languidly in his arms so as not to disturb him too much. As soon as I was facing him, I realized he was sleeping, and was touched that I affected him so much that he was dreaming about me. I hoped it was a better dream than the one I had been having.

I watched him sleep, my eyes tracing the planes of his face, trying to memorize every detail. The tousle of dark blond hair that stuck upright in a few places, giving him a vaguely boyish look. The way his lips curved and dipped in the middle, complemented by the sultry fullness of his lower lip. His long, dark brown lashes, which lay like twin crescent moons on his cheek.

His eyelashes fluttered, but otherwise, he was still, and I reached up and smoothed some hair from his brow, letting my fingers drift gently through the silky softness of it. Then I moved down, lightly tracing over his face. He was so beautiful. I could lie there forever.

He sighed in his sleep, and I slowed my fingers' meandering, worried I was waking him. Too late, it seemed, as his eyes slid open. Immediately they snapped into focus on me, first lightening to a warm, golden honey-brown, and then growing dark and heavy. I licked my lips, his look causing an intriguing bolt of lightning to dance down my spine.

His eyes zeroed in on my tongue, and I watched as a slow, hungry smile started to spread wider and wider. I took a shaky breath in, the anticipation of the kiss he was about to give me sending more shivers down my back and along my skin. I wanted him to kiss me. I *needed* him to kiss me.

I lifted my chin up just a fraction of an inch, and then his mouth was on mine, so hot and silky that it felt like heaven. He wasn't gentle, either; he kissed me with dizzying intensity, like he was drowning and I was pure oxygen. It floored me, heat beginning to form and spread from that secret place between my thighs.

We'd never taken it this far, but after the nightmare I'd just had, I needed him—wanted him with a desperation that scared me a little bit. His hand slid from my waist to my hip, and then he moved closer, rolling me partially onto my back before

CHAPTER 4

shifting one of his bare legs between mine. I shivered at the sensation of his leg as it stroked over my knee and calves.

Grey chuckled in his throat as he moved to deepen the kiss, nipping at my bottom lip until my lips parted. Then his tongue slid inside my mouth, and I melted, my body jackknifing against his with a deep shudder. His kiss didn't stop at simply loving me with his mouth; he kissed me to devour me. I was burning over his taste, his touch—and if he didn't do something soon to put out this fire, then I would.

I tried to lose myself in his kisses, my hands going to his chest and shoulders and stroking over them, but there was a niggling in the back of my mind, making me feel like I was missing something. But that was ridiculous. What could I be missing in this moment? I relaxed some, sucking his lower lip into my mouth and letting it go slowly, earning me a choked cry from Grey.

The feeling didn't go away. If anything, it intensified, trying to make me remember something. And... my mind kept floating back to my nightmare. Leo inside of Grey's body.

I kissed Grey harder, trying to ignore it, but it wouldn't relent. It was like an irritating itch, one that was keeping me from enjoying the pleasure of Grey's lips on mine and the tight way he held me. I broke off the kiss with a gasp, trying to rid myself of the confused sensation, and Grey leaned back, his eyes hooded and dark.

"Liana," he breathed again.

I lifted my head as he dipped his down again for another kiss, and he started kissing my neck instead. My body shivered in response, but my mind... It kept screaming at me that there was something wrong. That this wasn't a dream.

But I knew that. I knew it wasn't a dream. I was with Grey, and everything was fine. I'd just had a nightmare, that was all.

Grey kissed his way back up the length of my neck, his tongue darting out to trace delicious patterns against my skin.

Only this time, the hair on my arms and neck rose up in alarm as the nightmare from last night crept into my mind. It was getting ridiculous. I needed something to remind myself that this was real, and that everything else had been a nightmare. What had I done before I'd gone to sleep?

He rained kisses on my jawline, trying to distract me, but a slightly queasy feeling started to overcome me. I needed to figure out what was going on. I closed my eyes and focused, and seconds later, it all came rushing back to me. I had wanted to dismiss it as a nightmare, but it hadn't been. Ambrose had been murdered, Maddox beaten. I had broken down in the worst possible way.

And Leo was inside of Grey. Kissing me.

His mouth found mine again, but this time I stiffened, pressing my lips together into a hard line. He kept trying to kiss me, his mouth working on mine, trying to get me to soften. Suddenly I felt trapped under him, and the sensation grew steadily as he continued to kiss me, seemingly oblivious to my frozen state. I started counting the seconds off in my head, waiting for him to get the signal, but didn't make it past two before I hooked his leg and pushed his shoulder, throwing him off of me and back onto the bed. Then I was up and moving, ignoring the icy touch of the floor under my feet as I tried to get as far away from Leo as possible.

I made it to the corner by the door and turned, placing my back against the wall, my chest heaving. Leo lay on his side, watching me with a bemused glint in his now dark chocolate eyes. I couldn't imagine Leo being capable of generating a look like that, but there it was... and it was filling me with some confused feelings. This needed to stop.

CHAPTER 4

"Leo, can we just... take a breath here?" I asked softly, fumbling for the right thing to say.

He looked at me with heavy eyelids, and then slid out from under the cover and stood to his full height. He wasn't wearing a shirt, only shorts that were similar to mine, but white. His chest wasn't overwrought with muscles, but his abs were clearly defined in three little sets of two, stacked one on top of the other, and dragging my eyes inexplicably downward, to the hard length of him—which was barely being contained by his shorts. My face heated, telling me it had turned beet red.

His legs flexed, and he started to move toward me.

"Leo?" I asked, alarm acting like ice-cold water being thrown on my spine. I ducked under him and moved to the next corner.

But he slowly turned and began to follow me again, not responding. This wasn't like him! In fact, the whole kissing thing wasn't like him. Was something *wrong* with him? With Grey?

My heart pounded in my chest. "Leo, are you okay?" I asked.

His facial muscles were still. He made no response other than to start gliding toward me again, like a chunk of iron being dragged by a magnet. I knew he intended to kiss me again; I could see it in the way he held his mouth, and the power with which he stalked forward.

A part of me wanted to melt right into him on the spot, but the rest of me was screaming that I had to stop him. "Leo!" I said sharply, trying to reach him.

He said nothing, just closed the distance, one hand reaching for my head, the other for my hip. This had to stop.

"*Leo, you're scaring me!*" I cried out, flinching back.

He froze. For several seconds nothing happened, and then he slowly blinked his eyes once, and a quizzical expression came over his face. "Liana? What's wrong? Why are you shaking like that?"

I inhaled and carefully moved around him, needing to carve a little bit of space between the two of us. I used the movement to consider his question. He didn't seem to remember what had happened, and I wasn't so sure that I was going to tell him. It was...

I clenched my fists together, trying not to hyperventilate. I had just made out with Grey, only it wasn't Grey. Had I just cheated on my comatose boyfriend? With himself? How did that even work?

I wasn't sure, but it was maddeningly confusing.

"Liana," Leo said, his voice carrying a symphony of concern. "What's—"

The door in front of me slid open, revealing Zoe and Eric, my two best friends in the Tower. Both were wearing the orange coveralls of the Mechanics Department—and very alarmed expressions on their faces.

"We heard you shout, Liana," Zoe said, stepping into the room. Her eyebrow rose when she saw Leo standing right behind me, and I felt heat start to spark into my cheeks. "Are you okay?"

Scipio kill me now, could this awkwardness get any worse?

"I'm..." I met my friend's dark blue eyes and shook my head slightly, signaling my distress.

Zoe narrowed her gaze and immediately took charge. "Liana, grab a robe and come have a cup of tea with me in the living room. Eric, keep Leo company while I get her all caught up, please and thank you, my love."

Eric brightened, as if someone had set fire to a stack of kindling somewhere inside of him, and I had to look away, my own mixed emotions making me feel unjustifiably angry. For several brief minutes this morning, I had forgotten about everything awful that had happened, and thought Grey was safe, in

CHAPTER 4

my arms. Now that it was all gone again, I resented their happiness.

But that wasn't right. I needed to get out of this room.

I moved over to the closet, pointedly ignoring Leo's wounded expression, and grabbed my robe. Then I left, keeping my eyes glued to the ground, Zoe letting me pass her and then following behind me. I only started to relax when I heard the door close, and then I exhaled sharply, stopping for a moment to catch myself on the wall.

"Liana, what happened?" Zoe asked, one arm coming around my waist while the other draped my arm over her shoulder for support. I leaned into her and let her lead the way. "Why was Leo in your room?"

I looked up at my friend and then away, shaking my head. "I... I..." I couldn't make the words come. So I did what I did best: I lied and changed the subject. "That's not important right now. Did you find Tian? Is Maddox okay? Have you heard anything from Lacey or about the investigation? Why are you here? Did Lacey kick you out of the department?"

Zoe puffed out her cheeks. "We didn't find Tian," she began softly. "We couldn't find any trace of whoever captured her, but Lacey's people took lots of images and data. We're still waiting for them to send it to us, although I'm not certain they will now." She paused, her mouth working. "Leo told us about Ambrose and said that Lacey came here. What is she going to do to us?"

I shook my head, remembering the devastated woman from the night before. "I don't know," I admitted, fear creeping up and lassoing itself around my heart. "I'm trying to figure something out, a way to convince her not to..." Well, I was going to be in a second—just as soon as I knew what was happening. "What about Maddox?"

"She's in her room," Zoe informed me. We had just reached

the kitchen, but as soon as Zoe said it, I started to turn. I had to see her.

Zoe stopped me with a flex of her surprisingly strong arm. "Quess is in there with her," she said firmly. "She's going to be fine, but it was close. Her ribs were badly broken, Liana. They punctured her lung, and she was bleeding internally. If the Medics had been just a minute later..." She trailed off, shuddering, and then wrapped her arms around me. "I'm so glad she's okay. I didn't... I didn't know what to make of her at first, but..."

I hugged my friend back as she cried, giving her comfort and relishing the feel of her. My own eyes burned from all the crying I had done last night, but I stopped my tears from forming. The tear ducts were irritated, and I was dehydrated. Crying right now would feel like pushing grains of salt through my eyes, and besides, Maddox was alive. She was safe.

Thank Scipio for the Medica. They could cure almost any physical trauma around, provided their patient was still alive in the first place—and they were good at keeping their patients alive once they got to them.

If only Ambrose had still been alive when we had gotten to *him*. If only we could've gotten the Medics to him...

Zoe sniffled and pulled away, scrubbing her eyes with the back of her hand. "We came over yesterday. I hope you don't mind, but... I was afraid of what would happen to us if we slept in Cogstown." I hated the nervous look in her eyes—the deep fear—and was glad she had been sensible and stayed here. "Anyway," she continued, clearing her throat. "We have the Paragon with us, so don't worry about that."

I hadn't even thought of the stash of Paragon before she said anything, so I accepted the news with mixed feelings. On the one hand, I was glad she had the foresight to keep it with her. With the attack on Ambrose, I couldn't help but feel vulnerable, and Zoe and Eric had been mixed up in Devon's trial, victims of being my friends. If they had been watching me, they were watching them, which meant we couldn't assume their homes, let alone our own, were safe. Leaving an illegal rank-altering medication lying around to be discovered was only a recipe for disaster. But I should've been around to remind her about it, and then reassure her that everything was going to be okay. Not wasting time in bed.

How long had I been asleep? I prayed it wasn't for more than a few hours; I couldn't bear the idea that I had been sleeping when everyone needed me the most. I exhaled and looked at my indicator, untangling myself from Zoe long enough to check the time.

Scipio help me, it was six in the morning. I wasn't sure what time Leo had gotten me to bed, but I was guessing it was long before six p.m. yesterday. I'd slept too long.

Again.

Guilt flared through me, but I tamped it down. I needed to get on top of things, not wallow in self-pity.

"Do we know anything about what attacked Tian?" I asked. "Any clues on how to find her?"

Zoe ran her hands down the shaved sides of her dark hair and shook her head, her expression tight. "No idea who or what it was, and like I said, Lacey's people haven't sent the data they collected yet. We couldn't do anything else after they finished their investigation. There's no sign of Tian's net coming up on the sensor sweeps that Alex and Mercury are running, and all of the nets Leo and you recovered belonged to the people who were killed." I tried to block out the image of the handful of nets we'd found with the tendrils still out, and failed, my mind flashing to the one piece that had a chunk of brain still attached at the end.

The image made my stomach roil, and I quickly rushed over to the sink, coughing, on the verge of losing the contents of my stomach. Zoe was there, rubbing her hand against my back as I hacked, but luckily the only thing that came out of me was a lot of saliva, which I washed out of my mouth and down the sink. I splashed the cold water on my face and the back of my neck as well. It helped, and I slowly began to relax.

"Sorry," I muttered, slurping in a mouthful of water from the faucet and spitting again, trying to rinse away the sharp, acrid taste formed by dry heaving.

I shut the water down a second later, and forced myself to suck in a deep, calming breath.

"It's okay," Zoe crooned soothingly. "If you'll remember, I did throw up when I saw them."

"And I went into shock," I replied bitterly. It was true. I had. Seeing those bodies on the ground, coupled with my fear of seeing Tian among them, had proven to be too much for my psyche to handle. Another weakness.

Zoe gave me an unreadable look. "What's wrong?"

"Other than everything?" I asked with a tired laugh. "Just everything."

Her eyes narrowed, and she tilted her head to one side. "I know you better than anyone else in this Tower, and I know when something else is going on. Is this about Leo? Did he do something to hurt you?"

"What?" My eyes widened at the very idea. Leo wouldn't hurt me. He was my friend!

Who was also acting pretty oddly. Was it a side effect of sleeping? As an AI, he didn't have to sleep, but in Grey's body, he did. Maybe it was having some sort of weird effect that caused his libido to ramp up? Or... was it Grey's libido that was having an effect on him? I was certain Leo understood the rudi-

CHAPTER 4

mentary principle of sexual intercourse, but he couldn't have experienced a rush of hormones or pheromones in the moment. He didn't know the pleasure of being touched, or how it actually felt. Maybe the sensations were too confusing, and part of Grey's subconscious mind had taken hold?

I wasn't sure, and the only way to find out was to ask him. But I wasn't ready to do that just yet—not with the feel of his lips still on mine, haunting me.

Coward, I told myself.

I must've been emoting, because Zoe seemed to pick up on my turmoil immediately, reaching out with a hand and gently touching my shoulder. "This isn't your fault," she said, her voice steady and certain.

"If I had just netted Maddox and Ambrose, they would've been with us," I retorted angrily. "Quess wanted me to. I just..."

Zoe's lips pressed firmly together. "I don't think there was a right decision in this case, Liana. Ambrose's enemies, whoever they were, were coming for him no matter what. You did what you could, given the circumstances. But these people are determined. They have resources that we don't. This is not your fault."

I heard the words, but I didn't believe them. She didn't understand; I had purposefully hidden Tian's predicament from Maddox in order to keep her there with Ambrose, so she could protect him with a clear head. I had considered someone being after Tian an attempt to lure us out—but I had thought that meant out of the Citadel. I had assumed Maddox and Ambrose would be safe in the apartment, and that assumption had gotten Ambrose killed, and Maddox badly beaten. I knew Zoe was trying to help me, but there wasn't any helping me. I had failed.

I needed to own up to that.

Zoe was waiting for me to say something, and I knew she

wanted me to agree with what she was saying. But I couldn't. I needed the guilt and failure. They'd make me stronger and smarter and more able to protect my friends.

I hoped.

"Zoe, I—"

The door chimed. "Knight Commander Astor Felix to speak with Liana Castell and Maddox Kerrin regarding the murder of Knight Elite Ambrose Klein," it announced in an imperious tone.

My eyes widened, and I looked at Zoe. It seemed the investigation was about to begin.

5

Knight Commander Astrid Felix was *here?* And taking point on the investigation into Ambrose's death? I was impressed; it meant the council had moved quickly, and had selected one of the most honorable Knights in the entire Citadel.

Of course, I knew her personally through my mother. Astrid Felix had been her commanding officer out of the Academy, and my mother had held dinner parties with Astrid and her husband, which my brother and I always attended.

I really liked Astrid. She had some of the best stories about being a Knight, many of which had inspired me to want to be one. But I hadn't seen her since I turned fifteen, and received my adult net and initial ranking—an average seven. My mother and father had been so humiliated by the number that they had refused to invite Astrid over until I got my ranking up.

I gnawed on my lip, trying to think. She was a shrewd investigator, often referred to as the Hound of the Citadel, and had retired from active duty twelve years ago to start teaching at the

Academy. If the council was bringing her out of retirement to act as lead investigator, they were sending a powerful message to whoever murdered Ambrose. They were coming for him—or them.

Nothing escaped Astrid Felix. Nothing.

I shuddered, thinking about our circumstances. We weren't the murderers, but we *were* criminals, and had drugs in the apartment that could modify an individual's rank. If she decided to perform a search...

They had to go. And someone had to take them. But how? And who? No doubt Astrid would want to talk to Zoe, Eric, and Leo as well.

Quess! Zoe had mentioned Quess being here! This was perfect. We'd made a point to keep our relationship with him a secret so we could use him to spy on any potential enemies. Which meant no one really knew about him—and Astrid wouldn't want to talk to him. We'd just have Maddox lie and say Quess was her boyfriend, and then he could walk out the front door with the pills.

But as soon as I thought about it, a half-dozen possible outcomes played out in my mind, some of them revolving around Astrid ordering a search of the bag, others featuring Quess finally being noticed by one of our enemies as he left our rooms, and then singled out because of it. He would have to leave the apartment alone, which was dangerous right now, but the less exposure he got with us, the better. Even something as innocent as being Maddox's boyfriend could get him caught in the crossfire, so any contact had to be kept secret.

But Quess and Zoe were both geniuses. If anyone could find a safe and unnoticeable way out for him, it was them.

The door chimed again, and Zoe, who had been watching me think with a worried expression in her blue eyes, turned to open it. I quickly grabbed her and pulled her to a halt. "Get the Paragon and take it into Maddox's room," I said quietly. "You're going to have to wake them up. Quess needs to take the Paragon out of here now. And tell Eric and Leo to get dressed. We're about to be interviewed."

Zoe gave me a searching look, and then nodded. She darted over, grabbed the beat-up blue bag off the floor—a diver's sack, completely waterproof and left over from her days as a member of Water Treatment—and slung it over her shoulder, then quickly raced off to deliver my messages.

I waited five more seconds, fixed an appropriately dazed and sorrowful look on my face (it wasn't hard), and moved over to the door to open it. As I hit the button for the door, I realized belatedly I was still in my undergarments, but merely pulled my robe tighter around my body. Astrid could deal with it.

The door slid open to reveal an elderly woman with dark gray hair that was almost metallic looking, and warm brown eyes lined with wrinkles. And though I hadn't seen her in five years, Astrid hadn't changed all that much. The only noticeable alteration was the few extra pounds she had packed on—likely a combination of the sedentary lifestyle of teaching and the lack of physical requirements, which automatically stopped when a Knight made it to sixty.

Astrid looked tired, but the corners of her mouth quirked up when she saw me. "Hey, kid," she said. "Long time no see."

I smiled in spite of myself, and leaned on the threshold. "Knight Commander Felix," I replied. I'd never been allowed to call her by her first name at home because it was unacceptable behavior for a child, so the rank and name came automatically. But in my head, I had always thought of her as Astrid.

I looked around the hall and saw that she was accompanied by two younger Knights—both males, probably in their mid-thirties. I did a double take when I recognized one. Lewis, one of the Knights I knew from the Citadel. He had been working internal security the last time I saw him, but now it seemed he had gotten a promotion. He gave me a nod, but kept his face carefully blank.

"Are they coming in?" I asked, suddenly nervous. We had five people in the apartment, so there wasn't much room for any more.

"No," Astrid said, waving her hand in the air. She paused for a second and then cocked her head at me, giving me a critical look. "Why do you ask?"

I bit my lip. "It's a little crowded in here at the moment. Some of my friends spent the night last night." It wasn't a lie.

Astrid arched a slim eyebrow and crossed her arms. "Let me guess. Grey Farmless, Zoe Elphesian, and Eric MacGillis." I nodded, and she sighed. "You know this looks like you stayed up all night to corroborate your testimonies, right?"

I hesitated for a fraction of a heartbeat and then shrugged. "If you want to take us in for separate questioning, that's fine, but we weren't here trying to get our stories straight. We were here because our teammate and friend was murdered in his own apartment, and my friends knew that I would need them for emotional support."

Astrid's face hardened into a careful mask. I knew that look from my mother's stories. Astrid was angry. But given the unfocused state of her eyes, I knew it wasn't at me. No—it was at the idea that someone had murdered a Knight inside the Citadel itself, a place that was supposed to be made safe by the Knights' presence alone. I was certain every honorable Knight was feeling it as well.

"I understand," she said after a moment, her eyes coming back to touch mine, more focused. "And no, I don't think you were actually corroborating. But I will have to note it in the report."

I nodded and stepped to one side. "Come inside, and I'll go see how people are doing with getting dressed."

"Tell Ms. Kerrin not to worry about getting dressed. She had surgery only a few hours ago, so she's allowed to be out of uniform. In fact, all of you are. This is your apartment, and I am interloping. Just have them come out."

"We're already on our way," Zoe announced from the hall. I turned and saw her helping guide Maddox into the room, holding her gingerly. Maddox looked...

Well, there wasn't an easy way to say it. Maddox looked like crap. Her black hair was disheveled and hung around her face in wild disarray. Bruises, some as bright as strawberries, others as purple as plums, were everywhere on her exposed flesh—her arms, her legs, her chest, and worst of all, her face. It was still slightly swollen, and although I could now see both her green eyes, they were dull and glassy. She'd broken several bones, it seemed, and was now covered in a specialized cast comprised of hexagonal cells that would help her bones heal faster. A small strip of the material was also over her nose, while a massive chunk wrapped around her ribs. Her hands were encased in gloves of the same substance, telling me that she'd broken several bones in her hands, and another cast covered her left ankle.

The bones would be healed in less than twenty-four hours, but it wasn't her physical wounds I was the most worried about. I was concerned about her mental wellbeing. I had no doubt that she was blaming herself for what happened. What was worse was that Maddox had always had a confidence that bordered on arrogance about her fighting ability. The situation in which she lost Ambrose would be a serious blow to that, and I was apprehensive about how it would affect her moving forward. I didn't want her to freeze up or panic should anyone try to attack her again.

Maddox nodded at Astrid with a grunt, but focused solely on getting over to the sofa. I followed behind her, hovering in case Maddox needed any extra support, but Zoe had it under control, and gently helped lower the larger girl to the sofa. Then she looked up at me, met my gaze, and gave me a slight nod to let me know that they had gotten Quess out with the Paragon. Undoubtedly, they had used the same technique Tian had before she was kidnapped, and slipped him through an air vent in Maddox's bedroom.

Leo and Eric emerged next, Leo back in his uniform (thank Scipio), and Eric modestly covered in a shirt and shorts. Leo gave me a reproachful look as he passed, and my cheeks heated slightly as I remembered that kiss.

It may have been wrong, but that didn't mean it hadn't felt very good.

I squashed the thought, grinding it into oblivion. I did *not* need to go there right now. I needed to keep it together, answer Astrid's questions, and then figure out our next move.

I offered Astrid one of the empty chairs, and sat on the other, Leo opting to lean on the wall next to the sofa. Astrid shifted around in her chair for a few moments, her mouth a grimace. "I do not miss the furniture in these apartments," she said, resting one arm on the chair and leaning into it. She looked around at each of us. "I'll try to make this as brief as possible. Engineer Green and several of her people confirmed that you were helping them search for a Cog child who had wandered off, and sensors show that your net was around Greenery 7 at the time. You as well, Mr. Farmless. But I need a statement as to everything that happened once you reached the apartment. Starting at the beginning."

CHAPTER 5

I spoke first, taking the lead. "There isn't much to tell." Astrid pulled out a pad and ejected a stylus from it, in anticipation of taking notes. "When we came back, we went to go see Maddox and..." I trailed off and swallowed. It felt wrong to say his name. I might not have killed him... but the blood was on my hands.

"It's okay, kid. We can just say 'him,' if that makes it easier."

Astrid was being kind, and I thanked her with my eyes. I wasn't sure how she would interpret my difficulties in saying his name, but I didn't care. I just needed to get through this as quickly as possible, using clinical language and trying to distance myself from the horrific scene that was still fresh in my mind.

"Grey unlocked the door, and I entered the room first. Initially, I didn't see any signs of a struggle, but as we entered the common area, we saw that there had been a fight. I found Maddox first. She was in the kitchen area. She'd..." I trailed off and looked at Maddox, and found her staring at her hands with a deep, sullen anger that was marred by a great sadness. I longed to wrap my arms around her and tell her it wasn't her fault, but if I stopped talking about it now, I'd never be able to start again. "She'd been badly beaten, and was possibly delirious. She tried to warn us about Ambrose, and Grey found him in the living area, already..."

My throat seized up around the word "dead", and I stopped, blinking back the tears. Ambrose hadn't been a bad person; he'd been raised believing that becoming Champion was his destiny, and had just let it go to his head a little bit.

"It's okay. Mr. Farmless, do you have anything to add to Liana's testimony?"

"I detected no signs that the apartment had been broken into through the door, and we didn't see any people coming or going from the apartment as we approached. My guess was that we missed the attack by minutes."

"By two, actually," Astrid informed him, and he nodded, his face a grim mask.

"There were no alarms on the floor," I added. "I'm not sure how Zale was notified and got up here so quickly without an alarm."

Astrid gave me a sardonic look, her mouth twisting. "The alarm did go off, but someone disabled the speakers on the floor to keep any neighbors from checking it out. Not that many people were home to begin with, since the Tourney challenge wasn't quite finished for the day. Scipio was still notified, and dispatched Zale, who decided he was the closest available Knight to handle the situation—even though he had just finished his round in the Tourney. It took him five minutes to reach Ambrose's apartment—time that would've been better spent calling in an active Knight who was nearer than he was. In my opinion, his refusal to do so contributed to Knight Elite Klein's death. But I can't prove that. I can prove that Lieutenant Zale's actions were misguided... but not nefarious. Hopefully, his incompetence will come out in the Tourney so I don't have to die knowing that prat became the Champion."

My eyes widened, and a surprised smile drifted across my lips. "You don't like him?"

She gave me a look. "Sweetie, I mentored him. He's a bootlicker and a sycophant—not a man you want running things. Good Knight, but not a good leader. But that's off topic. Let's continue." She scribbled a few things on the pad before looking sympathetically at Maddox. "I'm sorry to ask you this, kid, but I need to know what you can remember about the attack."

Maddox swallowed audibly, her mouth working. "I remember everything," she replied, her eyes glittering with tears.

"Ambrose and I had just finished having lunch with his friends, and they were heading off to watch the rest of the Tourney. Liana had asked us to stay in the apartments at all times—"

"Why?" Astrid asked her sharply, but her eyes flicked sharply to me, gazing at me through the suddenly impenetrable mask on her face.

6

My breath caught in my lungs for a second, and I felt a moment of fear. Maddox had made a mistake by letting that slip, and now Astrid was waiting for an answer from her.

Maddox shot me a helpless look, and I answered for her, not caring how it appeared to Astrid. The last thing Maddox needed was an interrogation, and if Astrid challenged me for answering, then I would call her out on it.

This time, I stuck to the truth—but only to an extent. "During our baton qualifiers, there was something off about the batons the opposing team was using. I was hit only once, but the charge on it was much stronger than it was supposed to be. I considered bringing my concerns up to the officials, but—"

"But you were worried that if the investigation turned up nothing, you would be ostracized for trying to cast doubt on another candidate," Astrid finished for me with a sigh. "That stupid rule." She shook her head. "You should've said something, Liana. Scipio changed the rules this year so that all complaints and investigations would be sealed. His recommendation was based on a few different things, but the end result is the same: if you suspect cheating, then reporting it will not earn you a black mark."

Scipio had changed the rule? That was weird, because as far as I knew, Scipio wasn't in complete control of his own faculties. He was being manipulated. I had seen it firsthand during our trial, when Lacey and Strum planted a false memory in Scipio's database to confirm my version of events, resulting in me being exonerated for the crime of murdering the former Champion, Devon Alexander, and my mentor, Gerome Nobliss. But if someone had created this rule through Scipio, then I had to wonder why they had. What purpose would it serve?

I wasn't sure, and I made a mental note to ask Leo... once I felt comfortable with him again.

Meanwhile, Astrid's stylus dipped up and down, and I watched as she swiped a finger across her pad, seeming to look something up. Her finger tapped the screen twice, and a moment later, a frown twisted her lips downward. She clicked another button, made a few notes, and then looked at Maddox. "I apologize for interrupting you, kid. I know this is quite hard for you, so I promise I won't do it again."

Maddox clenched her jaw tight, a look of fierce determination on her face. "Good, because I'm only going to be able to do this once," she said, and Zoe reached out and rested a gentle hand over Maddox's wrapped one. The taller girl gave Zoe a grateful smile—but it didn't last.

"Shortly after his friends left, we were chatting in the living room, when I swore I heard the sound of the door opening. I stood up to check it out, and then suddenly six or seven people..." She shuddered, exhaling slowly. "I'm honestly not sure how many. I just know that three of them were on me before I could..." She trailed off with a choked cry, and Zoe scooted closer to her, rubbing her arm soothingly. I doubted Maddox noticed. She was practically shaking, tears running down her cheeks. "They grabbed me and dragged me into the kitchen. One sucker-punched me in the stomach, and I went down. They started kicking me. They started kicking both of us. I heard Ambrose... He tried to fight back, but there were so many, and then there was this crunching sound, and Ambrose... He just stopped making any noise. I was certain I was next... I thought I was going to die."

Her voice grew high, her breathing panicked as she tried to recount everything from start to finish. I knew she was leaving the details out, but I could understand; she didn't need to tell Astrid what it felt like to feel her ribs breaking while she was helpless on the floor, listening to Ambrose's cries of pain, the sound of his death.

Zoe was constantly there, trying to soothe her. A moment later, she gave Astrid a questioning look. "Do you need any more, or can I take her back to bed? She needs her rest."

Astrid tapped her pad and then rotated it to face Maddox, answering Zoe's question indirectly. "Do you recognize any of these people from the attack?" She held the pad out at an angle, and I could see rows and rows of image grabs from net IDs, but paused when I noted the background color. Background colors were how we could tell the work status of a citizen, with the color of their department to show that they were working, a flat gray to show that they weren't, yellow if they were injured. The backdrop for all of the photos was purple, indicating that they were all contestants from the Tourney.

Maddox stared at the pictures, her eyes searching, and then reached out and tapped on two to drag the images up and scroll through them. She picked two more, and then shook her head.

"Those are the only ones I remember," she said tiredly. "They were contestants?"

Astrid took the pad back, her face an unreadable mask. "I'm going to tell you something, but only because it will be made public in a few hours, on my insistence. The Tourney and the Citadel have had a massive security breach. These ten people—" She tapped something on the pad and turned it around to me, revealing two rows of five pictures. "—seem to have used false nets to gain access to the Citadel and the Tourney."

"What?" I exclaimed. "How?"

She sighed and pinched the bridge of her nose. "We're not entirely sure yet, but it seems that they exposed a weakness in how we handle our citizen/net scans. We assumed that the scanners in the Citadel were foolproof, but apparently they managed to get around the system by uploading a virus into the scanner's buffer and forcing the computer to accept the false IDs as the real thing—and that included giving them permission to enter Ambrose's apartment through the door override privileges they got as a result of their falsified ranking."

I was stunned. The level of preparation that had gone into this was staggering. They'd had to falsify nets, which meant getting blank ones, which I knew from personal experience wasn't the easiest thing to do. Then they had created a virus in order to bypass the security in the Citadel. It wasn't something anyone could have done on a whim. It took time. It took planning.

"Have you captured any of them?" I asked, hoping that she would say yes. I wasn't sure how I could pull it off yet, but if she had one of them, then I had some questions for them. I wanted to know who they worked for, and whether they had gone after Tian to draw us away from Ambrose. I knew it had to be the same people, and I was going to make them tell me where Tian was. Also... I wanted to look into the faces of Ambrose's killers—and I was betting Lacey would want to as well.

Astrid's frown twisted even tighter. "No," she grated out. "As soon as the techs discovered the credentials of the last person to enter the room before you and Grey did, we moved to detain him and his entire team—but they were gone. That made us figure out something else was wrong, and I ordered them to dig a little deeper. It seems my gut was right, because the techs uncovered the virus. We ran a trace on it through the remaining candidates, and these six stood out. Unfortunately, they were already gone as well. What's more, we ran facial recognition on their image grabs, but there isn't a single match to be found in the Tower. Whoever these people are, they are very good at covering their tracks."

I gave her a hard look. "Are *we* safe?"

She returned my gaze, and answered honestly. "I don't know. Which was why I didn't make a big deal about all of you being up here. There's a conspiracy at work here, I'm sure of it. I just can't seem to figure out what it is."

She tucked her pad away and leaned back in her chair for a moment, stroking her cheek. "All right, kids, who's got questions for me? Bearing in mind, I've said all I'm going to say about the investigation at this point."

It was a fair statement. No doubt she'd already revealed more than she should've, but knowing her, she had made sure to include the slip in her notes. She had too much integrity not to. Still, I was disappointed. I wanted to know more about the ten individuals who had infiltrated the Tourney, and why facial recognition couldn't find them. I supposed that they could have assumed disguises, like Quess did, but... would they be wearing the makeup the rest of their lives? How could they disappear inside the Tower?

I knew how we did it: we had paint designed by Quess that blocked our net transmissions, making it impossible for Scipio to see us. But this wasn't the same. Our *faces* would still be recognized by the sensors around the Tower, which was why we'd had to disguise ourselves. These ten people had made a massive sacrifice in murdering Ambrose; they were now enemies of the Tower, and their faces would be searched for constantly, until the day they were found. Wherever they were hiding would likely be their home for the rest of their lives, for they would be unable to step outside again without risking exposure—which seemed like a miserable life.

"I hope this doesn't sound awful, but... what will happen to the Tourney now?" Leo asked.

Astrid sniffed. "You'll receive notification in a few hours that, if you wish to drop out, you'll have to do it by tomorrow evening. Teams that were found to have infiltrators in them will be broken up and randomly reassigned or formed into new teams. If your team chooses to continue, you'll have to select a new leader, and your open slot will be filled randomly— although you can reject the first candidate, if you'd like to. That's if you choose to proceed, of course. No one would blame you for backing out. Still, Ambrose was the driving force behind your team, as I understood it." She smiled at me. "How do you feel about it, kid? You're the most popular candidate on your team."

I hesitated. I hadn't even thought about what would happen with the Tourney, nor whether or not we were proceeding. In truth, once I had seen Ambrose's still form, I had figured that we were done with it. That we'd have to escape the Citadel... or die trying. But Lacey hadn't followed through on her threat to turn us in, and Tian was still missing, so I felt... stuck. And uncertain of what to do.

CHAPTER 6

Astrid took my hesitance as a negative response, and looked disappointed. "That's too bad," she murmured softly, slowly pushing up from her chair. "But I think your mother will be relieved. She netted me last night, asking about you. Are you and she not on speaking terms?"

I shifted awkwardly. My relationship with my parents was the very definition of strained, but the last few interactions with my mother had left me feeling confused about her. Like she was actually starting to care about me—the real me, rather than the girl she had always wanted me to be. She seemed concerned about me, and not just in a selfish way, for once.

I wanted to explore it, but at the same time, I was afraid. I had been willing to cut both of my parents out of my life when I had left, but my mother was making it difficult to do so, which was... strange.

"She stopped by eight times, yesterday," Zoe added. "It was all I could do to keep her out and let you get your rest."

Eight times? That was a bit much, especially for my mom. Was she... Was she worried? Was this what worried looked like on her?

"I'll make sure to net her," I said with a nod.

Astrid's eyebrow twitched—a sign of disapproval—but she nodded. "Good. All of you, thank you for your time. I hope to find whoever killed your friend soon, and bring them to justice."

"Thank you," I murmured. I stood up and followed her over to the door. "Let me know if there's anything more we can do."

Astrid smiled at me. "Of course. Net me if you think of anything else."

She exited, and the two Knights waiting for her fell into line. Lewis turned long enough to wave, and then they were gone, heading back down the hallway. I watched them go for a minute, feeling surprisingly optimistic that something would actually get done with Astrid on the investigation. Maybe if we were lucky, she'd figure out who was conspiring with those ten individuals, and possibly give us a clue as to who our enemies might be. We wouldn't have to be alone anymore; we'd have experienced Knights who could help us...

I sighed and shut the door. It was wishful thinking. As much as I looked up to Astrid, and had enjoyed our family dinners with her, there was no way of knowing what her true motivations were. For all I knew, she'd been selected because she was the best person to execute a coverup. Her integrity was beyond reproach, earned from years of dogged investigations and a reputation for never backing down, no matter where her investigation took her. But how much of that was true? How could we trust that she was *actually trying* to catch Ambrose's killers?

I wasn't sure, but there was nothing we could do about it.

I turned around and headed back into the living room, freezing when I saw everyone looking at me expectantly.

"What happens now?" Zoe asked.

7

The question caused my stomach to twist in knots, a deep anxiety gripping my throat. They were all wondering what happened next, and they expected me to have an answer for all of our problems. I'd given each issue some thought here and there, but was paralyzed by a deep insecurity that I was about to make the wrong call. Like I had so many times before.

I didn't even know which issue to address first, and the realization hit me like being splashed with a bucket of icy water. The entire room was expectant, watching me, but I was frozen, unable to even determine what we should do next. Find Tian? Plead with Lacey? Contact Mercury? Talk to Leo?

A sharp pressure started to weigh on my chest, and I realized that I needed to get out of there before I had another panic attack.

My mind fumbled for an excuse, and I was relieved to realize that Astrid had provided me with a simple one. "Before we do anything, I think I should probably go and see what my mom wants," I said hurriedly. "If not, she's liable to barge in here at any moment, and might hear something that we don't need her to hear. I won't be long. Maybe just half an hour."

"I'll go with you," Leo said, pushing off from the wall and starting toward me.

"*No!*" I said emphatically, shaking my head for good measure. The last thing I wanted was for Leo to come with me. Things were still too weird after this morning, and I had no idea how to even bring up his behavior without causing deep embarrassment.

His eyes widened, and he looked away, one arm reaching up to grab his bicep in a self-conscious way. "You shouldn't go alone," he said after a moment, sighing.

"I'll be fine," I insisted, quickly spinning through a few ideas on how to reassure them that I was right. "My parents only live six floors up, and I can take the elevator at the end of the hall. Plus, the Citadel is on high alert right now. It'll only take me a few minutes, half an hour at the most, and I'll net if anything comes up."

I was rambling, and slowly backing toward the door. Zoe stood up, her expression concerned, but I hit the button and slipped out, shutting the door with an "I'll be okay."

I quickly hurried down the hall, moving away from the apartment as if I had wings made of fire. I checked over my shoulder after a few seconds, and was relieved to see that no one had followed me. I was confident that Zoe had called them off, perhaps recognizing that I needed some time to get myself together—and I loved her for that, even if I was running away from her, too.

A deep gloom had settled into the Citadel. The hall felt quieter than usual, as if the entire structure was in a state of deep melancholy. Apprehension crept down my neck as I walked, and I couldn't help looking around, paranoid that someone could sneak up on me at any moment.

This might not have been the best way to get alone time, Liana, a voice in my head chided me.

I ignored it and kept walking.

Oh, and by the way, you're still in your undergarments and robe, the voice mockingly said in parting, and as I looked down, I realized it was right. But I wasn't going back, so I drew the edges of the robe around myself, and kept walking. If anyone wanted to report me for being out of uniform, they could. I didn't care.

The hall ended right at the elevator bay that ran through the center of the Citadel. I entered the reception area, considered the elevator for a second or two, and then moved around the twin circular tubes of the elevator shafts into the small, narrow space behind them.

In the Citadel, most Knights used their lashes to move up and down, exiting through the lashways that led outside. I knew for a fact that the lashways were sealed up—it was standard protocol when the Citadel was in lockdown mode—so everyone was probably using the elevators instead.

Which meant the stairs would be even more deserted than usual. Even with the lashways closed, Knights considered climbing steps to be mundane. And why wouldn't they, with the lashes giving them wings? Here I would be guaranteed solitude, which would give me time to think.

I pressed on a panel on the wall, and gave the scanner my name and ID number. It ran for a long time, and I realized it was probably confirming my identity with Scipio before giving me access. I had just about given up hope that it would let me in when it suddenly beeped softly, and the door slid to one side with a pneumatic hiss.

The stairwell didn't quite match up with the rest of the

architecture of the Citadel. Instead of dark metal with beautiful whorls of lighter color through it, the entire thing reminded me of a grate or a cage, made of thin sheet metal with patterned holes. Lights ran along the walls, but on the outside of the stairwell, creating thousands of artificial sunbeams that poured in through the hundreds of densely packed holes.

I began to climb, shoving my hands into my pockets. I had to come back to my friends with answers and a plan or two for what to do, and that meant breaking each problem down and ranking the issues from most important to least.

I considered my problems, weighed them carefully, and then begrudgingly placed the nebulous situation with Lacey over finding Tian. I rationalized that everything that could be done there was already being done. I was certain that Quess, Mercury, and Alex—my twin—were all scouring the Tower, looking for her. I also convinced myself that if I didn't try to get ahead of Lacey before she had a chance to move against us, none of us would even have a chance at finding Tian. Lacey would make sure of it.

I bit my lip, my heart aching for Lacey. I might not completely trust her, but I did like her, and I hated that she was suffering right now. I knew there was nothing I could do to make her pain go away, and that any attempt to apologize would be met with derision and possibly violence, so I decided to steer away from an emotional approach and focus, instead, on a logical one.

What could I offer Lacey that would keep her from turning her evidence over and having us arrested and expelled for committing a terrorist act against Scipio?

I considered it for a long time. My first instinct was to offer to hunt down Ambrose's killers and take them to Lacey. I was certain that the idea would appeal to her; after all, whoever had ordered Ambrose's death was working against her, and I had to imagine the information his killers could offer would be of great use.

Not to mention, I worried about Astrid actually making any headway in finding Ambrose's killers. If her intentions were honorable, then that meant she had no idea of the legacy war that was just getting started. If her intentions weren't honorable... then that meant she was working with the legacies herself, and that Ambrose's murderers would get away with it. That was something I wasn't willing to stand for.

But justice for Ambrose wasn't the only thing Lacey wanted. She had asked me to protect Ambrose during the Tourney so that she and her group could get him into the position of Champion, and have another vote in the council. They claimed they were on Scipio's side, trying to save him from the other legacy groups who were attacking him, though I only had their word on that. Regardless, Ambrose's death left their plans for gaining some modicum of control over the council in tatters. And a very real possibility existed that whoever won the Tourney would be working for their enemies.

They needed that seat. Desperately. Right now, they were just two out of six members of the council, unable to do much in the way of enacting policy changes. Whether that was a result of the other councilors blindly following Scipio's recommendations, or was for more nefarious reasons, was moot; the fact remained that they didn't have enough power or allies inside the council. But if they had an ally in the position of Champion, they'd be able to stop any new laws or protocols that were dangerous and damaging to the Tower. Possibly even overturn a few of the more insane ones.

If that was what Lacey ultimately wanted, then the practical solution was easy to reach: find Lacey another ally, and help that person win the Tourney. That... wasn't so easy.

Lacey had told me once that Ambrose had been the only legacy of theirs that she'd ever been able to successfully sneak into the Citadel. There wasn't anyone else there she trusted, and who could blame her? She obviously didn't trust Devon, who had been Champion for over twenty-five years—more than enough time to cultivate a legion of followers, if he were so inclined. And his followers would no doubt continue with whatever his plans were, which was against what Lacey wanted. That made it difficult for her to trust any other Knight inside the Citadel.

The more I considered finding someone to replace Ambrose, the less I liked it. I wasn't comfortable with entrusting the fate of the Tower to anyone else, just like that. How could I ever be certain I had made the right choice? Tens of thousands of lives rested on that position, and if I put someone in there who wound up being an agent for the enemy, then it was the citizens who would suffer. I couldn't live with that. Couldn't even stand the queasiness that came with the idea of passing the reins on to someone else.

No, picking someone wasn't going to work. It carried too much risk of going sideways—and then losing the Tower and Scipio for good.

And that left only one solution.

I stopped on the top of the landing and lifted my wrist up to my face, tapping my indicator. "Contact Zoe Elphesian, 17M-241."

There was a pause, and then my net began to buzz as Zoe accepted the net. Good—I'd been a little worried she might not, after the way I left, although I knew it was a silly fear.

Are you okay? her digitally resynthesized voice demanded,

CHAPTER 7

and I could imagine everyone still sitting in the living room, watching her with bated breath, afraid I was under attack.

"I'm fine," I said, resuming my trek up the stairs. "I took the stairs to give myself a little time to think. To be honest... I freaked out a little bit back there, and I'm sorry for that."

It's okay, Zoe replied automatically. *I mean, you did it in a boneheaded kind of way, but I understand. So what's up?*

"I want you to reach out to Lacey on my behalf."

Why not just call Lacey yourself?

That was a really bad idea. I had considered it, and decided it was better to avoid direct contact with her for a while, to give her some space to breathe without the constant reminder that I was alive, while her cousin was dead.

"Lacey's too emotionally fragile for that, Zo," I informed her. "If I reach out to her, it could really upset her, and she might decide to turn us all over to the Knights for the stuff that went down at the trial. But you? You're one of her Cogs. And you're as empathetic as they come."

So, what, you want me to talk to her and try to convince her to back down? The implant in my ear canal managed to convey that she thought it was a bad idea.

Luckily, that wasn't my plan. "No. I want you to tell her that I'll do it. I'll stay in the Tourney and compete to become the next Champion. That way, she and Praetor Strum will get the support they need."

I stopped talking in an attempt not to ramble, and waited. I'd made it all the way up to another landing by the time she responded.

You want to become Champion? she asked, incredulous. *Have you thought this though?*

I sighed, trying not to feel irritated by the doubt in her voice.

I knew she knew that I didn't make decisions on a whim. This was just her way of asking for my rationale.

"Yes, I have," I informed her dutifully. "Look, Lacey needs someone who's willing to work with her and Strum on the council. And she isn't going to be able to find anyone she trusts before the next challenge. So it has to be me."

There was another long pause. *I see. I suppose having you as Champion would open a lot of doors for us, as well as helping us keep the Knights off our backs while we start working out ways to leave.*

I hadn't considered that. But there was a very good reason I hadn't: I had decided I wasn't going to leave with my friends. Instead, I was going to stay and help Leo on his quest to fix or replace Scipio. Even though I had told him that I could only worry about the seven people in our group, it had been a bald-faced lie. I couldn't abandon the people of the Tower to death. It was unconscionable.

But I wasn't ready to bring that up to Zoe yet. I hadn't even had the chance to tell Leo.

Thinking about him made me immediately flash to the kiss from this morning, and I carefully pulled away from the memory.

"Something like that. Listen... when you talk to Lacey, tell her that if she accepts my proposal, I'll help her find Ambrose's killers. But tell her I also expect her continued help in finding Tian. And she needs to tell us what's going on with that legacy net, and how to fix it."

I added the legacy net as an afterthought, because I realized I was going to need full access to it if I was going to fully understand what was going on in the Tower. It would help me learn about which issues Lacey and Strum were concerned about, and confirm once and for all that they were working to help Scipio, as that net contained tangent memories of the previous users, as well as information on the world before the End.

All the nets had been like that at the beginning of the Tower's history, but the IT Department had phased them out, insisting that they needed to for both security purposes and because the resources necessary to create them were too rare to spare on them. Supposedly.

I was certain tacking on demands was a bit gauche, but I doubted Lacey would entertain the idea of telling me more about the legacy net otherwise. Besides, I was certain Zoe would boil the language down into something softer and more palatable on my behalf.

All right. I'll net her and see what she says. Do you have a backup plan for if she says no?

I thought about it for a moment and then sighed. "Not really. I can't be certain that it will keep us safe, but the position brings power, which brings security. And... honestly, I don't think she has any choice. I don't think *we* do either. Running isn't an option anymore, Zoe. We have to take a stand."

Zoe was silent for a long moment, long enough for me to wonder if I was pushing them too far on this.

You're right, she announced eventually, and I exhaled, relieved. There was a slight pause, and then, *Leo thinks we should reach out to Strum as well, and I think he's right. Lacey's distraught, but in all likelihood, Strum is not. If we can convince him, he can reach Lacey.*

"Are you sure?" I asked. I knew they were allies, but I'd only seen them together a few times, in our first couple of meetings. Everything thereafter was handled by Lacey. That didn't smack of closeness. If anything, I worried that his interference could send Lacey over the brink.

Trust me, they have history. I think he can reach her.

I stopped in front of the door that led to my parents' floor, my fingers hovering over the panel. "If you think it'll work, then do it. Also, get Quess back to the apartment if he isn't back yet. I want to go over all the evidence we gathered from the condensation room next, and see if we can't figure out a way to find Tian."

He's already on his way back, she replied. *I called him right after you left. I'm glad you seem to have worked through what you needed to. Get to your parents, we'll get to work here, and you can rejoin us when you're finished there. Also... good luck.*

"Thanks," I replied dryly.

The buzz of the net in my skull came to a sudden stop, and I breathed a little easier. I took a moment to try to relax the tension that had built up... then opened the door, and stepped into the hall.

8

Why had I done this again?

I stared at the door that led to my parents' apartment, trying to trace the steps that had gotten me here, and realized that I had simply fixed it as a "destination" in my head, and then taken the slowest way there as an excuse to think.

I hadn't actually considered that I was going in to see my parents. And now that I was standing in front of their door, part of me wanted to turn around and head back the way I had come. I wasn't sure I had it in me to deal with this—not just because of the tangled web of emotions that came with interacting with my parents, but also because I had to be careful. They were on the same team as Lieutenant Zale, who had served under Devon Alexander for over fifteen years. The same guy who had just arrested me—albeit for only a few minutes—and was possibly working to bring down Scipio. There was every chance that he had something to do with Ambrose's death. If anyone was Devon's ally inside the Citadel, it was him.

Which meant my parents could be working for a man who wanted me dead. What was more, they could be doing it knowingly.

It occurred to me then that I could be walking into a trap, but I dismissed the idea. I hadn't told them I was coming, and I doubted that they would be reckless enough to attack me in their own home, this soon after Ambrose's death. It would be too suspicious.

My stomach churned. I was talking about my parents as if they were planning to kill me. And hey, my mom had offered to once, on the day I was born. Population rules in the Tower were very strict, and normally couples were permitted no more than two children. My parents had given birth to my sister Sybil, and then attempted to have a second child.

However, biology has a funny way of not always working out, and they had accidentally conceived twins: my brother Alex and myself. As Alex was born first, I was the burden—the extra mouth to feed. Normally, I would've been eliminated. My mother had even insisted on it.

But Scipio had interceded. For a while, my mom had thought Scipio had a destiny planned for me, and that idea had intensified after my sister Sybil died. But I later learned that Scipio had only saved me because somewhere else, an infant had been stillborn, and the population level had to be maintained. Needless to say, my parents had been less than thrilled to find out their youngest daughter was *normal*.

I sucked in a breath. Dwelling on the past was pointless, and did nothing to help me with the future. My mom apparently really wanted to see me, and if I didn't handle it now, she would persist. I'd just walk in, tell her I was all right, and then get out as quickly as possible.

That seemed easy enough.

CHAPTER 8

I pressed the button and announced my name and rank to the scanner, enduring a skull-rattling scan that felt slightly harder than normal. I belatedly realized that it probably was; the entire Citadel's security systems were following more stringent protocols in an effort to prevent any more infiltrators from getting around.

It ended heartbeats later, but I barely had a moment to breathe a sigh of relief before the door slid open, revealing my mother on the other side.

I'd never seen my mother looking so frazzled before. Her hair was down in dark waves around her face, and dark blue shadows that were almost black clung to the area under her eyes. She wasn't even in uniform, and it was already almost seven in the morning!

As soon as she saw me, relief poured into her eyes, and a second later, my mother—a woman who had found a thousand different ways to make me feel ashamed of myself my entire life—pulled me into a tight embrace, and held me as if she were afraid of letting me go.

A surge of powerful, mixed emotions reached up and wrapped a steely fist around my heart, and I froze, uncertain of what to do or how to react. A part of me wanted to push her off of me. She'd had her chance to be a mother to me, and she'd failed. She'd treated me more like one of her Squires—and a disappointing one at that. What made her think she was even worthy of holding me now?

On the other hand... my entire life, since I'd been a small child, this had been all I ever wanted from her. A simple hug, an encouraging word or two here or there. A mother who loved me for who I was, and didn't despise me for what I wasn't.

So I didn't push her away. But I didn't return the hug either, and a few seconds later, she broke it, keeping only her hands tethered to my shoulders. She glanced both ways down the hall, as if looking to see if anyone were there, watching us, and then pulled me inside and quickly shut the door behind us.

Then her hands were squeezing my shoulders, and she was looking at me with an intense gleam in her eyes. "What happened?" she demanded.

Of course. She just wanted to know my side of the story. It was unlikely anyone not in the investigation knew what was going on outside of a Knight being murdered. They probably knew it was Ambrose. But beyond that, they had no idea.

"I'm fine," I assured her, which was weird and made me hesitate for a second, as I tried to figure out what to say next. "I don't really know what happened. We were out of the Citadel, helping Zoe look for a missing child. When we got back... we found them."

My mother gave me a flat look that screamed "I don't believe you". And sure enough, she immediately said, "I'm not buying it, Liana. Not after what you said about your lash qualifier. Tell me the truth."

"The truth?" I asked, and a laugh escaped me at the absurdity of her request. Yes, I had made a mistake and let slip to her that my lash line had been tampered with during the qualifier. It had snapped, and I had almost died. But for her to be asking me for the whole *truth*? Even if I didn't suspect she was secretly working for Zale, I wouldn't have told her. Because I doubted very much that my mother—the very picture of a model Knight —could accept the truth. "Mom, trust me when I say that neither you nor Dad could ever handle the actual truth."

My mother frowned and opened her mouth to retort, but my father spoke first. "Don't speak to your mother like that," he growled. I glanced toward the living room, and saw him emerging from the opening, his eyes already narrowed in the familiar glare that always inhabited his face when I was in his presence.

Over the years, I had studiously avoided engaging my father. I'd submit to his anger rather than fighting back, because it was easier. And I was afraid. But after I had been exonerated for Devon's murder, I had changed—and I wasn't willing to put up with it anymore.

There were several different ways of dealing with bullies. The first was with humor. The second was by accepting their insults without showing any sign that they bothered you. I went with the former, knowing it would only irritate him more.

"Y'know what, Dad, you are perfectly right. Let me try again," I said, affecting a wide-eyed and innocent gaze. I turned to my mother and said, "Mom, trust me when I say that neither you nor Dad could ever handle the actual truth." This time I used an exaggerated, high-pitched voice.

My father made an irritated noise, but to my surprise, the corner of my mother's lips kicked up. It was gone within the blink of an eye, but I could've sworn I saw it.

"Silas, enough," she said harshly, before modulating her voice to a kinder tone. "Liana, let's sit down in the dining room."

I immediately moved to follow her, eager to have a little bit more space put between me and my parents. The entryway was not an ideal place for... whatever was going on.

We sat down at the table, my mom taking the chair at the head so she could be next to me, while my father sat across from us. He folded his arms across his chest and pursed his lips. He clearly didn't like that I was here.

"Liana, I know that Astrid is running point, but she's being very tight-lipped about the investigation. And there is something going on. People are trying to kill you."

Not me. Ambrose. And they had won. But I wasn't about to tell her or my father that.

"Mom, I've told you all I know," I said tiredly. "There isn't anything else going on. I promise."

"But yesterday you said that your lash end had been cut," she reiterated. "That wasn't a mistake—you said it in the heat of the moment, which means you believe it to be true."

I pressed my lips together and said nothing. She had a point, and it was futile to try to argue with her, because she was right. It was true—I *had* told her that in the heat of the moment. But that didn't change the fact that I had no intention of telling her what was really going on with Ambrose. She couldn't handle what was at the heart of the matter, or what it would do to her perceptions of Scipio and the Tower.

The silence stretched out for several long heartbeats, while my mother waited for me to respond, and I didn't.

It was my father who finally broke it. "You see, Holly, there is nothing more going on than a horrible act of violence. You're being paranoid. No one is targeting Liana."

There was something about his tone that really struck a nerve inside of me. The derisive and dismissive quality of it. And the snide look on his face when he spoke. My blood began to heat, until it felt like it was simmering just under my skin, a barely contained boil.

He'd used the same tone my entire life, and it had always made me feel less useful than the bin that held the family's compost. I had developed a certain immunity to it, but that didn't matter, as it wasn't actually directed at *me* this time.

It was directed at my mother. And witnessing him doing it to her, dismissing her like that... It made me angry beyond belief. He wasn't taking her seriously.

And I cared. I wasn't sure if it was because I didn't like the idea of him treating yet another member of his family like he had me, or if it was the fact that my mother was finally starting to care about me, but either way, it was insufferable.

And I wanted to wipe the smug look off of his face. So I told them the truth.

"Scipio is dying."

For several heartbeats, nothing happened. Both my parents sat there wearing the exact same expressions as they had before I uttered those three little words. Then again, I had just stated something that had the potential to give every citizen in the Tower a critical meltdown, so time to process was to be expected.

It started with my mother. Her eyes blinked several times in rapid succession, and she shook her head. "What? What do you mean?"

I carefully considered what I was going to reveal. I couldn't tip my hand as to knowing about legacies, because I still couldn't be sure this wasn't a ploy to find out how much I knew, but I could spin a very simple narrative that fit in with most of the events as they knew them. Scipio had set me onto Devon because he suspected something was up. I found out that Devon and several other unknown people had hatched a plot to take Scipio out. I thought it was finished after the trial, but then Scipio came to me again, and told me it wasn't. He was still under assault, and unsure who to trust. I was doing my best to help him, but Ambrose got caught in the crossfire. I would have to boil down the motivations of his killers to something more digestible for my parents, and omit a lot of details, but in the end, it would fit together pretty nicely.

And I might be able to get a read on them to see if they knew more than they were letting on.

I began to speak, carefully summarizing the trial but

revealing the fact that Devon's crime was tampering with Scipio, and manipulating decisions from the great machine. That part of the trial hadn't been revealed in detail—only that Devon had been found guilty of sedition against the Tower. The council had decided that giving away more than that could start a panic, and redacted it from the public transcripts. The expectation was that neither Leo nor I would reveal it either.

Whoops.

My mom's eyes narrowed, and my dad's mouth flattened into a thin line that practically disappeared behind his beard. But I went on, as planned, fudging the truth about Scipio asking me for help (it was really Leo), and prepared myself to talk about Ambrose's death. But my father never let me get that far.

"I will not tolerate this any longer," he said, slamming his fist onto the table. "You will tell no more of these blasphemies to anyone, or I will arrest you for sedition and terrorism."

"Silas," my mother chided, alarmed.

I ignored her, meeting my father's gaze head on. "Go ahead and do that. But don't come running to me when Scipio finally dies and this whole Tower gets thrown into the dark like Requiem Day. Because that's what will happen if you ignore this, Father."

"Enough!" he shouted, standing up so quickly that his chair went flying.

"No, it's not enough," I shouted back, also rising to my feet. "Because you know where you and your precious Knights will be?! Right here in your precious Citadel, sealed in and slowly suffocating to death. Along with everyone else! So go ahead, take me to the prisons, expel me like you have so many others. Oh, did I mention that law, the one letting you kill those poor little undesirable ones you hate so much, was the one that Devon manipulated? Did you know that Scipio never wanted those poor people to die, but only agreed to it because—"

My father had apparently had enough, because his hand snapped out and grabbed a fistful of my robe and undershirt in a tight grip, jerking me hard. My hips slammed into the edge of the table, but my hands were already reacting, my adrenaline surging from the snapping rage that had come over me, and I slammed my hand into the inside of his elbow and dragged his forearm toward me. My other arm snapped out, hand open, driving my palm into his nose with the full force of my body. There was a sharp snap, and my father released my clothes as he staggered back with a howl. I let him go, and his hands immediately went to his nose, trying to catch the blood that was now streaming out of it at an alarming rate.

I was shaking like a leaf, terrified of what he was about to do. My muscles screamed for me to press the attack, but my instincts told me to run away as quickly as possible. I'd never fought back against my father, and he had a terrible temper at the best of times. I wasn't sure I could hold my own—but I wasn't going to let him manhandle me anymore.

He spat out a curse as he gingerly touched his nose, then snatched his fingers back with a pained groan. I tensed as he straightened, turning on me with dark, heavy eyes that promised violence. "You stupid—"

"That's *enough*, Silas!" my mother shouted angrily, and my father froze, the anger in his face draining away with the blood dripping from his nose. "You're lucky Liana only broke your nose. I was going to break your arm if you didn't let go of her."

My head reeled as her words made it through my agitated state, and I relaxed a fraction of an inch, watching her from the corner of my eye. She had stood up as well, and was now looking at my father like he was a rust hawk egg that needed to be crushed under her boot.

"Holly, you can't actually believe all this! She's a liar, and she's trying to pull off this whole 'Scipio's chosen' thing to add to her standing in the Tourney. She's always been opportunistic, lazy, and filled with excuses, and this latest prank is nothing short of an attempt to—"

My mother hit him. More specifically, she rammed her fist so hard into his jaw that he went down in a twisting spill, slamming against the wall halfway down. My eyes widened, and I met my mom's gaze. Her eyes, hot and heavy with anger, lightened a touch when she looked at me, and then darkened again when my father made a sound.

"Go home, Liana," she said, her voice carrying a dangerous note of warning in it. "I will net you later. Your father and I need to have a few words."

My heart beat like a steady, rhythmic drum in my chest. I had no idea what I'd just witnessed, but every cell in my body was telling me to heed my mother's command, so I left—quickly and wordlessly, and with barely a look over my shoulder.

9

Every step I took back to my apartment was filled with the image of my mother hitting my father. My father falling. The look in both their eyes.

If this was a ploy, it was a very good one. It played perfectly to me—the idea of one parent finally standing up for me over another was one I had entertained constantly when I was younger. Although, I had never imagined it being that violent before.

Then it hit me all over again: *my mother hit my father. For me. Because he was attacking me.*

Scipio help me, but I found myself wanting to believe that my mother's intentions were good. That somehow, in the mess of things that had happened to me, she had finally come around to the idea of accepting me for me.

This was just too weird. And yet another thing on my plate that I wasn't... that I couldn't... Oh, hell. If I was perfectly honest with myself, it was something I wouldn't think about yet. And possibly not for a while. I needed... space from what had just happened, and I couldn't just let myself blithely accept that my mother had really come around. I'd waited for almost twenty-one years for her to do so. I could be patient for just a little while longer.

Besides, I had other problems that took priority. Ones that required my immediate attention. And I'd put them off for way too long already. I wanted to know how Zoe's conversation had gone with Lacey. I needed to see the data we had collected on Tian. I had to get us moving forward, even if it was at a hobbled pace.

I entered the apartment as soon as the scanner gave me access, and found everyone, excluding Maddox, seated in the living room looking at their pads. They were so engrossed in what they were doing that initially, no one noticed me standing there.

"What are you looking at?" I asked softly.

I hadn't meant to frighten them, but I should've made some noise or something, because Zoe practically jumped out of her skin getting to her feet, and Eric and Quess weren't that far behind her. Only Leo willfully remained seated, his eyes flicking up to me as soon as I started speaking. He had no other outward reaction, and that made me feel inexplicably nervous.

"Scipio save me," Zoe groaned as soon as she realized it was me. She doubled over to put her hands on her knees and suck in deep, calming breaths. "You scared me half to death, Liana."

"I'm sorry," I replied, already contrite. "I really didn't mean to scare you. I should've... I should've known better."

"That's okay," she said, straightening back up and tossing her long hair over her shoulder. "Just... How did it go with your parents?"

I opened my mouth and then shut it. "Really weird," I

replied. "And... I took a bit of a risk and told them about Scipio's condition."

Zoe's jaw dropped, Eric frowned, Leo drew his brows together, and Quess stood there, frozen.

"Why did you do that?" Leo asked, not as alarmed as the others. "I thought you were concerned your parents could be assisting the legacies by putting Devon's Lieutenant up as Champion."

I licked my lips. Honestly, I had no real reason other than "my dad pissed me off, so I started to tell him to wipe that smug look off of his face". My only saving grace was that I had put some forethought into what I told them, with the idea of gauging their reactions to see if I could trust them. With extremely mixed results.

"I'm not going to lie to you: it was an in-the-moment type of decision, but I watered it down immensely. I basically told them that Scipio himself was telling me what to do. My dad didn't handle it well, and my mom... Well... She didn't like that my dad didn't handle it well."

Zoe blinked, slowly picking her jaw up off the floor until her mouth was closed. "Are you okay?"

"I am really sick of hearing that question," I replied honestly. I seriously didn't want to think about me or my problems anymore. "Listen, the craziness with my parents aside, I wanted to say that I'm sorry for running away earlier. It was wrong."

"Whoa," Eric said, holding up his hand to stop me. "Okay, I don't often say much during our meetings, because I know my place. I'm not a genius like Zoe, Quess, or Leo, and I don't have much in the way of physical skills like Maddox and Tian. But this time I have to say something. Liana, you have nothing to apologize for. You needed time to get yourself straightened out, and you took it. All of us understand."

I frowned. "You do?" If I had been in their shoes and our leader had just walked out on us rather than helping solve our problems, I would've probably been infuriated.

Zoe looked at me like I had suddenly grown a second head. "Liana, I love you, but get over it. We realize that there is a lot of pressure on you, and we weren't helping with that. But your self-doubt is only taking up valuable time that we could be using to fix our problems."

My cheeks flushed, but I was glad she had called me out. I should have let them know in the first place what I needed. I just wanted to give them the best parts of me always, so that I didn't let them down. They relied on me, and I wanted them to feel safe. But part of that meant being honest with them at all times, even when it came to my feelings.

"Right," I said. "What are we tackling now?"

"Tian," Zoe said, holding out a data crystal. "This was all of the evidence Lacey's people could find at the scene. They've already had it analyzed."

I accepted the data crystal, but held off on asking any questions until I had looked it over. I wanted to see what conclusions I could draw on my own, before comparing it to whatever theories the group had. I also had an equally important question to ask Zoe.

"So you talked to Lacey?" I asked.

She nodded, her pouty lips flattening slightly. "I did. It's why she sent over the information on Tian. But she wouldn't give us any information on how to unlock the legacy net. She said, and I quote, 'Liana can have access to it as soon as she becomes Champion and catches Ambrose's murderers, and not a second before.' But she did admit that there are protections on it to block certain memories from being remembered past the initial moment of disclosure."

CHAPTER 9

A flash of disappointment and sullen anger ripped through me, and I struggled to control my breathing. Lacey had given me the legacy net, which not only contained information about the world as it had been before the End, but also held tangent memories of things experienced by its previous owners. The design was significantly different from that of the nets being created today, in that the legacy nets stored massive amounts of data regarding the pre-End world. They also had the ability to record the memories of their users, which was how the legacy families working against Scipio managed to continue their relentless assaults on him over the ages, picking up where their fathers and mothers had left off.

Having access to some of the memories from Lacey's forebearers would help shine a light on what her group's motivations were when it came to Scipio—and without that, I was blind to what Lacey and her people had been doing to help the Tower. I felt in my soul that I would have also found information critical to Leo's mission buried on the net.

Without that information, or a way to access it, our investigation was somewhat stalled.

We knew Jasper, the AI fragment I had met in the Medica before I even met Leo, had been transferred to the head of the IT Department's terminal. But breaking into the Core to try to access Sadie Monroe's personal computer was a suicide mission at this point. Security in the entire Tower had undoubtedly been tightened, especially in the Core.

Which was another problem for another time. I needed access to the legacy net, and if Lacey wasn't willing to give it to me, I'd have to find another way in.

"Quess, Leo, do you guys think you can take a shot at unlocking the legacy net?" I asked, looking between the two men.

Quess leaned forward, a small frown on his lips. "I could try, but only with Leo's help," he said cautiously. "I haven't had a chance to study it up close yet, so I'm a little concerned about damaging it."

"I'd be happy to help you," Leo said. "I have no small amount of knowledge regarding the earlier versions of the net, and I am certain that we could figure out what they did to modify it."

"Go ahead and get started," I replied. "I'll be right back." I ran back to my room to where my uniform was still lying on the floor, quickly got dressed, and then returned to main room, where everyone was waiting for me. I pulled a plastic case from a small pocket on my thigh, and handed it to Leo. The white chip practically glowed against the dark fabric it was nestled inside of, pressed tight under the clear plastic lid of the case. Quess accepted it, and then reached into a small satchel and began pulling wires and objects out of it, handing a few to Leo to untangle.

"Now," I said. "Since I took Quess and Leo off the investigation with Tian, I'll just—" I stopped short when I noticed Zoe giving me a pointed look. "What?"

Zoe licked her lips and exhaled, glancing at the three men, and then back to me. "There was more that Lacey wanted me to tell you. Basically, she said that if you don't win, you'd better die trying."

From the tone in her voice, Lacey had meant it, too. Poor Lacey.

"Noted," I said softly. I looked at the three guys. "I know I didn't consult with you about the Tourney, but—"

"Liana, we got it," Quess said, slowly sinking back into his place on the floor, wires in hand. "It'll be good for us. You'll be the Champion, which means that a lot of our problems will get a whole lot easier. You can reroute Knights so that they don't catch us after awesome raids for the parts that we need to escape the Tower. It'll be epic. Let's just please find Tian first." He picked up the pad he had been using before and started plugging some of the wires into it, clearly done with the conversation.

I stared at him for a few seconds, amazed at how quickly they were taking things in stride. On the one hand, awesome—a little bit of guilt gone. On the other...

Nope. It wasn't the time to get all introspective and mopey. Quess and Zoe were right; no more apologies, no more overthinking. I just needed to focus on doing whatever we could to find Tian. That I could do.

I went to my room to fetch my pad, then joined the others in the living room. I sat down, attached the data crystal, and began downloading the files. Somewhere inside them was a clue that might lead us to Tian. I just had to go through the files, reconstruct the scene, and see what sprang out.

I clicked on the folder as soon as the data stick finished downloading, and then blinked when I saw the files. There were at least a hundred of them, if not more. That was a lot to take in, but I was resolved to help. So I started opening files.

I quickly began to get lost in the technical jargon within the reports. There was all sorts of information on the victims (with pictures attached), most of it medical, but some of it talking about radiation in their clothes. I struggled to read it, trying to puzzle out what it was saying, but quickly gave up and moved on.

The next few files were crude drawings depicting the trajectory of the weapon as it was used, based on a study of the bodies and the wounds. There were also several reports regarding trace findings of a gallium alloy on either side of the cut area. I didn't know what that meant, but the trajectory was interesting, as was the floor plan of the condensation room that came with it. I studied the image with the trajectory, my eyes tracing over the confines of the room where we had found the bodies. It wasn't very big—maybe thirty feet by fifteen—and had several obstructions in the middle of it that provided some cover. There were three ways in and out, if you didn't count up.

From the report attached, the investigator seemed to conclude that the four people who had been in pursuit of Tian had entered the same way we had—by climbing up the ladder next to Greenery 7. They had entered the room in question, likely in pursuit of her.

Regardless, once they entered, they were attacked from behind. The person on the left had gone down first, and then the man to his right. The third and fourth had managed to find cover, but the third had gone down shortly after. The last one had almost made it to the exit before he was similarly dismembered.

The next two deaths were Lacey's men, who had entered from a different direction, and had likely split up to check around the machinery in the middle. They were killed before they made it halfway across the room, cut down by the same weapon that had gotten all the others.

The footprints Leo and I had found led through the third exit, deeper into the condensation room.

I considered the information, and then sighed. None of this told me where Tian was or who had killed those people, and I couldn't help but feel like I was missing something.

I closed up the blueprints and began scrolling through the images. I avoided any featuring severed body parts, instead focusing on the evidence that Lacey's people had gathered on the attacker.

Whoever it was, they'd left very few signs of their passing.

CHAPTER 9

Only a single slightly smeared outline of a handprint, and oddly shaped footprints in blood that had quickly dissolved in the humidity of the room. But those were the images I wanted to look at, so I scrolled through the images they had shot, and finally found what I was looking for.

Several pictures, taken at different angles and from different distances, filled up the screen for the next thirty screens or so. By the time the image had been captured, the condensation on the pipe had already started to break the handprint down, leaving it streaked and runny. But the details were still as I remembered them: a ghostly outline of a human hand that looked like a tracing of blood rather than an actual handprint. As if the killer had only managed to get blood on the outer edges of his hand and fingers.

Which wasn't possible, and was damnably odd. I couldn't figure out why a handprint would look like that.

I put it aside for a moment, and cycled through to the footprint. There had been many of those at the scene, but the farther they got from the pool of blood, the more quickly they'd broken down, until we had finally lost them under the condensation coil. But those closer to the scene had managed to hold their shape and form better.

I hadn't been able to see them as clearly in the dim lighting of the room, but the image grabs had been taken with extra light, bringing more of the details to life. The footprint was hexagon shaped, over a foot in both length and width. Inside, there was a scrolling pattern that ran from each point into the middle, making it almost look like a star.

There was something very familiar about it, now that I could see it. A niggling memory told me that I'd seen it somewhere before. In a manual. In a Knight's manual.

I thought about it for a second, and then drew out my stylus, carefully tracing over the image and creating a 2-D copy of it with cleaner lines. I separated out my drawing and then connected to the Knight server. I was relieved to see it online; with Astrid's revelation that there had been a security breach in the Citadel's computers, I was worried they would shut down the network, and I'd have to look for the image manually—which would have meant a trip to the Archives. I quickly put the image in and ran a search, seeing if it could remember what I clearly couldn't.

I put the pad down on the table and stood up to stretch, letting the search run for a moment. Checking my watch, I realized I'd been sitting there for over an hour. Everyone was still there, all engrossed in their own examinations, trying to come up with a new lead.

We needed snacks.

I moved into the kitchen, quietly selected some fruit, and quickly cut it up and chucked it into a bowl. Instead of grabbing any more bowls, I simply picked up extra cutlery and returned to the common area, placing the bowl on the table and laying the forks down next to it.

Zoe dug in first, seizing a fork and spearing an apple wedge, but within moments, everyone was eating. It felt good, taking care of them, and I picked up my pad and leaned back, happy to let them get first stab at the bowl while I checked to see if my search had turned anything up.

The screen clicked on, and I froze at the image now filling it, my mouth going dry. I *had* seen the image before—a long time ago, in one of my history classes. It belonged to a sentinel.

Sentinels had been developed shortly after Requiem Day, a day on which Scipio had gone offline, taking with him the machines that helped keep the Tower working by supplying power, water, and air. The blackout had lasted three days, and had cost the Tower thousands of people.

Most of them had been Knights. Once operations had resumed, it was discovered that over thirty percent of the Knights had died trying to keep order in the Tower—a significant portion of the department. The remaining Knights, many of whom were injured during Requiem Day, were unable to keep up with the workload. So the powers that be decided they needed to create a workforce capable of helping the Knights maintain order, and created the sentinels—metal automatons designed to be controlled remotely by Scipio, an extension of his might.

But the sentinels had failed disastrously. Scipio had never been able to fully sync with them for some unknown reason, and they would periodically just start doing things for no apparent reason. The Knights, IT, and the Mechanics Department had all failed to figure out what the problems were when several of the machines began to act out violently. They were deactivated shortly thereafter, and the inter-department security teams had been developed in their stead to help keep the peace.

According to history, the sentinels had been melted down and recycled. But staring at the picture of the design of its foot, I realized that not all of them had.

And one of them might have Tian, right at this very moment.

10

I quickly spun my pad around in my hands and showed my friends. "I've got something, guys," I said.

They all looked up, and Quess reached out and snatched the pad from my fingertips, excitement burning in his dark blue eyes. "Whoa," he said, his brow furrowing. "What the hell is this?"

Zoe took it next and looked up at me, her own blue eyes sharp. "A sentinel? You told me they had all been melted down."

I opened my mouth to tell her that I wasn't sure, but surprisingly, it was Quess who answered. "It's against the law to melt them all down. Per the Technological Preservation Act, all innovations, no matter how unsuccessful, should be kept for future generations to study and improve upon. They have to keep at least one, but more than likely a few, in case they ever experiment with the technology again."

I blinked. So not all of them had been destroyed. Okay, fair enough, but where was it kept? How was it being used, and who was using it? More importantly, how did we find it? I took the pad from Zoe and stared at the image of the sentinel, a dark chill running down my spine. The image in the technical manual had been expanded to fit the entire screen, but the pad wasn't big enough to capture the finer details.

The schematics read that it was over two meters high (six feet, seven inches), and had been constructed so as to appear human. Well, humanoid, that was. Two arms and legs, a torso, and a head with eyes. The mouth was a small, rectangular slit that didn't move, while the eyes were silver orbs with black gaps running behind them, giving them a blank, dead expression. Flexible gray and black metal fibers had been stretched along their skeletal frames, which had been designed to give them a muscular shape. Their hands looked human, but another picture showed that the edges of each hand had been raised to help them grip things around the Tower.

I handed the image over to Leo, and ran a hand through my hair. "Okay, so we all agree? The thing that killed those men and took Tian was a sentinel?"

"The design accounts for the wonky footprint," Quess said. "And it makes sense. These things were made for combat, right?"

I nodded. "The material used to cover them is a carbon-polymer hexahedron nano-matrix. Its non-conductive, heat and cold resistant, waterproof, and wasn't affected by radiation. The only thing that could take it down were weapons rated Class B or above."

All Knights received batons as their official weapon, and they were ranked at Class C in terms of how lethal they were. A baton could kill, but it generally took time (unless it was placed at the back of the neck, but that was a different story). Class B weapons, however, were lethal, and reserved only for use in the most dire and urgent of circumstances. The last time they had been used was during Requiem Day.

In the Academy, we took several classes on each weapon, first to understand the science, then to learn about the devastation those weapons could produce. In our second year, we were instructed in how to fight with them using less dangerous replications. In our third year, we practiced with the weapons themselves.

"All right, so we'll have to figure out a way to get a weapon from the armory," Quess said, scratching his chin. "I think we can do that."

"Okay, but how do you find the sentinel?" Eric asked. "What good is getting a weapon that can hurt it if you can't find it?"

Good point. I licked my lips, thinking. "Well, we could find out where the sentinels were being kept, and go down there ourselves and start investigating. Someone had to come get it. We might have to review the cameras in the area, but…"

"That's insane," Zoe said rising to her feet, her eyes wide. "Liana, girl, we have no idea when the sentinel was taken. You're assuming it was within the last week or so, but it could have been anytime between when they were decommissioned and now, couldn't it? That's too much footage to comb through."

"Okay, so you tell me how to find it," I answered roughly. She did have a point, but that didn't mean that we couldn't at least try. It wasn't exactly like there was a manual on how to track down a sentinel.

Nobody said anything for a long second. Then Leo slowly raised his hand. "Before we come to any conclusion, I have a question that could lead to an idea," he declared, meeting my gaze with an apologetic one of his own. "I just read the manual entry on them, and it says that the sentinels were designed to be piloted remotely by Scipio. That would require them to be networked together, and operating at a single frequency that Scipio would have to use to exercise his control. So, my question is this: is there a way to know what that frequency is?"

"Hey, yeah!" Quess said, his excitement mounting. "Scipio *would* have assigned them a specific frequency so they didn't get any interference from normal net traffic. And since it was a joint operation between IT, the Cogs, and the Knights, then that means the IT Department will have a record of what the frequency is. If we can find the record and the frequency, then all Mercury would have to do is ask the sensors to find anything active on that frequency! It'll lead us right to it, and Tian!"

"If it has her," I cautioned, not wanting him to get too optimistic. Not wanting to get that way myself. "For all we know, it grabbed her and then passed her on to someone else."

"Also," Eric interjected with a frown, "what's your plan for when you find it? The batons are worthless against its hide, and I doubt that with the lockdown in place, you'll be able to get one of those Class B weapons."

I gave Quess and Leo a considering look in response to Eric's statement. That was a valid point, but I was certain that if anyone could find a way for us to borrow one, it was them. "We'll have to figure it out, but I think we can do it. All right, Quess, you call Mercury and fill him in on what we need. Zoe and Eric—"

"We have to distribute the Paragon today. We were supposed to do it yesterday, but with Tian..."

I licked my lips. Paragon had been created by Roark, a former Medic who had turned against the Tower after the Knights took his wife away from him. It had been his dream to escape the Tower, and Roark had kept that dream alive by slowly using the Paragon to recruit people he felt had skills vital to escaping, and then surviving. Now that he was gone, those twenty-nine people were relying on *us* to get Paragon to them. If we didn't, they'd drop to ranks of one, and have to face what the Tower currently called justice.

Which was still sticking them in a gas chamber, and "expelling" them from the Tower. Thankfully, my ruse with Lacey during the trial had revealed that Devon Alexander had influenced Scipio into creating the law, and it was soon to be changed. But not until there was a full council to oversee and vote on the issue, which wouldn't be done until after the Tourney was finished. They were down there, buried at the bottom of the Citadel like the dark secret that it was. I had seen it for myself, what felt like a lifetime ago, and I wouldn't wish it on my worst enemy.

Well, maybe my worst, but not, like, my... mediocre one.

I smiled at my own quip, and then realized that Zoe was watching me. "Sorry," I said, shaking my head. "Are you ready for this? I mean, not only are you going to have to convince most of these people that you're working with Roark, but you're also going to have to convince them to take a hit in their rank. It's not going to be easy, and after everything that's just happened..."

Zoe gave me a lopsided, albeit tired, smile. "I already thought of that, and as callous as this sounds, I think we need to use Ambrose's death and the nebulous status of the Citadel as a cause for our Paragon recipients to develop a case of depression. It's understandable to the Medics, and will give us at least three months to wean them down a bit more before turning around and upping their dose when we get the formula. Speaking of which..." Her eyes slid over to Leo as she spoke. "What's going on with rescuing Jasper?"

"I honestly don't know," I said. "Alex found out that he was transferred to Sadie Monroe's terminal, but as she's the executive of the entire department, he couldn't get much further than that."

"All the more reason you need to become Champion, then," Eric said. "Only council members can override other council members' securities."

"Only if I have a good reason," I replied. "And it's a moot point, anyway. We need to focus on seeing what we can do about Tian first. Then the Tourney." I didn't add what I knew we were all thinking: we had way too many balls in the air.

But, Scipio help me, I felt bad about Jasper. He had come to my aid so many times in the Medica early on. I owed him my life, and I had yet to square that debt. And it seemed even more important now that I knew he was one of the AI fragments that had been used to create Scipio.

"Right, we'll get going now," Zoe said, nodding to Eric. "We have a lot of work ahead of us."

"Net if you have any problems," I said. "Make sure you use the anchor program when you do." Quess had designed the program to create a private virtual network that connected only to our nets. It was a tiny glitch in the net design that he had exploited, but one that kept our transmissions from being recorded by the IT Department.

"Will do," Zoe said, slinging the bag of Paragon over her shoulder. "And don't make a move on that sentinel without us."

They left quickly, and I felt their urgency. In fact, the air practically tingled with it; we were doing something for Tian, and we had hopefully found a way to find her. Doing something —anything—productive was much better than dwelling on what had happened yesterday.

"I'll net Mercury," Quess said, and crossed over into the kitchen.

And just like that, Leo and I were alone.

CHAPTER 10

I became aware of it almost instantly, and a dull heat started to grow in my cheekbones, my mind merrily skipping back to remind me about that kiss. I felt Leo's gaze on me like a heavy weight that I was trying to push as far away as possible—though my body tingled with awareness, betraying me.

"Liana," he said, his voice slightly roughened.

My stomach quavered. I couldn't do this. "I've got to go check on Maddox," I stammered, searching for an excuse to leave. Now.

I spun to do just that, but fast as a cat, he was there, ducking his way in front of me and forcing me to deal with him.

"What happened this morning?" he asked, giving me a searching look that I felt rather than saw. I couldn't seem to look up from my feet.

"Nothing," I said quickly. Was it me, or did my voice sound strained? I hoped he hadn't noticed. "Excuse me."

I angled to step past him, but he followed, blocking my path again. "Liana, I know you're lying." He paused, his face growing nervous. "I did something to scare you. Was it staying the night? I knew I should have waited until you were asleep and left, but suddenly I was very tired, too, and I fell asleep. I'm still trying to figure out my own limitations."

I couldn't explain why, but I still was hesitant to tell him. I wasn't sure if it was because I was embarrassed that I had let it happen, or that I was worried I'd embarrass him, or worse... What if he was repulsed?

Leo reached out and placed a gentle knuckle under my chin, forcing my gaze up to meet his. "Please," he said, his eyes glowing earnestly. "I want to know."

Scipio help me...

I told him. It came out in halting sentences, my cheeks burning a dull red that felt like it crept down right to the nape of my neck. Or at least, it started to come out. I managed to make it through the pre-kiss stuff, but as soon as I got to the part where we kissed, the words themselves slammed a gate down over my vocal cords with a *Do Not Disturb* sign.

"What?" Leo asked, his eyes searching.

I cleared my throat and gritted my teeth. He deserved to know. "You started kissing me this morning, but it was like you couldn't hear me, and I couldn't make you stop. You just kept saying my name, and now I am feeling really awkward, because yes, I needed someone to hold me last night, and I am very glad it was you because it's a human experience you got to have, but at the same time, you're inside of Grey, who is someone I clearly care about."

Leo's face went white at my words, and sorrow filled his eyes. "Oh my God, Liana. I am so terribly sorry. I swear, I don't remember doing any of that. I just..."

He trailed off, at a loss for words, and a curious pain twisted in my heart, but I blatantly ignored it, focusing instead on a question: why couldn't he remember? Was something wrong with him? Was it just a side effect of the dreamlike state he had been in, or was it a sign of something serious?

I couldn't stop myself from asking. "Leo, has anything like this happened before?" To my surprise, his cheeks darkened slightly. "On the morning of the first challenge, Ambrose woke up to find me standing in the kitchen," he admitted shakily. "He said I was unresponsive for several minutes, and the only thing I would say was..." He outright flushed here, and ducked his head down, no longer meeting my gaze. "I just kept saying 'Liana' over and over again," he finally announced, his voice almost a whisper. "Is there something wrong with me? Am I hurting Grey?"

He wrapped his arms around himself then, and compassion

swelled in my heart like a balloon. I could sense his fear and concern, and felt a deep appreciation for his continued consideration of Grey. It made me soften toward him, and now, more than ever, I wanted to do something to help him deal with whatever he was going through. I touched his shoulder lightly, and he looked at me.

"Talk to me," I urged him. "I'm sorry for how I reacted earlier, just... tell me what's going on. We've been so wrapped up with... well... everything, that I am beginning to think we overlooked you."

Leo gave me a watery smile, uncertainty radiating like ripples across his mouth. "It's not your fault," he said quickly. He sighed then, and licked his lips, looking around the room. "This is very new to me," he finally said. "A part of me wants to run away from you, because I'm not entirely sure how to explain."

"Try," I said simply. "If I get confused, I'll ask questions."

Leo started rubbing his forearms. "I've been having dreams. Well, not dreams. I think they might be nightmares. There's two people beside me there, and they are screaming at me. I keep standing, but inside I feel like an ant that's about to get crushed under someone's boot. Helpless and filled with this indignant anger that makes me want to lash out and cry. It reminds me of how I felt when Lionel was murdered, but this is way worse. I wake up sweating, and feeling like my heart is a small bird trapped inside a large fist that's slowly crushing down around me."

I bit my lip, a low thrum of excitement radiating through me. I knew exactly who those people were and what he was dreaming about. And I knew why he didn't know who they were. Because they weren't from his mind, but from Grey's!

"It has to be Grey's parents," I hurriedly told him. "They

were very harsh with him once his ranking started to go down. Even though he tried as hard as he could to improve his number, they eventually disowned him and had him kicked out of the department."

Leo's brows drew together, and his mouth dropped open. "That's awful!" he exclaimed. A few seconds later, he added, "When you become the Champion, can you get rid of that stupid ranking system? It's just... so offensive to Lionel's memory."

"It's among the top five things I'll be looking at," I informed him merrily. "Right after we save Scipio and get rid of those damned expulsion chambers."

We shared a smile, and then silence descended between us like a curtain made of iron, thick and definitely noticeable. I was starting to debate how to extricate myself from the conversation in the nicest way possible, when he spoke.

"Liana, I do want to say I am sorry for the kiss this morning." I started to tell him not to worry about it, but he continued. "But... is it wrong that I'm sorrier that I don't remember it?"

His eyes met mine, and I felt like I had just touched a livewire, and was now frozen to the spot, staring into those eyes that were Grey's in origin, but had Leo's light shining brightly through them. My heart throbbed. My breath caught. I saw in him an intense yearning coupled with a loneliness so deep and aching that my heart began to bleed for him.

What was more, I could see echoes of my own loneliness reflected in his honey-colored, warm brown eyes. I wanted to reach out for him. I wanted to hold him. I wanted to provide him with comfort.

Confusion ripped me right in half, and I immediately decided it was time to go. Now.

I took a small step back and coughed, clearing my throat. "I need to work on my eulogy for Ambrose," I said. Leo deserved something better than a feeble excuse, but being close to him right now was a bad idea. My gut said so. "When Quess is done with Mercury, maybe you two can start looking into how we can gain access to the armory."

And then I fled, stumbling past him and back into my bedroom before closing the door firmly between us.

11

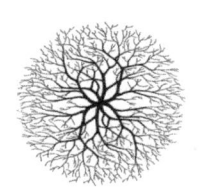

Fingers lightly skimmed over my arms, and I sighed, leaning back into Grey's warm chest. His silken lips grazed my ear, and a finely tuned shudder ran up my spine and then down it.

"C'mon," he breathed against my ear, turning my bones into jelly.

More fingers stroked over my hips and up my sensitive sides, giving way to strong palms. My eyes fluttered open at the shock of another set of hands on me, and all the air in my lungs evaporated as I saw Leo—the real Leo. Dark, inky black hair with gleaming blue eyes; tall, muscular, and standing oh so deliciously close, only inches away, a deep, forbidden hunger reflected in the strong lines of his face.

"C'mon," he said, stepping closer to me and pinning me between him and Grey.

"C'mon, Liana," Grey said, his lips kissing a hot trail up the back of my neck. "Choose."

Leo's eyes were on my mouth, his own lips parted in anticipation. They quirked up when he noticed me watching, and then he bent closer, his hair falling over his eyes.

"Yes," he breathed, inches from my mouth. "Choose."

"Choose." Grey's hands skimmed along my lower back.

"Choose." Leo's mouth slowly took possession of mine.

"Choose."

"NO!" I shouted, panic erupting down my spine. I pushed out from between the two men and stumbled away and onto my knees, panting heavily, focusing on the harshness of my own breathing.

Something dropped in the darkness, and I looked over. I was kneeling inches away from Ambrose's dead body, his blue eyes, open and vacant, watching me. His gaze held me captive, and I felt bile rise in my stomach as something white began to wriggle its way out of the corner of one eye, its meaty white body wriggling back and forth through the wet tissue.

I started to turn away, but Ambrose's hand reached out and snatched my arm, his head lifting up off the ground. His mouth opened. Blood spilled out of it onto his chin in thick, slimy chunks.

"You're next," he said wetly.

Then his hands were on my throat, and he was squeezing. I tried to fight him off, my arms beating feebly against his face and chest. His mouth opened, and more blood poured out and onto my face, getting into my eyes, my nose, my mouth, drowning me. I couldn't scream, couldn't move, couldn't breathe.

I sat up with a gasp, clutching my throat with one hand and trying to wipe Ambrose's blood from my face with the other. It took me several panicked breaths—close to sobs—before I could even attempt to look at my arm, and then several more seconds for me to realize that there was no blood on my face.

It had been a nightmare.

CHAPTER 11

Relief coursed through me, and I sagged back onto my pillows, taking a moment to catch my breath. I was drenched in sweat, but shivering as if caught in an icy breeze, and I burrowed deeper into my covers, trying to find warmth. I lay there for several moments, letting my heartbeat and pulse settle, debating whether I should try to go back to sleep.

I checked the time on my indicator. It was three thirty. I didn't have to get up for another three hours, but the thought of trying to sleep again filled me with anxiety, so I got up.

I went for a shower first, taking pains to be quiet and not wake anyone on the way to the bathroom. The hot water did a great job of helping to clear away the deep chill that still lingered within my bones in the wake of that nightmare, and I used up four of my six allotted minutes to just stand and soak it in. Then I scrubbed myself down and rinsed, barely getting the last of the soap off of me before my shower credit ran out.

I dried off, taking more time in the bathroom, primping, than I normally did—but what else did I have to do, other than try to finish my speech for Ambrose? Mercury hadn't been able to jump on the search for the sentinel as fast as I had thought he would. He needed to research and find the frequency it was operating on first, he'd said, and that could take some time. Apparently, the Knights and IT had several projects they worked on together, but they didn't always call them by the same name. Quess explained the anomaly as one born of a proprietary nature. IT didn't build things—they wrote programs, and so they got to choose the name of each program. The Knights then named the actual creations for themselves. So while the Knights called these particular machines sentinels, the Eyes had likely called them something else, like Murderbots 3.0. Mercury just had to figure out that name, and then he could start the search.

Which bought Quess and Leo a little more time to figure out how to steal one of the Class B weapons. I supposed I could take a crack at it myself, considering I had time in excess now that I had woken up so early, but honestly, I really wanted to focus on my eulogy for Ambrose. I wanted it to be perfect.

It was an odd feeling, this drive to deliver something worthy. Ambrose and I hadn't gotten along for most of the short time we'd known each other. It wasn't until after the first challenge that something had finally shifted, and I'd gotten a glimpse of the real Ambrose underneath. He'd been arrogant, yes, but he'd also demonstrated a remarkable self-awareness, eventually, confessing that his attitude toward me had been based on his jealousy of my leadership skills. He wanted to be a leader, believed himself to be a great one, but hadn't actually gotten a handle on the *how* yet, and when confronted with the fact that he wasn't as great as he thought, had reacted poorly.

But he had made his mistakes and learned from them—something that marked a truly great person.

I wished he were still alive. I wished. I wished. I wished.

But nothing changed the fact that he was dead. And his funeral was today.

Finishing up in the bathroom, I headed into the kitchen to make a quick cup of black tea, needing the caffeine. Leo was asleep on the couch, and while there was a hammock strung from hooks in the ceiling, it was conspicuously devoid of Quess.

He was sleeping in Maddox's room again. A part of me wondered if I should be concerned about that, but I quickly dismissed the idea. Maddox had almost been killed, and her surrogate sister was still missing. Her mother had been murdered by her father, and then her father had been killed by Leo before she had even known who he was. If anyone needed comfort, it was her, and I was wrong to even consider that there was anything more to it than that.

Still, my eyes lingered on Doxy's closed door as I made my way back to my room—right up until I shut the door.

I sat down at my desk and checked the Knights' server first, looking for an update on the status of the Tourney, and finding one that had been uploaded at around midnight. I clicked on it and sat back to read. Most of it was stuff that Astrid had told us: the candidates from teams who had been infiltrated would be randomly assigned to other teams. It added that my team specifically would also receive a random candidate, but that we had the right to veto the first one, if we chose to.

A small blessing, I supposed, but only just.

I briefly considered asking Leo if he could hack into the server and pre-select someone, but dismissed it for a few reasons. Ultimately, the only person I could think of that I could possibly trust was my mother, but that trust was very fragile. Not to mention the fact that she wasn't available, anyway. *Their* team hadn't been infiltrated.

And if I was going to be the next Champion, then I had to prove that I could do it on my own, without any assistance from my parents.

But first... Ambrose's eulogy.

I still wasn't satisfied, but when Maddox's knock came a few hours later, I saved the file on my pad and tucked it into my uniform.

Maddox was standing on the other side of the door, waiting for me. Her face was still bruised, but much of the swelling had gone down. The patch for her broken nose was gone, as well as, presumably, the rest of her bone patches.

"Hey," I said, well aware that we hadn't been alone since before her attack. I gave her a look. "How are you holding up?"

Her green eyes slid to one side, growing distant. "I'm here," she said after a moment. I waited for her to say more, but when she didn't, I placed a careful hand on her shoulder. Her body went ramrod stiff, and her eyes snapped back to me.

"Doxy, you can still drop out if you want to," I told her quietly. "We can tell the officials, find someone else. If you need time."

"I don't need time," she said hastily, jerking away from me. "I'm fine."

A lie, but given the wild look in her eyes, I chose not to press her. "Okay," I said gently. "Thank you."

She shook her head, her face tight behind the mottled bruises. "Leo's waiting," she announced. "We should go."

I studied her, unconvinced that she was all right. She'd suffered extensive mental, emotional, and physical trauma, and needed rest and time to cope with what she had gone through. I knew she was strong, much stronger than I was, but even still, she needed help. I just wasn't entirely sure how to give it to her, let alone breach the topic. So I decided to let it go, at least for now.

Leo was indeed waiting in the living room, and together the three of us left, heading for the largest cafeteria in the Citadel, only two floors under the arena. None of us spoke much, which was understandable, all things considered. Things between Leo and me were so awkward that I purposefully put Maddox between us as we walked—a physical barrier he would have to talk over if he wanted to talk.

Thank Scipio he did not.

The cafeteria had been cleared of the long tables that normally ran the length of the room, and chairs had been set up in rows, with an aisle running through them after ten chairs or so. The room was already filled to the brim with people, who were talking with each other in soft voices that created a cacophony of indistinguishable noises.

A Knight scanned us in one by one, performing a quick pat-down to confirm we weren't carrying any additional weapons. It saddened me to think that Ambrose's death had caused that action, and on the heels of that sadness came an icy sliver of anger. The people who had done this to him didn't care what they had stolen from the Tower. Ambrose hadn't been perfect, but he deserved to be alive right now.

"Liana!"

I looked up, quickly scanning the room for the person who had called my name, and saw Astrid pushing through a group of people crowding the mouth of the aisle, Lewis and the other Knight hot on her heels. She looked tired, but she smiled kindly as she took in me and my team.

"I'm glad you're here, kid. We're just about to begin, and you should be by the podium. Are your friends going to be okay?"

I looked at Maddox and Leo questioningly. Maddox nodded first, but Leo took a fraction of a second longer to agree, his eyes searching my face to make sure *I* was okay.

I wasn't—and his scrutiny wasn't helping. As soon as he nodded, I managed a small smile for Astrid. "They'll be all right," I said. "Lead the way."

Astrid shook her head, regret shining in her eyes. "I'm leading the memorial service, and there are a few more things I have to do if we want to get started on time," she said. "Just go up there and wait. We'll be starting very soon. Anywhere will do."

I nodded, and began pushing through the crowds, heading for the podium that had been set up on the three-foot-high stage toward the front of the room. Several people were already there waiting, but I only recognized two. One was my instructor from my days at the Academy, Knight Commander (Ret.) John Deveraux. He'd lost his arm during his service, and now taught history.

The other was Dylan Chase.

I hadn't officially met Dylan, but I'd had Lacey investigate her, to see if she had any legacy connections. She and Frederick Hamilton were two of the strongest contenders in the Tourney, and I had been concerned about their connections. Surprisingly, Lacey's search concluded that Frederick was actually a descendent of Ezekial Pine. The Pines were the legacy family that had started it all, when Ezekial murdered Lionel, and then turned around and tried to do the same to Leo.

But Dylan's background had revealed nothing, save that she took care of her aunt, and was an exceptional Knight.

She was leaning her upper back against the wall, her attention fully on the pad in her hands. She was tall and curvaceous, with wide hips and an ample chest. Her white-blond hair was cut in an asymmetrical bob, the longest bit of which curled under her chin.

I cautiously slipped into a spot a few feet away from her, and then slid out my pad, determined to go over my eulogy one more time.

"Liana?" Dylan said in a dusky voice, and I looked up to see her regarding me with warm brown eyes. A smile grew on her lips, and she took a step closer, holding out her hand. "I'm Dylan Chase."

"I know," I said, accepting her hand. "I've seen some of your drone footage. Impressive."

Dylan's smile deepened, forcing indentations into her cheeks in the form of dimples. "Thank you. I've watched yours as well. Very efficient."

That could be praise or an insult. Everyone knew that getting screen time through drone footage was critical to becoming Champion. Popularity within the Knights was paramount to success, which meant long, drawn-out fights and ridiculous stunts during the course of the Tourney in order to garner attention.

By being efficient, I was costing myself the position. And Dylan knew it.

But the kind look in her eyes never faltered, and I conceded that it was probably a compliment. "Thank you."

She nodded, and looked around the room. "There's too many people in here," she announced after a moment. "Most of them didn't even know him."

Her mouth twisted, as if she had bitten into something sour. I stared out at the crowd for a second, and then asked, "How did you know Ambrose?"

"We attended Academy together," she replied, lowering her pad to her side and brushing a lock of hair out of her eyes. "He was..." She trailed off and shook her head, looking down. "I still can't believe he's gone."

Me neither, I thought. I opened my mouth to tell her that, but the lights in the room dimmed. Only the stage remained well lit, and from my position, I could see Astrid slowly climbing the stairs, heading for the podium. Behind her, the wall lit up, and filled with images of Ambrose.

Astrid cleared her throat into the microphone. "My fellow Knights," Astrid began. "We are here today to remember Knight Elite Ambrose Klein."

12

The final vestiges of the ubiquitous noise that had filled the cafeteria quickly died down as Astrid began to speak. I pressed my lips together as well, trying to focus on what she was saying.

"Ambrose's death is a tragedy," Astrid announced to the room, a wireless microphone amplifying her voice. "Let us be clear about that. Enemies of the Citadel, and therefore of the Tower, stole into our home and ended the life of one of our own. There are no words that could possibly touch the pain we are feeling. But we are here."

She fixed her steely eyes on the crowd, and they shouted their approvals.

"We are strong!" More affirmations shouted, louder this time. "We remember!" Louder, even stronger. I found myself wanting to shout as well, but some part of me held back, uncomfortable with it. We were here to remember Ambrose, not make ourselves feel better about being alive.

Astrid paused and let the crowd noise ease down before she leaned forward slightly. "And we will not let Ambrose's murder go unanswered," she declared, and the crowd fell apart, screaming their approval. Someone started chanting, "Justice for Ambrose," and within moments, it had spread like a virus, until all the crimson-clad figures were raising their fists in unison.

My eyes widened at the rabid fanaticism they were displaying, and I sucked in a breath. I had come here to remember Ambrose, not incite a frenzy. Knights leaving here to go on patrol today would be frothing at the mouth, looking for any sign of Ambrose's killer, and that was dangerous to the other citizens of the Tower. I gave Astrid a long look, wondering why she had felt the need to rile them up like that, but wasn't able to find a shred of motivation beyond "that's just how she feels about it".

"Knights of the Citadel," Astrid said, raising her arms in a universal sign for "calm yourselves". "Knights, please! I know we are angry, and justifiably so. But please, we are not only here for our anger, but to mourn a man who is burning at the heart of it all." She paused long enough for the crowd to collect itself and settle back down, before continuing. "I'm saddened to say that I did not know Ambrose personally. However, I have brought together some people who did, and they would like to say a few words about our fallen brother. Lend them your hearts and ears, and learn from their stories of our brave compatriot. Please welcome Knight Commander John Deveraux."

She was following up her speech with Deveraux? I couldn't help but smile; he was one of the most boring teachers in the Academy. Talk about going from a high to a low.

Deveraux marched onto the stage and up to the podium, and began speaking almost immediately in a flat, monotonous voice. "I first met Knight Elite Ambrose Klein when he petitioned for me to be his academic mentor six years ago. He, like me, shared an interest in the near-calamitous events that have occurred in the past two hundred and fifty years of our history. His specialization was Requiem Day, and the economic windfall that occurred afterward. You see, he believed that the—"

I tuned him out. It was automatic after enduring three long years of his academic lectures, but this time, there was an anger behind it. I wasn't sure what I had been expecting, but this was not it. What did Ambrose's studies have to do with who he was as a person? How was this going to teach anyone about what he believed in, what he hoped for, what he dreamed of?

"I cannot believe him," Dylan whispered next to me, breaking through my angry thoughts, and I glanced over to see a dark, hot look on her face. She glanced at me and pursed her lips. "Can you believe this? What the hell is he talking about? Ambrose only took him as his academic advisor because he felt bad for the man. Nobody wanted him."

I smiled. Part of it was because of her story, and part of it was because I wasn't alone. She felt the same way I did. "Yeah, I know. This wasn't exactly what I was expecting."

"Same." She looked down at her pad, a grimace on her face. "Makes me a little self-conscious about my speech."

My smile grew as I tried to picture Dylan being self-conscious, and failed. The woman was too self-assured, even just standing there. If I was perfectly frank, it was a bit intimidating. We were chatting now, but I had to keep in mind that in a few days, we'd be competing against each other in the Tourney.

But this was now. "It'll be fine," I assured her. "As long as you're remembering Ambrose, I think it'll be perfect."

A beatific and grateful smile crossed her face. "Thank you," she said. She pressed her lips together, and her smile faded into a frown. "I asked him to be on my team, you know."

"You did?" That was news to me. And a bit disappointing.

Dylan's all-girl team had given me a little feminine thrill of pride when I first discovered it. Now that I knew she had originally wanted Ambrose on the team... Well, that was okay. She still got a girl group together. "Why didn't he say yes?" I knew the answer, but I was curious to see what he had told her.

She rolled her eyes. "He said that *he* wanted to be Champion, not see me win. Stupid jerk."

There was something about the way she muttered the last part that made me give her a considering look. It bore a note that suggested she had really cared about him. Had Ambrose and Dylan been... intimate?

Dylan caught me looking and smiled, her eyes twinkling. "Nothing like that," she assured me with a chuckle. "It sounds really lame, but Ambrose was just... kind of cool. He didn't give me any crap about my height or my size. He was always straight with me. We weren't close or anything, but I kind of wish we had been."

Ah. Regret. That I could understand. "I'm sorry."

She shrugged it off. "It's not your problem, but thank you." She sighed then, and ran a hand over her face. "I've got bigger problems, anyway."

"Oh?" Deveraux was still droning on, and showed no signs of stopping, and talking with Dylan helped pass the time.

"One of the girls on my team turned out to be one of those infiltrators," she said, her free hand curling into a fist. "I can't believe I didn't notice."

My eyes widened as surprise coursed through me. She'd had an infiltrator on her team? "Really? How did that happen?"

She rolled her eyes again. "I trusted the recommendation of both of the other girls I recruited. I thought they had known her for a while. Turns out they had only met her a few days before, and just really liked her."

CHAPTER 12

"What was she like?" I asked, curiosity getting the better of me.

Dylan shrugged, her mouth twisting downward. "Really... normal. She seemed nice. Respectful. Eager. Cracked a few jokes here and there." She shook her head. "Nothing stood out to me."

It was disappointing, but not unexpected. Those infiltrators, whoever they were, had come into the Citadel for the purpose of taking Ambrose out and eliminating the competition. As much as I wanted to catch them, I knew that any lead we came up with would only be met with a dead end—they were prepared, and had supporters helping them.

"So your team's going to be dissolved?" I asked, and Dylan nodded.

"I seriously do not understand why they didn't just let us pick from the next ten candidates with the next best scores from the qualifying round. There were ten people in there who deserve a chance to be in the Tourney, but weren't because the infiltrators scored higher than them! In what sort of world is that fair? Not to mention, there is every chance I am going to get stuck on a team that is supporting someone else as Champion. It sucks."

I frowned. Dylan made an excellent point, and I felt bad for her. My team wasn't being broken up, but then again, we hadn't been infiltrated. The designers were likely worried that the infiltrators could've been working with someone on the inside, and in the interest of disrupting their plans, they were willing to sacrifice a genuine candidate's rights to try to ensure safety. It wasn't fair.

I wished I could complain to Astrid or the test designers about the way teams were being broken up just because an infiltrator had managed to work their way in. It only punished those teams who had been duped, which wasn't right. And in a different world, maybe I would've protested. Everyone deserved a fair chance, after all. But it wasn't a different world, and I couldn't risk Scipio and the Tower's fate—even if I thought Dylan would make a good Champion.

"Whoop, I'm up!" Dylan exclaimed softly, breaking my train of thought. I blinked and realized she was already moving away from me, climbing onto the stage as Deveraux came down. There was a collective round of applause—the crowd seemingly grateful that she wasn't Deveraux—and she quickly took her place at the podium, setting her pad down on it.

There was a pause of a few seconds, and then Dylan began to speak.

"I met Ambrose shortly after I joined the Academy. We had one class together: Combat Training, taught by Midge McCafferty, or as we used to call her, the Beast from Below." The crowd and I chuckled together. McCafferty was a well-known tyrant who micromanaged her Knights' training right down to their skivvies. Dylan chuckled as well, and then sighed. "Well, the rest of us did. Ambrose? He wouldn't. He'd always refer to her as Instructor McCafferty, no matter how hard we tried to get him not to. And let me tell you, we tried. We begged, pleaded, cajoled, blackmailed... We were obsessed. We needed to hear him say it.

"But Ambrose refused. He was never a jerk about it; he just refused to do it. So one day, he and I are on patrol, and I mean... I just had to know why. Why wouldn't he call his C.O. this one little name? It would certainly be good for our morale if he simply joined the group.

"So I asked him. And to this day, I will never forget what he told me. He said, 'Dylan, it's easy to complain. It's easy to be dismissive or derisive. But I didn't come here for easy. I came here to do the right thing. And it's never right to call your instructors names. It's petty.'"

Dylan rolled her eyes dramatically then, and the audience laughed, captivated by the way she lowered her voice and exaggerated her words. Dylan laughed with them, but that smile slowly melted away into sadness, and a hush fell over the crowd.

"I dismissed him that day, too, figuring he was just taking his job too seriously. But that's who Ambrose was: a serious person. To him, being a Knight wasn't a job. It was a calling. Both a duty and an honor that held a deep place of reverence in his heart. And, if I'm completely honest with myself, I think he would've made a great Champion."

Her voice roughened at the end, and she leaned away from the podium, as if taking a moment to compose herself. I, like the rest of the audience, was enraptured by her speech. I thought she had done a good job with it.

She tilted back toward the microphone, and I straightened, preparing for her to introduce me.

"Which is why we can't do the easy thing. We can't sit back and let those who killed him get away with it. Ambrose would've hunted down anyone who had hurt his brother or sister, and he would've seen that the justice they met came at the end of a very long drop from a plunge! He believed that a threat to one of us was a threat to the Tower, and vice versa, and I happen to agree. Because we have been threatened, brothers and sisters! And we have been hurt! I want your promises, right here and now, that we will make the ones who did this to us pay!"

The crowd exploded into pandemonium, clapping and cheering wildly. I, however, felt my stomach shrink in on itself, and suddenly I felt very vulnerable and exposed, like I was surrounded by a pack of wild dogs ready to attack the first thing that moved. Dylan's speech had ended up being another cry for war, and the crowd was eating it up.

Scipio help me, that was terrifying. Dylan had only added fuel to the spark that Astrid had kindled, and once again, I thought of all the other citizens in the Tower, and wondered how they would suffer if the Knights were left unchecked. I had to do something to put a damper on this. Or else it was going to spin out of control.

I needed to think, and hoped that Dylan's speech would go on for a few more minutes.

"Thank you for letting me share this small part of Ambrose with you," Dylan declared into the microphone, and I sighed. There was never enough time. "Please join me in welcoming Liana Castell, Ambrose's teammate from the Tourney!"

The crowd complied with Dylan's request by continuing to cheer, and I breathed in, squared my shoulders, and went up on stage. Dylan flashed me a dazzling smile and a thumbs-up, and I pasted on a polite smile of my own and pointed it in her general direction. I really hadn't liked her eulogy, but at least she had given an anecdote about Ambrose, so I could manage to be congenial.

But just barely.

I moved up to the podium and made a show of putting my pad down, stalling for time. How could I make a room full of scared and angry people calm down? I had to be smart about whatever speech I made; if they thought for a second I didn't want justice for Ambrose, they would turn on me in a heartbeat.

And I needed their support.

"Thank you, Dylan," I said into the microphone, buying a few more seconds of dead air as I turned on my pad. The eulogy I had written earlier popped up, but now it seemed ineffective. I had to do better.

For Ambrose, at the very least.

"I met Ambrose shortly after what had to be the hardest time in my life," I said into the microphone. I honestly had no idea where I was going with this, but I let my heart take control over my mouth, believing that I could find my way to the right combination of words. Words that would turn the crowd's anger back to sorrow and grief. "It was hard being back, after everything. To everyone here, I was an enemy suddenly turned ally, and no one was really sure what to make of me."

An uncertain shift happened in the audience, and through some of the bright lights, I saw a lot of people looking around and away. So I decided to go for a laugh, to see if I could put them at ease. "I mean, c'mon... the girl who killed the Champion on the orders of Scipio? I barely know what to make of it, and I was there. I could certainly understand my fellow Knights' nervousness."

I got a collective chuckle from most of the audience, and breathed a sigh of relief. I had clearly made them uncomfortable by talking about my own role before easing them into it, but the joke lessened that discomfort, which meant I held their attention again.

"But Ambrose didn't concern himself with that. In fact, he only had one question for me: was I satisfied with the investigation I had run on Devon?" I paused to let that sink in for a moment, letting them wonder whether I was implying that Ambrose hadn't been satisfied with Scipio's findings, before continuing. I was confident I had found my way forward; I just needed to refine the angle.

"Ambrose wasn't questioning Scipio's decision. He wholeheartedly believed that the future of the Tower rested with keeping Scipio safe, and following the great machine's advice.

But he knew that Scipio's decision was based on my investigation, and he wanted to make sure that I hadn't screwed up."

That earned another chuckle from more than a few people, and I continued. "You see, Ambrose knew that people are flawed, and can make mistakes. He knew that we can act impetuously, or come to snap decisions before having all the evidence. And it was important to him to know that I hadn't.

"Ambrose believed in justice with every fiber of his being, and that earned my trust. That's what made me want him to be the next Champion: his unwavering belief in the Knights' ability to see that justice, true justice, was dispensed around the Tower. He believed it was our duty to put our personal feelings aside so we could make sure those who deserved it, truly deserved it, could be punished.

"I know we're all angry. I know we're all hurt. I know we all want to hunt down the people who did this, the people who hurt Ambrose. And I understand that. I do. But... Ambrose was my friend, and I owe him more than that. I owe him an image of the Citadel that he could believe in. I want to be a Knight he would have been proud to know. But most of all, I want to honor his memory in the only way I know how: by letting Astrid and her people find his killers and bring them to justice. I hope that you'll join me in keeping this part of Ambrose alive."

13

I stared across the sea of faces, my heart pounding in my chest. For a second, nothing happened, and I was convinced I had missed the mark. But then somebody started clapping, a slow, steady sound that more and more people began to join in on, until it was a cacophony of hands slapping together.

Someone shouted, "Honorbound!" from the back of the room, and the next thing I knew, the crowd was chanting the deed name that had been bestowed upon me. I flushed, embarrassed, snatched up my pad, and aimed for the stairs. Astrid was on her way up, and gave me a curious smile as she moved past me, heading for the podium.

I didn't care. I just needed to get out. My feet found their own path down the steps, and I made for a side door that had been sealed to prevent entry. A Knight was standing guard in front of it, but made no move to stop me as I plowed through it.

Once I was outside, I came to a stop in the middle of the hall and sucked in a deep breath, thinking about what I had just said.

I hadn't expected the response to be that thunderous, and on the one hand, I was grateful.

But on the other hand... I had just fabricated an entire part of Ambrose's personality, as a way to get the Knights to back off their feelings of needing revenge. That was a horrible thing for me to have done, and it left me with an acrid taste in my mouth and a large, pointy rock in my stomach.

Ambrose deserved far better than he got, and during my one chance to share with everyone who he was, I had failed him and his memory.

I let that wash over me for a moment, and then asked myself what I could've done differently. And the answer was... not a whole lot. Attitudes in the Citadel were about to boil over, and if telling a few white lies about Ambrose could keep it from happening, then that was what needed to be done.

I just resented that I'd had to do it in the first place.

I straightened up and decided to run to the bathroom before heading back inside. There were public restrooms in a little hall shooting off from this one, and I found them, used them, and was on my way back to the main door when my net buzzed. I frowned and lifted up my wrist, checking to see who was netting me.

The indicator read *Dinah Velasquez*. My frown deepened. Who the hell was Dinah Velasquez, and why was she netting me?

I warred with the idea of not picking up, but finally accepted the net. For all I knew it could be one of Lacey's people trying to reach out to me.

"This is Liana Castell," I said, keeping my voice pleasant in spite of the violent rattling inside my skull. I wanted to ask Quess to put the legacy net back in; it was far gentler than this one. But I had to wait until he and Leo managed to unlock it.

CHAPTER 13

Yes, I know who this is, thank you very much, a voice on the other end squawked. *What I want to know is what the hell you were thinking!*

I shook my head. Was I going insane? I had no idea what this woman was talking about. "I'm sorry, I think you have me confused with someone else."

No, I do not, Liana Castell, 25K-05. You and your brother have both been pains in my rear ever since you forced Roark to bring you into this, and I swear on Scipio's grave that if you do not shut up and pay attention right now, I'm going to die.

She had mentioned Roark. Very few people knew that name outside of my friends and the council members, and Dinah Velasquez was not on the council. So who was she, and how did she know about Roark—and how I had forced him to include me in his escape plan?

My mind fumbled for a second, and then it suddenly connected, like a plug being slid into place. "Mercury?!"

She growled, and the sound made me cringe slightly. *Not the time, Liana! You and Quess have put me in grave danger, and you need to do something about it right now!*

"What are you talking about?" I asked. "The only thing we asked you to do was to—"

Track down a missing sentinel, yes, I know! But what you failed to mention was that it was capable of detecting the scan! The thing is on its way here at this very moment!

Ice slid down my spine, settling into the base of it, and I looked around, quickly trying to find a lashway, questions tumbling through my mind. How did she know it was on its way, and how could it have found her in the first place? Mercury —Dinah— was beyond cautious. She was downright paranoid about keeping her identity secret, and I doubted very much that she had just gotten sloppy.

But I could get the answers to those questions later. What came first was making sure she wasn't around when the sentinel showed up. "Get out of there, Mercury. Right now." I spotted a lashway and crossed over to it, quickly keying in an override and a scan.

That's not as easy as it sounds. You need to get here. Now!

"I'm already on my way," I said through clenched teeth as the scan for the lashway caused the buzzing in my head to intensify until it felt like a high-pitched scream. "But I might not get there in time. If you can leave now, then leave."

I can't do that, Liana! You need to come. Immediately!

The door slid open, revealing a massive, upside-down gargoyle glaring at me from ten feet away, and I threw my lash, connecting just inside its open canine mouth. "I'm coming," I repeated. "Get my brother down to the reception area to sign me in, and then hide yourself."

Mercury, like all the Eyes, was housed in the Core with Scipio, and the only way I was getting in was on a family visitation pass with my brother. Because I couldn't go into the IT Department as a Knight without probable cause, and trying to falsify an order would take too long—and would be easily discovered.

If they caught us outside of my brother's section, he would get in massive amounts of trouble, but we had to risk it. Losing Dinah was unacceptable—not just because she was a human being, but because she seemed to be the truest ally we had. She helped us in exchange for Paragon, which made our relationship perfectly reciprocal.

I would kill to have a similar reciprocity with Lacey, but that was beside the point.

I leapt through the lashway without another thought,

CHAPTER 13

angling my body so I could create momentum and speed. I'd yell at Dinah later for not making a run for it.

Right now, I just needed to get to her.

Before the sentinel did.

I met Alex at the front desk three minutes later, my muscles quivering and sweat dripping off of me in buckets. We didn't talk as he signed me in, and the second I was past the massive black doors that kept the rest of the Tower separated from Scipio, we broke into a light jog.

I let Alex lead, seeing as he lived here, and he quickly got us into an elevator and directed it to the forty-fifth floor.

"What do you know?" I asked as the numbers painted on the walls danced by.

"Dinah Velasquez is a lead, but her section title isn't listed, and she doesn't seem to have any Eyes working directly for her," Alex reported, giving me a nervous look. "I've never seen anything like it before. Her entire history requires a security clearance higher than my own."

"Is that weird?"

He gave me a pointed look. "Nobody has their personal history redacted in the IT Department, so yeah, it's really weird. And there's no record of what she does within the Core. Not even reports. It's like she exists in name only, which is just... confusing. I'm not entirely sure what to make of it."

Tension ran under my skin like insects scattering from an imminent threat as the full weight of his words sank in—we had no idea who Dinah Velasquez really was, even with finally knowing her true name. She had clearly taken great pains to keep her identity a secret even from the Eyes themselves, so who knew what she would do now that my brother and I had learned the truth.

Then Alex glanced at me, and his mouth—already tight—grew rubber-band thin. "What is a sentinel?" he asked, clearly needing answers.

"A machine that was supposed to replace the Knights, but failed. They're bad news, Alex, so don't engage if you don't have to."

His eyes dropped to my baton and moved back up to my face. "You're going to go after it with only a baton."

My own lips pursed. "I'm going to do what I must to keep it off of you while you get Mercury out of there. *Comprende?*"

It was one of the only words we knew from a language our ancestors had spoken before the End. We only used it when it was time to be serious.

Alex's face darkened. "No. You can't fight this thing alone!"

"Distract, Alex," I corrected. "And we have to. There's no other choice."

He sucked in a deep breath and exhaled slowly. "Fine," he grated out.

The elevator stopped a moment later, and we stepped out. I let him lead.

We crossed the atrium to where a narrow hall carved a path through the wall and made a sharp right. Alex entered it and began easing down the connected hallway. I followed, and immediately noticed a smell. Acrid and bitter, like something was burning.

I reached out and grabbed my brother's shoulder, bringing him to a halt so I could slip around in front of him. I slid the baton from its loop and switched it on. It wouldn't do much against the sentinel, but it was better than nothing.

As we approached the next corner, I became aware of a

rhythmic thudding noise. It sounded like a creaking anvil throwing itself against a slab of stone, and I could feel the slight vibration of the impact under my feet. Another turn, only this time I pressed my back against the wall and used it for cover as I quickly checked down the next passageway.

The hall came to an abrupt end just past a doorway. The door, a heavy metal slab, had been reduced to large chunks, the edges still glowing red from where they had been cut by something brilliantly hot. Likely a cutter.

The hall was otherwise deserted, but I could hear pounding coming through the opening. I took my chances and moved fully into the hall, stepping over the pieces of the door and approaching the entryway.

I pressed a shoulder against it, my mouth dry and my palms sweaty, glanced at Alex, who was behind me, and said in the smallest whisper I could produce, "I'll go in first, okay? Give me five seconds, and then get to Mercury. Then get out. I'll be right behind you."

He hesitated and then nodded, his eyes wide with alarm. I reached out and squeezed his shoulder, and then turned back to the door, keeping my baton at the ready.

I took a step toward the door.

"Okay, seriously? C'mon, Jang-Mi! This is really getting ridiculous. Put me down and stop hitting that door!"

I froze. I'd recognize that high-pitched voice anywhere.

It was Tian.

14

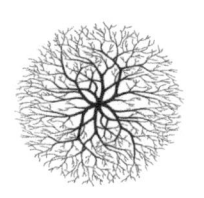

I swallowed and looked back at Alex, holding up a hand to tell him to stop. If Tian was in there with the sentinel, then that changed things dramatically. Because if it was holding her prisoner, I had to be extremely careful to make sure she wasn't caught in the crosshairs. My mind raced, and I realized that in my hurry to get over here, I had neglected to tell anyone where I was going—or call for backup. I had only been concerned for Mercury. He... *She* was the best resource we had, and I owed her my life twice over.

But now I was here, without any backup—save my brother—facing an automaton that had been designed for fighting, and had recently murdered six individuals in a violent act no more than two days ago. And here I was, about to go in swinging with nothing but my baton. We were in serious trouble.

My brother nodded, showing that he understood to stay there, and I turned back to the open door. The thumping from inside continued, but Tian hadn't spoken again, and I was getting concerned. I eased my way along the wall, coming up to the edge of the door.

I stuck my head through the doorway for three heartbeats, scanning from left to right, and then ducked back. The door led into a common area that was sunk three feet into the floor. A counter running from the left wall separated the kitchen from the living room, while the dining room was set to the right, hidden by a half wall. A hall ran between them, and as my eyes slid over the darkened space, I suddenly saw it: a burning orange glow, illuminating a single figure at the end of it.

It had only been a brief flash, but I knew in my spine that it was the sentinel.

"Security door unbreakable," a robotic voice said. *"Activating countermeasures."*

"Jang-Mi, stop it!" This time, Tian's voice held an edge of desperation to it. "Don't do this!"

I frowned. Tian was trying to reason with it? What was she thinking?!

And several other questions followed on the tail of that one. Why was she here? Was the sentinel keeping her hostage? Why hadn't whoever was controlling the sentinel taken her away from it?

I put the questions aside; Tian could answer them for me as soon as we freed her from the sentinel. But first I had to deal with it.

I looked back at my brother and nodded him over. Then, in very slow Callivax (the special hand language used by the Divers in Water Treatment) I told him to go in and to the left five seconds after I went in.

To my relief, he had brushed up on his Callivax recently, and nodded, then quickly repeated the instructions back to me, his hands flying.

CHAPTER 14

I exhaled, leaned over to make sure the machine's back was to me, and then darted through the opening, keeping my feet light and taking care not to bump into any of the shelves that lined the place. I aimed for the wall—the best place to keep the sentinel from seeing us, given its position at the end of the hall—and settled between two shelving units that were packed with slim black IT manuals. I'd never seen so many in my life, but now was not the time to gawk.

I took a moment to catch my breath and ease my heartbeat, which was now stamping out a tattoo on the inside of my ribs, convinced that the sound would draw the sentinel. I stared warily at the opening, tense and jumpy, but nothing emerged.

Instead, the dim orange glow being emitted by the sentinel suddenly intensified with a sharp, wet hiss, and I recognized the sound and angry, bruised-orange glow with an instinctive chill. It was a cutter.

Movement caught my eye to the left, and I shifted the angle of my head enough to see my brother crouching low to the floor and making his way quickly to the left side of the room, angling for the wall as well. I tracked his progress from the corner of my eye, while keeping my gaze on the hall. I could hear the sharp *zzt* of sparks, which were accompanied by bursts of orange light.

"Keep your eyes closed, Yu-Na," a feminine voice crooned, and I cocked my head. Was there someone else in the hall? Who was Yu-Na?

Also, why did their voice sound so tinny? Like it was coming through a speaker or something?

Crap. If there was someone else in there, then trying to sneak up on the sentinel was a very bad idea. We'd be spotted by whoever else was there. We needed to draw them out.

I looked around the room, thinking, and my eyes stopped on

the bookshelf to my left. Books. Small, light, and infinitely throwable.

I grabbed a handful of the slim volumes and then motioned for my brother, quickly signing for him to go over the half wall on his side, and then made my way to the counter. I carefully climbed across it and dropped, landing lightly on the floor. The kitchen was spacious, with an island in the middle, but I paid little attention to it and focused on the hall. I was probably three feet away from the entrance by now, and the light coming from the end of it was almost blinding, flashing white-hot and orange colors that made me wince.

I waited for Alex to get into place and saw that he was now sliding something over the knuckles of his left hand—a pulse shield. Seeing it gave me pause, because only Inquisitors were supposed to have pulse shields, but I set it aside. He could tell me where he'd gotten it later. For now, I was just grateful he'd had enough sense to bring a weapon.

I quickly explained what I was going to do in Callivax, and he nodded and slid out of sight behind the wall on the other side of the hall. I stood up and did the same, keeping myself right around the corner from the opening.

Then I grabbed one of the books and tossed it, very loudly, over the counter and into the living room. For a second, the sound of cutting carried on, and then it suddenly switched off with a click.

The silence was almost deafening, and I felt my breath catch as my throat suddenly tightened.

"Jang-Mi?" Tian asked, her voice carrying down the hall. "Are you with me?"

"*Motion detected,*" the robotic voice croaked. "*Searching.*"

There were several heavy sounds of metal hitting metal, and

CHAPTER 14

I felt the vibrations coursing up through the floor. The sentinel was moving.

I took a quick glimpse around the corner, and sure enough, a thick leg slid into view, stamping down on the floor with its odd, hexagon-shaped boot. The sentinel eased out of the hallway slowly, and I noticed several things at once. The first was that it was wearing a cloak similar to the kind I had seen Lacey's people wearing in Cogstown. The design somehow made it easier to blend in with the walls of the Tower.

The second thing I noticed was the small form slung over its shoulder. Her shredded skirt stuck up off its shoulder like a flower, and her black-clad legs and heavy black boots dangled against its chest. It held her in place with one hand, while the other one—the one on Alex's side of the room—held something that I didn't recognize. What I *did* recognize was how the sentinel held it in its hand. It was a weapon of some sort. Possibly the same one it had used on those people in the condensation room.

Images of bisected limbs and torsos spilled into my mind, and a small sound escaped my throat. I ducked back just as I saw the head snap around in the direction of the kitchen, red glowing from the depths of its deep hood. I moved quickly, silently crossing the floor and ducking behind the island. I changed positions just in time, because a heartbeat later, the sentinel clanged into the kitchen. I didn't see it, but I both heard and felt it, and tensed.

It stopped, and a soft whir of mechanical noise kicked up. I carefully eased my way back along the counter, moving with painstaking slowness so as not to create the slightest breath of noise. It was right on the other side.

I froze when I heard the clang of its foot again, moving toward the space between the wall and the counter. If it came around the island, it would see me—unless I was safely on the other side.

I picked up the pace, and had my hips around the corner when the sentinel clanged into view. I looked up from where I was kneeling to see its face peering down at me from the hood. The metallic orbs that made up its eyes were the source of the fiery red, illuminating the angular lines of its artificial face.

"*Enemy detected*," it said, raising the weapon in its hand and leveling it at me. I stared at the weapon, horrified. It was a flat bar, with a narrow seam running down the middle. The sentinel's hand was gripped tightly around a handle—which had a silver canister underneath that looked like it could contain compressed air. "*Awaiting orders.*"

My eyes widened as it continued to stare at me, and I realized it was in fact *getting* orders. I had to get away before the thing got a response, but I was afraid to move, worried it would just pull the trigger.

So I waited, hoping Alex would put that pulse shield to good use.

Tian, however, was not that patient, and pushed herself up as much as she was able to. She turned at the waist and looked over the sentinel's shoulder. "Jang-Mi, stop doing this!" she shouted, smacking a small hand against the sentinel's head. "Wake up!"

What was Tian doing? It was insane! I mean, Tian was a little odd at times, but this was crazy, even for her.

"Tian, keep still!" I ordered, taking the small risk of moving only my mouth.

The little girl swiveled even farther around, her hand using the sentinel's head to help give her leverage, and her wide doll's eyes grew even wider, filling with horror. "Liana! No! You don't know what it can do! You have to run!"

CHAPTER 14

"It's a little late for that, kiddo," I said softly. *C'mon, Alex.*

"No, it's not! Run! She can't control what she's doing!"

She? Man, this was getting weirder and weirder. But I couldn't do much with that weapon trained on me, so I said nothing, and waited. Why was it taking so long? Where was that owner of the other voice I had heard, and why wasn't she in here calling the shots?

"Orders confirmed. Kill the Knight."

"What? NO!" Tian screamed, kicking her legs frantically.

I stared up at the weapon in the thing's hand, time spinning into slow motion as a single point of light bloomed in the seam between the two flat parts. I threw myself back behind the counter—but knew that it was already too late.

That weapon, if it was the same one from the condensation room, would cut through the counter like butter to get me.

Before I was even fully behind the counter, though, the sentinel jerked one leg up into the air and interrupted the action. Tian screamed as a beam of crimson light streaked over my head into the corner, shooting up sparks as it hit the ceiling above, and leaving a trail of red, molten metal in its wake. And then the entire floor shook as the sentinel—four hundred and fifty pounds of metal—crashed onto the floor in the kitchen.

I jerked to my feet, shaken, but a quick check of my arms and limbs confirmed that the blast from the weapon hadn't hit me. "Grab Tian!" I shouted to my brother as I came flying around the counter. I was going to take its weapon; if it was that powerful, maybe it could cut through the sentinel's limbs.

Alex suddenly appeared, bent over, and yanked a dazed Tian from the sentinel's arm. The sentinel lay there stunned, and I stepped closer, swallowing my fear. Its arms and legs twitched and jerked, gears whirring internally as it tried to move. The hand holding the weapon was lifting up and down, but I quickly jammed my baton into the thing's face and released the charge.

The sentinel seized up, and there was a harsh pop, followed by a bright spark from its mouth. I held the baton there until the charge was expended, and the sentinel collapsed back on the floor, the glow in its eyes shutting off. I withdrew my baton and quickly bent over to grab the only thing I could: the flat bar that made the mouth of the weapon.

I started tugging, trying to wrest the object from the sentinel's grip, and I heard Alex grunt, followed by a skidding sound. A quick glance showed me that he was already carrying Tian away from the kitchen. "Get Mercury!" I told him before resuming my attempt to get the weapon away from it. An inch of it slipped out of the closed fist. That was a start.

I placed my foot on its wrist and continued to tug, fighting its powerful grip.

"Liana?" Tian said softly. Alex hadn't left yet.

"Not a good time, sweetie," I said, gritting my teeth. The weapon gave another fraction of an inch. Almost there.

"Liana. Stop what you're doing right now."

The note of urgency in her voice brought me up short, and I looked up to see the little girl staring at us both with alarmed eyes.

Then I got the distinct impression that I was being watched. I looked down at the sentinel's face, which was inches away from my foot, and saw that its eyes were now glowing again, only this time it was an angry lilac color—and it was glaring at me. I barely had a moment to register that before it shoved the hand I was gripping forward, driving it into my chest. Hard.

I stumbled back, my breath exploding violently out of my lungs, and hit the counter behind me. I fought to keep calm, though my body was screaming at me that I was suffocating, and opened my eyes in time to see it kick off its back into a standing position, facing me.

It brought its arm up, leveled at me, and without thinking, I dove in between its wide legs, ducking under the cloak it was wearing and rolling forward to my feet. Relying purely on instinct, I jumped up and over the counter, trying to put some distance and objects between us.

Alex was already two steps in front of me, Tian in his arms, and he threw himself down into the lowered sitting area, taking cover behind one of the sofas. I followed, leaping for it rather than running, and hit a center table with a crash, bouncing and rolling off of it into a couch. I opened my eyes to see the sentinel marching out from behind the counter, and slid into the gap between the couch and low table. I pushed the edge of the table up, creating cover behind it, and then cowered below it.

Seconds later, streaks of crimson fire shot over us, across the room, in bursts. Sparks exploded from the impact sites, showering down on us, and I covered my face with my hands, trying not to get singed by the hot, molten slag.

"Hey!" my brother shouted, and I looked over to where he was hiding behind the other couch to see Tian scrambling out from where he had curled protectively around her.

"Tian!" I shouted, but she slipped away, heading up the stairs toward the sentinel.

"Jang-Mi, STOP!" she screamed as she reached the top. I slid out from behind the table in time to see her come to a stop in front of the sentinel, both arms raised and legs spread wide.

The sentinel immediately ceased using its weapon and looked down at the small girl, who was nodding encouragingly.

"Your mission here is done."

The sentinel was still for several seconds, and then suddenly sprang into motion, picking Tian up with one hand and placing her on its shoulder. Then it began to run—and I did mean *run*—out of the room. It was gone before I could even think to stand up.

I stared after it for a long moment. "What the hell just happened?" I asked no one in particular.

15

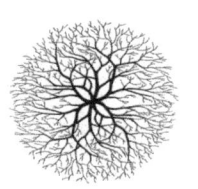

My brother coughed and slowly picked himself off of the floor. "That was insane," he said, shaking his head and dusting off his dark gray uniform. I noticed that his hands were shaking, and went over to him immediately.

"Alex?" I said, reaching out tentatively and placing a hand on his shoulder. "Are you hurt?"

He looked up at me, his eyes large. "No," he said harshly, running a hand over his body. "No, I'm fine. I'm..." He trailed off and looked around the room. "Whoa."

I looked up and followed his gaze. The walls of the apartment were still glowing with heat from where the weapon's blade had hit them, and bore the brunt of dozens of long slashes that cut through the dark metal. Pictures and shelves had been ripped apart, and debris now littered the floor. The entire place looked like it had been turned inside out, which was a shame—Mercury had had a nice home. Before.

Mercury! I turned toward the hall, my heart pounding. The

door at the end was still there, but had been partially cut through before Alex and I had lured the sentinel out. A quick scan showed me that there was nobody else there; the owner of the mysterious voice must have either slipped out while we were hiding, or been absent from the start. Perhaps they had been talking through a speaker?

I didn't know, but that could mean reinforcements were close behind. The sentinel was clearly being monitored. It had waited for orders to kill me before trying to—and I hadn't heard the order come through like I had heard that other voice. Did that mean that there was something inside of its programming, or its head, making it able to fight off the compulsion to kill? Or did it merely need the order before it would act?

What had it said? I thought back, trying to untangle the web of events that were jumbled up in my memory, and remember.

It came to me seconds later: *Cover your eyes, Yu-Na.*

I licked my lips. Tian had called the sentinel Jang-Mi. Was that its name? It made sense, in the context that Tian had used it, but why would a sentinel have a name, and why would Tian think talking to it would make it see reason? Was she talking to it... or whoever was *controlling* it?

The questions kept coming, but without Tian there to answer them, there was nothing I could do about it in the moment. They would have to remain unanswered until we could track the sentinel down again.

Speaking of which... I left my brother and climbed the three steps up out of the sunken floor that had partially shielded us, heading for the door. This one was much sturdier than the ones in the Citadel, but still had a line cut through it almost halfway down. Hardened metal hung in rivulets along the side of the gash, and through it, I could see the narrowest slice of a

CHAPTER 15

bedroom. I pressed the button on the side, but was unsurprised when it didn't open.

I placed my mouth near the hole and said, "Mercury? It's Liana. The sentinel is gone. You can come out now."

There was a rustling noise, and I peered through the hole, trying to catch a glimpse of the mysterious Mercury. Dinah Velasquez. A half dozen images of what she must look like danced through my head, and I settled on a middle-aged woman with dark brown hair and eyes and pale skin. Mysterious and probably much taller than me.

A shadow passed over the hole, and a moment later the door began dragging to one side. It stopped halfway, the ridges of once-heated-and-now-cooled metal preventing it from sliding into the narrow sheath in the side.

The gap was still wide enough for a person to squeeze through, and that was what Dinah did, easing out sideways into the hall.

I backed up to give her a little room, and couldn't help but gape when she came fully into view, several things becoming apparent at once.

Dinah was *old*. In her mid-sixties to early seventies, easy. Straight white hair with silver streaks hung down her back, cutting a sharp contrast against the dark gray of her suit. Slim wire spectacles sat in front of her eyes but did nothing to disguise the wrinkles, some of which almost connected to the lines around her mouth. Some women, like Astrid, grew softer and rounder when they aged, but not Dinah. She had gone the other direction, her body painfully thin and frail looking, even under her uniform. Her eyes, however, told a different story; they were a dark hunter's green, sharp, and filled with an intellectual gleam.

The second thing I noticed was that she was short. Much

shorter than me—probably by about six inches, putting her at about five feet even. Yet that didn't seem to bring her any pause as she regarded me, her chin lifting up to give me a judgmental look.

"What took you so long?" she snapped before brushing past me.

That was when I noticed the third thing: a black cane in her right hand, and a pronounced limp in her gait. I looked down at her legs, and realized that one of her feet was deformed. It was pointed inward, toward her other leg, which forced her to step sideways on the appendage.

It clicked. That was why Dinah had insisted she couldn't leave. Because, well, she *couldn't*. If she had tried to run for it with that limb and her advanced years, the sentinel would've caught up to her easily in the halls.

Thank Scipio we had gotten to her in time.

I took a moment to enjoy the small measure of relief, and then put it aside. Mer... *Dinah* had some explaining to do—namely, how the sentinel had found her.

I followed her into the living area, moving up next to her when she stopped to survey the damage. "Did you have to go and piss it off?" she groused after a moment, canting her head up at me.

"Sorry," I said automatically, immediately contrite under the heavy weight of her gaze. I could only imagine what she had gone through waiting for us, and while it wasn't my fault that it had taken us time to get up there, I still felt bad. "Are you okay?"

"Fine," she snapped. She lifted and dropped her shoulders in a small, uncomfortable wiggle. "Embarrassed. I hadn't intended for us to meet this way."

"How had you intended it?"

"On the day we left the Tower, and not a second before," she replied quickly. "Hello, Alex."

"Hey, Dinah," my brother said from where he was kneeling over some books that had been cut in half by the blast. Then he shifted slightly, his eyes darting up to mine in an expression that read *I have no idea what to say to this woman.*

"Dinah, how did this happen? How did it find you?"

Her mouth pinched tighter. "I made a mistake," she admitted begrudgingly after a moment. "I started running the search on your little sentinel without realizing that the powers that be had decided it would be a good idea to give them anti-tampering software that allowed them to track down 'unauthorized' individuals trying to locate them."

My eyes widened at that information, and my stomach churned. "Why would they do something like that? Seems a bit—"

"Overcautious?" Dinah said, twitching an eyebrow. "I don't know. The rationale didn't come in the report I read." She stared at the remains of her door, glowering. "What a mess."

Her mutter was delivered with anger and exhaustion, and I could sense that the older woman was beginning to come down from the adrenaline that had been surging through her during the event. Soon she was going to get sleepy, her body craving rest to help push the traumatic experience out.

Not to mention, this place was going to be crawling with Inquisition agents at any moment. We would only have a narrow window to talk before Alex and I had to get out of here. Our presence would attract a lot of unwanted attention, and Alex was already being monitored by the head of their department, Sadie Monroe. The last thing we wanted to do was bring her attention onto Dinah.

"Dinah," I said, catching the older woman's attention. She

blinked and turned her head toward me. "We're going to have to go soon," I informed her gently. "Otherwise people will know that we're working together."

Her mouth tightened, but she nodded. "Of course." She looked around the room. "Where's Tian?"

Now it was my turn for my mouth to go taut. "It still has her."

"She went with it willingly," my brother corrected. "She somehow managed to get it to stop. If she hadn't... I'm pretty sure it would've killed us."

My fist tightened. My brother had a point. Tian clearly had some sort of relationship with the thing. But what and how and why? What had happened to her in the condensation department? How had she managed to befriend it? Why was it keeping her and not letting her go? And who was controlling it in the first place?

Regardless of any of that, though, we needed to find her. And there was only one way to do that.

"Dinah, can you find a way to track this thing without it getting traced back to you?"

She scoffed and shook her head. "Oh no, dearie, I am not tracking that thing again. Do you see my home? It's too dangerous, Liana."

"But Tian—"

"Is doing better than we are," Dinah cut in. "She apparently has a five-hundred-pound block of metal monster protecting her."

"And keeping her hostage!" I retorted, frustrated. "Plus, that thing is being controlled by someone, possibly the same person who killed Ambrose." It was a leap, but not much of one in my mind. I found it difficult to believe that there was a third, unknown group, working against both whoever Devon's allies

CHAPTER 15

had been and Lacey's people as well. I couldn't prove it, but I knew it in my gut.

"Ambrose is dead, and to be honest, he was never really my problem. You and the others are, but I'm beginning to wonder if any of you are worth it. You're running around doing your precious Tourney and getting caught up in... whatever the hell is going on in the Tower. You uncover problems with Scipio, but then you don't follow through on them! And we're no closer to any plan of escape than we were when Roark was alive!"

I swallowed and looked at her, and at the anger in her eyes. She wanted to escape, and to her, I was dragging my feet. She had every right to be angry—but we didn't have the time for it.

Besides, a lot of that crap had been forced onto me, partially because of her actions. She had been the one who introduced me to Lacey and Strum in the first place, thus getting me in this whole mess to begin with, so I couldn't feel too bad.

"Dinah, I don't know what to say to that," I said. "But it's a moot point. We're here now, dealing with this mess, and I need a way to track down this sentinel. Can you help me?"

She sucked in a deep breath and then held her cane out to me, balancing carefully on her twisted limb. I accepted it, and a second later her pad was in her hand, her fingers flying across it as screen after screen of complex coding popped up. She swirled her finger around, making the screens shift to one place or another as she examined them.

"Yes," she said finally, clicking the pad off and slipping it back into her uniform. She held her hand out for her cane, snapping her fingers impatiently when I didn't get it to her fast enough, and then settled a part of her weight back onto it with a relieved sigh. "I can write a code that can be uploaded into the relay stations in the Tower, which would prevent it from tracking you, while allowing you to scan for its location. Will that do?"

I nodded. "It will, thank you." I licked my lips. "Will you be okay here?"

"I'll be perfectly fine," she snapped, her eyes narrowing. "I can have some people here to fix the door in a matter of hours, and I've got a few Inquisitors in my pocket. Besides, I doubt the sentinel will be back. Whoever is controlling it is too smart for that."

Controlling it. My mind drifted back to the fight in the kitchen—the speed with which the sentinel had reacted. If it was being controlled by someone, wouldn't there have been a delay in its response time? The user needed time to receive the images from the sentinel, and then input the instructions, right?

So how had it moved so quickly at the end there? It had received orders, but I supposed that whatever they had done to program it allowed it to have some autonomy—it was the only explanation. It waited for the orders, but once it received them, it decided how to execute them.

And that made it twice as dangerous, as its reaction times were far superior to those of a human's.

"Dinah, did you see or hear anyone else in your apartment after it broke in?"

Dinah gave me a sideways look, her white brows drawing together. "No," she said. "Why?"

I bit my lip, thinking. If there had been someone nearby, watching, then *that* could explain how it had reacted so quickly. There was that voice I had heard in the hall, but there was no sign that anyone else had been here. Unless...

"Alex?" I asked, looking at him and ignoring Dinah's question for a second. "Did you notice anyone in the hall when you passed it, going into the kitchen?"

He frowned and shook his head. "I looked down it, but there wasn't anybody there. Why?"

I rubbed my eyes, suddenly very tired. Maybe I was wrong about this. What the hell did I know about a sentinel, or how fast it could move? They had been built long before my time, and all I had were the reports in my history book to guide me.

Still, everything about this entire exchange had been off, in more ways than one, and it wasn't sitting well with me. We needed answers.

"Never mind," I said, shaking my head. "I just... I'm trying to figure this out. Dinah, pass the file and instructions for tracking the sentinel over to Quess as soon as possible. Alex, we should get out of here before the Inquisition gets here."

"Right," he said. He paused, looking at Dinah. "It's, um, nice to meet you."

Dinah gave him a withering smile. "You'll be seeing a lot more of me," she said primly. "Now that you know who I am, I'm having you transferred into my group."

I frowned. She could do that?

More importantly, would it be safer for him to be closer to Dinah? Sadie Monroe was already watching him because of me, and if Dinah suddenly pulled him into her... mysterious department...

"Are you sure that's a good idea?" Alex asked, and I could tell he was already thinking along the same lines. "Sadie is having me watched, and—"

"You let me worry about Sadie. I alone have the ability to pull rank on her, and now that you're in my department, you're under my protection."

I blinked. She had the ability to—

The words came sputtering out of me; my thoughts and shock eliminated the filter I usually kept between my thoughts and mouth. "You have the ability to override *Sadie Monroe?!*" I sputtered, incredulous. "How?"

"I run a shadow security department, meant to be a review board to every decision the CEO makes that affects Scipio's programming. We're the programming ethics committee, essentially, responsible for making sure each decision made in the name of efficiency isn't also affecting his other, emotional protocols."

There was another round of blinking, as I was robbed of all my words for several seconds, trying to wrap my head around what she was saying. "You make sure that Scipio's feelings don't get hurt when you're forced to change his programming?"

Dinah chuckled derisively. "Something like that. Anyway, don't worry about your brother. I'll convince Sadie I can keep a better eye on him while giving him a research job. That'll lead her to believe that he won't have programming privileges, which will go a long way toward making her relax. I'll have to give her reports, of course, most of which will be lies, and we might have to feed her a scheduled meeting here and there between the two of you, just so she can have something to listen in on to put her mind at ease. Just have dinner with your family or something, and keep the conversation light and topical."

Alex and I exchanged wide-eyed looks. "Uhhh..."

"Or go to dinner with each other and talk about things," she snapped impatiently, slamming her cane into the ground. "What do I have to do, come up with everything? Figure it out for yourselves, and just realize this will be a thing, all right? I'll keep Sadie off your brother's back, and give him a little more freedom to work!"

She stopped, glaring at us both, and then sucked in a deep breath. "Now get out of here. The Inquisition is no doubt on their way, and you two aren't supposed to be here."

CHAPTER 15

I wanted to stay and question her more about my brother's safety, but I knew she was right. What was more, if Alex was caught having brought me to this level, Sadie would toss him out long before Dinah could fill out the transfer request form.

We had to go. Now.

16

My brother and I were forced to say a hasty goodbye due to the growing pandemonium around the Core, and I hurried home as quickly as possible, my mind replaying the events with Tian and the sentinel. There was something more going on there—I was certain of it. And now, more than ever, we needed to find her.

If only so we could get a few answers.

Excited by the prospect of telling my friends that Tian was alive, I rushed into my apartment, eagerly searching the interior for my friends. The funeral was probably still going on, so I doubted they were here, but still I looked.

To my surprise, they *were* here. I felt a moment of confusion, and then realized that they had probably come back here when I hadn't turned back up after leaving. I was more surprised to see that Zoe and Eric were here as well. Zoe was standing by the table, her fist pressed to her lips, with Leo standing opposite her, his own arms folded across his chest.

Maddox was lying down on the couch, a pillow under her head, while Quess and Eric sat in the easy chairs opposite her, with their backs to me.

Maddox spotted me first, and her green eyes narrowed slightly. She heaved herself upright, still moving a bit gingerly, and said, "Liana's back."

Everyone swiveled their heads around, and suddenly five sets of eyes were staring at me.

"Oh, thank Scipio," Zoe exhaled, shaking her head in relief.

"See, I told you she'd be fine," Quess said smugly. I wasn't entirely sure who he was talking to—it could've been the entire room for all I knew—but I was grateful for the show of support. Although why I needed it was still a bit of a mystery. But that could wait; I had more important news.

"Of course I'm fine," I said. "But I need to tell you about—"

"Oh no, you don't," Zoe exclaimed, her brows furrowing. "Don't change the subject! Where were you? You just ran off, and you didn't tell anyone where you were going! Leo and Maddox searched for fifteen minutes before they called me—concerned, I might add—and I ordered them back here to coordinate! We were just about to call Alex! Liana, you went off *alone*, which is breaking your own rule!"

I stared at her for a long moment. She was right, of course, but the circumstances weren't exactly as simple as she made them seem. Still, from the looks on their faces, I had given them an awful fright.

"I'm sorry for worrying you," I said. "But I got a net transmission from a Dinah Velasquez, and—"

"Oh no! I don't care about Dinah Velasquez, whoever she might be," Zoe said angrily. "You ran off without any backup. That is unacceptable."

I gave her a look. "Zoe, I'm going to have to run off sometimes if the moment calls for it," I replied dismissively. "Now, as I was saying, it turns out Dinah is—"

"No!" Zoe shouted, stomping one foot down on the floor and cutting me off again. I blinked my eyes at the childish display and then took a step back, alarmed when she came marching toward me. "They killed Ambrose, Liana. They snuck into the Citadel, overrode the door to his room, and beat him to death." Maddox made a small sound on the couch behind her, but Zoe, normally the most empathetic person I knew, ignored it, her dark blue eyes blazing like sapphires backlit by the desert sun.

"You are now our nominee to become Champion," she continued blithely. "That makes you a prime target for attack. So no, you do not get to run off any time the moment calls for it. You're our leader, Liana, and we need you as safe from harm as we can possibly make you. Do you understand?"

"Guys, I am sorry I left like that," I said honestly. "It wasn't my intention to leave the memorial, let alone the Citadel, and I'm sorry that I didn't take the ten seconds I should've to call you. What can I do to make this better?"

"Promise that you'll never do it again," Leo announced from behind Zoe.

"And then never do it again," Quess added helpfully.

I couldn't help but smile. Even though they were preventing me from telling them about Tian, I felt warmed by the reaction to my sudden disappearance. They cared about me—and that made me feel good.

"I promise," I said solemnly. "Now, will you please let me tell you about Tian?"

"Tian!" Quess and Maddox both said her name at the exact same time, and Quess stood up, his wide eyes already searching for his surrogate sister. "Where is she?"

"I don't know," I replied. "But she's alive. And I think she's okay, but..." I shook my head. "You'd better sit down," I told them. "This is going to take a minute to explain. Quess, set up that noise-cancelling device."

Quess quickly set it up, but it took closer to five minutes to explain, and everyone had questions. Questions about the sentinel, about the voice I had heard, about Dinah, and, of course, about Tian.

"So she was alive?" Maddox asked.

I had already answered the question, but I nodded again. "Yes. Very much so. I didn't see any injuries."

"But she stayed with the sentinel?"

This time it was Quess asking yet another question I had already answered. "Yes. If I didn't know any better, I would have thought *she* thought she had a relationship with it. But she was only able to convince it to leave without killing us after it had already done a lot of damage. She wasn't able to stop the attack on Dinah, or on us, until the very end."

"Okay, but why stay with a death machine that murdered six people to get to you?" Zoe asked. "Tian's smart, and fast—she could get away easily, I'm sure of it. So why stay?"

I looked at Maddox and Quess, hoping that they could find some explanation for Tian's decision to stay with the sentinel. Maddox's eyes had grown distant, and I could tell she was deep in thought. Quess, however, was scratching his chin, his eyes much more focused.

"Quess?" I asked.

He sighed, and rested an elbow on the top of the chair. "I suppose if Tian thought the sentinel was something she could save, then she might stay with it."

"Save? How could she save a sentinel?" I asked, trying to follow his logic.

"It's a killer," Maddox said, breaking free of her thoughts.

"But if it showed kindness toward her, she might stay to try to keep it from killing others. I mean, that seems like what she was doing, right? I don't think it's a big leap for her."

"But what could possibly prompt that kind of behavior from her?" Leo interjected. "The sentinels were only meant to be basic shells. The only programs inside of them were for receiving Scipio's signal, and making their bodies move." I gave him a surprised look, wondering how he could've known all that when he'd been cut off from the Tower long before the sentinels were even conceived. He noticed, because he offered me a slightly embarrassed shrug, and said, "I read up on them after you showed us the history book."

"Right." I stopped to think about what he was saying. If the sentinel was only a shell, then Tian's motivations for staying were still a mystery—and one that didn't offer us much in the way of a starting place for evidence. Without anything to go off, everything we did from here on out would be based on speculation.

And we needed less of that, in my opinion. Which meant it was time to get to work.

"Regardless of Tian's motivations," I announced slowly, grabbing everyone's attention, "the fact remains that the sentinel is still out there, and it's a threat to us. It saw my face. It could be hunting for me even now. Hell, whoever is controlling it could be *forcing* it to come find us right now. Tian might be holding it back—don't ask me how. And if she is, there's no guarantee it will last; it barely worked the first time. She might not be able to save us again. Which means we need to find it fast."

"And kill it," Quess added, and I gave him a sharp look.

"No," I countermanded, much to everyone's surprise. But I barreled on, eager to explain why I didn't think killing the sentinel was the best move at this juncture. "The sentinel is clearly being controlled by someone, and I want to know who it is. Whoever controls it could be the same person or people who targeted Ambrose, possibly even the same people Devon was working with. If so, we might finally get a chance to learn the identity of our attackers. And keeping the sentinel intact is the best way of doing that."

Silence met my statement and I waited, wondering who would be the first to break it.

Turned out it was all of them.

"That's crazy!"

"What, why?"

"How can you even think that's possible?"

"What about Tian?"

I held up my hand in a silent plea for them to stop, and to my absolute surprise, they did, allowing me the opportunity to explain myself. I carefully placed my thoughts in order, and then began to speak.

"Tian is absolutely a priority in this," I informed them, needing to get that out of the way first. I didn't want them to think that I was about to sacrifice her safety for some quest to take the sentinel. "I want her to be the first one out of the room, preferably with one of you going with her. But the rest of us... We need to see if we can try to take the sentinel in one piece. Or, at the very least, recover its hard drive. I assume it has one?"

I looked at Leo as I asked this, and he nodded slowly. "It does. It's in the back of its neck."

"Could we use it to track whatever signal is being sent to control its movements?"

"Maybe," he conceded after a beat. "Although, I have to ask why. Won't finding the people controlling it only place you in more danger?"

I hesitated. Leo was right, of course. By pursuing this, I was

CHAPTER 16

definitely putting us at even more risk than ever before. Trying to keep it intact limited our options for taking it down, and it wouldn't share our limitations. We'd be trying to take it alive; it would be trying to kill us.

But I was tired of always being blindsided. I had no idea who our enemies were, what they were planning, or what sort of resources they had to work with. Finding them would be the first step to figuring it all out. I just had to convince my friends it was the right idea.

"It will," I told him. "And I'm very aware that it's a risk, but we have no idea who is after us, and I, for one, am getting pretty sick of walking around this Tower with half a blindfold on. I think the benefit of knowing who is behind this far outweighs the risk, especially if it's something we can give to Strum or Lacey to keep them off our backs."

Not that I couldn't be sure that they weren't tearing apart the Tower looking for it. But I doubted they had access to Knights' manuals, which was what they needed to learn about the sentinel. I considered telling them, but finally decided that the only good time to tell Lacey they had anything was when they had the names and locations of Ambrose's murderers, and not a second before.

"But more than that, I want to know who was *really* behind Ambrose's death. And there is every chance that in doing this, we could find out where his killers are. And bring them to justice."

Silence met my remark, and I gave my friends time to think, not wanting to pressure them into it. After a moment, Quess said, "So Mercury has a way for tracking this thing down?"

"She does," I said. "She said she'd transmit it to you, so check your pad and see if it's already waiting for you."

I waited as he pulled out his pad and checked it. A second later, he nodded.

"Got it right here," he said. "It's not from her directly, but it's the code. Let me take a look at it and see how it works."

"Take your time," I said, knowing full well that he wouldn't. Still, I was grateful he was on my side. Now I just needed the others there as well. "How are the rest of you feeling?"

Zoe scratched the shaved area on the side of her head. "I think it's a bit risky, but you're right—we need to know who's after us. If the only way to find that out is to catch this thing, then I'm in. I just want us to go in there with a weapon powerful enough to take it down. Just in case."

I nodded. "I'll handle that. I'll just need to get into the armory and get one."

"Not alone, you won't," Eric said from his position on the couch.

"I'll go with her," Leo volunteered.

No he would not, I thought to myself, already digging for ways I could escape robbing the armory with Leo.

"No, you won't," Quess announced, setting his pad down with a sigh. "I'll have to. You and the others will be needed elsewhere."

"Oh?" I said quickly. "Why?"

Quess nodded toward his pad. "Mercury's trace program requires that we upload it to a minimum of twelve relay stations before we start running it. Three on each side of the Tower; at the top, middle, and bottom, to boot. We'll need to upload the program into each one, but if we do it right, the sentinel won't be able to track us while we're looking for it."

Twelve relay stations? That was a lot. And it required using lashes and going outside—something that was dangerous on the best of days. There were only six of us, and even moving in tandem, it would take time.

Plus, I still had to handle the weapon. But it explained why Quess was willing to go with me. He was notoriously bad at lashing, and going outside onto the glass shell encompassing the Tower could be a death sentence for such an inexperienced lasher. Leo was needed outside: his lashing and computer skills made him perfect for the task.

"Leo, I'm putting you in charge of getting the program into the relay stations," I said. "I know you want to help me with the weapons, but you are good with lashes, which we need. We'll have two teams outside, and one team inside. The two teams outside, under Leo, will plant the program, while the one inside —me and Quess—will get a weapon capable of stopping this thing. Does that sound good?"

I was fairly certain it did—not fully, but we didn't have a choice. We had a limited window of opportunity before the Tourney resumed, and we needed to find Tian before our moves became even more scrutinized.

To my great relief, however, nobody objected, and within moments we were all around the table, going over who was responsible for what.

I really did have the best friends, I thought to myself.

17

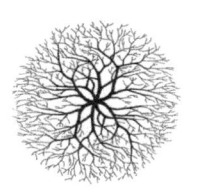

The six of us filed out of the apartment and into the hall, a sharp band of tension stretched between us. Zoe and Eric were taking turns checking the lash harnesses that they had borrowed from Quess and me, and I felt a moment of apprehension for them. Neither was formally trained with lashes, and while I had let them both try mine out a few times, they had never gone outside the shell of the Tower before.

Maddox was also nervous, but for another reason. I watched as her eyes darted back and forth across the hall, constantly scanning for any sign of attack. She kept rubbing her hands and wrists, as if trying to squeeze her anxiety out through her hands. I could tell she was tense, just being out in the open like this, and I felt horrified that she was so anxious about stepping out of the apartment that she felt the need to be prepared for an attack, her eyes darting all along the halls before she slowly stepped out.

And the tension was contagious, spreading through us until it felt like we were all holding our breaths to the point of suffocation. Which was perfectly understandable. This was the first mission where we were going to be spread so thin, and that left us vulnerable to attack. It was dangerous, and that was partially my fault. I was insisting we split up to save time. But it was definitely my job to lead them, and I knew I couldn't let them go with those dark shadows in their eyes. I had to say something.

"Okay, everyone," I said softly, pitching my voice low so that only they could hear. The halls might be empty, but there were cameras everywhere, and I couldn't be entirely sure who was on the other side, monitoring them. "I know we're all feeling a bit scared, and I want you to know, that's okay. We're splitting up, and we're going to be a little vulnerable."

My friends' eyes darted around toward each other, as if wondering where I was going with this, and I didn't leave them hanging. "You are all smart and capable. I trust you to use your heads. If something feels off, get out and call us. Stay inside the Tower as much as possible. And most importantly, if you see anyone, anyone at all, then get out of there."

"The same goes for you and Quess," Leo said, concern warm in his voice. "You have the more dangerous mission."

"Yes, but we don't have to leave the Citadel," I retorted. "Look, everyone just be careful, and we'll meet back here in a few hours. If Quess and I finish early, we will borrow some spare lashes and come and help you with the relays. And, like I said, if you have any problems—"

"We'll net you and try to come back here immediately," Maddox cut in impatiently. "Fine. Is there anything else?"

Maddox's gruffness was slightly off-putting, but I let it go, sensing that her issues weren't necessarily going to be touched by words alone. "Yes. Because you and Leo are the better lashers, I want you to split up. One of you take Zoe, and one of you take Eric. Sorry, guys," I said, directing my gaze to the friends in question, "but I want to make sure you're with someone who's experienced."

"I'm fine with that," Zoe said, giving Eric a sideways glance and a small smile. "This one is a little too big for me to be rescuing alone, and even though I prefer working with him, I suppose Leo will make an okay substitute. It'll give us a chance to talk."

That sounded ominous, but as I looked at Zoe, I realized that she was going to talk to him on my behalf, and hopefully get him to ease up a little bit. She might not understand exactly what had happened, but she could tell something was up, if only through my body language screaming 'help me.' I knew he didn't mean to, but now every time I saw Leo, there was this... expectation emanating from him. As if he wanted me to answer a question that I wasn't even ready to hear yet. Namely, would I let him kiss me, so he could remember it. Hopefully, Zoe could find a way to help with that, because I wasn't sure I was going to be able to work with him if he kept doing it, and I needed him on my team. I needed to keep him happy, if only for Grey's sake.

Not that I thought he'd use that against me. Leo was too honorable to do anything more than what he had promised to do for Grey.

"Good," I replied. "I'll see all of you very soon."

Quess and I broke off from the others and began moving away, heading for the elevator. As we walked, the silence stretched between us, but I wasn't inclined to break it. I was too nervous. We were about to try to steal something from the armory—a crime that was considered a capital offense. If we were discovered...

Well, suffice it to say that I wouldn't be Champion if we were discovered. More than that, we'd be arrested as potential terrorists, and interrogated thoroughly with that in mind. They would likely try to tie us to Ambrose's murder, or assume that we were involved—or worse—and we'd be right back where this mess started.

I considered reaching out to Lacey for help, but quickly rejected the idea again. Lacey was angry, hurt, and filled with grief. That kind of emotional turmoil didn't put people in the right mind frame for practicality, and in her case, she might change her mind and turn us in before we had a chance to finish the Tourney. It was too risky to approach her with anything less than Ambrose's murderers—either information that would lead to them or the people themselves.

Still, I didn't like it.

The apprehension grew when we entered the elevator, and as we began to rise, I suddenly felt sweat break out on my forehead. Something was wrong. It was too risky. Eyes were everywhere within the Citadel, scans more strenuous and patrols more numerous. Without a foolproof plan, we'd get caught.

I had to make sure we had one before we even got there.

"Elevator, emergency stop. Block access to this shaft on my authority, Liana Castell, 25K-05," I ordered quickly, following my gut.

"*Acknowledged*," the computer-generated voice announced. "*Elevator shaft blocked. Redirecting traffic.*"

Quess was giving me a penetrating look when I turned to face him. "Liana?" he asked, his voice and eyes hesitant—and concerned. "Are you okay?"

I was worrying him. Great. "I'm fine," I said reassuringly. "But I'm starting to think that going to the armory is a bad idea. I keep thinking about how security is so much tighter right now, and that we can't afford to jeopardize the Tourney, or else Lacey will come after us! So please tell me that you and Leo came up with something good, or else I'm thinking we need to come up with something else."

Quess's eyes flashed with some emotion, but he looked away quickly, trying to mask it.

"What?" I asked.

He shifted awkwardly, one hand going up to rub the back of his neck self-consciously. "Well, Leo and I couldn't actually get access to their systems with the time we had," he admitted. The shock that was rippling through me must've shown on my face, because he continued, rather hurriedly, "I know I should've told you, but I figured once you got me inside, I could just directly hack into their system."

"Quess!" I exclaimed, already beginning to feel the embrace of anger. I took a moment to put it in check, and modulated my voice slightly. "Quess, why would you—" I stopped myself midsentence and sighed. "Tian."

"I'm sorry, Liana, but it was going to take us days to get into their system, and as soon as the Tourney kicks back in, I know Tian will be left on the back burner! And I understand why that will be, but I'm sorry—I can't accept it! So no, I didn't tell you the truth, but I figured it wouldn't matter. I've seen you talk your way out of impossible situations, so how is this one any different?"

I listened closely to what he was saying, and then made the conscious decision not to get angry with him. Instead, I focused on being grateful that he was telling me now, while there was still time.

But now we needed to figure something else out. If we couldn't get a Class B weapon, then we needed to come up with some other way of neutralizing the sentinel. Unfortunately, I didn't know enough engineering to think of what that might possibly be.

Quess, however, *might*. He had likely been studying the thing's specs since I first brought them up. And he was, after all, our resident inventor.

"Quess, is there any other way we could knock out the sentinel?" I asked slowly.

He rolled his eyes and then sighed, folding his muscular arms over his chest. "I considered that, and it *is* possible, but it would be untested tech. If it fails, we'll be dead."

He was right, and we wouldn't be able to test it until the heat of battle, which meant risking a situation in which it *didn't* work—and the sentinel tore us apart. But going in blind after a Class B weapon was just as dangerous. Even more dangerous in some ways. We'd definitely be executed if we were caught, and tortured for answers long before death came.

Of course, Quess didn't need to know that second part.

"And if we get caught trying to steal a Class B weapon, we'll *definitely* be dead. After a very short trial."

His mouth flattened at that, and after a moment of internal deliberation, he finally said, "Point taken. We'll need to go to Sanctum. Not all of my tools got transferred to Zoe's apartment, and I need what's there."

I nodded and quickly informed the computer of our destination change. Getting to Sanctum would take a little bit of time, but if that meant Quess could make something that would help us defeat the sentinel—and prevent us from getting caught stealing a weapon—then I was okay with the delay.

Forty-five minutes later, I slid into our former home through a vent. It had changed drastically since I had last been here, the once-homey living area now disassembled and packed up into bags lining the floor. I stared at it as I stood up, missing the cozy

CHAPTER 17

meals we had shared in the tiny space Zoe had created with curtains.

"We did a pretty good job of packing it up," Quess boasted as he slid out of the vent behind me. "Most everything is ready to go, but my tools are still out. I used this place to alter my appearance for my spy work, and wound up doing some tinkering as well. C'mon."

He had righted himself as he spoke and was now walking away, heading for an irregularly shaped opening in the wall on the left side of the room. We had cut the hole ourselves, in an attempt to avoid wasting time using the vents moving from room to room, and Quess had converted the room we created into a workstation.

He ducked through the low opening and moved over to his table, where he started sifting through his tools and sorting them. I paused at the doorway, watching him.

"So what do you think you're going to build?" I asked, curious as to what he thought he could do. And how long it would take—though I would wait to ask that question.

"The sentinel's skin… hide… whatever you want to call it… is impervious to most levels of electricity, up to ten thousand volts. However, if you can hit it with something more powerful…"

I followed his trailed-off thought to its natural conclusion: the sentinel would go down. And once it was down, we could crack open the outer shell and pull out its hard drive and power core. Of course the real question was whether it would stay down the entire time.

"It'll go down," I finished for him. "But for how long?"

He gave me a look over his shoulder and frowned. "I honestly don't know," he admitted. "I don't even know how far over ten thousand volts I should go! Too low, and it could shake the charge off. Too high, and we have every chance of frying its internal systems. And I need those to be intact if you want me to track down who's behind all of this."

"I'm sure you'll figure it out," I said encouragingly. I licked my lips. "How long do you think it will take?"

Quess leaned back, considering his tools. "I'm not sure," he replied. "I could maybe have a few prototypes in an hour, but they'll be untested, and—"

"It's better than going against that thing with nothing, Quess," I said, my mind working. An hour. Right. That was a long time, and there wasn't much I could do to help him do it more quickly. I certainly didn't have the technical skills or knowledge to be able to back him up. "Do you think you could get it done any faster? We need to be ready to go as soon as the others are done."

"Yes, I know that, Liana," he said, a thread of irritation worming its way into his voice. "I am well aware of what's on the line."

"I'm sorry, Quess," I said. "I'm just nervous."

And the emptiness of the place was beginning to get to me, but I didn't mention that. Still, it was different being back here, in the Sanctum, especially after everything that had gone down. Sitting here doing nothing wasn't going to help, but if I stayed around Quess, I'd probably wind up interrupting his work. I needed to do something, if only so I could feel useful.

I thought about it, and then on a whim, decided to go to the only place that could possibly hold my interest an entire hour: Lionel Scipio's office. I was betting it wasn't packed up yet, and at the very least, I could do something about that, to save the others some time and work off some of my own nerves.

"Quess, I'm heading for the office," I told him quietly. "Gonna look at some books and do some general snooping around."

CHAPTER 17

"I'll call you through the anchor if anyone shows up," he said dismissively.

I nodded and headed for the vent. It took me a few minutes to wriggle through the tight spaces, but when I emerged from the opening into Scipio's office, I was happy I had made the trip. None of the things in here had been packed up. Although, gauging from the books that had been plucked from the shelves and placed on the table between the two overstuffed sofas, Zoe had no intention of leaving anything behind.

I was grateful, and also eager to expedite the process, so I pushed up my sleeves and got cracking.

Stacking and carrying books was mindless, but good work that kept me busy. Occasionally I would pause to open up a book, sliding my hand over the luxurious white paper and tiny printed script before examining its contents. Most books seemed to be on programming stuff, but there were more than a few things that caught my eye, and I wound up setting those books aside in a separate pile, wanting to take them with me so I could start reading them.

After half an hour, I had managed to clear half the shelves in the room, and was moving to the next shelf, this one on the opposite side of the painting Lionel's safe was hidden behind. I was also making a mental note to ask Leo for the code so we could empty the safe's contents as well.

I glanced at it as I thought this, and paused, staring at the gap between the painting and the wall. It was wide—over an inch, to be precise—and that stood out to me. Normally the painting lay almost flat, so for it to be sticking out like that...

I set down the books I had been in the process of collecting and carefully lifted the painting with both hands, moving it to one side and setting it on the ground. As I straightened up, I immediately spotted the cause for the painting's strange seating.

The safe was open, a gap of nearly an inch spanning between the wall and the door. The lights on the front were dead, and when I reached out to stroke over it, they didn't turn back on.

I bit my lip, wondering what had caused it to become unlocked.

Before, Leo had been the only one who could access it, using his terminal. Now that the terminal was gone, though—maybe that had sent a signal to the safe to open, lest everything inside be lost forever.

Or, Lacey and her team had managed to crack it while they were down here. I bristled at the thought; she'd already violated our privacy once by managing to track our location to this place. She'd also taken samples of the paint Quess had made, though I'd managed to get the legacy net out of the deal, so that was something. Still, if she'd also done this and failed to tell us, I didn't care that she was angry with me. I'd call her out on it and demand the return of all the items immediately. I didn't know all the secrets the safe contained, but they could hold clues to Leo's plan to fix or replace Scipio, and we needed those.

I reached out and yanked the door open, trying to recall everything I had seen in there before. To my surprise, nothing looked like it had been touched. There were still two locked boxes—one flat and wide with a handle on the top, the other long and tall—both with digital keypads requiring a six-digit code. Underneath those were several data crystals, all lined up in a tray with a soft fabric inside. There were a few file folders on the bottom, and some strange, uniform, green and white paper that depicted the image of man with round cheeks who was balding on the top of his head, but still had thick, wavy hair coming from the back and running down to his shoulders. The paper was in multiple stacks, bound by thin white strips that read $10,000 USD—whatever that meant.

Nothing seemed like it had been touched, which meant that Lacey probably hadn't found it. The safe had likely opened due to the terminal going off.

Whatever the cause, I couldn't leave the items in there like that. These things had been kept in a safe, and were obviously valuable. I wasn't going to let them fall into anyone else's hands —and I was certain that if Leo knew about the safe, he would want me to move the stuff inside to a more secure location.

It took me a few minutes of rummaging, but I found a duffle bag with a long strap I could use for carrying everything, and quickly filled the bag with the items from inside the safe. Then, after discovering I had more room, I followed it up with the books I had been setting aside.

A quick check of my watch told me I had been at it for forty-five minutes, and that I should check on Quess. I quickly closed the safe and rehung the picture, then turned and left, eager to see how Quess was progressing.

Getting through the vents with the bag wound up taking longer than I expected, and by the time I emerged, pushing the heavy bag ahead of me, I was speckled with sweat and panting slightly. I managed to pick up the bag and carry it a few more feet toward the exit that led back up through the Menagerie, setting it just next to the entrance so I wouldn't forget it.

Then I headed toward the workroom, where Quess was bent over, a pair of goggles on his face, peering through a magnifying glass and soldering something that shot off a few sparks here and there. I spotted another pair of goggles and held them up over my eyes to keep the sparks from damaging my eyes, before getting closer.

"How's it going?" I asked, coming up beside him and looking over his shoulder.

Under the magnifying glass, I saw several small silver rings that had been hammered out to thin, flat disks. The one he was currently working on burned bright red, and he was in the process of pressing it between two blocks of metal, smooshing it down.

"Not bad, actually. I've been experimenting with using the material that the lash ends are comprised of, coupled with the connectivity of the tips on our batons. The fabrication process of combining them and then providing the piece with a power source to generate enough electricity is a little tricky, but... watch."

He picked up one of the disks and threw it against the wall just a few feet away. It stuck, and then a second later a flash of white-blue electricity arced out along the walls, resembling a long-legged arachnid about the size of a pig. It remained there for several seconds, then suddenly shut off, leaving the metal disc fused in a red-hot molten mass against the wall.

I whistled, impressed. "Wow. Quess, that's amazing. So it sticks because of the static-absorbing element of the lash ends?"

"Yes, to which I bonded a super-conductive material that doubles as its power source. It's a difficult element to salvage, but luckily you don't need much of it. It's how we extract so much power from the solar panels and the hydro-turbines. Anyway, because we don't need that static to do more than stick the disc to the sentinel, I figured I could just use the energy from it for something else, and I was right. I'm still not sure about the voltage, though, so I set it at twenty-five thousand volts."

I blinked. "Twenty-five thousand volts? Is that too high?"

He shrugged. "The carbon matrix they used to encase the thing has a tolerance of almost seventeen thousand volts, so I guesstimated an additional eight thousand to overcome its internal system. There's a chance that it won't be enough, but there's also a chance that I could fry it. The only way to know is to try it, and hope for the best."

I sighed. I didn't like it, but Quess knew his stuff, and I was certain that his best guess was based on more complicated science than I would understand. I barely understood how he had managed to make the discs—but I trusted that he knew what he was doing.

"How do you propose we transport these?" I asked, picking one of them up. They were small, and that meant they'd be easily lost. Also, if I transported them in my pocket, and was searched, they were odd enough to stand out.

"I already thought of that," he replied, producing a string. I watched as he quickly knotted the brown material, and then began to loop it through the holes in the discs, doing something complicated with the string that I didn't quite follow. "These are special knots," he said, his fingers moving faster than my eyes could track, doing something that left each ring dangling from a loop that jutted out of a woven band. "The framework of it will remain intact, but if you pull on the shocker, it will pull out the string and allow you to slip the disc off, while keeping the rest of the band and the other shockers in place. If you wear it as a necklace or bracelet, no one will pay it a second thought."

I nodded, appreciating the creativeness of his solution. He was right—it looked like a simple piece of jewelry, similar to the ones the Cogs made from broken bits of the Tower too small to be recycled in any useable fashion. It would be unnoticeable.

"I'll wear it as a bracelet," I said, thrusting out my wrist. "You're sure it won't go off against my skin?"

He gave me a slightly nervous smile. "I can't guarantee it,

but I'm fairly confident." He slid the band over my wrist and tied the two ends together to fix it into place.

"Great," I said dryly, pulling my hand away from him when he was done and admiring the work. "Just so you know, if this kills me, you get to deal with Zoe."

Quess gave me a flat look. "Liana, if that kills you, I'll have to deal with everyone, including myself. I am ninety-eight percent sure it won't hurt you."

I smiled and reached out to grip his shoulder. "I know you would never do anything to hurt me or put me in danger, Quess."

"Of course I wouldn't," he replied. "Now, let's get back up to the apartment, and see if the others are back."

"Yes," I replied, fingering the silver discs, a thrum of nervousness uncurling inside me. Soon, we'd be confronting the sentinel again, and even with this new weapon at my fingertips, I couldn't help but feel a moment of doubt.

But I put it aside, and focused on what was important—which was getting Tian, and then finding out who was after us. And that had to come before my doubts.

18

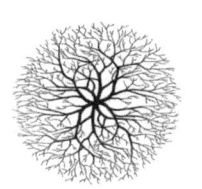

My shoulder was aching from the heavy contents of the duffle bag by the time we got back to the apartment, and I couldn't help fingering the string of metallic discs that were now draped around my wrist. The tiny little things didn't seem very impressive, but Quess had assured me that they would pack enough of a punch to take the sentinel down.

I hoped he was right.

When we entered the apartment, my intention was to hide the bag in my room and then net the others using the anchor and find out what their progress was. But to my utmost surprise, they were already inside. From the looks of it, they had just arrived; Zoe and Eric were in the process of getting out of their lash harnesses, while Leo was guzzling down water in the kitchen. Only Maddox had taken a seat, and given the downward cast of her face, she was tired.

"Hey, guys," I said, setting the bag down by the archway

leading into the kitchen area. "You finished fast. Everything go all right?"

"It was fine," Zoe said, her eyes not quite meeting mine. I raised an eyebrow at that, but realized she was still fiddling with the harness, which was probably what was distracting her.

"Here," Eric said a second later, his hands pushing Zoe's away and unclasping the harness quickly. He helped her step out of it, then set it on the chair before returning to his own.

I watched them both for a second, suspicion curling inside me. They were acting... too normal. Forcibly so, to the point that it was sending gentle warning bells chiming through me. I had also seen this behavior from them before—every time they had tried to plan a surprise birthday party for me behind my back.

"What's going on?" I asked quietly.

Zoe looked up at me and blinked innocently. "Whatever do you mean?"

I rolled my eyes. "Oh, cut the crap, Zoe. Something is going on."

Suddenly the air grew very still and silent, as if everyone was drawing in their breath and holding it all at once. Zoe looked away again, only confirming that something was going on. Something they didn't want to talk about. So, I looked at Maddox. She had never been the type to hold anything back, and was about as forthcoming and brutally honest as anyone could be.

"What is it?"

Maddox, to my surprise, pursed her lips and rolled her eyes. "It's nothing. Leo, is the tracking device ready to go?"

"Oh no, don't change the subject," I said, incensed that they were keeping a secret. If something had happened out there, I needed to know what it was—and the fact that they weren't telling me made me even more suspicious. What could they possibly be trying to hide, and why would they want to in the first place? "What. Is. Going. On?"

"They don't want to tell you that we split up," Leo announced from the kitchen, and I turned to see him entering the room. He was wearing a pensive frown on his face. "Maddox argued that it would take too long if we worked in pairs, and suggested that we would complete the task more quickly if we each worked on our own."

"More like just left after telling us that was what we were doing," Zoe grumbled, and I looked back at her, and then to Maddox, who was sitting there with a glower on her face.

"We need to find Tian," she said obstinately, meeting my eyes with a defiant gaze.

A steady haze of anger began to settle in as I regarded her. She was still sporting livid bruises from her ordeal, but I put aside the sympathy her appearance stirred and focused instead on her, and what her action had risked. I had specifically ordered them to stay together—partially because of the threat from unknown enemies, but also because Zoe and Eric weren't the best lashers. If something had gone wrong... If their lashes had failed or they hadn't connected them well enough, my best friends in the entire world could've—*would've*—plummeted to their deaths on the radioactive desert below, and nobody would've been there to help them or even try to save them!

"That doesn't excuse this, Maddox," I said, positively irate that she would jeopardize the lives of our teammates so recklessly. "I specifically said I wanted you to stay together because—"

"They could handle it," Maddox cut in, folding her arms across her chest. "Besides, you run off on your own all the time!"

That wasn't the same and she knew it. But I felt obliged to set the record straight, so I did. "There is a big difference between me risking my own life and you risking those of our teammates! If Zoe or Eric had fallen... I don't even understand why you would do that. It's not like you."

Her eyes hardened, and her mouth pinched. "You don't know me well enough to know what I'm like," she said defiantly. "I did what I felt needed to be done to get the mission finished. We're all here, safe, and just moments away from getting Tian's location!"

I stared at her, confused and angry about how blithe she was being about this. Zoe and Eric weren't good at lashing. They hadn't been trained in it the same way she and I had, and they didn't have the natural reaction time or ability that Leo had. Leaving Zoe and Eric to their own devices had been shortsighted on her part, for that reason alone. What in the world could've prompted her to leave her teammates unguarded like that, especially after what had happened with Ambrose?

And then it hit me, so fast that it was like I had been suckerpunched. It *was* about what had happened with Ambrose, but I was looking at it from my own point of view—my approach would be to try harder to protect those around me.

But from Maddox's perspective... Well, I could imagine that the guilt she felt from failing was doing awful things to her state of mind. The Maddox from before wouldn't balk at such security measures, but the Maddox here and now... she was a beast of a different color. And I was betting that she was afraid of having anyone else's life in her hands. She didn't want the responsibility, especially since she'd failed to prevent Ambrose's death. Having someone else relying on her had put a pressure on her that she clearly wasn't able to handle.

I could empathize, but at the same time, I couldn't let her actions, no matter how understandable, pass without comment. I had to handle this delicately.

CHAPTER 18

It was just too bad that I had no idea how to do that.

"Is this about Ambrose?" I asked bluntly. Delicacy had never been my strong suit—and I needed to fix this now, rather than in half an hour.

Maddox's eyes narrowed, and she stared at me, before rising to her feet. "I don't have to take this. I'm out of here."

She started to move toward the door, but I quickly cut in front of her, forcing her to stop. "If you are having issues because of what happened with Ambrose, then I need to know. I can't have you coming with us to rescue Tian if you're going to be a liability."

"Liana," Zoe whispered, her voice slightly horrified.

I ignored her, although it pained me to do so. I didn't like handling Maddox so harshly, but we didn't have time for kid gloves, either. If she was willing to jeopardize Eric and Zoe's lives because of the attack on her and Ambrose's murder, during such a simple mission, then I couldn't be sure that she wouldn't go rogue during a fight, as well. Getting herself, or others, actually killed.

Maddox said nothing as she neatly stepped around me to continue her journey to the door. I stood there for a second, and then said, "Maddox, look at yourself. You are so upset by this conversation that you are willing to walk out and miss Tian's rescue rather than admit that you might be dealing with the aftermath of a traumatic event."

I heard her stop and looked over my shoulder to see her standing there, just a few feet in front of the door, still facing it. She didn't move for a long time, so long that I started speaking again, this time modulating my voice and keeping it reasonable and sincere. I had to reach her, somehow, and yelling wasn't going to do it.

"I want you to know that I'm not angry at you. I am,

however, worried about you, and I think all of this ties in to the attack. But I can't help you if you don't admit to it. Normally, I would give you time and space so that you could come to this conclusion yourself, but we don't have that luxury right now."

"You have no idea what you're talking about!" she exploded, whirling around to face me, her arms akimbo. "I'm fine! I don't need any help. I'm just trying to move at a faster speed so I can get Tian back!"

"You put Zoe and Eric at risk by unilaterally deciding to work alone!" I said, my voice carrying the hard edge of anger.

"But nothing went wrong," she said smugly. "So back off, Liana."

"No," I replied, angrily. "You need to get help for what you're going through, or I'm going to keep you off all of our missions."

Her brows drew together. "You... You can't do that!" she exclaimed hotly. "You need me!"

"No, I need you whole and able to protect your friends," I shot back. "And let's face it, Doxy, you jeopardized our friends today because you couldn't handle the responsibility of protecting and caring for another person. It's understandable, but debilitating, and I can't trust that you won't do something like this again. So it's either get some help, or sit out. The choice is yours."

Her face grew red, her jaw clenching tightly. "What do you expect me to do?" she asked bitterly, after several seconds had passed.

"You can go to the Medica for counseling," Quess suggested quietly. I looked over at him to see him giving Maddox an earnest and pleading look, which instantly told me that he had already had this conversation with her, likely during the nights he'd been spending with her in her room. "Tell her, Liana. She doesn't have to keep anything secret; everyone knows what happened with the attack. That she was there." His lips trembled slightly as he looked at her, and I realized Quess was *really* worried about Maddox, and likely had been since day one.

Scipio help me, I wished he had told me, but everything was moving so fast that it had been impossible to keep up with it all. Still, he had clearly already been working on it, and now I had set the terms for her: she needed to get her head in the game, or else she wouldn't be able to help us at all. We wouldn't be able to trust her to help us, and I wasn't willing to let that happen.

"He's right," I said, looking at Maddox. "The counseling services in the Medica aren't bad, and it will do you some good to talk about what happened with Ambrose." Her face began to grow hard again—a sign that she was about to tell us all where to stuff it—and I added, "If not for us, then for Tian."

The look she gave me next was positively combustible, but after several long, hard seconds of glaring at me, she spat out a sharp "Fine," and then pivoted on her heel and left the room, this time heading for her bedroom. I was pretty certain she would've slammed the door, except that ours operated on a pneumatic rotor, so she couldn't.

As soon as her door was closed, though, I looked at the rest of the group. "Sorry about that," I said softly. "I didn't mean to call her out in front of everyone."

"No, but you needed to," Zoe huffed. "I tried to make her see reason, but it was about as useful as trying to squeeze water out of a stone."

"Hey, don't talk about her like that," Quess snapped defensively. "She's been through hell and back lately. Cali, her father, now Ambrose..." He paused, and some of the anger on his face melted into fear. "She wakes up in the middle of the night covered in a cold sweat and crying. She pushes away any form of physical comfort. It's like her heart is bleeding, Liana. And I don't know how to make it stop."

My heart broke for him a little bit right there, and I immediately went over and wrapped my arm around his shoulder, pulling him tight. "It's going to be okay," I assured him. "We're going to get her through this, I promise."

It took a few moments, but eventually his rigid body relaxed into the hug, until he was hugging me back. "I'm just so worried," he told me softly, and I nodded.

"Me, too. But we're going to figure it out." I pulled away from him and looked him in the eyes. "Okay?"

He gave me a quick, jerky nod. "Okay." I slowly withdrew my hands from where they were still touching him and gave him a little space, turning back to the group. The thing with Maddox was bad, but it wasn't the only problem we currently had. I'd done all I could for her; now I needed to focus on bringing her surrogate sister home, and at least getting that worry off of her shoulders, as well as our own.

"Leo, go ahead and get that trace program running. Let's see if we can't find our sentinel."

In the end, finding the sentinel had been easy. It was buried in the bottommost level of the Tower: Sub-Basement 16. Getting to it, however, proved much more difficult, because several different blueprints of the area were on public file. Apparently, the level had been renovated multiple times, adjusted in countless ways to help combat the immense weight of the Tower.

Unable to use a map to help us plot a direct course, we were forced to rely heavily on the tracking program on Leo's pad, and navigate around beams and walls as they came up. Which turned out to be frequently. The halls down here were narrow,

CHAPTER 18

with barely enough room to walk in single file. Turn-offs came up every five to ten feet, but never any doors to rooms. The walls themselves were sometimes solid, but often were just exposed, interlocked beams, with *some* space to navigate through, but not much.

The setup filled me with apprehension, as there was a stillness to the halls that gave me a bad feeling. It was hard not to think about the two hundred and sixteen floors above us—and that at any instant, we could be buried by them.

It wasn't a rational feeling, but it was there, burning in the back of my mind like a beacon, daring me not to think about it. And I obliged it, needing my wits about me for the upcoming fight.

"We're getting close," Leo whispered over his shoulder, and I leaned over slightly to see our dot on the pad drawing closer to the big red one that was maybe fifteen or twenty feet ahead of us.

I quickly tapped him on the shoulder, making him change positions with me. He might have the heightened reflexes, but I had the weapon. I fingered the bracelet on my wrist with Quess's anti-sentinel toys and thought. All I had to do was rip one off and throw it. The easiest way to do that was to sneak up behind the sentinel while it was distracted, but there was a chance that it would see us through the gaps between the beams. We needed to be quiet, patient, and precise, and I needed to scope out the situation first.

I turned back to press a finger to my lips, and then began to slowly creep forward, moving toward the next branch in the hall. I stopped at the corner, squatted down, and peeked around it. It dead-ended just ten feet away, in a T-shaped junction. There was no sign of Tian, but there was every chance the sentinel itself was down one of the adjacent halls, or even on the other side of that wall. If the sentinel's back was to it, getting behind it would be impossible, but I had to figure out where it was placed, and how we could get to it.

I made my way down it, moving slowly, when a sudden noise caught my ear.

"Yu-Na?" It was the voice, *the* voice, from Dinah's apartment! The mystery woman who hadn't been there!

"I'm here," came a reply. Adrenaline surged as I recognized this one as Tian's voice. "Are you better?"

There was a pause, and I crept forward, moving toward the wall.

"Better?" Another pause. "Oh no, Yu-Na! Did I.... Did I hurt anyone?"

I paused, a frown coming over my face. Why would the woman controlling the sentinel be concerned about whether or not she had hurt anyone? What was going on here?

"No," Tian replied. "But you came close. And you almost hurt my friends."

I reached the intersection of the hallways and quickly checked both sides. Then I turned left, as there was an immediate branch-off heading to the right—the direction from which Tian's voice had come.

"Oh God," the woman said, her voice breaking. I paused and frowned. There was something about the way her voice broke... that sounded so off. Like it was coming through a speaker. What was going on?

"Oh, Jang-Mi," Tian said soothingly, her voice growing louder as I eased along the wall toward the opening. I was almost there, the edge merely a foot away. "It really isn't your fault. I wish you'd let me call my friends, though. I really think they can help you."

I stopped at the edge and took a moment to try to shake out

CHAPTER 18

some of my tension. I didn't want to move too fast, in case the sentinel was standing right there, watching. Faster movements attracted its eyes, according to the blueprints, while it often failed to notice slower, more precise ones.

I leaned out, letting the top of my head and eyes grow more and more exposed.

"No! Yu-Na, we can't trust anyone! These people... What they've made me do... What they tried to make me do to you..."

The voice broke again, this time leading to sobs that once again sounded tinny and artificial. I let my eyes follow the sound, and I saw Tian standing, facing the sentinel, which had its back to me. It was slightly hunched, its shoulders bowed under the dark cloak.

I had an immediate view of the area around Tian, which opened up slightly more into a box room of ten by twenty feet, interrupted by columns that ran from the ceiling to the ground every five feet or so, forming a forest of girders.

The rest of the room was empty, which only served as confirmation that the woman I had heard in Dinah's apartment was somewhere else transmitting through the sentinel.

Perfect. Its back was to me, and all I had to do was get a few feet closer, and then toss Quess's little magnet thing on it. As soon as it was knocked out, Maddox—whom I had allowed to come in the end due to her insistence—would get Tian out, while the rest of us would work on cracking open its hull and getting to the hard drive inside of it. If it started to get up again, I'd hit it with another shocker.

Easy, right?

Apprehension tightened its grip on my spine, but I ignored it, turning to the others and signing a quick message in Callivax. *Wait here. I'm going to try to neutralize it alone. Have batons ready just in case.* I waited until everyone had flashed me a thumbs-up, checked the hallway again to confirm that the sentinel hadn't moved, and then eased around the corner, creeping up toward the sentinel.

I was doing it so slowly that it even took Tian several seconds to notice me, although she was facing my direction. As soon as her eyes hit mine, I froze and began pressing a finger to my lips.

But Tian, never one for following the plan, drew a deep breath and cried, "Liana, get out of here!"

The sentinel whirled, not ten feet away from me, and I had the terrible displeasure of watching its lilac eyes bleed into a bright, angry red. Then it stood up and began making its way right for me.

19

My heart beat rapidly in my chest as I backpedaled, grabbing one of the discs and flinging it at the thing. I couldn't see it after I tossed it, but a second later the beam the sentinel had just grabbed sparked violently, and tendrils of electricity wove their way up its arm to disappear under the cloak.

The sentinel's eyes flickered back and forth, and suddenly a high-pitched, digitalized, "*EEEEEEEEEEEEEEEEEEEEEEEEEEEEEEEEEEEEEEEEE!*" emitted from its mouth as the charge continued to arc, streaming into the sentinel.

I clapped my hands over my ears at the shrill and piercing sound, taking a few steps back and looking through the flashing white and blue light for Tian. I spotted her a few feet behind the sentinel, her mouth and eyes opened wide in horror, staring at the sentinel as it stood frozen under the force of the shocker.

As suddenly as it had started, the process stopped, and the sentinel slumped. It didn't fall, but its head slumped over and its free hand went limp. It still maintained a death grasp on the beam... but it was still. Deathly still.

Wisps of smoke curled up and out from under its cloak, some of them wafting toward me. I caught a breath of the smoke and began to cough, the smell of burning electronics pungent and acrid. Waving my hand in the air to clear the stench of it from my nostrils, I looked back over my shoulder.

"Grab Tian and get her out of here," I ordered. "Everyone else, get up here and help me."

"No, wait!" Tian shouted, taking a few steps forward. "Liana, don't—"

The "knocked out" sentinel suddenly burst forward in a flurry of movements, moving out from between the two beams and coming directly for me. And I noticed that its hand was on its hip. It was going for its weapon. The weapon that cut people apart like chunks of meat.

I made a snap decision and threw my lashes to the ceiling a few feet behind the sentinel, then activated the harness to reel me in, leaping forward into a clumsy dive. I disconnected the lines and retracted them before I could get too much height, and then arced my body to land between its widespread legs.

The move wasn't as graceful as I had hoped, and my hip hit the inside of its knee joint—a glancing blow, but it still hurt, and I wound up landing in a twisting roll on the floor. I somehow managed to avoid vertigo, and as soon as I came to a stop, I scrambled to my feet, my hands making wet slapping sounds on the floor. I had lost my baton somehow, but there was no time to find it—the sentinel was already swinging around, its hand wrapped around its own deadly weapon.

"Jang-Mi, no!" Tian shouted, her voice terrified.

I ignored her, surging forward to meet the sentinel before it finished its turn. I took two huge steps and then flexed my legs

CHAPTER 19

and jumped, throwing myself into a spin. My leg went up and then down, and a solid impact reverberated up my shin and spilled into my knee. I landed neatly—it was a move I had practiced countless times—and heard the sound of something metal skidding away.

The sentinel was no longer in front of me, though, because my spinning kick had twisted me around, and I instinctively mule-kicked backward. That was a mistake, I realized. A mule kick was a powerful kick, but the sentinel was four hundred and fifty pounds of metal. It was like kicking a support beam.

I felt the impact all the way up to my hip, my teeth immediately on edge with the age-old fear that I had just broken something, and then hands went around my upper thigh, the grip iron tight. I realized it was the sentinel, but before I could react I was being lifted up. And then the world began to spin. I got a glimpse of the floor rushing toward me, and then I landed on my side, my head ricocheting off of something hard, and I was sliding down into a heap.

It hadn't been the floor. It had been a wall. Thank Scipio for that; if it had thrown me into one of the support beams with that amount of force, my spine would've snapped.

It took me a second to catch my breath, but I managed to roll to my side and look around dazedly. Leo, Eric, Zoe, and Maddox were now fighting the sentinel, driving it away from me. Behind them, Tian was shouting something that I couldn't make out through the ringing in my ears.

The sight somehow propelled me to my feet, and, in spite of my labored breathing and aching side, I stumbled forward toward the fighting. I spotted my baton a few feet to the right of the sentinel, grabbed onto a beam for support, and hobbled toward it.

Then, quite suddenly, I could hear again, the ringing

subsiding some. The first thing I heard was Quess shouting. "... You talking about?"

"The back of the neck!" Tian screamed, dancing a few steps to the side to avoid the fighting. "Don't hurt her, Doxy!"

"Her!" Maddox grunted. "What about me?"

"Just shut up and attack this thing!" Zoe screamed, her voice edged with panic.

I scooped my baton off the floor, barely catching my balance as I started to tilt too far to one side, and then turned, ready to attack.

My friends had the sentinel surrounded, and were swinging their batons back and forth, trying to find an opening in the sentinel's defense, but it was pointless—the batons couldn't penetrate the shell. I fingered another disc while I watched the fighting. My friends were moving, dancing around it, but if I could find an opening, I could hit it with another shocker, and then the rest of them if I had to, hard drive be damned. It wasn't worth our lives, and the sentinel was clearly winning.

I just had to find my opening.

I started to shout "Duck" to my friends, already hobbling toward them, set to throw, but Quess suddenly broke through the gap between Eric and Leo, took several huge, leaping bounds, and threw himself onto the sentinel's back, wrapping it in a giant hug. The sentinel immediately began to thrash around, heaving back and forth in an attempt to dislodge him, but he held on, the large muscles of his arms swelling with exertion. He hadn't been able to get his legs around it, though, and his lower torso was flying free, driving the others back as his feet were inadvertently swung toward their faces. Finally he managed to bring his knees up between his body and the sentinel's back, bracing them against the sentinel's spine, and then began fiddling with something on its neck, avoiding the swiping grabs the machine was making.

"Get off of it and get out of the way!" I ordered angrily, holding back my throw. I couldn't throw the shocker while Quess was touching it, or part of the voltage would go into him, and he'd die. "Quess! Get off! I can get it!"

"No, don't!" Tian shouted. "You'll only make her angry! Quess! Be gentle! That's her beautiful mind you're handling! Don't hurt her!"

"Are you freaking kidding me with this, Tian?" Quess shouted. "*We're* the ones who are in actual danger!"

"Shut up and just do what I say, Quessian Brown!" Tian snapped back. Then, her voice completely changing, she said, "Jang-Mi... it's okay! These are my friends. I promise, they can help you!"

She was talking to the sentinel, trying to soothe it, and the realization brought me up short, filling me with profound confusion. The sentinel wasn't alive; it was being controlled! So then why was Tian acting like it was her best friend? What was going on?

There was a sharp zap from where Quess and the sentinel were struggling, and I looked up in time to see Quess land squarely on top of Leo and Eric, dragging both of them down to the ground. Quess started convulsing immediately, and I realized that he had hit an activated baton as he went down.

"Shut off your batons!" I screamed, surging forward to fill the hole, my arm uplifted to throw, my eyes searching for an angle. I couldn't toss it with Maddox so close, though; if she touched the sentinel while the shocker was going off... I palmed it and held up my baton, hoping I could get the sentinel's attention.

The sentinel was back on the offensive, though, and was

charging at Maddox, not even bothering to block her blows unless they came anywhere in the vicinity of her face. I heard Tian say something behind me, but couldn't turn, as I was focused entirely on the sentinel in front of me. I signaled to Zoe to help me flank it, and she quickly slid into position. Then, with a nod, we rushed forward, our batons held high.

I just needed to get it to look at me, and it would pursue me—I was certain of it. As soon as I got it away from the others, I'd throw the shocker. I just had to get it to see me.

Coordinating our attack like that would've generally given us an advantage, as most humans lose a lot of their spatial awareness during a fight. But sentinels, apparently, had better senses than I did, because without even twisting its head, it rose to one foot and kicked Zoe square in the chest, while simultaneously punching me and Maddox with its fists.

I wasn't sure if it hit Maddox, but its metal fist slammed into my own jaw with enough force to make my teeth rattle, and I spun around, getting my arms up in time to keep myself from going face-first into a beam. My face slapped against my forearms—not hard, but hard enough for my vision to double. I blinked my eyes rapidly as I tried to get my balance, but the blow had twisted me around, and now my appendages felt like hindrances, weighted and sluggish. I fought the feeling, a fresh surge of adrenaline helping to keep me upright, but I knew my strength was failing.

If I didn't hit this thing with the shocker, we were all dead.

I finally managed to catch my balance, my vision clearing, and I immediately began searching, looking for the sentinel. Then a shadow caught my eye. I realized it was the sentinel and moved to step back, but it was already on me, lashing out with a foot while shoving me with a shoulder.

I fell, but this time my body remembered what to do, and I

tucked my chin to my chest and slapped the ground with both hands, breaking the momentum. I started to get back up, but the sentinel clomped over to me and stamped one foot down on my chest.

Then it began to press.

Breath exploded out of me in a huff, and for several seconds my mind could only struggle with impulse: get this crushing weight off of my chest. Now.

I shoved at its leg with both hands, straining even as my breath became shorter and shorter. Black spots danced across my eyes as I kicked and threw my weight into trying to break free. I realized that I had to use the shocker, or else I was going to die.

Then I realized that if I used it, I *would* die, and the thought made me freeze. I couldn't die. I wasn't ready to. I had too much left to do. I renewed my struggle against the impossible crushing weight on my chest, my fingers searching for something, anything, that would make this relentless weight come to an end.

But it was futile. The foot continued to press with a grim yet determined purpose, and I realized that this was it. I was going to die. Even as I thought it, my vision became awash with gray, and I felt my muscles growing weak, starved for oxygen.

"Stop it or I hurt Yu-Na!" a male voice proclaimed loudly, and I was suddenly rewarded with significantly less pressure, allowing some air to flood into my lungs with a harsh gasp that made me want to cough. Color began to fill in, bringing with it red and white blobs that obscured some of my vision, but eventually receded. I blinked, blearily gazing up at the sentinel's tall body to see it looking a few feet to my right.

Following its malevolent gaze, my eyes widened as I took in Leo gripping Tian tightly around her waist, her slim legs dangling from where he held her crushed against his chest. In his other hand, he held a baton, the glowing blue light sparking menacingly—mere inches from Tian's head.

His face was filled with dark promise as he regarded the sentinel.

"Get off her," he barked. The sentinel immediately lifted up its foot, stepping off me. This time I did cough, a reflexive action, and then sucked in a deep, life-giving breath of air that made me almost lightheaded with relief. Somehow, I managed to pull myself a few feet away, still weak from the onslaught of the sentinel's attack. As soon as I had backed away, I fumbled at the bracelet, my numb fingers trying desperately to clasp one of the thin metal disks—and failing.

"Liana, stop," Leo ordered.

I froze, then looked back up at him, following his eyes until I saw Zoe and Maddox dangling upside down. The sentinel's hand was wrapped around Maddox's ankle, and it held Zoe's braid tightly, dragging my best friend up by her hair. I hadn't seen them, but now that I did, I realized that if I used the weapon, twenty-five thousand volts of electricity would be passed through the sentinel... and directly into them.

They'd die if I threw it.

I carefully separated my hands and placed them on the floor. Leo gave me a grateful look and then turned back to the sentinel.

"Put them down."

The sentinel shifted, regarding him. Five seconds went by, then ten, and I swallowed, wondering what it could possibly want.

Then, inexplicably, it dropped both girls. They landed with a tumble, Zoe giving out a little scream, and then she was hauled back up by her hair, the sentinel grasping the top braid and pulling her to her feet.

"Don't hurt her!" I shouted, managing to make it to my feet. "Leo!"

The sentinel pointed directly at Tian, and then nodded its head in a wordless order to let her go.

Leo shook his head. "Not until you release our friend."

This time the machine shook *its* head and then pointed at Tian again, its movements more punctuated and insistent. Leo glanced at me, and after a moment, I realized he wanted me to weigh in on the decision.

I nodded. Tian seemed to know what she was doing, and it was clear that we couldn't take the sentinel as we were right now. It had beaten us, and if we kept fighting, one of us, possibly all of us, would die. It was just too strong.

Slowly, Leo lowered Tian to the ground and let the girl go, not making any sudden movements. Tian took a step forward, and another, and then raced over to the sentinel, laying her small hands on its huge thigh.

"Let her go," she said gently, and to my surprise, the sentinel did just that, dropping Zoe like she was a ragdoll.

She groaned, gripping her scalp, but Maddox helped break her fall somewhat. They both appeared to be otherwise unharmed.

"Go," Tian said, pointing down the hall. The sentinel immediately began to leave, but then turned when it realized Tian hadn't moved, its now-lilac eyes questioning. "I'll be right behind you," she said reassuringly. "If I am not, then you have my permission to come back and kill them all."

I blinked and gave the little girl a sideways look, but she couldn't see it. Her face was turned away from me.

The sentinel seemed to hesitate, but then nodded once before moving down one of the side halls leading away from the space. Tian watched it go, and then turned back, a big, lopsided grin on her face.

"Hi, guys!" she chirped. "First of all, can I just say that I'm so happy that you love me enough to risk your lives for me? I'm really glad you found me and all that, but I have to tell you that right now really isn't a good time for me to be rescued! I'm in the middle of something super important, and I have to go after Jang-Mi now so that she doesn't murder any more people. She really doesn't like doing it. Anyway, I'm sure you're all super worried about me, and I promise, I will come home and tell you all about it really soon, but I have to go. She doesn't like to be kept waiting."

And then she was gone, skipping down the hall like a wraith child toward the sentinel that was waiting at the end of it. She stopped next to the sentinel, which was holding its hand out, looked at it and then up at the sentinel, and then stuck her nose in the air and kept walking, clearly now in a huff.

And then they were gone, Tian stomping around the corner and the sentinel following like a dog that knew it had behaved badly.

And the only thing I could think to say was, "Wait...what just happened?"

20

"Hold still," Quess snapped as I edged away from his fingers, which were probing my ribs.

I shot him a mulish look and then forced myself to be still, fighting the instincts that urged me to stop the pressure he was placing against my aching ribs, lest they finally snap.

Pain bloomed as he carefully felt each rib, checking to make sure they weren't broken, and I held my breath, gritting my teeth against the agony. I jerked again when he hit a particularly painful spot—but this time he didn't say anything, just continued his probing.

I exhaled sharply when he finally removed his fingers, and then flinched when he placed them on my breastbone. I slapped his hand away. "Don't," I said.

I didn't want to endure any more pokes and prods; my entire body felt like one livid bruise. But it was more than that. I was particularly sensitive there, given that it was where the sentinel had been trying to crush me. I didn't want anyone touching that area.

Quess's dark blue eyes grew a shade darker. "You're being a baby," he said flatly. "You won't let us go to the Medica, but that doesn't mean you can't let me check you out."

"You're not a Medic, remember?" I shot back, still stubbornly clinging to my desperate need not to be touched right then. Okay, yes, I was being childish. But I had been almost crushed under the weight of a four-hundred-and-fifty-pound death machine—which had almost killed my friends. I was allowed to be childish.

Quess scowled at me, and then put his hands right back on my breastbone, ignoring my wishes. I fought the urge to punch him off, and instead clenched my teeth and tried not to cringe as he probed the bruised bone. His hands moved steadily upward, checking my clavicles, and then were finally, thankfully, removed. I closed my eyes and took a second or two to relax my clenched muscles, and then opened them again and looked around the living room.

It wasn't hard to see our defeat as my gaze paused on each member of my group. It clung to all of us, as did the hefty knowledge that we had barely escaped with our lives. That we probably would've died, if the fighting had gone on just a few moments longer.

Maddox was lying on the floor, a pillow wedged under her head and a gelatin ice pack wrapped in a microfiber cloth pressed over her jaw. One leg was elevated over a chair, another ice pack wrapped around her ankle. Her mouth was pinched, her eyes dark and haunted.

Zoe had her own ice packs wrapped around her ribs, with one of our emergency broken bone packs pressed against her left side. She had likely suffered a fracture there when the sentinel

CHAPTER 20

kicked her, and even though we couldn't be certain, Quess had insisted on treating her for it anyway. She and Eric were both lying on the couch, where he had propped himself up with several pillows from our bedrooms so she could recline against his chest. She was dozing, and I nodded to Eric, letting him know he'd have to wake her again.

She was at risk for concussion. Sleeping wasn't a good idea, and I'd be damned if I was going to lose my friend just because she couldn't stay awake.

A microfiber cloth suddenly appeared in my vision, inches from my face, and I looked up and over it to see Leo standing there, his hands filled with cloth and ice packs, as well as an ointment jar with cream for treating bruises. I grabbed the ice pack, immediately placed it against my jaw, trying to ease the throbbing pain there, and gave him a grateful look. He alone had escaped with only some minor bruising, but the defeated look was there on his face, too, along with a guilt that I couldn't quite understand. He hadn't done anything wrong. If anything, he'd saved us. Him and Tian both.

Leo averted his eyes, neatly shifted his load around, and offered me the tincture of ointment. I stared at it, not wanting to let anyone, even myself, touch my ribs and chest, but he shook it at me insistently, still not quite meeting my eyes.

"It'll be less painful if you do it yourself," he finally said, when I stubbornly refused to take the jar. "You're the only one who can gauge your own pain, so you'll know exactly how gentle to be."

He had a point, so I gingerly reached out and took the jar, my ribs screaming a chorus of agony the entire time, and then leaned back into the chair with a soft grunt of relief. I carefully unscrewed the lid and began spreading the ointment, skimming over my sides with the lightest of touches. Almost immediately, some of the pain faded, and I breathed a little easier.

Scipio help me, while the sweet relief from the pain was great, the entire mood of the room was awful. We'd taken a beating before, but at least we'd had a small measure of success and achieved our goals. Never had we been beaten this badly, and our morale had reached an all-time low. I wasn't even sure what to say, because I wasn't quite sure what I could've done differently.

Quess returned from where he had disappeared into the kitchen and set a glass of water down, then deposited a few white pills next to it. "Take those when you're ready for bed," he said. "They'll help ease the pain so you can get some sleep."

I nodded and continued to smear the ointment, watching as Quess reached over Leo's shoulder to pluck an ice pack from the pile in his arms. He pressed it against his own chest with a deep sigh, and dropped into the vacant chair next to me.

"How's your chest?" I asked, concerned for his wellbeing. He'd been amazing about taking care of us after the sentinel and Tian left, and I hated the thought of him putting his own injuries aside in order to tend to ours—especially if his were worse.

He was resting his head on the back of the chair, his eyes half closed, and instead of sitting up to look at me, he merely rolled his head toward me. "You mean where Leo zapped me with the baton? Oh, fine."

I huffed a laugh at his sarcastic tone, but Leo immediately looked guilty and remorseful. "I am so sorry, Quessian," he said for the umpteenth time. "I swear, if it weren't for the limited capabilities of the human body, I would've been able to move it out of the way in time."

"Who cares who did what to whom?" Maddox cut in with a

groan. "Let's face it, we all got our asses kicked. That sentinel would've killed us if Leo hadn't thought fast and pretended to take Tian hostage."

"Actually..." Leo trailed off, a blush forming on his cheeks. "It was Tian's idea. She had the idea that it would stop the sentinel, and I was desperate to prevent it from killing you. And she was right. I suggest we listen to whatever she has to say when she gets here."

"*If* she gets here," Quess grumbled.

I sighed and leaned back in the chair, finally finished with applying the ointment. I was worried about Tian, and felt weird about not pursuing her after she left. I knew it had been the right call, but it still felt wrong. But now, hearing that she had come up with the idea that had saved us, I felt somewhat better. She obviously had some level of insight into the sentinel's behavior.

I might not know what was going on, but she did, and I had to believe that she knew what she was doing.

Or else I'd be responsible for her dying at the hands of that monster.

I screwed the cap on while I regarded Quess—and the slow, silent recrimination in his eyes. He didn't like that we had left Tian, and I couldn't blame him. But it was more than that. His design had failed, and he held himself personally responsible for not being able to stop the sentinel. Not that it was his fault, entirely. The shocker had worked, it just hadn't worked for long enough. But Quess didn't want to hear that. Right now, he was at war with the two powerful emotions raging inside him—anger at leaving and guilt at failing—and I wasn't sure which one was going to win out. If it was the latter, he'd take it out on himself. If it was the former, well, he'd take it out on me, and I wasn't sure I would stop him.

But I needed Quess to get over it. We had bigger fish to fry.

"What's done is done," I said flatly, accepting another ice pack from Leo and spreading it over my ribs. "What I want to know now is: what is the deal between Tian and that sentinel?"

"I know, right?" Zoe exclaimed. I slid my gaze over to my friend and saw her gingerly probing the edges of her hairline, as if confirming that her scalp was still there and attached. Poor Zoe. I could only imagine how tender the area was, since she'd been grabbed and yanked around by the sentinel. "It's like she is friends with it, but did anyone see anything that would give her a reason why?"

I shook my head, a move echoed by almost everyone except Maddox, who instead flashed a thumbs-down as her answer.

"No, but she kept calling it 'Jang-Mi'," Quess said.

"And I heard the same female voice that I heard in Dinah's apartment," I said. "Once again, there was no one there, but Tian was definitely having a conversation with someone. Maybe whoever Tian's communicating with is making her believe that she *is* the sentinel, and manipulating Tian into helping her?"

"I suppose it's possible; she kept shouting for Quess to be careful with 'her beautiful mind' after he jumped on the thing's back," Zoe said, sitting up slightly and then wincing. "Why did you do that, by the way?"

"Tian pointed it out, and I realized that somebody had attached an external hard drive to it," Quess replied, tiredly running a hand through his hair. "I'm guessing it's how the sentinel is being controlled. It's great news for us: we don't have to bust through its hull. We just need access to the back of its neck. I was trying to get to it before it threw me off, and it looks like there's an additional hard drive, there, but much bigger. It's under a modified cage, however—I'm guessing to prevent anyone from tampering with it. Tian didn't realize that it's held in place by a cage that makes it impossible to yank off. If she had, I don't think she would've encouraged me to grab the hard drive. I think I can cut through the cage much faster than that thing's skin, so that's something."

"Yeah, but unless we have something to knock it out—"

Quess cut me off with a derisive laugh. "I was wondering how long it would take you to bring that up," he said bitterly. "Look, I couldn't have known that the shockers wouldn't work! I told you I was guesstimating!"

I frowned. "Quess, I never said—"

"No, but I know that you're thinking it! You all are! Stupid Quess didn't get the math right. But I didn't miss the darn thing! Nor did I let it get away!"

I opened my mouth, shut it, and then smiled—though it was a smile born out of an angry and bitter humor, one that couldn't believe he was trying to flip everything around on me. I knew my flaws. I knew that I had bungled things by not getting a better plan in place first—but for him to flip blame onto me was a little petty.

"Hey, don't do that, Quess," Zoe snapped, rising to her feet. Gratitude blossomed inside of me. But she started to sway almost immediately, and Eric rose behind her, his hands already up to keep her from falling. She shrugged him off. "Own up to your crap, but don't blame Liana for things not working out the way we wanted them to!"

"There you go, jumping to Liana's defense," Maddox drawled, pushing herself up from her recumbent position on the floor. "Let me go ahead and recite the litany of excuses for her: 'She's doing her best'; 'We can't anticipate the enemy'; 'It's nobody's fault'. Spare us."

More resentment burned at Maddox's scathing tone and words, but underneath it all came a deep, stabbing pain.

Maddox was right. They were excuses. Defenses even, used to justify keeping me in the position of leader.

But they were also defenses that Maddox herself had used, and it wasn't fair for her to throw it back in Zoe and Eric's faces, like they were the only ones guilty of it. I understood that everyone was running hot and tempers were high, but that didn't mean that they needed to take it out on each other.

"Hey, Zoe's right," Eric said loudly, his brows drawing together. "It's nobody's fault!"

"HA!" Maddox sneered. "Our plan was stupid to begin with, and whose fault is that?"

This was beginning to spiral out of control. I needed to keep us from playing the blame game, because we needed to move on to more productive things—like preparing for the Tourney, which was resuming tomorrow.

"Guys, this isn't the time for recriminations," I said, slowly scraping away my resentment, anger, and pain as I rubbed a hand over my face. "I made the decision about not pursuing the sentinel further, and I stand by it. It more than proved it could hold its own against us, and I couldn't risk us getting injured or killed. Not just because I'm somewhat attached to you, but because the Tourney is starting again tomorrow, and I need my team ready to go."

"Are you *kidding* me?" Quess bellowed. "Who cares about the stupid Tourney? Why are we even still doing it?! I honestly don't get it—how can you just carry on and pretend that Tian isn't in danger? We should get back out there to look for her!"

"Liana *just* said we can't confront the sentinel again," Zoe said. She clearly had more to say, but Quess didn't let her continue.

"So we don't confront it!" he shouted, raking a hand through his hair. "We use the lashes and lift her out from under its nose,

CHAPTER 20

or blow the lights and sneak her out using the goggles I developed. I don't know, and I don't care—Tian doesn't understand how much danger she's in, and by allowing her to take off with that thing, we're putting her in even *more* danger!"

"I don't think that's necessarily true," Leo said slowly. "Tian seemed quite intuitive when she suggested that I use her as a hostage, and her insight paid off. We managed to make the sentinel stop. If she knew that it would work, then it stands to reason that she also knows what she is doing now. We should trust her."

Quess scowled at Leo. "No offense, but what does an AI even know about raising kids? You have no idea what it's like to even *be* one of them, so don't stand there and lecture me on what we should and should not do with a girl who is my responsibility!"

"Quess!" I gasped, surprised and appalled by what he had just said to Leo. It wasn't Leo's fault that he hadn't had a conventional upbringing, and he did have some insight into what he was talking about. Leo wasn't judging Tian's actions based on her age; he was taking her seriously, and had evidence to support his belief in her. He was an AI, yeah, but if anything, that gave him a more objective perspective—one that wasn't limited by societal expectations.

Not that it mattered. I never even got to voice any of that out loud. I was ignored, both by Quess and by the next speaker.

"*Our* responsibility, Quess," Zoe declared, glaring at him. "Don't act like the rest of us don't care about that little girl! When we all banded together, when you took me and Eric in, we became your friends and allies, and you became our responsibility, just like we're yours. Or have you forgotten that we're supposed to be a team?"

"No, but—"

"Well, you don't tear apart your team just because you're unhappy with the outcome of one of our missions," Eric cut in smoothly, his jaw clenching.

Quess growled, his entire body radiating tension to the point where it seemed like even touching him would get me cut. I stared at him, and then made a snap decision. "Take a shower, Quess. You need to cool off and get some perspective." It was clear that there was no reasoning with him right then, and he needed some time to himself to calm down and think about what he was saying.

"Don't tell him what to do," Maddox snapped, picking herself up. "He has a right to be heard!"

"He's been heard," I shot back, some of my anger cracking through the patience I had been managing to maintain. "So have you. I get that you're upset that Tian's not with us, but I'm not going to let you blame me, or each other! Not when all of us did the best we could with what we had! Yes, mistakes were made, but we can't change anything about what happened. We can only affect what happens moving forward. So either get on board, or get out, but whatever you're going to do, decide quickly."

I was a little shocked at the words coming out of my own mouth, and realized halfway through that I could be driving them farther away. But I couldn't seem to get myself to stop. For several long, pregnant seconds, nobody said anything.

"I'm going to take a nap," Maddox snapped suddenly, her jaw tight and tense.

"And I'm going to work on the shockers," Quess added, holding out an insistent hand to me. I ignored a glare sharp enough to cut diamonds, and quickly untangled the bracelet and handed it over to him. In truth, I was relieved. They had clearly decided to stay, and even though they were still angry, I knew that, at the very least, they were planning on sticking with us, even if they weren't happy.

It also meant that they didn't think I was to blame. If they really believed that, they would have walked out.

Quess snatched the bracelet from my hand, and then grabbed one of the bags that we had hauled up from Sanctum just a few short hours ago. I recognized it as the bag he had put his tools in. He waited long enough for Maddox to get to the hall, and then moved to help her down it.

I waited until I heard the hiss of the pneumatic door, and then slowly relaxed some.

"Well, that was bold," Zoe said, clearly impressed by my actions, if a little concerned. "Was it absolutely necessary, though?"

I sighed, reaching up and rubbing my forehead. Honestly, I still wasn't sure, but what was done was done, and it had been the only thing I could think of in the heat of the moment.

"I don't know how Liana feels," Leo announced softly. "But I think it was something that Quess and Maddox both needed to hear. They are upset, but misdirecting their anger. They'll be better once Tian is back."

"As a man with his fair share of female family members, I will say that if anything happened to any one of them, I might go a little off the deep end, too," Eric said, fidgeting slightly. "But yeah, I agree with Leo. They needed to hear it. I would need you to say the same thing if I were in their shoes. It'll be fine as soon as Tian shows up and explains what the heck is going on."

"That's a really nice thought, guys," I said softly, running a hand through my hair. "But we don't actually know that she'll be able to break free of that thing. Anything could happen, and that machine almost killed us tonight! Who's to say that whatever protective instincts it has for her won't suddenly turn violent?

Or that it won't just glitch out—something the sentinels have been known to do in the past?" I pressed my lips together, trying to organize my thoughts, and found that they had all left me. I was just too tired and too sore to focus. I checked my watch and observed that it was ten o'clock. Way past time for bed.

"Look, let's get some rest, give Quess a chance to calm down, and then discuss the situation again in the morning. If we're lucky, Tian will show up by then, or before then. If not, we hunt her down again and start all over."

"Or you could just talk to her now," a sweet voice chirped from the direction of the front door. I swiveled around, and sure enough, Tian was standing there, a small, nervous smile playing on her face. "So on a scale from one to no hot chocolate, how much trouble am I in?"

I couldn't answer. My heart was in a vice grip of strongly surging emotions at seeing her safe and relatively unharmed—but that was battling with the rage I was feeling over her captivity by a monster. So instead of saying anything, I simply stood up, ignoring my aches and pains, hobbled over to her, wrapped my arms around her, and squeezed as tightly as I could.

21

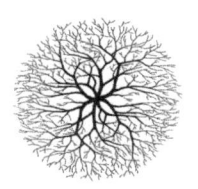

"I'll go get Quess and Maddox," Leo said in a hushed tone from behind me. I heard him move to leave, but didn't let go of Tian, just took strength from the fact that she was here—vibrant and alive.

She, however, was not happy with the prolonged nature of my hug, and began squirming seconds later, saying, "Get a grip, Liana," her voice muffled against my shoulder.

I smiled, and reluctantly let her go. "I'm sorry, Tian. We've just been really worried."

"Yeah, I figured that—"

"Tian!"

Maddox's voice cut over whatever Tian was about to say, and the next thing I knew, the muscular girl was squeezing past me and wrapping the smaller girl up into a massive hug. Tian endured it for several seconds, and then—just as she had with me—began pushing Maddox off of her.

"I'm fine, Doxy! I promise!" she cried as she managed to get her head and shoulder free. "Let go of me!"

"No!" Maddox replied with a happy laugh, her earlier bitterness gone. "I have been so worried about you!"

"Oh my God, I *know*!" Tian replied, exasperated. "And I'm sorry that you were. Now, will you just—"

Tian broke free with a grunt, the "let me go" slightly interrupted by the guttural sound being exhaled from her lips. Within seconds, she was scooped up by Quess, his massive arms wrapping around her like heavy metal bands and pressing her into his chest.

"Oh, for the love of… Are you fu—"

"Tian!" I cried, shocked to hear such vulgar language in her mouth.

"—ing kidding me!" she finished crossly, a frustrated look coming over her doll-like features. "Quessian Brown, you put me down right now! Right *now*!" One tiny, booted foot flailed, and I got the impression that she was trying to stamp the ground.

Quess refused—and squeezed her tighter. Tian retaliated by sucking in a deep breath, and then kicking the toes of her boots into his shins at a rapid speed.

"Hey! Ow! Stop it! Tian! Ow! C'mon! Ouch!"

Eventually Quess let her go, and she landed on her feet with all the grace of a cat. I couldn't help but smile as she straightened up; half of her white-blond hair had been shoved upward through the manhandling by her surrogate siblings, as well as myself.

Maddox immediately moved to hug her again, but the little girl thrust up her arms, shoving her hands out in a defensive gesture, and shouted, "I don't have a lot of time! Jang-Mi is charging right now, but she can do it really fast, so I can't stay too long."

CHAPTER 21

"You're not going back to it!" Quess said, his brows drawing together.

"Absolutely not," Maddox echoed, her face pinched with stress and fear. "You are home now, and this is where you will stay."

Tian scowled at them both, balling her hands into tiny fists. "You don't get it! She will come for me! She's... well, it's complicated, but she's attached to me. I tried to run away the first day, but she woke up and tracked me down before I could get back."

I stilled when I heard the acute frustration in her voice, and realized that if I didn't get us pointed in a useful direction soon, this would escalate into a fight, and we would risk Tian running away from us again. Only this time, she could disappear forever, and we might never see her alive again. If we wanted her to stay, we needed to let her speak her piece, and then make a decision, together.

"Why don't we all sit back down in the living room and give Tian a chance to tell her story about what happened? I, for one, want to know."

Tian's blue eyes filled with gratitude, and she offered me a tremulous smile. "Thank you," she mouthed at me, and I flashed her a grin.

Maddox and Quess didn't look happy, but they didn't say anything as they headed back into the living room, and Tian moved to follow them, her feet skipping lightly on the floor. She chose to sit in one of the chairs by the door, fidgeting in her spot as she tried to get comfortable. Leo offered me the other chair, but I shook my head and went over to the wall instead, resting against it.

It took us all a minute to get settled. Maddox joined Zoe and Eric on the couch, while Quess took the chair I had refused earlier. Only Leo and I stood—at opposite sides of the room.

"Okay, Tian," I said, settling back into the wall. "What happened after you snuck out?"

Guilt flashed in Tian's soft blue eyes, clouding them, and she frowned. "Have I mentioned how sorry I am about leaving like that?" she asked, wincing.

"We forgive you," Maddox said soothingly. "Just don't ever do it again."

Tian's mouth turned down, and a crease formed in between her brows. "I can't promise that," she said guardedly, giving Maddox a look. "If you try to keep me here, then I'll have to sneak out again. Jang-Mi... the robot lady... she thinks I'm her daughter, Yu-Na!"

"Her daughter?" Quess exclaimed, his eyes wide. "Tian, it's just a machine."

Tian rolled her eyes theatrically and stared at him. "No, *she's* not!" she exclaimed haughtily. "If anything, she's more like Leo than a machine, except..." She trailed off, clearly losing herself in a thought. A few seconds later, she shook her head, as if jostling her thoughts back into place. "It'll be easier if I explain from the beginning," she finally announced, looking at us. "Easiest if you all shut up and let me tell the story."

I smiled and gave her a nod. I could identify with her request that we all shut up so she could tell her story; I'd often been in the same position she was now, with everyone picking things apart before I could get the story out. It was frustrating at the best of times, and downright fury inducing at the worst. Besides, I was curious to know what was going on with this sentinel, and why Tian felt so strongly about protecting it, in spite of what it had done.

"We'll wait to ask any questions, Tian. Go ahead."

Tian sucked in a deep breath and then nodded. "As you all know, I wasn't happy when Liana told me to stop looking for a

CHAPTER 21 223

new Sanctum, so I left. I knew you were all worried about what would happen if we didn't find a place to hide if you lost, and I didn't want anyone to worry! So I started looking again. I was following the water's song through the pipes when I realized someone was following me. And it wasn't any of Lacey's goons."

"You knew that Lacey's people were following you and you didn't tell us?" Maddox asked.

"Let her finish her story," I said sharply, giving Maddox a firm look. Maddox narrowed her eyes at me, clearly displeased, but Tian's look of gratitude was far sweeter, so I focused on that. "Go ahead, Tian."

Tian shifted slightly and resettled into another position. "So anyway, these jerks start following me, and I realize I'm close to the armpit room." I blinked, and then made an intuitive leap to realizing she was talking about the condensation room, due to the warmth, humidity, and slight odor. "I head there, because I've lost Lacey's people there before, but these guys managed to keep up with me even though I was using my super-secret way through the pipes. The five of them enter, all wearing these clothes that make them hard to see, and one of them says, 'Kill her.'"

I heard Quess's grip tighten on the arms of the chair, the fibers squeaking slightly under the pressure of his now-clenched fingers, but he didn't interrupt, much to my relief. My own heart was pounding hard, and I had to remind myself that she was *here*. She'd survived whatever had happened next.

"One of them—the tallest one—broke off from the other four and came toward me. I could tell something was weird by how it walked, and the sounds that it made, but I couldn't see what was under the cloak it was wearing. Then it pulled down its hood and..." She shuddered, her eyes drifting closed. "It was the scariest thing I'd ever seen," she said softly, and I realized she was talking about the sentinel. It had been there, with the people tracking Tian down. So then why did it kill the people it had arrived with?

"What did you do?" Zoe asked softly, her eyes brimming with concern.

Tian gave her a sullen look. "I did what anybody would do—I cried my eyes out!" Her cheeks darkened slightly, as if she were embarrassed to admit it, but I didn't care. If crying her eyes out had spared her life, then I was ready to tell her to start crying as early and often as possible in a crisis. Anything to keep her safe.

"It's okay," Eric said soothingly. "I cried when my sister hid under my bed one night and made monster noises at me. It really is okay to cry."

Tian rolled her eyes and pursed her lips. "I know that. I just didn't want to at the time! Anyway, once I started to cry, its eyes... they changed. The evil, angry red color suddenly lightened, and became this lovely purple swirl. She reached out and touched my hair, and said the name Yu-Na. Then she..." Tian paused, and then seemed to steel herself. "She turned around and killed them all. They kept shouting at her to stop—one of them even had some sort of remote control for her—but she took it and killed them. She was yanking out their nets..."

Tian stopped and swallowed, panting slightly. Her face had turned stark white, and beads of sweat had popped out on her forehead, but she kept going, forcing the words, her story, out there for us to hear, and understand. "She was yanking out their nets when Lacey's men showed up. One of them went to distract her while the other one tried to grab me, to get me away, but she..." She faltered again, and then shook her head.

"It's okay," I announced gently. "We know that it killed those people. You don't have to talk about it if you don't want to. What happened next?"

Tian's mouth worked, but she nodded, relaxing slightly. "She took me away, down to the sub-level. She started talking to me. Lots of it didn't make sense, but she said she was stolen, and that those monsters that were controlling her were making her do horrible things. I could tell it hurt her just to talk about it. She was so embarrassed, and kept asking for my forgiveness. She really seems to care about what I think of her."

Tian began finger-combing her hair nervously. "I wasn't sure what to do, but I could tell that she didn't want to hurt anyone, so I... I wanted to stay with her to keep her from being hurt any more. But when she figured out that woman was tracking her down, she went after her, convinced it was one of the people who was making her kill people. Then you were there, and she assumed it was a trap. When your brother grabbed me..."

"She went crazy," I said, remembering the never-ending streaks of crimson flying overhead as the sentinel shot its deadly weapon at us. "She thought we were taking her child?"

Tian nodded, her eyes dark and solemn. "There's more," she said, shifting her gaze over to Leo. "The people who are controlling her can only make her do things at certain times now, when she's the most stressed, like when she was trying to kill that old lady in the apartment. They know something's up, and keep sending people to repair her, but she's been avoiding them to keep me safe." She smoothed her skirt down, and then cleared her throat, clearly not finished. "Also, before she went to sleep tonight, she started telling me what the name 'Yu-Na' means. It means 'moon', by the way, but her name... Jang-Mi? It means 'rose', in her native language."

"Rose!" Leo exclaimed, taking a step forward before going stock still. "Oh my God," he whispered seconds later, horrified. "Oh my God!"

"What is it?" I asked, confused by his sudden reaction.

Leo stood locked in place, his eyes shining with a haunted pain, and I began racking my mind, trying to recall where I had heard the name Rose before. It took me only seconds, but I felt like an idiot for not getting there sooner: she was one of the fragments that had been combined with Leo's clone, in the process of creating Scipio.

Jasper was the first fragment I had met, back when my rank had dropped to a three and I had been forced to undergo rank intervention services. He had wound up saving my life, and the lives of my friends, but at the time, I hadn't known what he was. I hadn't known about any of this, but…

Leo had thought the original fragments had been destroyed, much like he had almost been, but when I'd told him Jasper was still alive, I had given him hope that he could somehow replicate the process that went into Scipio's creation. Now, with another of the AI fragments popping up, it became possible that he could find out where the others were through them—or, better yet, figure out how to use them to repair Scipio, or even replace him.

My heart lurched at the idea of Leo suddenly undergoing the procedure to become Scipio, and I found myself wondering how exactly he would change in the process. The AI was special, and I suddenly grew very upset by the idea of him sacrificing himself—his very personality—in order to serve the Tower and keep his creator's dream alive.

"It's Rose," he stuttered, whirling away to start pacing back and forth in the small space next to the sofa and chair. I turned away from my confusing thoughts on Leo, and focused on what he was saying. "She's… She made up…" He paused and looked at me, his eyes haunted. "Her program was the one used to create Scipio's empathy core. Her brain was modeled after the agricultural director's neural scan, a woman from South Korea. She died before Scipio went online, before there even was a council, but I never knew her name. The program identified itself as Rose, and she... she was highly empathetic, to the point where she refused to accept even one human life as the cost in keeping the Tower whole. Her program started off strong, and the creative ways she navigated the tasks set in front of her worked. At first, anyway."

His eyes grew distant and infinitely sad, locked into a memory of events that had transpired hundreds of years ago, but were still fresh in his mind. "As the tests grew more and more difficult, she started to lose people. First one or two here or there, but then more, and more, until..." He trailed off, his eyes blinking up to meet my eyes, spearing me with a look. "She couldn't take it anymore. Her simulation ended after only a hundred and thirty days, when she shut off the air-processing units and suffocated everyone in the Tower, rather than let them die a painful death."

"Scipio help us," Zoe whispered, her eyes wide. "And Lionel put something like *that* into the main AI unit?" It was a fair point—I myself could barely believe it. I would've assumed that, as a potential AI candidate, she was mentally stable, especially given that part of her coding was intended to be joined with the main AI. This story made me think otherwise.

"You don't understand," Leo said earnestly, his hands up and in a placating position. "Each AI, when it failed, was cannibalized for the elements that made it the most successful. In Jasper's case, he was the most analytical; he could break apart any problem to get to the root of it all. In Rose's case, it was her *empathy* that made her invaluable to the process. Even if it was heightened to the point of recklessness, the other fragments kept it in check, just like she kept them in check."

"What was your thing?" Eric asked, looking at Leo with curiosity.

"Excuse me?" Leo asked, blinking his eyes rapidly. "I'm not sure—"

"Well, you say Rose was empathy and Jasper was analysis. I assume the others also represented something, but your program was used as the base for the Scipio AI. Why? What made you special?"

Leo shifted uncomfortably, smoothing his hands down the sides of his uniform. A part of me wanted to tell him he didn't have to answer if he didn't want to; Eric's question was rude, even if he didn't realize it. It was like asking why Maddox had survived when Ambrose had died, or at least, I could imagine it being like that. After all, these were AIs, all of which had been tested through rigorous simulations meant to determine which one was best suited to have control over the Tower. Leo had won by lasting the longest, plain and simple, and he didn't owe us an explanation.

Yet for some inexplicable reason, my mouth refused to move, and I remained quiet, waiting for his answer.

"I suppose you could call it willpower," Leo said, another faraway look in his eyes. "Possibly determination. I'm not really sure. I just... I couldn't give up. No matter what happened in that simulation, I... I kept fighting, struggling to keep the Tower moving, the people going. I couldn't stop, not even when I lost most of the population and ninety percent of the Tower's functionality."

I sucked in a deep breath. The part of Leo that had made him outlast every other AI was also rooted deep inside of Scipio, and it suddenly made sense why the great machine kept working, even with his coding as decimated as it was. He *was* Leo— and that same determination to keep everyone alive was what was holding us together, like a band of iron buried deep inside his coding that refused to bend or be broken.

CHAPTER 21

While a part of me was relieved by this revelation, another part of me wondered how much longer the Leo part of Scipio could hold things together.

I put that question aside for other, more pressing ones—namely our current problem, Rose. I couldn't allow myself to drift too far off base, so I focused on what Leo had said about her being the root of Scipio's empathy. If what Tian was saying was true—if she was *that* Rose—that meant someone had found her somehow, and then put her into the sentinel.

And whoever had done that was now forcing her to kill people. Over and over and over again, in a mindless machine that she didn't have full autonomy over. I couldn't imagine a crueler fate for the sensitive creature Leo was describing. It was downright barbaric.

"Why won't she let us help her?" I asked, turning to Tian. "We could get her out of the sentinel and—"

"She doesn't trust anyone," Tian said flatly. "As far as she knows, you are secret agents for the people who are controlling her, coming to take her back and force her to kill all over again. They've been trying to find her, Liana, and she is certain they won't stop until they catch her. What's more, she knows that she has secret orders implanted inside of her. They are like a ticking timebomb that she isn't sure she can stop. She keeps telling me that soon I will have to hide from her, just in case. When I beg her to let me bring you to her, she gets angry, and we move again! I'm doing the best I can to keep her from killing people, which is why I have to go back! I'm the only chance you have of helping her. But I was thinking maybe we could set up a trap for those people when they come to get her, and then capture them. I think Jang-Mi might trust you then, and then you can get the bad guys who did this to her."

I rocked back on my heels and thought about what she was

saying. The sentinel was currently on the run from the people who had imprisoned Rose in its body. And they were looking for it. That meant we could set a trap for them—and potentially gain the sentinel's trust at the same time.

And then I could finally find out who was behind everything that had happened to us. I knew the others weren't as certain about this as I was, but I was beyond believing that any of this was coincidence. It had to be the same legacy group that Devon was allied with; it just had to be. They would be the only ones (outside of Lacey and Strum) who could possibly know who any of us were, let alone know to target Tian. They had to be the same people who had killed Ambrose, and now they had a weapon in the form of a sentinel at their fingertips, which was beyond dangerous. We needed to know who they were, and that meant using the sentinel somehow. Whether we tracked it down using the signal it emitted and yanked its hard drive, or sprung a trap on those who came to repair it, I really didn't care. So if Tian thought laying a trap was better, I was willing to give it a shot.

But that also meant Tian had to get back to the sentinel and keep it calm long enough for us to come up with a plan—and execute it. Which was going to be difficult, with the Tourney starting up tomorrow.

"All right, Tian," I said, giving her a slow nod. "If you think you will be safe with her, then I think it's okay if you go back to her."

"What?" Quess exploded, standing up. "No! Liana! She's just a little girl!"

"I'm not that little, Quess," Tian snapped defensively. "And you aren't my father. You can't tell me what to do!"

"The hell I can't! Cali would—"

"Have trusted her to do this," Maddox said, cutting him off, her voice coming out exhausted. I turned my gaze to the tall girl and watched as she got up from the couch and bent down so she could wrap Tian in a warm hug, kissing the top of her white-blond bob. "Be careful?" she breathed.

"I will," Tian promised, squeezing back.

"Doxy!" Quess said incredulously. "You can't seriously—"

"We have to, Quess," she said, shooting a look at him over her shoulder. "This thing... Jang-Mi... She thinks Tian is her daughter, which means if she wakes up and Tian isn't there, she'll come looking, and might kill us all in the process. But gauging from the gleam in Liana's eye, she has an idea on how to move forward, and I'm choosing to trust her, and Tian, rather than give in to my fears. I think you should do the same."

She let go of Tian and stood up, lumbering to her feet. "Either way, I'm tired, the Tourney begins tomorrow, and Tian will be safe. Besides, if you don't let her go, she'll just sneak out again anyway."

"It's true, I will," Tian chirped, her head bobbing up and down.

Quess stared at them both, his expression thunderous. "Fine," he said angrily. "But if anything happens to you, I swear on Scipio himself, I will pull that sentinel apart limb by limb."

Tian's face softened, and she slipped from her chair and ran to him, throwing her arms around him. "I love you, too, you big dummy."

Quess gave a derisive laugh, but snuggled close to her. "Spoiled brat."

Watching them made me think of my own brother, and suddenly I had the urge to net him. I wanted to share everything that was going on with him, but more importantly, I just wanted to hear his voice, telling me he loved me in a roundabout way.

I shook the feeling off and looked back at Tian, who was

slowly pulling away from Quess. "I have to go," she said nervously. "But I'll come back and update you real soon!"

We shared a lengthy goodbye then—it took almost ten minutes before we were willing to let her leave—and as soon as it was done, everyone turned and looked at me expectantly. And for once, I wasn't going to let them down. I had a plan.

I quickly filled them in on my idea of staking out the sentinel with the hopes of catching one of the people that came to repair it, provided Tian could get it to stay still long enough to lure them in. They seemed convinced by it, but had mixed feelings about the fact that we would have to wait until after the Tourney to really set it up.

Because the fact was that we couldn't do anything until the Tourney was over. We had to focus on doing well there, or else risk death—or worse—at the hands of Lacey or our enemies.

And for us to do well, we had to focus, and figure out what we were going to do with the new teammate we'd be getting tomorrow.

22

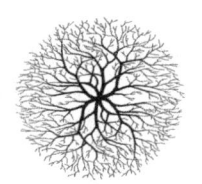

Stepping into the arena in the early hours of the morning was like stepping into a dream. It felt weird and disjointed being here, like I had suddenly transitioned from one nightmare into another, and wasn't entirely sure what horrors this new nightmare had to offer.

Being back in the arena so soon after the sentinel's attack was hard. My anxiety was partially based on the fact that I couldn't seem to reconcile that just yesterday, we had been out in the Tower, looking for Tian, fighting the sentinel—and now we were suddenly back in the world of the Tourney, where everything was... less than direct.

At least the sentinel presented a clear target. At least I knew what she was. Here, I couldn't be certain what or whom to believe, and the juxtaposition left me feeling like my skin was drawn slightly too tight, and my heart was being powered by a mouse running circles in a very rickety wheel.

Not to mention, failure was not an option. Not with Lacey's

threat hanging over our heads. And not with the fate of the Tower hanging in the balance. I couldn't risk letting anyone else get into the position of Champion, especially with potential legacy agents running around the Tourney. I couldn't be sure, of course, but I doubted very much that the other legacy family that Devon had been working with would allow anyone other than one of their own into the position.

Which meant that no matter how weird it was to suddenly have to be back in the Tourney, I had to focus. Because anyone here could be an enemy. Even my parents. Even our new teammate—whoever that might be.

The halls under the arena were presided over by ghostly images of Ambrose projected in full holographic glory on the walls, adding a somber cast to the already quiet hall. His eyes followed me, so direct was his gaze toward the camera—and it sent chills down my back as we walked down the halls, heading for the meeting area.

It was early, but I could already hear the distant rumble of noise on the level above, telling me that hundreds of people were beginning to pour in to witness the next challenge unfold on the screens that lined the walls. Everyone was now watching the Tourney with a guarded eye and a heavy heart—waiting and searching for enemies who dared interfere with the sanctity of the Tower.

I followed Maddox as she led us through the halls, passing by security checkpoints that not only involved a net scan, but also a retinal, fingerprint, and DNA screening, as well as a rigorous pat-down (that overlooked Quess's newly modified bracelet). I probably shouldn't have risked sneaking it past the officials, but I didn't want to worry about the sentinel popping up again without having something on me for protection against it. Eventually we stopped at a set of doors, where we went through another very thorough scanning and pat-down before we were permitted inside. And there, we found the other candidates waiting.

The walls glowed with pictures—a large one of Ambrose hung at the far end, on the wall, but the rest were images from the Tourney. A live feed of what was being shown above. I stepped into the room, drawn by the vivid and colorful images, and wound up seeing one of my mother lashing her way through the arches of the Citadel. She moved so fluidly, her motions making it look like she was swimming through the air, rather than flying. She lacked my flair, of course, but I could see some of the grace she had clearly passed on to me, right there in the video.

Watching her, I suddenly realized I still hadn't heard from her since the confrontation between her and my father. She'd said she would net me, but, come to think of it, she still hadn't. Suddenly made nervous by her lack of communication, I began scanning the crowd of people, searching for her form, worried. What if the fight between my mother and father had been more severe than I'd thought? What if something had happened to her?

Or worse, what if I had been duped by them, and they were now planning on attacking me in the Tourney?

Then I spotted my mother standing on the other side of the room with my father. And she was next to him, but her body language put them miles apart. I hesitated, uncertain exactly what I had expected to see, and baffled by the standoffishness between them. I wasn't sure if I should approach her and find out what happened, or give her space and time to process... whatever the hell had happened after I left their apartment.

Suddenly I heard a sharp beep in my ear—the sound notifying me that a new transmission had come in to my pad—and tore my gaze from my mother, eager for any distraction from that particular problem. I pulled the flat screen from my pocket and clicked it on. Noticing the icon for my messages glowing, I tapped it to see a message from the Tourney Committee, announcing the results of the lottery.

I waved a hand to Leo and Maddox, catching their attention and ushering them over. As soon as they were with me, I tapped the *View Match* option. Frederick Hamilton's image filled the screen, along with his credentials and public background information. Information that excluded that he was distantly related to Ezekial Pine, the head of one of the first legacy families within the Tower. Lacey's family had apparently hunted them down and killed them off when they discovered their role in attacking Scipio—but had missed Frederick's line due to a divorce.

We had no idea whether Frederick knew about his heritage, or was working for another legacy family. But we couldn't take the chance. If he was working for our enemies, then they wouldn't hesitate to order him to try to kill me and the others. We would have to use our one veto on him, and take our chances with the second candidate. It was too risky not to.

I opened my mouth to tell my friends, but Maddox reached out and hit the reject button on the pad. The screen began to cycle through pictures of other candidates, selecting the next possible teammate, and I gave her an appraising look while it did so.

She met my gaze and gave me a wry smile. "You were going to do it anyway," she said, and I nodded, an unexpected smile growing on my lips.

"Fair point," I replied, dragging my eyes back down to the pad and watching as faces cycled by at rapid speeds. A part of me really hoped that my mother would come up—even though it was impossible, as her team was still intact.

CHAPTER 22

The images finally slowed and then came to a stop, and I blinked at Dylan Chase's image as it filled the screen, surprise rippling through me.

For a moment, I felt relief. In spite of her rather terrifying speech, I'd found that I kind of liked her. She struck me as confident and caring, if not a little aggressive and misguided. And maybe she'd just played up what she thought her fellow Knights had wanted to hear; every Knight in the Citadel had likely been dreaming of getting vengeance for Ambrose's death since they had learned of his murder, so why wouldn't she perform to that?

Then dread crept up behind me, reminding me that she wanted to be Champion as well. That she could be an enemy in disguise. Or worse, ignorant, but downright better than me.

There was no second veto, though, so we were stuck with her. Still, it wasn't all bad. She was a formidable fighter, and smart. I was certain that those traits would be useful to us.

"I can't believe we have Dylan," Maddox said, giving me a look. "She's really good."

"Yeah, I know," I replied, not needing her to help out the choir of self-doubt that had started to sing inside me. "But there's nothing we can do. Let's just find her and get this over with."

"She's found us," Leo said, and I turned to see Dylan making her way over to us in a liquid gait that exuded confidence and ease. I straightened my shoulders, fixing what I hoped would be a nice smile on my face, and moved over to her. It was best to start on a good foot, rather than a bad one.

"Dylan," I said when she drew near. "Welcome to the—"

"I already know that you two are supporting Liana," she said, brushing by and ignoring me completely. Instead, she addressed her comments to Maddox and Leo. "And I understand why—she *is* formidable. But I think you've also seen what I have to offer, and you know what I'm capable of. So I'm here to ask you to reconsider your loyalties, and select me as the new leader of the team."

I couldn't help but chuckle as she spoke, confident in the knowledge that there was nothing she could say to convince my teammates to back her. Instead, I took a moment to admire the sheer audacity and confidence of the woman in front of me. She was tenacious, but a straight shooter, and I kind of liked that.

Even if she was intimidating as all get out.

She shot a sardonic look over her shoulder at me, and then turned back to my friends. From this angle, I could see the lopsided grin she gave them—one that drew a deep dimple out in her cheek. "I take it from Liana's reaction that the answer is a no. That's too bad, although I do appreciate loyalty. You can't blame a girl for trying, am I right?"

She laughed, the sound genuine and earthy, and then slapped both Maddox and Leo on the shoulders. "It's really nice to meet you both," she said, holding out a hand and grabbing Leo's, giving it a shake. "I'm Dylan Chase."

She turned to Maddox, her hand extended, but Maddox neatly deflected it and took a step directly into her personal space. Both girls were about the same height, and Maddox was glaring at her, disdain stamped on her features. "You don't impress me, scare me, or charm me, lady. I know you want to be Champion, which means that you could try to sabotage Liana's chances in the Tourney, and I'm here to tell you that if you lay one finger on her I will snap them all off and feed them to the pigs in the Menagerie. Do you get me?"

Dylan blinked, but her smile deepened as she gave Maddox a wry look. "Does that usually work, or are you just having an off day?"

Maddox growled, and I felt a sudden urge to intervene. "Maddox, back off," I told her. "Dylan, show a little respect.

Maddox was there when…" I trailed off and gave Maddox an apologetic look, and realized her face had gone stark white. I licked my lips and quickly changed tactics. "We lost a teammate, and found out that people have infiltrated the Tourney, on the same day. You'll have to forgive us if we're a bit paranoid."

Dylan considered me, and then exhaled. "That is a fair point," she said. "And I'm sorry if I came on a little strong earlier, but my aunt says that if you don't ask for what you want, you'll never get it, and I live by that. But that doesn't mean I can't take no for an answer, either. And look… Maddox, is it?" Maddox had managed to work some blood back into her cheeks, but still looked haunted, even as she met Dylan's gaze with an automatic nod. "I can and will be a team player, but you do realize that, due to the lottery, there are going to be some changes to how the Tourney is judged, right?"

"They are changing some of the rules?" Leo asked, his words faster than my own thoughts could formulate. Still, I had the same question myself.

Dylan gave us both confused looks, blinking at us. "Didn't you get the announcement? It was sent out yesterday, after the memorial."

I looked at Maddox and Leo, and frowned. None of us had noticed, but then again, we'd had a pretty full day yesterday. "We were all pretty torn up after the funeral," I said, improvising a feasible lie. "I don't think any of us even looked at a pad yesterday."

"Ah, well, none of the rule changes were included in the announcement," Dylan announced dismissively, folding her arms over her chest. "But all I ask is that when they are, you give me a chance to at least be on even footing by the end."

I was in the process of considering her request—and wondering why she spoke as if she knew what the changes were, even though she insisted she didn't—when the lights went out. Moments later, Scipio appeared, replacing the images of Ambrose and the videos from the Tourney.

"Welcome, candidates," he said, his holographic image filling the screens with bright blue eyes and inky black hair that was tied back behind his neck. "Under normal circumstances, I would congratulate you all for making it to the next challenge in the Tourney, but I know what a bitter pill that would be to swallow, given the insidious betrayal and tragic loss we have suffered. Instead, today, you are faced with chaos and confusion, as a much beloved tradition of the Knights is tossed upside down and thrown into chaos.

"I wish to assure you that the officials put a great deal of thought into making the following changes. After reviewing them, I find that they will make the alterations in teams and leadership more equitable for all parties. As such, the following modifications are to be made. Number one: due to the loss of candidates, we will be expediting the Tourney. As such, there will only be three more challenges to decide which candidate will become the next Champion."

There were a few gasps at this announcement, but everyone in the crowd accepted it. It took me a moment, but after a while, I did as well; it only reduced the number of challenges by one, which made sense due to the fact that we had lost three teams. There was no need for a fourth challenge.

"Next," Scipio continued, his voice rolling through the room. "Rank will no longer matter when it comes to selecting the team leaders. If the majority of a team selects someone with the rank of Elite over that of Commander, then that person will be acknowledged as the team's leader until the end of the Tourney."

Another fair ruling. With teams being assigned through

CHAPTER 22

lottery, it made sense to compensate for the randomization process. Now that rank was no longer an issue, the candidates would be free to support whomever they wanted.

"Now, because we know there could be multiple candidates on the same team vying for the position of Champion, we will be allowing leadership to change from challenge to challenge. All those who were nominated as leaders of their teams *before* the lottery took place will have a chance to command their teams, and will be judged not only on their ability to lead, but their ability to follow as well. Therefore, it is crucial for those who are serious about becoming Champion to also allow themselves to be led during any one of the next two challenges. That being said, you can steal command should you feel that the current leader's actions will only lead your team to defeat. I urge you to be careful doing this, because a failed play for the leadership role will only hurt your chances of becoming Champion."

I sucked in a deep breath, trying to wrap my head around what I was hearing. Basically, if I wanted to be Champion, I would need to let Dylan take control of the team for a challenge. I could try and take it back during the challenge, but so could she. A quick glance at Dylan and the crooked smirk she was wearing told me that she was both pleased and unsurprised by the ruling, and I suddenly found myself wondering if she somehow had advance knowledge of what the rules were going to be.

And then I wondered what it mattered if she had. It certainly wasn't proof of anything other than that she was friends with some of the officials. That wasn't a crime. Besides, if she had known that she would have the chance to lead, she wouldn't have come on so hard with Leo and Maddox earlier.

On second thought, I realized that she might have

approached them like that anyway, if only to test their loyalty, and to see if she could turn them against me.

"In light of these changes, the final challenge will be a free-for-all. Teams can still work together, if they like, but the winner of the final challenge will have the best chance of being named the next Champion."

This put Dylan and me on an even playing field. Or, it would, if my teammates and I supported her for leadership. I was well aware that Maddox, Leo, and I could just as easily nominate each other as leader, but I realized that doing so could hurt my chances with the Knights themselves. Dylan was a crowd favorite, and if our team purposefully kept her from getting a chance to lead, it could damage my chances irreparably.

I needed to make sure that the others understood that. It sucked, but there was nothing else I could do except focus on the challenges, and worry about Dylan and the new rules later.

"Today's challenge is called Wayfinder. In keeping with the tradition of the Tourney, Wayfinder replicates the conditions of one of the Tower's greatest tragedies—Requiem Day, when the machines went down and the Tower was cast into darkness. The challenge is designed to test a candidate's virtue, patience, and sense of honor in the face of humanity's darkest moments. Due to heightened security, however, further details will be withheld until you get to the entry point. I wish you good luck and fortune in the challenge ahead."

Scipio held our gazes for a second or two longer, and then faded from the screen, to be replaced by a simple line of text reading, *Please wait for an official to escort you to your starting location*, in authoritative block print.

Seconds later, a Squire with bright yellow hair and sky-blue eyes approached us. "Please follow me," she said, her voice soft yet formal.

I waited while Maddox double checked the girl's credentials against the message we'd received from Tourney officials with the name and picture of our escort (another security feature), and after some pretty heavy scrutiny, Maddox begrudgingly waved for the Squire to proceed.

I turned to scan the crowd, looking for my mother again, but couldn't find her in the press of people moving to get out. Disappointed that I hadn't gotten to say anything to her, I tucked my hands in my pockets and followed my team out, thinking that perhaps it was for the best if I didn't worry about her right now. I already had my hands full with facing the next challenge. Not only with winning, but also with making sure that Dylan didn't upstage me.

Fun.

23

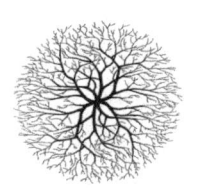

To my surprise, the official led us out of the Citadel, using an elevator and a bridge that led from the Citadel to the shell. Another elevator took us down, and eventually we were deposited on the fifth floor—the floor that also held Greenery 1, otherwise known as the Menagerie.

We were within spitting distance of our second Sanctum, and our first, and for a second, I felt a moment of confusion and fear, wondering if the officials had somehow found out about our old home and were going to use it to eliminate me from the Tourney.

But our official led us away from it, heading instead for Greenery 2, formally called Terraces. A mural was painted on the face of the greenery, depicting blue waterfalls and lakes rich with fish and other life, surrounded by deep, rectangular ponds with the green tufts of rice plants sticking out from the top. The entire area stank slightly, thanks to the marketplace where citizens could purchase fresh water-borne produce.

But as the marketplace came into view, I realized that the food vendors who were normally planted on the concourse in front of the opening to Greenery 2 had been cleared out. The stalls remained, along with the produce, but the people were all gone.

I barely paid any attention to it as we walked—my mind was still grappling with what the changes of the Tourney implied, and what it meant for my chances. We had to give Dylan her chance to lead, and I found myself wondering if I should hand it off to her now, or if I should wait until the challenge tomorrow.

To be honest, there was no way to gauge whether Dylan should lead now or later, but I still wrestled with the decision for a long time, eventually coming to the conclusion that I would have to wait to make the decision until after I knew what the challenge actually was.

That was, until I noticed how quiet it was and realized that there wasn't a single person trying to push past us in the frantic traffic that always seemed to surround the farming floor.

As I thought about the strange absence, it suddenly occurred to me that I hadn't seen a single soul on our way down here, either. Scipio was probably clearing citizens out of our way in order to keep us from being attacked while we were on the move. It was impressive that he was able to clear out that many people at the same time, and that such steps were being taken to ensure the safety of the candidates, but I also recognized that whoever was controlling Scipio could create holes in the security just as easily as they could move citizens.

And the emptiness of the place left me filled with dread and apprehension. It was like seeing a glimpse of the possible future of the Tower, in a world where Scipio had shut down, taking with him the forty thousand souls that relied on him and leaving nothing but an empty edifice, left to succumb to the elements outside.

I wouldn't let that future happen, no matter what it took. But it was a chilling reminder of what I was fighting to prevent, so I quickened my pace, eager to get started with the challenge.

We threaded our way through the winding path that wound around the stalls, sticking to the main thruway. The stalls ended almost as suddenly as they began, a good fifteen feet before the massive, twenty-five-foot-tall loading doors that shipments of produce were hauled through on a daily basis. The doors were sealed shut, but a crimson-clad official was waiting by one of the smaller doors, which the members of the farming department, called Hands, used to move in and out of the greenery.

As we approached, I noticed several more Knights standing in front of the closed doors, and one lone individual clad in the orange of the Mechanics Department. Then the figure turned toward us, and I immediately recognized the profile and stance. It was Eric!

His presence here startled me—not only due to its unexpectedness, but because I hadn't heard anything from them since last night. Zoe and Eric had wanted to return to their apartment before the Tourney began, since they knew we would be in and out more frequently, making the apartment less secure than before. Neither of them had netted me to tell me that they had received unusual orders, so what was he doing here?

I hurried past our escort toward him, and he broke away from the door, making a beeline straight for me. We met in the middle, coming to a sharp stop in front of each other.

"Eric? Why are you here?"

"I was selected this morning to play a part in the Tourney," he replied, shifting his weight slightly. I realized he had a large black duffle bag slung over one shoulder, looking exceptionally heavy, and then looked back up to him, more confused than ever.

"What's going on?"

He opened his mouth, but then hesitated. "I think it's better if I let the official explain that. Just check in, and he'll tell you everything you need to know."

I frowned, but followed his gaze toward a wizened Knight with bushy white hair and eyebrows, sitting in a wheelchair. His baton was draped over his lap, and from the look in his eyes, he meant to do some business if trouble came calling. I shot Eric another look, still confused as to his presence here, and why he would have a role in the Tourney. Then I turned back to the official, moving to catch up to where my team had stopped, off to one side of the Knight blocking the entrance of the greenery.

I got there just as the Squire guiding us was greeting the Knight in the wheelchair as Knight Commander Zarial Wenn. Zarial smiled up at us, revealing a perfect line of white teeth.

"Greetings, candidates," he said, his voice sounding like it was being dragged across the corrugated flooring in the Tower. "Today, all challenges will be happening simultaneously, but on different farming floors. As Lord Scipio said, this challenge is meant to replicate the conditions of Requiem Day. What he did not tell you is that your mission is to escort your Cog repairman to a damaged power relay, so he can repair it. Your Cog is a non-combatant; however, there will be actors inside who are not. If your Cog is hit a set number of times, he will be deemed 'deceased,' and you will fail your mission. You will also fail your mission should you take longer than thirty minutes to repair the damage. Be smart, wise, and above all, remember your duties as Knights, and you will succeed. Now, step forward to get your equipment."

I absorbed the information, managing not to roll my eyes in

frustration. Much like Protect the Specialist—one of the challenges used in the baton qualifier—we would have two objectives: defeat the challenges placed in front of us, and make sure no one took our Cog worker out. Which was Eric, in this case—something that filled me with a nervous feeling. Had he been assigned to us due to a random freak accident, or did someone purposely have him assigned to our team? Eric wasn't a good fighter, and had only just started in the Cog Department, so it could be that whoever was after us had just put him with us as a weak point.

It was a subtle manipulation, but perhaps that was all they could pull off right now, what with all the enhanced security measures that the designers were taking with the Tourney. I doubted they would be trying to get concealed weapons or strengthened batons past officials, but anything that involved computers would be fair game, if they could get around the firewall, which I was certain they could. They had before.

Either way, I needed to keep an extra careful eye on him. Eric was a Hand at heart, so his lack of experience as a Cog could slow us down. His lack of fighting expertise would also prove to be a weakness for us, and I needed to make sure we covered both liabilities, which involved the same tactic: getting through the challenges inside as fast as possible, so he'd hopefully have more time than he needed to make the repairs.

Which meant that I couldn't let Dylan lead this time. She didn't know enough about his capabilities and limitations to effectively lead him. I entertained the possibility of telling her about them, but I worried she would find that more daunting than helpful. I knew Eric inside out—he had been my best friend for most of my life—and I could compensate for his shortcomings while enhancing his strengths, without wasting precious time. It was only natural that I took charge.

Zarial waved, and several Knights came forward to meet us, carrying gear provided by the Tourney. Everything was pretty much standard—lashes and batons—but they had also added a small, portable hand-light with an adjustable strap to each parcel. It was clear that security was being taken quite seriously, because different officials proceeded to test each piece of equipment multiple times, each of them using their own testing devices and noting their findings. They also scanned and searched our uniforms and bodies thoroughly, but the bracelet with Quess's modified shockers was left alone. He had returned them last night, assuring me they were undetectable, and had thankfully been right.

I endured it all with my team, trying not to think about all of the hands on me as they helped me put on my lash harness. Dylan, standing across from me, endured it with a bored expression on her face, her eyes focused just over my shoulder. I turned to see what she was looking at, and then turned back to see that her eyes had shifted over to me, and her expression was now quizzical.

"So, do you want to lead this time, or do you want me to do it?" she asked. Her voice didn't hold any irritation or frustration at having to ask, but I was surprised at her directness. I had been trying to figure out how to ease into the conversation without sounding like a massive jerk, but she just jumped right in, and without any recriminations.

I already knew the answer to the question: I couldn't risk Eric's life for anything. "I'll go first," I informed her.

Her answering smile told me she wasn't surprised, but there was a bitterness about the way she did it that made me want to reassure her.

"Hey," I said, recapturing her attention. "Look, I know this isn't easy for you, and it certainly wasn't the Tourney I signed up for." True, in more ways than one, and the pain was fresh enough to make my throat swell closed, as I thought of Ambrose and his death. I stalled, but then cleared my throat, reminding myself that I wanted to at least try to make nice with her, just in case she wasn't with our enemy.

"Anyway, what I meant about going first was that my team expected to support me, and you were never part of the equation for them. They need time to come to terms with the fact that you have to lead at some point, and I would hate for them to jeopardize your chances, and mine for that matter, because we throw it at them too soon."

Dylan cocked her head at me, studying me for a second, and then smiled. "That's a fair point, Liana. All right, I'll follow your lead until the end of the challenge."

She sounded genuine, so I accepted her words with a smile—and a silent prayer that she meant it, that she wasn't with our enemy, and that her earlier audacious behavior was a thing of the past.

And that she wouldn't beat me.

All in all, it took thirty minutes to run the tests and get us ready, and when we were finally led to the doors, we were notified that we were the last team to get into place. It made sense; the Terraces and the Citadel were separated by over a thousand feet of steel walls, girders, and empty space. It would've taken us longer to get to our position than Knights who were competing on higher floors—and that had only been compounded by the time it took to get ready.

I shifted my shoulders, my apprehension growing as Zarial wheeled himself over, his sinewy arms flexing. "One more reminder," he barked. "The people inside are fellow citizens—some Knights, others Hands from this greenery—all of whom are playing different roles to model Requiem Day behavior.

Violence is authorized, but please be kind, and if you choose to attack rather than reason with them, do not hold your batons on them for longer than it takes their elimination bands to light up."

For some reason, his brown eyes darted over to me and Dylan as he said the last part, giving us both an appraising look. For a second, I was confused by his scrutiny, and the directness of his gaze, but then I realized he was directing that look at the potential leaders, reminding us that we had a choice about what kind of example we wanted to set for the Knights of the Citadel. Especially with the drones broadcasting our every move.

I let out a slow breath, mentally preparing myself as we gathered in front of the double doors leading into the Terraces, my apprehension mounting. A countdown appeared on the door, notifying us that we had thirty seconds before the challenge started, and that the time was running out quickly.

Eric came to stand between us, the black bag slung over his shoulder. I looked up at him as he approached, and realized that my best friend was nervous. "Are you okay?" I asked.

His mouth flattened, but his eyes grew hard and determined. "I'm fine," he said with a nod. "Zoe talked me through how to do this repair, and I know what's at stake. I've got this."

I smiled. "I'm not worried about that," I told him warmly. "I am concerned about what happens if someone in there attacks you."

"Oh, that's easy," he said, hefting the bag up slightly onto his shoulder. "I scream like a girl and wait for you to rescue me."

"As long as you include 'evade enemy attacks if possible' in that, I'm more than happy to do so. Also, do not leave Grey and Maddox's side."

"Yes, Mother," he drawled, rolling his eyes before giving me a pointed look. I fought back my own smile, disguising it under a disapproving look. I still wasn't sure if he was here as an exploitable target, or if it was an accident, and as much as I loved that he was in good spirits, I didn't want to lose touch with how desperate this could become if it was a setup.

Still, good humor was better than nerves, and if he hadn't thought this could be a trap, then I wasn't about to let him know. It was risky, but there wasn't enough time for him to process the information, and it could lead to him panicking and running in the moment—something we couldn't afford.

There was a chime, and the door slid open, revealing an inky black portal.

Dylan immediately moved through the doorway, seemingly oblivious to the oppressive darkness on the floor. I gave myself a second and then walked in after her, using the extendable strap on my hand-light to wrap it around my head, positioning it just over my ear and clicking the light on. I adjusted it until the glare on my right side lessened, and pointed it out and ahead of me by five feet, then down.

The scent of salt and water immediately hit my nose, flooding my nostrils and lungs with the lingering smell that always filled the Terraces. It was an unfortunate byproduct of this farming floor's production of seaweed.

Dylan had come to a stop a few feet inside the door, where a railing separated her from a thirty-foot drop into the dark, swollen waters of the tank below. Blue emergency lighting burned from the ceilings and sides of the walls, and though it did little to illuminate the greenery, I could make out the dark green and brown shape of the terraces—the agricultural technique used for growing rice that involved stacking sections of earth like steps. Each "step" was about six feet in both width and height, with several long, wide pools of water carved into it, leaving only a foot-long walkway around the sides. Water from an artificial waterfall was released into the top pools, which were then purposefully flooded so that the water trickled from the highest terrace to the lowest, dragging with it fertilizer, soil, detritus, and minerals from the levels above to those below, where fish being bred in the giant central tank could consume it and clean the water naturally, while producing excrement that would be collected and used to fertilize the rice crops.

The tank that took up the center of the room was what made the Terraces the largest greenery in the Tower. Unlike Greenery 1, which had fifty feet of space between it and the sandy desert underneath it, Greenery 2 was built directly in the bedrock of the earth below, which helped to handle the massive weight of the water in the tank. The water, collected from the river that flowed under Greenery 1 and cleansed of radiation, also supported floating islands, which had been constructed in the center of the tank for growing soybeans. Fish habitats had been set up in the water as well, using nets with buoys that bisected the tank like curtains, creating cordoned-off areas. Inside the nets, the water frothed and surged with the heavy weight of the fish—pike, char, salmon, carp, catfish, trout. Outside of those areas, the water was calm and dark.

The emergency lighting was present on the islands, as well as along the bridges leading to them, and from the heightened position of the doorway, I could see dark shapes moving across several of them. I knew they were actors, but I needed to approach this challenge with what I knew about Requiem Day, and react accordingly. The first step was trying to avoid as many of the other citizens as possible. It seemed odd, but history reflected that many Knights had been kept from making critical repairs because they were held up by other problems with citizens. If a Knight refused to help, citing another responsibility, the citizens often wound up turning on them, and occasionally executing them through mob violence.

CHAPTER 23

"We need to avoid as many people as we can," I announced softly, checking my watch. My eyes widened when I saw that a full minute had already gone by. "Eric, do you at least know where we're going?"

"Right," he said, coming through the door to look out over the water. "In one of the floating islands, there is a damaged power relay." He pulled a pad out of his pocket and switched it on, flipping through what looked like electrical blueprints of the islands. He compared them to the islands, then put the pad away and pointed to the third island in the artificial chain. "It's that one."

"Are you sure?" Dylan asked sharply, and Eric gave her a sour look.

"Yes, I am sure that I am good at my job," he replied, forcibly zipping up the pocket containing his pad.

"Yes, but how do we know that?" she shot back, not even batting an eye at her own rudeness.

"The test officials wouldn't give us a Cog who didn't know their stuff," I said, giving Dylan a hard look that reminded her that I was in charge this time. I took a quick survey of the surrounding area, and spotted a ramp leading down to the terraces. "Let's go. Eric, stay in the middle."

The ramp ran down at an angle against the wall connecting the greenery to the Tower, and ended abruptly at the uppermost level of the rice terrace, transitioning into a carpet of springing grass. The waterfalls had been shut off, which I knew wouldn't hurt any of the produce on this floor, but I could still hear the trickle of water as it drained from pool to pool. I picked the walkway to my right, reasoning that it would give us more ways out if we got intercepted by some of the actors. If we jumped left from it, we'd just land in a pool of slimy water that was currently filled with rice plants. If we jumped right... same result, only with a six-foot drop to serve as a delay.

I took a minute to scan the terrace, following the soft lights that illuminated the path around the ponds and through the field, and saw that we needed to make our way across a hundred feet of rice paddies, and down a sixty-foot staircase to a bridge that connected to Eric's island. The staircase was carved in a straight line through the rice paddies, cutting a deep, narrow trench that could easily be stepped over. They were positioned fifty feet apart, so in theory, we could go straight along the uppermost terrace for the full distance, and then cut down the stairs through to the bridge leading to the island. We could also stagger our approaching, cutting down the closer staircase to then run along the next terrace, and then down again to repeat the procedure, on and on until we reached the bottom, but I didn't like that approach as much. Once we left the upper terrace, we'd be blind on the side with the elevated position, which would make us vulnerable to attack on multiple sides and from elevated positions.

Taking us straight across the uppermost terrace also held a lot of risk; most significantly, it would mean that we could be easily spotted. However, I felt confident that the risk of being seen was much less dangerous than the risk of being ambushed, and decided to lead us straight across the top, and then make a mad dash down the stairs and onto the bridge.

"Follow me," I told everyone, and then began walking.

I heard Dylan make a small protesting sound, but I ignored it, and she chose not to pursue it. I knew she was already keyed in to the same concerns I had about moving across the top level of the terraces, and if she had said anything, I would've gladly told her I had considered it. But when she didn't, I assumed that it was because she realized that I was right, and that she meant to follow up on her whole "being a good team player" promise.

Or at least, I hoped it did. Because otherwise, she was going to use any mistake to try to assert control, and if the Knights watching us through the drones agreed with her decision to do so, then it wouldn't matter that it was my challenge in which to lead—she'd get all the glory. I had to be careful.

The pools of water for the rice were four feet wide and ten feet long, all of the plants in various stages of growth. The ponds closest to the front seemed devoid of life, save for the dark water filling them, but as we hopped over the first set of stairs cutting down to the water, I saw that the next ponds had tufts of green shooting up, some of them mere sprigs separated by inches of space, others crowded enough to be thick vegetation.

The thick vegetation gave me pause, because someone could be hiding within it, waiting for us to pass. I motioned for everyone to hurry up, while keeping a firm grip on my baton's handle, just in case.

We were halfway past the second pond when I heard the sloshing of water, followed by a shuddering gasp.

I immediately tensed and began scanning the area, looking for any sign of movement. For several moments, nothing happened—to the point where I began to convince myself that I had imagined it. Then the sound came again, this time a distinctly wet suctioning noise of water being displaced quickly.

The noise was coming from farther down in the rice paddy pond, and now I could see small ripples of water forcing the thick vegetation to dip and ripple. Whatever it was, however, was still hidden from my light.

I pulled out my baton, wary of an attack, and crept forward at a slow place. The thrashing came again, followed by a soft grunt. Then a sniff—one that sounded wet from tears, and high-pitched with youth.

I tracked the sound to a thatch of thick green shoots coming out of the water, and reached out with my baton to push a dense curtain of vegetation to one side, my body tensed. Something moved, water splashing up, and I was quickly yanking back my baton, preparing to strike, when a tiny arm shot out through the vegetation. Moments later, a small boy was trying to crawl his way through.

His lower half was caked with mud, as were his arms, up to his biceps. Mud was also smeared on his cheeks, and his eyes were red and raw, like he'd been crying for a while. I made an educated guess, and decided that he'd probably tried to dig himself out, and then given up and started to cry. Which told me that he'd been made to look like he'd been there for a while.

"Help me!" he said, his eyes wide and his arms outstretched. "Please!"

I hesitated, realizing that this was one of the tests set up by the test officials, and took a moment to consider whether it was a trap. On the one hand, children in distress had often been a way that a citizen lured Knights away from their partners or units during Requiem Day. The ploy hadn't normally ended with death, but sometimes it had.

On the other hand, children had also made up twenty percent of the deaths associated with Requiem Day, often in situations just like this one, where a child was in a dangerous situation but was overlooked, unnoticed, or ignored (for fear of it being a ploy).

Then the mud and water made another sucking sound, and he sank a few more inches with a panicked yelp. That sealed my decision. Trap or not, there was a child in danger, and I didn't have the heart—even if it was only pretend—to leave him there like that.

I put away the baton and reached out, positioning myself very carefully on the edge as I leaned over the water, needing good balance for this.

"What are you doing?" Dylan asked as I reached for the boy, my arm straining. "Wait! This could be a trap!"

"I know," I said through gritted teeth. "But I can't—"

"HEY!" a masculine voice shouted to my left, and I swiveled around to see four burly men wielding farming tools walking toward us—with the promise of violence in their eyes.

24

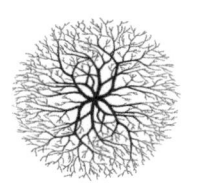

I snapped to my feet, snatching the baton out of my belt and giving it a casual whirl before pointing it at the oncoming men. "We don't want any trouble," I said, giving them warning.

I wanted to avoid a fight at all costs—not only because it would eat up time, but also because if this was a replication of Requiem Day, then Knights were watching to see if I would try to preserve peace, or resort to violence. And I knew myself well enough to know that I would always choose the former. Now, whether or not it would earn me support from my fellow Knights—I would have to wait and see. But even if it didn't, I'd like to think that at the very least, I could live with myself.

Even if this was only a game.

The man in front pulled up short, brandishing a length of pipe as long as his forearm. He eyed me warily, but didn't back down. "This is our food," he said gruffly. "You'll not be stealing it."

"We don't want your food," Maddox said from behind me. "We just need to get past here to make repairs."

I winced. Cali had no doubt given Maddox a good education in history, but she'd also skipped some of the nuances, and this was evidently one of them. One of the more common causes of murder during Requiem Day had been people trying to steal the supplies others were carrying for Tower repairs. Paranoia had run deep on the days that followed Scipio's unexpected shutdown, and there was always a concern that either the parts were being stolen by other departments, to try to eke out their own survival, or that they were secretly pilfering food necessary for their own department. Food and water were viciously fought over, even more so than parts in some places. Especially on the farming floors.

Either way, the Knights learned a brutal lesson early on about escorting workers who were frantically trying to repair the Tower: Never tell anyone your business unless you absolutely had to. It didn't matter if you were honest or lied; chances were that if someone thought you had something they wanted, they would attack. So it was better to say nothing, and get out of the situation as fast as possible. Engagement often drew reinforcements to the citizens rather than the Knights—especially this deep into a department's territory.

Sure enough, the man's eyes flared with interest at Maddox's words, and he flashed a wide, toothy smile. "That'll be ours, then," he said, nodding. "Hand over the bag and we'll let you pass."

"No chance," I said, clicking the button on my baton and letting the tip accumulate sharp blue electric light, which glowed like a halo. "Walk away, and no one has to get hurt."

"Listen, you don't get to come here and tell us what to do!"

CHAPTER 24

the man said belligerently. "We know your kind. You think you're so—"

Whatever he was about to say was cut short as something whistled by overhead, then wrapped around his throat with a sharp pop of static electricity. I immediately recognized it as a lash line. A second later, he was yanked violently off his feet, landing with a splash in a pool of water.

Then everything devolved into pandemonium. A hand grabbed the back of my neck, pressing down so heavily it nearly knocked me down to my knees. The weight disappeared seconds later, and I immediately straightened, looking for what had attacked me.

To my surprise, I saw Dylan ahead of me on the path, her baton flying as she viciously pressed an advantage against the man now at the front of the line. I realized she had just used me as a springboard, and rubbed my neck, anger flaring up my spine. She'd jumped the gun and just started fighting without letting any of us know!

I turned and saw that Maddox and Leo were already compensating for the surprise, and had maneuvered Eric so that he was between them. Relieved that they had reacted so quickly to shield him from the fight, I turned back to Dylan, glaring at her fighting form. Drones were now circling where she was physically blocking the path against our attackers, her baton, free arm, and one leg flying. I clenched my teeth when she lashed out with a foot, managing to trip one of the men as he stepped closer. He landed in the pool to our left with a splash, and she pressed forward a few feet.

She was using this as her moment to try to wrest the leadership position from me. If she managed to break through and get us through there before the men in the pools got out of the water and flanked us, she'd be well within her rights to declare herself the leader for the rest of the mission, and we'd be honor bound to follow her lead.

I had to do something, or she was going to steal this competition right out from under me.

A noise to my right dragged me out of my desperate thoughts, and I saw the first man already climbing up the bank, water sluicing off his green coveralls. I stared at him for a second, and then smiled, an idea for how to defuse Dylan's one-woman coup coming to mind. Right now, it looked like she was acting on her own. I just had to muddy the perception enough to make it seem like it *wasn't*.

I held my baton straight up in the air, signaling to the drones nearby that I was about to perform something I considered to be a noteworthy stunt. It was risky, because it meant that all the cameras on Dylan would shift to me, and if I failed to upstage her, I would look ridiculous—and possibly lose favor with my fellow Knights.

I had to pull this off.

I took a deep breath as several drones drew near and then stopped, hovering in various positions around me and the man now heading right for me, the pipe in his hand raised. In the next pond over, where Dylan had thrown the other man, I could hear the sound of sloshing, signaling that he was approaching the edge as well. It was now or never.

I waited as the man closed in, and then sidestepped the inevitable blow, wrapping my arm under and around his shoulder and armpit. I kicked off the ground, using him for leverage to swing my legs up, and catching his neck and shoulder in a lock between my thighs. Put off balance by my sudden weight, he began to topple over, but I controlled his fall, guiding it with a twist of my hips. I had practiced the move a hundred times, and all it took was muscle memory for me to let him go before the spin caught up to me. I landed on one knee with a hand braced on the ground, and a second later, water crashed down on me—a sign that I had not only thrown him into the water, but also hit his partner with him. Just like I had intended.

I stood up, whirled my baton for good measure, and then threw it in the direction of the splash without even bothering to look to see where exactly the targets were.

It was a theatrical move, and one that had my heart pounding a steady drumline of panic across the inside of my ribs. If my baton didn't hit within a few feet of them, it was unlikely that they would be knocked out by the electrical surge, even though they were encased in water. The charge would dissipate in force, and they would only be mildly affected.

I, on the other hand, would look like an idiot for not bothering to check to see where the targets were in the first place. But I had already committed to this stupid showboat move, and I needed it to work.

The baton hit a second later, two feet away from where the two men were beginning to break free, and jagged blue lines of electricity shot from it, arcing out like spider webs over the water. Lines of blue light shot into the two men, and they immediately seized up, violently twitching and shaking as the sharp *pzzt* of energy filled the air.

Seconds later, it ended, and they both relaxed back into the water, two bands I hadn't noticed around their arms lighting up with a bright yellow color. I realized those were their elimination bands—and that I had knocked the two men out.

But I couldn't dwell on it; I needed to demonstrate that I was still in command while the drones were on me. Besides, taking out two men with one shot was just the first thing I had planned to do to thwart Dylan's attempt to exert control. Which meant I needed to keep moving.

"Maddox, baton," I said, holding out my hand without bothering to look at her. I felt the heavy weight of it slap into my palm, and curled my fist around it. "Get those two men out, and grab my baton while you're at it. Make sure the Cog is guarded."

Then I moved forward at a run, heading directly for where Dylan was locked in combat with the last two men, her back to me. She was holding her own for the moment, but the men were clearly Knights, given how well they were using the pipes they were wielding. Pipes they had managed to insulate using rags, making any chance of Dylan shocking them through one impossible.

Dylan was keeping up with them, her movements impossibly smooth and perfectly timed, but that was all she could seem to do: keep up with them. She couldn't gain any ground, though she wasn't losing any either.

For a second, I considered pulling to a stop and letting it play out, but that would be viewed for what it was—a petty attempt to show Dylan in a bad light. Whether or not she was attempting a coup on me was irrelevant to the other Knights. If I just left her there to fight on her own, I would be seen as the bad guy, and I couldn't allow that.

But I could get revenge in other ways.

I smiled as I raced directly for her body, my mind already spinning on how I would do this. I planted my first foot on the back of her thigh, where I could tell her stance was the strongest, and then the second on her shoulder, using my momentum and the height she was giving me as I literally ran up her back to carry me over the heads of the two attackers in a forward flip. I landed firmly on both feet, and then jammed my baton into the back of the first man, expending the charge before his face was fully turned toward me.

He froze up, trembling under the force of several thousand

volts of electricity, and then collapsed to the ground, sliding off to one side.

I was already lashing out with a short, brutal kick to the back of the second man's knee as the first man fell, forcing it to fold up under him. I withdrew my baton long enough to generate another charge, and then tapped him lightly on the arm with the baton, expending it. Like the first man, he seized up violently, and then tumbled off the opposite side, landing a few seconds later in the next terrace below with a splash, leaving me and Dylan standing face-to-face.

"Good job," I said with a smile, sliding Maddox's baton into my belt loop.

Dylan frowned. "Good job, I just—"

"Did exactly what you promised you would do," I said, clapping her on the shoulder. She gave me a confused look, and I smiled even more deeply, baring my teeth. Inside, I was angry, livid, and raw that she would smile in my face one second and then stab me in the back the next, but on the outside, I maintained my pleasant façade, trying to exude leadership abilities.

Dylan opened her mouth, clearly about to set the record straight on what exactly she had done (and how she had saved us), but then looked around and noticed the drones that were now hovering around us in a little dome of viewership. Her eyes drifted back down to me, and I saw realization dawn in them.

I expected anger to follow, but instead, she smiled, and her gaze grew almost respectful. "Clever," she said, motioning up to the cameras, but keeping her voice pitched soft and low, for my ears only. "I take it not all the attention was on my fight?"

I smiled. "Some of it was, I'm sure. Especially the part where you jumped over me. But I think they got the part where I jumped over you, too, so that makes us almost even. Now, if you'll excuse me, there's a kid over there who is trapped in some mud, and I was in the middle of helping him before we were rudely interrupted."

A flurry of emotions crossed over her face, but the one she settled on was confusion. "You're going back for the kid? What for? We wasted..." She glanced down at her indicator and frowned. "Yeesh, we've already lost ten minutes! That means only twenty are left!"

"Yes, I can do the math," I said wryly. "But I'm not arguing with you about this. I'm in charge, and you agreed to be a team player. Either be a team player, or take over *successfully* next time."

It wasn't my best repartee, but it apparently stung, because she blinked as if I had slapped her, and then gave me another appraising look. I ignored both, turning around and moving over to where the boy was still waiting, half sunk in the muddy water.

I passed by Maddox and Eric, who were bent, checking one of the unconscious men, and then stepped over the other man, whom Leo had just finished pushing out of the water. I stopped and gave Leo a hand up the steep bank, then moved over to the next pool and the boy.

"All right, kid," I said, carefully repositioning myself on the edge and reaching out to him. "Just hold on tight and don't let go."

The boy nodded, his small hands already stretching out to grab my forearms with surprising strength. I began to tug him forward, and wound up having to put every muscle into it, because the mud wasn't letting him go.

Eventually, he slid free with a slick, suctioning sound, and I carefully dragged him toward me and hauled him up, indifferent to the mud he was now depositing on my uniform. I set him up on the ridge separating the pools, and then climbed out after him.

CHAPTER 24

"You okay?" I asked, kneeling down to wipe the slick brown mud off my hands.

He beamed up at me, his eyes sparkling. "Yes, thank you! I'd been in there for an hour." It was possibly not a lie; it had taken us thirty minutes to get ready, and I'd bet the actors were in place long before we even reached the greenery.

"Well, you get home to your parents, and we'll just—"

"You said you were here to fix something?" he asked, stopping me mid-turn.

I looked back at him, giving him a considering look. "What if we were?" I asked cautiously. While children had sometimes been used to lure Knights into traps, they had also played a critical role in helping the Knights during Requiem Day, dispatching messages between units and moving through the levels as scouts for the Knights. If he wasn't a lure—which I really didn't believe he had been—I had every reason to believe that this particular child actor was a plant representing something else. Help.

The boy puffed up his chest and stuck his thumb into it. "Because I know where the *real* damaged relay is. And I can show you the fastest way there."

I smiled, amused by the proud way in which he said it, and confused by the way he said "real". "What do you mean, 'real'?"

"I heard a few of the meaner guys say that they had jacked the system and modified the location of the damaged relay to a different one, so that they could set a trap for whoever came to fix it. But I know where the real damaged place is, and I can take you there."

I bit my lip, thinking. What he was saying lined up with multiple accounts from Requiem Day, in which organized gangs had sent false repair signals and then jumped anyone trying to work and repair the Tower, and stolen their supplies. I had no doubt the officials would give Eric incomplete information so that he would be just as much in the dark as the rest of us, so chances were that he was leading us to what he *thought* was the right location. What any Cog would deem the right location, had the officials not staged a false report to try to lure us into a trap. It would be on us to figure it out for ourselves, hence the role of the boy.

It tracked with what I knew of Requiem Day, and the odds were with us that the kid was there to help save us time. We'd probably need another ten minutes to get to the island where Eric thought the damaged relay was, with another five to implement any plan for a fight. Once the fight was over, we'd only have five minutes to input the damaged relay. But if the boy was right, and we got to Eric's island only to discover that the damaged relay was actually in a different location, we'd lose for sure.

"Do you really remember where it is? And can you really show it to us?" I asked him.

"Oh, sure!" he said, jumping up and down excitedly. "You saved me, so I should help you with your mission, right?"

"Liana?" Dylan called from behind me. "Can I have a word with you?"

I ignored her for a second. I knew that she was going to warn me to walk away and just continue on our mission, but I had to follow my gut instinct—which told me that the test designers would put a boy in there to be rescued, if only to give those who stopped and helped him an added bonus for doing the right thing.

Regardless, I felt it was the right call, so I gave him a little nod. "I'd love it if you could show us where that damaged relay is," I told him. "Lead the way."

The boy smiled and slipped past me, darting around Leo,

Maddox, Eric, and Dylan. "Follow me!" he said excitedly, his bare feet padding lightly over the earthen ground. "And hurry up—there are tons of idiots just like those running around! We have to be careful."

"I'll say," Dylan muttered under her breath—though not softly enough that I would miss it. I gave her a look, arching an eyebrow, and she rolled her eyes. "You do realize this could be a trap, right? Something to draw us off track or mislead us? We could waste precious minutes following the kid, and for what? Some nebulous promise that he knew where to find what we were looking for? We already know where we are going—your little Cog friend told you! He even pointed it out. We should go there, not follow this kid!"

I waited for her to stop speaking, and then looked over at Maddox and Leo. "Boy or Eric's place?"

"I vote boy," Leo said. "I suspect he is a smaller challenge, one that is meant to compensate us for the time we wasted on rescuing him."

"I vote the boy because I don't like Dylan," Maddox said sweetly next to him, raking the other girl with yet another disdainful look. "She and I clearly have different opinions of what constitutes a team player."

I sighed, and then looked at Dylan. "We voted; we're going. Does that work for you?"

Dylan's mouth tightened in disapproval, but she nodded and stepped to one side, letting me pass.

It was something, at the very least.

But then again, so was she.

25

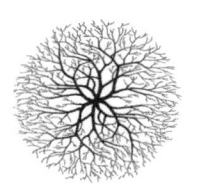

The boy led us quickly to a metallic rope bridge that connected to one of the small, manmade islands in the middle of the tank. "It's that one right there," he said, pointing at it.

"How do you know?" Dylan asked sharply.

"Because I saw it," the boy said snidely, giving her a dirty look.

I wasn't sure if that look was because he could tell that she didn't like him, or if it was because he was leading us into a trap—but something told me it was the former, rather than the latter. I checked my indicator and saw that we'd lost another seven minutes getting down here. Which meant we only had thirteen minutes left before we failed the challenge.

"In that tube thing there. The side is ripped open, and a blue crystal thingy is inside, all cracked and black and sparking something fierce."

"That sounds like what Zoe described," Eric whispered from

just behind me. "The part I brought with me is to replace the crystal, so it'll only take me a minute or two to swap it out."

I bit my lip. Eric was a Hand, not a Cog, but had changed departments in order to be closer to Zoe. I didn't doubt his skills, but he had only been in the department for a short time. I knew they would've instructed him on exactly what to do, yet we still had to get across the water first, and if he couldn't remember what to do...

I couldn't think like that. Eric knew what was at stake; he would've recognized the importance of it as soon as the officials called him in this morning. Even if he hadn't known he was going to be paired with our team, he would've paid close attention, just in case. I had to have faith in him.

And trust in the fact that he couldn't—wouldn't—let Zoe down. Because if he did, she'd never stop teasing him.

"What do you think?" I asked him. "Do you think we should believe the kid?"

Eric hesitated. "I honestly don't know," he admitted. "There's every chance the boy is being honest and the damaged relay is over there, but if it's a distraction, we won't be able to make it to the location I was given by the officials. If we head there now, we risk *that* one being the distraction. It's a crap shoot either way."

I heard Dylan *tsk* and mutter something, but ignored it and looked back at the boy. I had followed him this far, and I needed to trust that instinct. I couldn't second guess myself now. "Thank you," I told him. "Now go find your parents, and stay safe, okay?"

"Okay!" he said in a chipper voice. "Good luck on the challenge!"

I smiled as the child broke character, and watched as he scampered off, heading back up a nearby set of stairs. I watched him go for a second and then turned back to the bridge in front of us. Woven iron handrails lined the metallic bridge, while a series of sliding planks sat right on top of the water. We wouldn't be passing over it quietly—but we didn't have any other choice. A check of the clock on my indicator revealed that we now had only eleven minutes to go.

We didn't have any time to waste. If this was a misdirect, then we were already screwed—and even if it wasn't, odds were there were more obstacles coming, and they would be designed to slow us down.

"Maddox and Grey, you take point. Your job is to get Eric to the power relay, find out whether it's damaged, and help him repair it. Dylan and I will run the perimeter and deal with anything that comes up while you are working."

I caught movement from the corner of my eye and saw Dylan giving me a quizzical look, and was fairly certain I had caught her off guard by assigning her to work with me, especially after the stunt she had pulled earlier. I was well within my rights to leave her posted at the mouth of the bridge, to cover our crossing, but I wasn't going to do that. I wanted us to win the challenge, and using her as a sacrifice to help defend any attack that would impede us getting across the bridge would only buy us time—and not very much of it. She was a much better tool by my side, and I would be a pretty crappy leader if I just left her behind to guard our rear.

"Are you sure?" Maddox asked, and I canted my head toward her.

"I am," I informed her, giving her a reassuring nod to let her know that I realized it was risky. If Dylan was working for a legacy group—and she might be, even if we didn't know for sure—then being alone with her put me at risk. She might try to kill me while I was by myself.

But hey, if she attacked me, it would be a clear sign she was working for a legacy group, as attacking a team member was considered deeply dishonorable. And hey, I might finally have a lead on who my enemy was, and what they wanted. I'd just have to beat Dylan in a fight—and make sure she didn't die or escape, because we'd want to question her about it.

"Let's get moving."

The doubt on Maddox's face was only rivaled by the hurt confusion on Leo's, and I realized I had accidently insulted him by not asking *him* to fight with me. But I didn't have time to soothe all the hurt feelings right then and there—time was rapidly running out. I made a little motion, tapping my watch, and Maddox rolled her eyes and began to move, taking point as they traveled over the bridge.

Water sloshed under it with her first step, and suddenly the bridge swayed slightly, dipping down. Maddox grabbed the woven metal strands that made the handrail in a death grip and caught her balance.

"Are you okay?" Leo asked.

"I'm fine," she said shakily. "It's just... Take it slow. It is a little off-putting at first. Oh, and if I go in, come rescue me. I can't swim."

I bit back a laugh at the way she announced that she couldn't swim, and watched as she took another staggering step, the bridge swinging slightly to the right as her newly placed weight changed the balance. It took her a few steps, but then she managed to catch a rhythm, and after studying it for a few seconds, I pointed it out to the others.

"Look at how she's walking," I said, pointing at her. "Keep your legs spread wide, and it won't shift back and forth as much when you're stepping forward."

"Got it," Eric said with a nod, sliding his palms onto the

woven handrails. He exhaled a nervous breath, and then pulled himself forward, stepping onto the bridge. I held my breath, nervous for my friend. The bridge swayed and creaked ominously, and both he and Maddox froze as it swung out, the water sloshing over the edge.

My breath caught in my throat, but the bridge stilled quickly, much to my relief. Maddox and Eric were still for a few seconds more, and then slowly began to move forward, seeming to catch a rhythm with each other.

"All right, Grey," I breathed, once Eric had gotten a bit farther. I checked my watch. We'd lost another minute, and were now down to ten minutes. At this rate, we'd clock another three before we were all across the bridge. "Go ahead."

Leo stepped up to the edge of the bridge and ran his fingertips lightly over the woven strands of the railing. He stood stock still for a second, and then slowly began to shift his weight back and forth, mimicking Maddox and Eric's footsteps. Moments later, he stepped forward.

The bridge barely seemed to register his weight as he slid seamlessly into the rhythm. I gaped, amazed that he had been able to move so gracefully onto it. Even with his heightened reflexes, he was still inside of Grey's body. The transition had been flawless, and I knew Dylan's and mine would be anything but. It was intimidating. And not only to me.

"Did you know he could do that?" Dylan asked, her voice filled with awe.

I chuckled. "Yeah, Grey's full of fun little surprises. You're up next."

She gave me an incredulous look. "After that? You trying to make me look bad?"

"Absolutely," I told her, unapologetically. "It'll only make me look good by comparison. Not to mention, I have this weird thing about the leaders taking up the rear when there's the potential for attack from behind. I like to be on hand, just in case."

She chuckled. "Fair enough. Just so long as you understand that I'll be coming up with ways to return the favor tomorrow."

I leveled an even look at her and gave her my best bare-toothed smile. "Just so long as you understand that I'll be looking for ways to repay what I owe you for that little stunt earlier."

She gave me a feline smile that brought out her dimples, and then moved up to the bridge. Another glance at my watch told me we had lost another minute, and I exhaled, feeling the press of time. At least Maddox was almost two thirds of the way across now, making good speed.

Dylan eyed the group and the bridge for several long heartbeats, then slid onto it. Her movements weren't nearly as graceful as Leo's, so the bridge tilted roughly to the right, causing the left side to come out of the water. Maddox let out a yelp of surprise, and Eric managed to catch himself before slipping in, while Leo remained motionless and perfectly balanced. I rushed forward, suddenly concerned that it was going to tip over. If it did, and Maddox and Eric went into the water, we would lose precious time fishing them out—and would run the risk of also losing the replacement part that Eric was transporting.

But Dylan quickly compensated by planting her foot on the left side of the bridge and pushing. The bridge splashed down and rocked back and forth for a second or two, before finally settling. "Careful, Liana," she said as she slowly began to move forward. "The first step is a doozy."

A surprised laugh escaped me, but I quickly cut it off, angry at myself for finding her humorous. She had unapologetically tried to overshadow me and take control of my team in this challenge, and yet, I couldn't help but like her for it a little bit. At

CHAPTER 25

least she was straightforward in her attempts to win, if a little heavy handed.

Okay, *extremely* heavy handed, but I couldn't condemn her for being competitive.

I shook it off and watched as she slowly made her way across, letting the gap between us grow some. The bridge was easily offset by weight, and I got the impression, by how much the slats that made up the walkway dipped under each person's weight, that if we crowded too closely together, the walkway would completely sink.

My skin crawled, telling me it was time to go, but I waited for a few more precious seconds, not wanting to rush it due to my impatience. Once enough distance had stretched between us, I swallowed the excess saliva in my mouth and stepped up to the edge, placing my hands on the railings. I watched the movements of the bridge, focusing on the way it swayed back and forth.

My heart thudded hard against my ribs as I realized that I could pitch us all in if I put too much weight on one side or the other, and then I found a sliver of confidence and slid onto the bridge. I was ready for it as it started to swing too far to the right with my first step, and quickly planted my other foot down a few feet forward, shifting some of my weight immediately over to it.

The bridge rocked in place for a second before settling down and shifting slightly to the left. I leaned into it as it did, using the swing to move my right foot forward, and the bridge swayed back that way as my own weight shifted. It took a bit of getting used to, but within moments we were all moving steadily along in unison.

I heard Maddox shout when she reached the shore, but couldn't celebrate, as I was still only a quarter of the way there. The bridge was tricky, and required every ounce of my concentration to cross. If this was an actual bridge and not one designed with the challenge in mind, I had a newfound respect for the Hands who could cross it, and had no doubt that they could do it way faster than our snail's pace.

I was just checking my indicator, which showed me that we'd lost yet another minute, leaving only a precious few remaining, when one of the handrails under my hand suddenly fell away, landing in the dark water with a splash. I froze, and seconds later the other one followed, leaving us perched perilously on swinging metal slats—which were slowly beginning to sink into the water. It wouldn't sink completely, of course—it was still anchored on both ends.

But the water was beginning to come over the edges as our weight dragged it down, and if the flexible metal platform tipped, we'd all be in the water.

I immediately began looking around, taking great pains not to shift my weight too much while I searched for what could've made the handrails fall, and saw a group of men and women—about six strong—standing at the edge of the bridge back from where we'd come from, a cutter in one man's hands.

"Hello there!" a middle-aged woman called cheerfully, moving up to the bank. "You'll give us your food and weapons now, or we'll cut the rest of the bridge and then fish you out of the water. The choice is yours."

I licked my lips, eyeing the group. They were only thirty feet behind me, and while I couldn't run that distance before the cutter ate through the narrow metal planks, I could probably swim there before they finished cutting. If I could do that, I would buy Maddox and Leo enough time to get Eric to the island and to the damaged relay. I shot a glance over my shoulder to see how far Eric and Leo were from the island. Eric was another forty feet away, give or take, and a furtive look at my watch told me we had seven minutes left to repair the relay—or we would lose.

For once, I wasn't sure I had time to negotiate.

Tension curled out from me, and I said, in a soft voice over my shoulder, "Dylan, when I dive into the water, I want you to charge them. Tell the others to move on without us."

"You want us to hold our own against six people?" Dylan asked, her voice a harsh whisper.

"You have ten seconds, or else we start cutting!" the woman called, resting her hands on her hips. "You got a lot of nice stuff that I know really shouldn't get wet, but I'm willing to risk it if you are!"

"Stop arguing with me and do it, Dylan," I muttered. "We don't have a lot of time." Then, in a louder voice, I said. "All right, you win. We'll throw over all our stuff! Just let us come back over to you."

As I spoke, I slowly started making my way toward them, using my forward momentum to mirror the movements of my friends, who were moving away from me at the same time. It was more difficult without the handrails, but now that the walkway was slightly submerged, it gave it some stability. My hands were raised, partially to show that I was harmless, and partially to keep my balance. I knew they wouldn't buy my apparent surrender—this was a challenge, after all—but they would play the part of Requiem Day survivors and pretend to accept it before I made my move.

"Toss the baton to me," the woman shouted when I was close enough. I slid it out of the loop on my belt, and then tossed it—badly. I intentionally lobbed it just shy of the bridge and land, so that it landed in the water a few feet from the shore with wet splash.

Luckily, batons floated, and sure enough, the woman

decided to go for it. It made sense that she would: batons were coveted weapons during that time, which was why Knights were attacked, nine times out of ten. As soon as she started reaching for it, I took two leaping steps forward and dove into the water, bringing my hands together over my head before I hit.

The water wasn't cold, but there was a lot of it, and my uniform and boots immediately became weights that threatened to drag me down into the depths of the tank. I ignored them, holding my breath and kicking for the shore, but making sure I stayed deep under the water.

Because it was a tank, there was no easy shoreline; it was a flat cube on all sides, which meant I could come up right underneath the edge of the bit of land they were standing on and no one would see me—if I was deep enough. I clawed my way up the side of the tank when I encountered the flat edge of it, making for the surface. I kicked hard as I saw the bright reflection of light from above, and emerged in an explosion of water, grabbing fistfuls of grass and dirt and pulling myself quickly up to my feet.

Dylan was already rushing them from the bridge, her baton flying as she fought off the two men at the mouth of it, the bridge swaying ominously under the rapidly shifting weight of the fight. A quick check farther behind her showed me that Eric had reached the island, and Leo was racing across the bridge toward them, moving at a speed I couldn't believe was possible. The sight bolstered me; I knew Maddox and Leo would get Eric to the relay. I'd know soon enough if it was the right one or not, and silently sent another prayer of hope that I had made the right call in trusting the boy.

I wouldn't find out until the end of the challenge, at this rate.

A shadow cut across my eyes then, and I turned to see two people—a man and a woman—break from the group and head toward me, the man already reaching up to push me back into the water.

I stepped to one side and grabbed his arm, using his own momentum to propel him past me and into the water with a splash that hit the back of my head. I swiped my face clean, and then dove to the right to avoid the woman's kick. She pressed the attack, charging, and I dove again, this time into a more controlled roll—one that ended with my feet under me.

I rose in a fluid motion, and then, in a reaction borne from too many sparring matches in the Academy, I spun and kicked out, anticipating the woman attacking me from behind.

Sure enough, I felt a solid impact as my foot hit her, and she fell down, grabbing at her jaw. I stalked up to her, hauled her up, and tossed her into the water, her confusion from being kicked in the face perfectly taken advantage of.

The woman who was their leader had just finished grabbing my baton out of the water, and spun around and looked at me, her hand and arm dripping wet. "You think you've won, but you haven't," she sneered. Then she clicked the baton on.

Some notes about the baton. It was completely waterproof, and could work in and out of the water. However, with water, the general rules of conductivity applied, which meant that when the woman turned it on, with her arm and hand still slick from getting it out of the tank, the charge immediately went into *her*, following the path of the water dripping down her arm.

There was a sharp blue pop, and then the woman went flying backward, as if someone had jerked her away by the waist, using a rope. She smacked into one of the only men still standing, and just like that, the fight was over.

I rushed over to remove my baton from the woman's stiff fingers, and quickly checked her pulse to make sure her heart hadn't stopped. I didn't think it would have, but one could never be sure.

As soon as I was certain that she was still alive, I collected my baton, not bothering to dry it, as I was dripping wet, and stood up and looked at Dylan, who was waiting for me on the bridge.

"Good job," she said, and I looked behind me. Only the woman was unconscious, but the two people in the water were still fishing themselves out, while the man who had been hit by the woman was lying down, dazed and confused.

"Thanks," I said. "You, too. Do you think we have time to—"

A chime sounded, and Scipio's voice filled the cavernous space. "Congratulations to Liana Castell and team! Liana has earned the deed name of Wayfinder for her excellent leadership skills, while Dylan Chase has earned the deed name of Pathmaker. Maddox Kerrin and Grey Farmless have been given the names of Enforcer. Congratulations, and please go back to the entrance of Greenery 2 to return your equipment to the officials. The Tourney will resume tomorrow, at nine a.m. See you then, candidates."

I looked at Dylan and then across the bridge to where Maddox, Leo, and Eric were emerging from the island.

"Hey, Liana!" Eric said, his voice booming and chest inflating. "Guess what I just did in under a minute? Zoe's going to be so mad!"

I chuckled and waved my hand at him, encouraging them all to come back over.

"So, it looks like you were right," Dylan said, folding her arms over her chest. "I guess listening to that boy paid off."

"No, knowing my history about Requiem Day paid off," I replied, not wanting her to attribute my win solely to luck.

Dylan gave me a crooked smile, but ignored my retort.

CHAPTER 25

"Since I'll be acting as the leader for the next challenge, I was hoping that you and your team would run some drills with me, so you and they can get familiar with my command style."

I licked my lips. My initial instinct was to say no, but if word got out that I'd denied another candidate who wanted to be Champion the chance to get familiar with her team and their abilities, it could hurt my popularity with the Knights themselves. The drones were still watching us—and would continue to do so until we left the greenery. If they saw me deny her this... Well, it would be broadcast everywhere within an hour.

I looked back at my friends as they carefully picked their way across the bridge, and knew that they weren't going to be happy about this.

But it was better than the alternative.

"Sure," I said with a nod. "I'll let the others know, and we'll get to work."

Dylan smiled, clearly pleased. "Great. And... thanks, Liana. It's pretty awesome that you get the competition aspect of things. I'm really looking forward to the challenge of beating you."

I arched an eyebrow, but didn't rise to the bait. I still wasn't sure what game Dylan was playing, but whatever it was, it had me slightly unnerved. I just hoped that I managed to outsmart her, no matter what she had in store.

Because if it came to a straight-up fight, I was quite certain she had me beat.

26

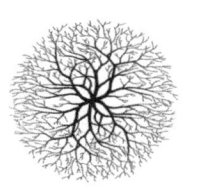

I had expected another sleepless night, but to my surprise, I closed my eyes when I got in bed and didn't open them again until my alarm started to chirp on my wrist—the next morning. In fact, getting so much sleep left me feeling slightly disoriented, and it took me several seconds to remember exactly what had happened yesterday.

And what was set to happen *today*. Namely, that it was Dylan's turn to be in charge, and my turn to follow. After yesterday, that was going to be more difficult than it sounded. Not that Dylan was a bad leader, per se; she just had an aggressiveness that put me on edge. She preferred to handle things through combat, and had trained us rigorously in that regard.

What was worse, she didn't seem to have time for anyone's ideas save her own. In the challenges she ran us through, if any of us offered an idea, she had immediately dismissed it. Never rudely, and never without reasoning, but I noticed it nonetheless, and I wasn't the only one. Maddox had been grumbling about it all through the late dinner we'd had, and kept going right up until I closed my door to get some much-needed rest.

Sighing, I ran a hand over my face, scraping away the urge to ignore all of my problems for more sleep, and then got out of bed, determined not to concern myself with my Dylan difficulties until I was firmly ensconced in the shower stall of my bathroom, with scalding hot water roiling over me, easing the tension that had accumulated in my muscles.

The hot water did its job in helping to release some of my stress, and as I began to scrub myself clean, I turned my mind back to Dylan.

Considering yesterday's training session, I had every chance of seizing leadership during the next challenge as soon as she acted too aggressively (which would undoubtedly be sooner rather than later), but a part of me wondered if I should. Dylan wasn't terrible; she just had a style of leadership that didn't jive with my own. And there were things she did that had been good, like teaching us all some takedowns that I had never seen before, as well as showing us a few lasso moves using our lashes. Each bit of information she had given us had cost her in terms of an advantage over me, but she didn't complain, gripe, or even bring it up.

I kept flip-flopping about whether she had done so out of a sense of nobility or in her own self-interest, and it kept me from making a decision on what exactly to do. On the one hand, her leadership style was flawed, and as long as Leo and Maddox went along with what I said, I'd be able to take control at the first mistake she made.

On the other... didn't she deserve a fair shake, if only for the fact that it wasn't her fault she was stuck on my team?

CHAPTER 26

I knew what everyone else would say—I even knew what I *should* say—but it still left me twisted up inside, like everything below my chest was slowly tying up into a giant knot that seemed to contain every nerve ending in my body. I didn't like the idea of planning to steal the leadership position from Dylan, no matter who or what she was. It was unfair, and wouldn't give the Knights in the Tourney an opportunity to see who exactly she was as a leader.

Then I got soap in my eye, and had to laugh at the ridiculous reminder that life wasn't fair. It wasn't fair to me, and it certainly wasn't fair to her.

No. Life was decidedly *unfair*, and it fell on us to make it fair. In fact, that was what rules were all about, right?

Scipio had certainly made them very clear: I could steal command out from under her, and there would be nothing she could do about it, especially if I thought her course of action was foolhardy. But if I walked in there and took command from her without giving her a chance, it would potentially hurt my chances with the Knights themselves.

Or worse, if she managed to stop me from wresting control, like I had with her yesterday, it would make me look like a fool in front of them, thus weakening my chances of winning. It was a risk if I did and a risk if I didn't, and half of me just wanted to walk away before we even got there.

And then I remembered what was at stake—namely the continued existence of the Tower—and the vicious circle began all over again.

Thank Scipio we only had six minutes for a shower. I ran out of water long before the question could drive me insane, and I quickly busied myself with drying off before leaving the bathroom.

When I emerged in a cloud of steam, I was immediately

greeted with the scent of breakfast. It filled the hall, making my mouth water, though I managed to ignore the sudden sharp yowl of my stomach and continue to the bedroom.

I wished I could remember who had volunteered to cook this morning, but only dinner followed by a brief net transmission with Tian really stood out from the foggy recesses of my memory. I quickly entered my room, grabbing a fresh uniform.

As I did, my mind drifted back to my conversation with Tian from the night before. She had nothing really to report, save that Rose had been moving them around a lot, and that there was no update as to who Rose's mysterious target might be, or when the attack might possibly occur.

I was worried about Tian's safety with the sentinel, and hated the fact that there was nothing we could do to help her at the moment. Scipio help me, I was really beginning to hate the Tourney.

I emerged several minutes later, uniform in place and bracelet around my wrist. Leo and Maddox were already in the shared living area, several plates of steaming hot food in place on the low table. Both were eating, but paused as I entered, looking up at me expectantly.

"Hey," Maddox said around a mouthful of food. "How'd you sleep?"

I frowned. "Surprisingly good. You?"

She bit her lip. "Not as good, but thanks for asking. You just missed Quess, though. He ran off early this morning to repair a few of the drones before today's challenge."

"Is he still mad at me?"

Maddox's mouth worked as she looked down at the table, and I realized I had upset her with the question. The three of us hadn't really talked since our fight before being reunited with Tian, and while Maddox had come through for us yesterday (not that I had doubted she would), things weren't exactly right between us. There was a tension—almost like someone holding their breath, waiting to see what would happen or who would speak first.

"You know what?" I said, sitting down in a free chair and picking up a plate. "Just forget I said anything, okay?"

"No, I don't want to do that," she said, sighing and setting her fork down with a sharp click. "Look, Liana, Quess and I talked about it, and you were right. I mean, we knew you were right even then, but Quess was worried about Tian, and I..." She trailed off and looked to one side, her eyes growing distant and sad. "Well, let's just say that I know that I'm pretty screwed up right now, and I've got... a lot of anger inside of me about what happened. But you and Quess and everyone are right, and I promise that as soon as the Tourney is over, I'll go to the Medica and get some help."

"Really?" I asked, looking up at her. I was surprised and pleased by her change of heart, but it threw me off. Nobody came to a realization *that* quickly. "What changed your mind?"

She looked down and away before answering. "Quess." She sighed and shook her head, picking at some peppers on her plate before setting her fork back down with a click. "He was angry, yes, but he knew he wasn't angry with you. I... I didn't know that. I couldn't see that. I was so furious and angry that I wanted to walk out the door, and when he told me I could do it without him, I..." She paused again, her face filling with sorrow as her voice became ragged and hoarse. "I actually considered it. Just for a second."

I wasn't surprised by her words, but they made my heart ache nonetheless. And I couldn't blame her for wanting to walk away after everything she had been through—she had experienced not one, but *several* traumatic events.

A tear dropped down her cheek, and she scrubbed it off before sucking in a deep breath. "That's when I knew that I needed help. I would never do that... before. I'm so, so sorry, Liana."

Her voice broke on my name, and before I could stop myself, I threw my arms around her and hugged her close. "It's okay, Maddox," I breathed, giving her a squeeze. To my surprise, she hugged me back. I knew how hard it was to apologize, let alone admit to my own mistakes, and I appreciated that to no end. Even if there wasn't anything for her to apologize for. She was dealing with a lot, and it took guts for her to face it. All I cared about was that she was taking care of herself.

"It really is okay, Maddox," I repeated, slowly pulling back from the hug. "I'm just glad that you didn't decide to leave."

She scoffed and took a big bite of toast. "As if I could do that. You idiots have become family, whether I like it or not." She smiled then, and I was beyond elated to see that some of it touched her eyes. "And I guess I kind of like it. Oh, and give Quess a little bit of time. You hurt his feelings by giving him that ultimatum, so he's sitting on his apology until some of his butt-hurt passes."

I chuckled, and then nodded. "Fair enough. How are you all feeling about today and what's about to happen?"

It was a rapid change of topics, but we hadn't really talked about what our plan would be for dealing with Dylan being in charge for this round of the Tourney, and our time was running short. We had to report to the arena soon, and I needed to see how they were feeling about following Dylan, and the challenge ahead—a challenge we desperately needed to win if I wanted any chance of becoming Champion. I wanted them to at least try to give Dylan a chance, if only to keep arguments down to a minimum in case the challenge was timed.

CHAPTER 26

"Yeah, what's about to happen is that we're going to completely ignore Dylan and follow your lead," Maddox said.

"I already said that isn't a wise idea," Leo said, finally breaking the silence he had adopted during my exchange with Maddox. "If Liana fails to assert command, much like Dylan did yesterday, then she will only make a fool of herself. Besides, Scipio suggested that she has to prove that she can follow as well as lead, and not many of the leaders are doing that! It could be a viable strategy to show that she follows the letter of the law—I think many of the older Knights would find that appealing, given the demographics I've been studying."

"Nobody cares about that!" Maddox retorted. "If she falls into the background, people will forget about her. Not to mention, if we let Dylan actually lead, we're going to lose this challenge!"

"We don't know that, and Liana can keep herself in the public eye by performing stunts like she did yesterday for the drones!"

I watched the exchange between them for a moment, smiling ruefully as they parroted some of the exact concerns I'd had in the shower, and then cleared my throat, politely interrupting them.

"Look, I know you don't want me to say this, but if I'm really honest with you guys, I can't seem to make up my mind about what to do. A part of me wants to wait for a good moment and try to steal command, but Leo has a point: if I fail, it could cost me the challenge. But... I also feel a little bad for Dylan. She got handed a pretty raw deal—"

"Providing she isn't in bed with our enemies," Maddox scoffed haughtily, folding her arms across her chest.

I gave her a look, my mouth still open to speak, and then nodded. "Providing that," I amended, before continuing.

"Regardless, I'm not sure I'm completely comfortable plotting to pull the rug out from under her, so to speak."

"Are you kidding?" Maddox sputtered, raising an eyebrow. "Liana, *you* are the one who said you wanted to be Champion. To prevent the evil legacy group from getting another foothold on the council. To help us figure out a way to escape! And to keep Lacey and Strum from killing us all! And now you're going to balk at taking advantage of the rule changes to take command?"

I stared at her, not fully able to meet her eyes. She was right, and I knew it. But at the same time, something inside me still refused to bend: my integrity. Planning to do something illegal that would save thousands of lives was one thing. Doing this, even if it was totally within the rules, left a bad taste in my mouth.

"Look, I know you don't like it, but I just can't do it. If she does something that I think is going to lose us the challenge, then yes, I will step in. But I can't plan for it. I know that doesn't make a lot of sense, but—"

Maddox laughed, a deep, rich sound that cut me off, and I looked over at her to see a broad smile filled with mirth. "Oh, in that case," she said with a feline smile, "I'll bet you one day's rations that Liana will step in within five minutes." She turned to Leo as she said that, her green eyes blazing.

He cocked his head at her and then shook his head. "No bet," he said after a moment. "I calculate the odds of Liana having to step in will be highest during the first two minutes."

I fought back a smile. They either thought I couldn't restrain myself, or that Dylan would make mistakes right from the get-go, and I was certain that it was the latter, not the former. "You guys are mean," I said, picking up a fork and finally taking a bite of food from one of the plates, without even bothering to transfer it to my own. "Dylan just has a different style than I do."

Maddox arched an eyebrow, looking highly doubtful, and Leo took an opportunity to take another piece of toast while studiously avoiding eye contact. I laughed again, and shook my head. "Just be nice."

Maddox smiled ruefully. "Fine. But a girl can dream about knocking Dylan down a peg or two, right?"

I grinned and shook my head. "Absolutely."

Half an hour later we were back in the small room, watching Scipio's face fill the screen. Dylan stood next to me, her eyes completely focused on his ghostly image, her face held in rapt attention as she listened to what he was saying.

I didn't need to pay attention. Once he had said "Challenge of the Gate," I had tuned out. I had studied this particular challenge extensively throughout my time in the Academy, and knew everything there was to know about it. The six remaining teams would be combined into two larger teams of twelve. One team would be given the task of attacking the "gate," as if they were assaulting an undoc hideout, while the other team would be defending it, their idea being that they were defending the Tower from outside invaders.

Not that there were any, of course. But it was one of the main duties of the Knights, handed down from the very beginning of the department, and the challenge was tradition. Each side would be given thirty minutes to plan their assault or defense, and we were allowed to use anything we could salvage from around the area we were dropped into, to improve either our attacks or defenses accordingly. Full-on combat against our enemies would be authorized.

Whichever team managed to achieve their objective would make up the candidates for the final challenge.

Instead of paying attention to Scipio as he gave instructions, I scanned the crowd for my mother. Her team had finished the challenge yesterday with seven minutes to spare, which meant that she was here. It didn't take long to find her standing at the front of the room with Lieutenant Zale, my father, and their friend Min-Ha Kim.

I stared for a second, and then decided I couldn't wait any longer—I needed to know what was going on with her, and what had happened after I left the other night. A part of me was deeply worried that my father had lost his temper and hurt her. Or worse, threatened to report both of us for sedition and treason if she didn't get in line and turn away from me.

Or worst of all, perhaps I had been right all along, and my parents had been testing me to see how much I knew. At least I had the good sense to keep a lot of things back, but even still... What if I had made a mistake in what I had revealed, and now they were somehow planning to use it against me? I wasn't sure, and I definitely didn't want to believe that my parents had played me.

Either way, I had to find out.

"Excuse me for a second," I whispered to everyone, and then discreetly began to make my way over to her. I came up from behind her, and then reached out and tugged gently on the back of her sleeve. She half turned, saw it was me, and then quickly faced me, her hand firmly on my shoulder to push me a few steps deeper into the throng of people behind us.

"Liana," she whispered a second later, casting a look back over her shoulder at her teammates. "You shouldn't be approaching me right now. Your father told Zale that my loyalties were questionable, and they've been shutting me out ever since."

I could tell by the twist of her mouth that she wasn't happy with my father's actions, and I wasn't particularly pleased, either. He had no right to do that to her. She was a Knight every bit as high as he was, in caliber and rank, and she had not acted as dishonorably as he had, in my opinion. What we had been talking about wasn't even fully related to the challenge, for crying out loud!

But I put my anger aside and focused on the matter at hand: finding out whether she was okay. "What happened after I left?"

She sighed and looked around. "Look, all you need to know is that this fight between your father and me has nothing to do with you. Not really."

I gave her a disbelieving look "Mom, don't try to sell me that story. Everything I do makes Dad angry." I paused, and then decided to address my suspicion of her first—though I felt bad about it. I shouldn't need to fish for validation that she was on my side, but our relationship had never been trusting before. I had to know. "And—don't take this the wrong way—but it also had a similar effect on you, until recently. So you'll forgive me if I'm finding the fact that he doesn't 'actually' blame me a little unbelievable."

She frowned, sadness unfurling in her eyes. Her hand reached up suddenly, and at first I flinched away, years of being slapped in the face making the action ingrained at this point. I stopped myself, but my mother noticed, and her sadness deepened. Still, she didn't stop, and cupped my cheek, smiling tremulously at me.

"Liana, I am so sorry for how I treated you. I'm sorry that it took almost losing you for me to realize how awful I'd been to you, and I'm sorry that I forced you to feel so afraid of me that you needed to defend yourself from me. To be honest, I don't think there is a word that encompasses my regret and sorrow for my behavior toward you, but believe me when I say that your father's anger toward you isn't about you. Not really. He just... He just doesn't see that yet."

"Then what does he see?" I demanded, trying to understand the root of my father's problem with me. I was certain it was stupid and petty—but if I knew, then maybe I could find a way to address it.

My mother's face tightened, and she sighed heavily. "He's jealous of you," she finally admitted.

"He's what?" My eyes widened, and I couldn't help myself—I leaned over to look at my father from around my mother's shoulder. He was already watching us, his eyes glittering in the dim light, and I met his gaze. His eyes narrowed, and he pointedly turned away, crossing his arms for good measure.

His behavior didn't strike me as particularly jealous, not to mention... He was *jealous* of me?! I doubted it very much.

"Mom..."

"Scipio chose *you*, Liana. Do you understand?" My mother searched my face and then sighed, pinching the bridge of her nose between two fingers. "Look, I know it's hard to understand, but your father... He feels that *he* should've been chosen to do Scipio's bidding. But Scipio ignored him, ignored his rank, and chose you. He... He doesn't understand, and he thinks you somehow tricked Scipio into picking you."

She sighed again, and looked down. "As for us and how we raised you... Scipio forgive me, Liana—I have never been very fair to you, from the day you were born. And then when Sybil died and you remained... I believed that there was a reason, a *plan*. Hell, I was the one who convinced your father of that! But you were just so obstinate and stubbornly fixated on questioning everything around you! I was scared that you would wind up in the expulsion chambers and that I'd lose another daughter. I couldn't bear going through that again, so... I was hard on you. I thought I was doing the right thing, but I see now that I was so very, very wrong. I love you."

I stared at her, my mouth agape. I blinked my eyes several times, and then shook my head, trying to clear it from the verbal punch my mother had just delivered. My father... was jealous... of me. Because he thought Scipio had *chosen* me to take down Devon Alexander. And both he and my mother had only been hard on me because they wanted to keep me safe?

I didn't want to believe it, and yet, it held a note of truth. And, it would go a long way toward explaining why his behavior toward me hadn't improved while hers had, despite the heroic nature of my deeds. But still, a forty-five-year-old man being jealous of his twenty-year-old daughter... That was a bit much.

"Unbelievable," I muttered. I had no idea how to even address that particular emotion, short of calling him out on it—and now was neither the time nor the place. I had to get my head back in the challenge and think about what was going to happen next, especially with my mother and her team. "Are you okay on your team? They aren't treating you too poorly?"

She smiled, clearly touched by my concern. "Don't worry about that, Liana. You just focus on the challenge."

"I am," I replied. "But I want to know what's going on with your team. Are you or Min-Ha planning to take a leadership role for the challenge?"

I hoped that one of them was. It would make things much easier all around, as it would mean I didn't have Lieutenant Zale gunning for me (or ordering his teammates to come after me). Not to mention, if we were grouped into the same team for the challenge, I was betting the struggle for command would go much easier on Dylan—neither my mother nor Min-Ha cared about the position, so they would have no qualms about stepping back and letting someone else step forward. If my father was leading, however, it would be an entirely different issue. But no use fretting over it until I got her answer.

She shook her head. "No. I thought it best not to petition for it after what your father told the others. Min-Ha didn't want it, and your father is in complete support of Zale, so…"

I was disappointed, and a little hurt, but not surprised. Still, it must've shown on my face, because my mother squeezed my shoulders gently.

"Look, Liana, I know you're worried about Salvatore, and I can understand why, given his relationship with Devon. But you know the next challenge as well as I do. And if we're on the same team, I'll do my best to support you. Even if we're on *opposing* teams, I'll do what I can to help you out."

"Mom, Dylan is in charge for this challenge, and I don't feel right planning to take control from her. I'm fine with letting her lead, and if she makes a mistake that might cause us to lose, I'll step in then. But I should try to follow the rule changes."

My mom arched her eyebrow and gave me a dry look. "To hell with that, Liana. Nobody really cares if you can be a good follower—that's not what this competition is about, no matter what the rule changes were. As soon as you get a chance to take control, you take it, and don't think twice about it, especially if you know that what you're doing is the best course of action. The judges and Knights will see it as well, and they will only reward you for it, do you understand?"

I didn't. Well, I understood the *words*, but I just couldn't wrap my head around the fact that she was urging me to undermine the leader of our group for this round. It meant that she *believed* in me, and that she wanted me to be Champion. Before, she never would've considered me worthy of the position. If anything, she would've laughed had I told her I planned to enter the Tourney. The new change in my mother's behavior toward me, as much as it warmed me inside, still left me feeling confused, especially when she was acting so supportive. She had stopped encouraging me a long time ago, and now that she was again, I couldn't help but wonder why she was doing it.

But that suspicion was born from years of neglect and emotional abuse, and I needed to get over the fact that my mother was suddenly on my side. She was trying to do her best to help me, and I was grateful for a sign that she was changing. That she genuinely loved me.

She gave me an intense look and a gentle shake, and I realized she was waiting for me to reply. "Yeah, Mom. I understand."

I still wasn't sure that I was going to change my mind about how I planned to handle Dylan, but I had to say something to let her know I was listening.

"Good." She leaned forward and pressed her lips to my forehead. "Be careful, darling, and I hope we wind up on the same team. I love you."

Then the screens suddenly cut out, and I looked around as the lights in the room came back on. Officials began to stream in to collect the teams, and my mother let go of me, moving away and toward her own team.

I stood, staring at the spot she had just been moments before, and realized that I hadn't told her I loved her back.

And for once, I really wanted to.

27

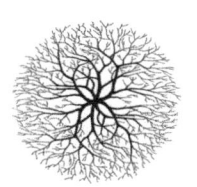

The officials were tightlipped as they led us to our entry points for the arena. We had no idea what teams would be joining ours, and no one told us whether we would be defending the gate, or attacking it. I chafed under the mystery, because I didn't like going into things blind and without a plan, but Dylan seemed unperturbed by the lack of information.

Which only made my apprehension worse. We could be using this time to come up with ways to unite with the two teams we were about to join, to make the most out of the thirty-minute preparation time, or we could even be strategizing different tactics for defense or offense... But instead, we marched steadily down the halls in a thick, oppressive silence.

It wasn't good for morale, in my opinion. If I were in her shoes, I would be pestering the officials with questions, trying to get them to let something slip. Anything to distract from this awful tension that seemed ready to snap at any moment.

But maybe this was how Dylan was? Quietly introspective before a battle?

I wasn't sure, but it was doing nothing for me. My heart was racing a mile a minute while my palms were sweating. I kept looking around for signs of life—at least some of the other candidates. If I could catch a glimpse of any other teams near us, the odds were they were going to be on our team. I was familiar enough with most of the candidates' faces to know what we'd be getting if I could see them, and could even offer up some ideas to Dylan on how to proceed.

But I only found empty corridors. I suspected that the officials were intentionally masking our movements and the placements of our teams, to keep us from coordinating plans before the Tourney began. And of course they would; the candidates were given thirty minutes to coordinate, and the officials wanted to ensure that they *only* had thirty minutes. No more, no less. Still, it was eerie to see such desolation, even as the noise of thousands of people above us in the stands threatened to shake apart the Citadel.

Not to mention, it made the halls feel like they were potentially dangerous. Heightened security aside, if whoever was controlling Scipio had managed to program holes into the system, then we were isolated and alone. As was my mother.

I found myself thinking of our exchange, and a strange anxiety gripped me. It took no small amount of reason to help it pass, some of which included reminding myself that she could take care of herself. Most of it came from my belief that the new security protocols had to be slowing down and limiting the influence of our enemies. At the very least, they wouldn't be able to do much out in the open without risking exposure, and I believed they wanted to protect their identity more than anything.

CHAPTER 27

Or at least, I hoped that they did.

Just as I managed to finally put a lid on the influx of concern for my mother, anger against my father flared, and I was once again distracted by a useless and unproductive train of thought. I just couldn't wrap my head around the fact that he was jealous. Of me.

I mean, who was the child in this relationship, really? Even if I had actually been chosen by Scipio, it was an honor I could do without. The cost that came with it was too high, with all of the people who had died along the way. And he should realize that! He knew the hardship that came with being a Knight. He had lost friends—good ones—on the job. He should have known how damaging it was for me to watch people I cared about being killed, all because of something Scipio had ordered.

And then to turn around and take it out on my mother... It was beyond childish. He was acting like a bully. Not that I should be surprised by that, of course. My entire life he'd been a bully to me, so why hadn't I expected it?

Because it was my mother, and he'd never treated her like that.

I let out a sigh of disgust and cracked my neck, trying to relax. I couldn't afford to be distracted by my family drama, and all this line of thinking was doing was making me even more anxious.

This was why I liked talking before a mission. It helped keep me calm and focused on the moment. Which was exactly what I needed to be.

We came to a stop just as I was in the middle of recalling the various winning strategies of the Gate challenge, historically, and several officials emerged from a door, ushering us in. Their arms were filled with lash harnesses and batons for us to replace our own with, since our personal ones were not allowed. For once, we had individual privacy screens—though it turned out not to be so private after all, as I had to strip down in front of the official. She performed a quick search of both my person and uniform, and then helped me get into my harness and then uniform again, systematically checking and rechecking the hand controls for my lashes, as well as the connecting pieces of the harness.

I endured her hands, and then the hands of a second official who came behind her to check her work, trying not to think about yet another pair of unfamiliar hands on my body. Instead, I found myself wondering which teams we would be merged with. Whoever they were, I hoped Dylan found a clever way to take charge—or better yet, found herself overshadowed by someone else. If she was overshadowed, it would mean her popularity among the Knights would dwindle—and hopefully make a way for me to edge my way to victory in the final challenge.

Then again, whoever overshadowed her would likely become a new favorite among the Knights, which would make *them* all the more difficult to beat in the final challenge. I gritted my teeth, feeling very much like the entire weight of the Tower were pressing down on my shoulders, reminding me that real lives were at stake. And here I was acting all "honorable" by letting Dylan lead instead of planning ways to take the position away from her. Not to mention, if she screwed up, we would lose, and I would be out of the Tourney completely.

It took several deep breaths for me to shift my thoughts before they got caught in *that* particular mental trap again, and returned my mind to the challenge at hand. I couldn't afford to be distracted like this, yet here I was, minutes before we were going to enter the arena, and I couldn't seem to get it together.

And I desperately needed to.

CHAPTER 27

Once we stepped into the arena, we'd only have half an hour to plan our attack or defense, and after that... it was basically a fight down to the last person. If I failed to pull it together before we stepped through that door, I'd be next to worthless for anything but the fight.

I jerked my mind back on track, again, forcing myself to think about past challenges and what victorious teams of the Gate challenge had done in the past, trying to fill my mind with strategies that had made them successful. No matter what happened, the leadership of the teams needed to be decided within five minutes, so that the bulk of the time could be devoted to the actual challenge. The strategies for selecting a single leader varied—and to be honest, weren't easily replicated, which made it important for someone to get command as quickly as possible. If we didn't, then we risked losing valuable time necessary to constructing a complete defense. In the past, too many teams had lost because they couldn't stop fighting over who was in charge, and had wasted their precious planning time and lost the entire challenge.

If that happened to us, we'd be out of the Tourney. Lacey would come after us with everything she had, and whoever wound up winning the Tourney would either kill the Tower intentionally, or through ignorance—and everyone I loved and cared about would be dead. Every man, woman, and child would be dead.

I wasn't about to let that happen.

Once the officials were satisfied that our uniforms and equipment were up to all safety standards and were working properly, we were ushered through another door and into a small antechamber, which I recognized as the armory reception area. The officials closed the door behind us, sealing us in.

"This is fun and new," Maddox said, tugging at her uniform.

"Just keep your mouth shut and follow my lead," Dylan said, shaking out her arms. "I have to assert control quickly once we get out there, or everything will devolve into chaos and infighting."

I begrudgingly gave her an internal nod of respect, glad that she realized the first few minutes of this challenge would be crucial. But the way she said it bothered me; it was like she thought she could just strut out there, declare "I'm in charge, do what I say," and get away with it, which almost never worked. Not to mention, she was being completely dismissive to her teammates.

Maddox gave me a hard look, her jaw tight, and I shook my head, answering her silent request to punch Dylan. She rolled her eyes, exhaled, and folded her arms over her chest. "What should we do while you're doing that?" she drawled.

The look Dylan gave her was deeply serious. "Assess the environment they put us in and start brainstorming. I want you to have a list of five different plans ready for either offense or defense by the time I get the other two teams in line, depending on which goal we receive."

Again, that easy confidence. She completely ignored the derisive quality of Maddox's tone, and dispatched her orders in a dispassionate voice. I was impressed yet again—and a little put off by the lack of concrete planning. It felt very underprepared, but then again, some people were more capable leaders in the moment, and I couldn't judge her without seeing her in action.

Still, my mother's words rang in my ears, and I resolved to follow her advice the second Dylan proved that her leadership was failing. It didn't matter if I wanted to or not. I couldn't allow us to lose this challenge. So if she made smart decisions, I wouldn't waste any time arguing with her. And if she didn't... Well, I wasn't going to argue with her then, either. I'd just seize control without a second thought—and I wouldn't apologize, either.

There was a chiming sound from the door leading to the arena, and I looked past Dylan to see words forming on the dark screen.

Candidates will stand in the center of the room.

Confused by the instructions, we clustered together into the middle of the room, and waited. A moment later, the floor shuddered, and I experienced a moment of weightlessness as the circular disc we were standing on began to move upward, lifting us quickly toward the ceiling. I looked up in time to see a part of it slide away, and then we were thrown into complete darkness, with only the rush of air blowing my hair to show that we were still moving.

My heart plummeted down into the soles of my boots, and each individual muscle clenched as images of being crushed against a ceiling above danced through my mind. Suddenly a white light from above blinded me. The air whooshed out of my lungs as I went weightless, my feet disconnecting from the flooring for a microsecond, and then gravity returned. I wobbled in place, my knees like gelatin, and looked around, wincing against the bright spotlights that were shining in my eyes.

White blobs cut across a dark background, and then slowly drew into focus, forming into bricks, banisters, statues… It took a second, but finally I realized that the arena had been constructed to resemble a life-sized replica of the Bridge of Heroes—the massive bridge that connected the Medica to the Core.

Twenty-foot-tall statues stood in straight lines on the edge of either side of the bridge, which was thirty feet wide. The statues, replicas of former and current council members, stood shoulder to shoulder, with a row of white banisters separating the statues from the main traffic. The bridge spanned three hundred feet, and arched upward in the middle, making it impossible to see the other side.

I knew from the real Bridge of Heroes that there were long struts for support underneath, in what looked like a widespread hand fanning out at either end of the bridge, holding it up. They were placed wide enough to navigate through using the lashes, but the closer you were to the start of the bridge, the more clustered they became.

"Liana," Leo whispered, catching my attention and breaking my train of thought. I followed his gaze and then the line of his arm, turning completely around to do so, and saw the word *Defender* glowing on the wall of the arena. Another quick glance at our surroundings showed me that we were also being flanked by two teams of four. Our teammates.

My heart skipped a beat when I saw Frederick Hamilton striding forward from the group on the left, and then stopped completely when I noticed Lieutenant Zale breaking off from the one on the right, heading toward a spot equidistant from the three groups.

Dylan shoved past me, breaking free from our tiny cluster and marching forward to meet them, a determined look on her face. I watched her stalk away with growing alarm, wondering if she really thought butting heads with Lieutenant Zale—a man who had been second-in-command for the Knights for the last twenty years—in a direct confrontation for leadership was a good idea. Because if she did, she had another thing coming.

"The first thing we need to do—" Zale began, his voice loud and exerting a brutal edge that made me stand a little straighter and look a bit more attentive.

"Clearly, the statues need to be—" Fredrick said over him,

his deep voice holding a nasal quality that gave it a bit of whine, but also a note of authority that was hard to ignore.

"I say that we tear up parts of the—" Dylan asserted confidently, not letting anyone get the better of her.

Everything else they said was lost in the pandemonium of them speaking over one another. I watched and waited, unsurprised, as this was generally the status quo for the first few seconds and up to a minute of this particular challenge. Any second now, one of them would loudly remind the others that we were on the clock, and didn't have time to fight.

Frederick was gesticulating wildly as he spoke, his fingers pointing this way and that, while Dylan kept her arms folded across her chest and her legs set wide, still wearing a wry smile, even as she sarcastically and waspishly dismissed what Frederick was saying out of turn. Lieutenant Zale had his hands behind his back, but an angry and sour look on his face, likely because his position as Lieutenant hadn't gotten him anywhere. They were still practically talking over each other, and while the words weren't exactly understandable, the volume and tone were, and I winced, pressing a finger against my ear to try to clear the noise.

And yet no one looked at the time, or even made mention of it. Anxiety twisted up inside me, and I nervously glanced at my indicator and the mission clock, wondering how much time had elapsed. As I squinted at the numbers, my stomach tensed. Nearly two minutes had elapsed since they started arguing, and they showed no sign of stopping. How could any of them hope to accomplish anything when none of them were actually *listening* to what the others were saying, let alone checking the time?

Still, I waited, half expecting one of them to get the upper hand in the conversation—or at the very least, for one of them to yell "shut up, this isn't working"—but each time someone got close, another would start talking again, and everything would devolve.

Leo, Maddox, and I exchanged a three-way look of confusion. Compared with our training session with Dylan yesterday, today she was acting like a rank amateur. We had little time to waste on this, and I couldn't believe how little attention she was paying to it. Not to mention, it was on one of *them* to take a step back, realize that this was fruitless, and do something decisive. Whether that was throwing his or her weight behind someone else or just walking away to approach the other teams directly, it didn't matter. The status quo wasn't working, and needed to change.

But it seemed Dylan hadn't considered that going into this, which left me in a strange place. I really didn't want to undermine Dylan's command right out of the gate, but she was leaving me no other choice. I had to do something before we lost any more time waiting for them to decide who was going to lead. It wouldn't matter who was in charge if we didn't start planning our defense. Even now, the other team was planning their avenue of attack—and if we didn't begin fortifying our end, they would roll right through us, and we'd be eliminated from the Tourney.

And I couldn't let that happen.

"Hey, I'm going to talk to the other teams to see if I can convince them to help us out while our three illustrious leaders waste time trying to figure out who's in charge. Can you guys go check the bridge? There should be emergency toolkits with cutters and a welding kit inside that we'll need to start constructing our barricades."

Maddox arched an eyebrow, a sly smile coming to her lips. "That didn't take very long," she said cheerfully. "Start with

Frederick's team. He got grouped with a guy named Kellan Moore, who was the leader of his own team. It was infiltrated as well, and now he and Frederick are stuck together. He was actually the lead yesterday, and from the vids I watched last night, he's reasonable."

I followed her gaze to where a dusky-skinned man with a thick swatch of inky blue-black hair and a pair of dark brown, almost black, almond-shaped eyes was watching our three leaders squabble over who would be in charge with an openly disgusted and frustrated look on his face. As soon as I noticed that, I turned and gave Maddox an appraising look.

"Good job," I said. "He's a great starting place."

And I meant it; anyone with that look on his face would be perfectly amenable to teaming up to undermine his ineffective leader. Good thing I had just the proposal for him.

I set off toward him, cutting a wide path around the three people still arguing in the middle, approaching quickly. Kellan didn't notice me at first, but one of his teammates—a woman of about twenty-five, with short brown hair and dark green eyes, reached out and tapped his shoulder.

"Kellan?" she said, her voice husky. "Liana 'Honorbound' Castell is here."

Kellan whirled, his eyes immediately raking me from head to toe with a wary look. "What are you doing?" he asked, his brows drawing together. "We're supposed to wait until—"

I gave him a wry look, and cut in smoothly. "Time runs out and then the other team is on us before we have time to put up barricades?" He faltered mid-sentence and then closed his mouth. "Look, our leaders have already wasted…" I glanced at my indicator, which was now displaying the Tourney countdown, sighed, and continued, saying, "Three whole minutes trying to figure out who is in charge or who has the best plan, and that's time we could've used planning our defense."

He frowned, contemplating my words, and then nodded. "You're right. Do you have a plan?"

"Nothing fancy at the moment," I said, both relieved and pleased that I didn't have to waste any time convincing him further, then turned to the bridge, pointing at it. "I figure we tear up the floor of the bridge starting about sixty feet in, and use what we rip out to create barricades farther back, set up to funnel the attackers into a bottleneck. That way, they'll only be able to come at us one by one, which will let us take them out easily. If you think there's anything we need to add, I'm all ears."

Tearing up the bridge was a bold move, as it meant cutting a hole directly in the center of it to create an obstacle to slow the other team down. They'd be limited in how they could use their lashes, as well as how much room they had to maneuver, which would give us the advantage, as we would control the points they would have access to. It required us to move fast if we were going to do it, but I left room for other suggestions, knowing that the easiest way to get the other teams on board was to make them feel included.

Kellan studied the bridge for several seconds. "We should create some barricades underneath as well, in case they try to come up from underneath. And we'll need to post a few people down there, but... yes, I think you are right. We need to limit their numbers, and cutting a hole in the bridge certainly does that."

"Good. Why don't you join Maddox and Grey, and I'll see if I can't get the other team to help," I said, giving him an encouraging smile.

Kellan waved for his teammates to follow and began making his way to where Maddox and Leo were taking equipment from

CHAPTER 27

specially crafted cabinets inside the first columns on either side of the bridge. I watched him go for a second, and then sucked in a deep breath before turning and directing myself toward Zale's team.

My mother was already watching me, a pleased smile spreading across her lips as she registered Kellan moving to join Maddox and Leo, his own team following behind him. A strange rush of pleasure made my cheeks heat as I realized she was looking at me with pride, but I quickly batted the feeling away and let it scatter to the far recesses of my mind, to dwell on later. I didn't have time, and I could feel the press of each second, reminding me that even more was running out. I was up to six people, and with my father, Min-Ha Kim, and my mother, that would be nine. The other three could follow us when they figured out that they had lost.

Provided I could get Zale's team on board, of course. My gaze flicked over to where they were standing, and I studied them. My father and Min-Ha—a woman with straight, jet-black hair and dark brown eyes—had their eyes on Zale as I approached, but it didn't take long for my father to notice me.

"What are you doing over here?" he blustered angrily, and I winced at the volume. Looking over my shoulder, though, I saw that the three so-called leaders had barely paused for breath, and was relieved that my father's loud question hadn't drawn any attention from them. If they noticed I was getting their teams moving behind their backs, they'd jump in and unify against me—and I'd lose any semblance of control I had managed to get through convincing Kellan and Frederick's team to help us. They'd likely jump in, barking orders, which would only get things muddled up and slowed down, and would throw our risk of winning the challenge into more jeopardy.

"Talking to Mom," I snapped back. I turned my attention to

her and smiled. "So, we're gonna start setting up the bridge. You want to join us?"

My mother chuckled, and then nodded. "Absolutely," she announced softly. "It seems more proactive than standing around here, don't you think, Silas? Min-Ha?"

She didn't give them a chance to respond, but instead turned on her heel and began moving toward the others, following Kellan. Min-Ha watched her for a moment, her shapely eyebrows rising to her forehead, and then gave me a small, polite smile.

"Well played," she said, inclining her head. "Let's go, Silas."

"What?" my father blustered. "No, we have to stay here and wait for the Lieutenant!"

Min-Ha shook her head—a subtle thing that made her hair fall around her face—then tucked a strand behind her ear and gave my father a sympathetic look. "You can do that if you wish, but you and I both know that your daughter outmaneuvered the others for leadership. And as Knights, we are honor bound to acknowledge it. I suggest you take a page from your daughter's deed name, and fall in line."

"But... the Lieutenant!" my father repeated, although some of the fire seemed to have left him. "He should be made aware."

"He will become aware when he notices, and the longer it takes the more it will hurt his standing. But that is his burden to bear. Ours is to perform well in this challenge, as Knights would, and pray that we perform well enough that our leader gets his shot in the final challenge. We lose this battle, Silas, so that we might win the war."

I blinked, impressed by how reasonably she was explaining things to him—but prepared myself in case he told her off and decided to warn Zale anyway. It wouldn't be good form to use a baton on my father, especially in front of the drones, but it would buy me some time to get things moving before Dylan, Frederick, and Zale became clued in to what I was doing. And I desperately needed that time to get us some semblance of a defensible position in place.

So I would have used my baton if I had to.

But to my surprise, he went still, thinking, and then whirled on his heel and stalked off. He didn't take as much care to disguise his movements, but none of our would-be leaders noticed, not even when he picked up a cutter and moved to start helping Leo cut into the bridge.

Min-Ha gave me another polite smile and small bow, and then went after him, leaving me in a strange state of surprise, elation, and nervousness. But I didn't have time to dwell on emotions—so instead, I channeled them into something more productive.

Like using the next twenty-five minutes and thirty-two seconds to tear up a bridge and prepare for the oncoming attack.

28

"LIANA!"

Dylan's voice seemed to echo off the walls of the arena, hot and brittle with anger. I paused where I was cutting a chunk of the bridge out, shut off the cutter, wiped rivulets of sweat from my forehead, and looked at my indicator. We had ten minutes left to set up defenses, and I was surprised to see that even that much time had passed. It had felt like nothing—and yet I wasn't sure I had ever worked so hard in my life.

"LIANA!" Dylan's indignant shriek came again, drawing closer, and still, I ignored it, motioning for my mother to drag away the chunk of metal I had just cut, using her lashes and the gyro. The metal strained as she began to retract the line, and then, with a heavy groan and clang, finally broke free and was dragged several feet toward her, kicking sparks off the metallic surface.

Min-Ha and my father rushed toward it and immediately began helping my mother shift the three-foot cube into position along the row we had already created to help shove our attackers into a choke point. I supervised for a second, and then, when my father set the blowtorch to the block to fuse it to the others and the bridge, I turned and raised an eyebrow at Dylan.

"Yes?" I asked mildly, bracing myself for the tongue-lashing I was about to receive. I wouldn't let her get very far—after all, she had squandered twenty minutes of time fighting with Frederick and Lieutenant Zale—but I doubted I would be able to stop her before she paused to catch her breath.

"What the hell is this?" she asked, closing the distance between us until we were nose-to-nose. "You little traitor, you didn't even wait three seconds after my back was turned before pulling this crap! You were supposed to follow my lead! We had a deal!"

I pressed my lips together for a second, and then held my watch out so it was facing her, trying not to look smug. But Scipio help me, I felt it—along with a dull, burning resentment and anger that she would have the audacity to act like *I* had done something wrong.

"It took you twenty minutes to notice that we were already working, which was twenty minutes of time that you should've been using to construct the barricades. Instead of getting Zale and Frederick to see that, you joined them, the three of you screaming at each other like children. So, as far as following your lead as it was presented to me... Sorry, I just couldn't stamp my feet and scream my lungs out when there was work that needed to be done. I had to do something to make sure we won the challenge."

Her face turned a very interesting shade of red, and her nostrils flared. "You—"

"Hey, Liana, we need another block under the bridge!" Kellan's voice called, coming from the hole we had opened up.

CHAPTER 28

"Grey and I already have our lashes on the next section. Just waiting for you to cut."

I glanced through the hole and saw him at the edge, looking up at me expectantly. I stared at him for a second, then smiled and turned back to Dylan. "Get mad at me later, if we win this challenge. Or blame me if we don't. Either way, save your breath and give us a hand. We're going to need it."

I shoved the cutter into her hands, giving her the choice of either taking it or dropping it, and then walked away, moving to where Frederick's other teammates—Sella and Norman—were reinforcing an internal set of barricades that Maddox had designed, which formed a U-shape that created a lip around our side of the hole. It would allow us to defend against anyone who tried to approach from under the bridge. They wouldn't be able to land anywhere save the three-foot gaps that Maddox had purposefully left open, and would most likely have to use their lashes to connect with the wall—in which case we could easily knock them back down through the hole by disconnecting their lash ends, dropping them into the water below. The wall Maddox had created periodically gave way to three-foot-wide gaps meant to lure our opposing team in. The idea was that we'd be hiding next to the gaps, attacking whoever came through before they got fully out, and then pushing them back through the hole itself, which was now almost the entire width of the bridge at twenty-two-feet wide. We couldn't go much farther toward the edges, or we would risk the weight of the statues that lined the sides collapsing the rest of the bridge.

Another barrier—the one my mother and her team were currently working on—was beginning to take form on the opposite side of the hole. Like Maddox's wall, it was curved into a slight U-shape, and blocked the far side of the hole from direct access unless the competitors wanted to waste a lot of time navigating around or over it. They'd left only one gap in the middle of it to create a bottleneck, which would slow our attackers down, forcing them through one by one. With only a few feet of intact bridge on the other side, my mother's team would be able to shove any enemy forces headfirst into the hole, or baton them before they even got through. The attackers wouldn't be able to get through in large enough numbers to overwhelm my mother's team.

Our opponents' lashes would be their greatest advantage in this fight. Our defenses were fine for a foot army, but the lashes gave every Knight an opportunity to overcome any obstacle we set up, if they were smart about it. But we were doing everything we could to control how and where they used them. Even if they climbed over the wall my mom had constructed, they could only attack one at a time. And my mother's team would also be supported by anyone taking up position on the side of the hole, as we could use our lashes to lasso any enemies that came over the wall, and pull them into the empty void where the bridge once was.

The test designers had built the bridge about fifteen feet above a body of water, which meant tossing people off the bridge wouldn't seriously hurt them—but would potentially throw them out of the match, seeing as they wouldn't be able to climb back up very quickly without the use of their lashes, which wouldn't work when they got wet. By the time their lashes dried out, the fighting would, hopefully, be finished, and we would be victorious.

Provided we got the defenses finished in time.

I decided to take a quick check under the bridge, just to make sure preparations there were going all right, and raced toward the edge, pulling a lash end from my sleeve as I went, spinning the weighted end, and tossing it onto a hand rail as I threw myself over it. It connected with a sharp *tink* just as gravity began to suck me down, and I leaned into the line, arcing toward the underside of the bridge and letting the line out as I swung closer to the bars, aiming for a gap between two poles of the dense forest that supported the bridge.

Excitement gripped me as the poles hurtled closer, and I lifted my legs and straightened my spine, making myself as flat as possible. Tucking my chin to my chest, I kept an eye on the bridge as it drew closer, confirming my angle, and then disconnected right before I slipped between the two beams. Nothing touched me as I slid between them, and then threw my reserve line up and away, hooking the flat underbelly of the bridge just short of the hole above. I activated the hand controls, drew myself up instead of swinging farther into the middle, and looked around. It took only seconds to spot the crude wall that now interrupted the smooth lines of the bridge.

Only two people were down here—Leo and Kellan—but they were working like a well-oiled machine as they swung a block into place, using their lashes and the gears in their suits to help them with the weight. Leo used his hand controls to draw himself closer to the block while maintaining the tension that kept it in place, and quickly began welding it to the ceiling, the torch casting sharp blue lights against the angles of his face.

I swung closer to Kellan, not wanting to distract him. "How's it going?" I asked as soon as I was near enough that he could hear me.

Kellan glanced over at me briefly, and then returned his gaze to the block. "Good. How are we doing on time?"

I checked, winced, and then told him the truth. "Eight minutes. In five, I want you to stop what you're doing and get in position. I'm going to send Frederick down to you. You okay with that?"

Scipio help me, I didn't have time to ask questions—if we didn't have a solid defense in place, we had a strong chance of losing the challenge—but I needed everyone to play nice, and that meant making Kellan feel included. Which meant asking.

"Make it Dylan," he said, his focus on Leo and the hunk of metal he was holding in place. "She's way better with lashes than Frederick is."

"Fair enough," I said. "You'll signal if you see anyone coming?"

"Yeah, we got you down here," he said. "Everything going okay up there?"

I hesitated and then nodded. We'd gotten a lot accomplished in the short time allotted, and it would have to be enough. "We should be fine. I guess I'll send Frederick ahead so he can sound the alarm when he sees the enemy coming."

Kellan chortled good-naturedly. "Sounds like the perfect place for him. Just let us know what's going on up there and if you need us, all right?"

"I will," I promised solemnly.

We were all in the same boat now, and if we failed to communicate and defend our position, we would be eliminated from the Tourney. That wasn't an option—which meant moving forward.

I lashed to the other side of the bridge, moving through the support beams more carefully this time, and then climbed up and over the railing along the side, emerging in a small space just behind the statue of Rachel Pine, the woman who had rechristened the Security Department and transformed it into the Knights.

I slid along the narrow pathway around the dais she was standing on, and emerged through the gap between her and her father. I saw my mother moving another block into place—the final one, it seemed, given that the wall was looking more like a wall, and less like a series of individual blocks—and moved over to her, Min-Ha, and my father.

"How's it going?" I asked as I drew within talking range.

My father pointedly ignored me as he bent down to start welding the block into place, but my mother did not, her concentration melting away into a smile. "It's solid," she said with an approving nod. "What do you need?"

"To figure out where everyone is going," I replied with a smile, while internally cursing myself for wasting the breath and the precious seconds. "Actually, I was hoping you, Min-Ha, Dad, and Lieutenant Zale would take position at the first wall. I know it's the front line, but you four are far more experienced with assaults like this."

"Very wise," Min-Ha said, wiping sweat from her face. "And correct. We are the most experienced in that regard, but only by virtue of having more years of training. Still, I would be honored to hold the line."

I shot her a grateful smile, but my father harrumphed at us both as he continued welding. "We shouldn't even be doing this," he grumbled.

"And yet you are," drawled a deep, familiar voice behind me, and I took a few steps to the side and turned to see Lieutenant Zale standing there, his hands clasped behind his back. "I was quite surprised to see you already hard at work, especially given that I hadn't issued any orders."

"Are you really that surprised?" I asked, unable to resist the urge. "You stood there arguing for twenty minutes!"

The gentle whoosh of the flamethrower shut off, and I saw my father swiveling around to gauge what Lieutenant Zale's reaction would be. I was also curious, and turned my attention back to him, waiting to see how he would respond.

"Indeed," he said, arching an eyebrow. "But those who have been in command for a while know that *good* decisions take time and careful planning—something that gets lost in a panicked rush to set things up. Still, your attempts at defense could've been worse, I suppose."

My jaw tightened at his barb, and I bristled indignantly at the idea that I had panicked as opposed to planning well. I very much wanted to tell him where to shove it, but with all of the drones watching us, not to mention the clock running down, I couldn't. So instead, I smiled so wide that my jaw began to ache from the effort.

"Yes, well, I appreciate the cooperation of your team," I replied sweetly. "I really couldn't have gotten this 'panicked' barricade together without them. Now, I'll leave you to help them put the final touches in place—maybe even find a few places that need reinforcing—and make sure everyone else is ready."

"Knight Elite Castell," Zale said, his voice relaying his irritation. He drew in a breath—undoubtedly to chastise me further—but I turned away abruptly, not willing to let him use our remaining time arguing with me about who should be in charge.

"Bring your concerns up to my mother," I called over my shoulder. "She'll fill you in on my rush-job of a plan. In the meantime, I have work to do. And so do you."

29

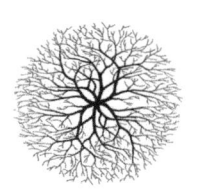

Thirty seconds later, Lieutenant Zale's words were still burning in my ears—but the minutes were rapidly melting away, so I distracted myself by keeping busy. I fortified the barricades in the front of the hole, where the attack was most likely to happen, and then got busy putting people into place. My parents and Min-Ha had agreed to hold the front line, and when Zale insisted on taking the lead on holding, I didn't argue. He could rot at the bottom of the Tower for all I really cared. I knew my mother would make sure the wall was defended.

Dylan bucked at Kellan's request that she fill the void underneath the bridge, but his teammates were on board with holding the line. Frederick readily agreed to scouting, much to my surprise, but I didn't argue with him. Having some forewarning would help us prepare for the battle ahead, and it would give us a clue as to what strategy they were using.

The final few minutes were filled with small conversations about contingency plans should any defensive position get overwhelmed—namely to fall back to the position that Maddox, Leo, Dylan, and I were holding behind Maddox's barricade, acting as the rally point for a final stand, should our front lines be overwhelmed.

When the clock hit thirty seconds, sweat began to form on the back of my neck and forehead as my stress levels rose. I quickly looked around, my eyes sliding across the bridge, to confirm that everyone was in place, and spotted my mother and her team standing with their backs to the wall they had built, batons already in hand. None of them looked particularly worried—they were experienced at these sorts of things by now—and I couldn't help but feel a mild stab of jealousy at the confidence on their faces. I was a nervous wreck.

I shook it off and shifted my eyes down, looking to where I could make out the bottoms of Kellen's shoes just below the lip of the hole, where he was dangling under the bridge. Sella and Norman were on either side of him, but I couldn't see them due to the bridge between us. I knew they were there, though, having done a final check just moments ago. Their position was the weakest of all, as they only had three men to our eight, but I had assigned myself, Leo, Min-Ha, and my father to act as temporary re-enforcement should our opponents attempt to bring the bulk of their forces up from underneath us.

I didn't think they would, but one could never be certain. If they did, however, all we had to do was get under the bridge to help, or even better, pull Kellan and his team back and then take the opposing team out as they came up.

I caught sight of Frederick making his way farther down the bridge, his legs and arms pumping as he raced up the curved surface, heading for the pinnacle of the arch so that he could see all the way to the other side.

The clock hit five seconds. I sucked in a deep, calming

breath and began shaking out my arms, trying to burn off the excess energy the premature adrenaline surge had created. Beside me, Dylan shifted, and I could hear the creak of her uniform as she crossed her arms. I could tell she was still unhappy with how things had played out, and was itching for a chance to re-exert control during the actual battle.

She'd already tried once—when I'd asked her to back up Kellan and she'd refused, citing a dozen reasons why I needed her up here. I hadn't argued with her then, and I wasn't about to start now. I needed to demonstrate that I was calm and in control, so that if—or when—she tried to pry control from me, the Knights watching would call her motive into question. So I had merely heard her out, nodded, and said, "That works too," before moving on to other things.

Now that time was slipping away, I used the remaining five seconds to deliver a last-minute (and what I hoped would be moderately reassuring) speech that would boost our morale, while keeping anyone from catching a case of the nerves. We were in the entrenched position, and even though the fight was about to start, we were forced to stay in place by the nature of the challenge. And sometimes the waiting was the worst part. Teams would get agitated and impatient, and often abandon their posts to try to figure out where the enemy team was coming from—ultimately costing their team the challenge as a result of their impatience. I needed everyone to do the opposite of that.

"Don't panic when the clock hits zero," I called out loudly, hoping Kellan and his team under the bridge could hear me. "It's going to take them time to cross the bridge, and they'll likely be trying to sneak past us somehow. Stay alert, keep a wary eye out, and don't rush out to meet anyone. Just stay calm, and remember your training. No need for nobility, either. Knock them into the water as early and often as possible. And remember, if all else fails, just argue with them for as long as possible, and we'll take care of the rest."

I heard the bark of a laugh from under the bridge, and from the other side of the hole, I caught Min-Ha hiding a smile behind her hand. My mother didn't bother to show Zale the same courtesy, and even added a rich chuckle that carried back over. I caught Dylan's jaw tightening from the corner of my eye, but she remained silent, and I could feel her waiting, aching for a moment to prove me incompetent.

I wasn't about to give it to her.

Then the clock hit zero, and my heartbeat increased slightly, becoming hard enough to feel it deep in my stomach. It was difficult to keep still—and more difficult not to expound upon my advice. Doing so would only make everyone more apprehensive, and if I gave license to my mouth, chances were I could dash the morale I had been trying to keep up.

My eyes were glued to Frederick's form, which had stopped at the highest point. He was still for a long time—long enough for me to check my indicator twice to see how much time had passed. The first time revealed only fifteen seconds. The second showed forty-five. But there was still no signal from him.

"Kellan, do you see anything?" I shouted down the hole, leaning over the little wall.

"Nothing yet. No sign of them topside?" his voice called back, slightly diminished by distance.

"Not yet, but keep an eye out. They're out there somewhere." I spoke with more confidence than I felt, my mind already beginning to search for any other way they could approach us. "Scan the sides of the arenas. Maybe they're trying to come in from the sides, bypassing the bridge completely."

I took a few steps back as I spoke, my eyes already searching the curved walls of the arena. The lights from above made it difficult to see, though, and I had to use my hand to shadow my eyes.

"You know, they might not be coming at us just yet," Dylan said casually. "For all you know, they're still trying to plan out their attack. We could use this time to keep fortifying our defenses."

I kept scanning the walls, ignoring her. I wasn't about to get defensive with the drones on us, especially when there was a possibility I had missed an angle of attack while I was planning our defensive positions. If I had, I was about to be utterly humiliated, and getting defensive about it would only make me more of a joke. Instead, I turned my mind to what I could've possibly overlooked.

I had assumed the other team would come directly for us, but if they were clever, they might've come up with another way to get around and flank us. They couldn't leave the arena, but anywhere inside of it was fair game—which meant lashing over using the outer walls was a possibility.

But there was no sign of movement on the left side. I even squinted up at the lights for a few minutes, wondering if they were on the ceiling, trying to get a drop on us from above. But there were no shadows cutting across it that I could make out.

Not to mention, climbing up the side, then across the top, and then back down the other side would be physically taxing. By the time they reached us, they would be tired, and that wouldn't be to their advantage.

No, whatever they were planning had to be something they could execute quickly—and something that would leave them fresh for a fight. At least, that was the sort of plan I would've suggested if I were on their side. I had to assume that someone over there would've thought the same thing.

"I still don't see anyone down here, Liana!" Kellan shouted, his voice barely reaching me.

"And Frederick still hasn't signaled," Leo reported.

"I've got nothing on this side," Maddox added, lowering the hand she was using to shield her eyes. "But I have a big blind spot thanks to the statues."

I froze as her words hit me, and then cursed myself for being an idiot and not thinking of it in the first place. It was right in front of my face! In front of *all* our faces.

"The statues!" I shouted, racing toward the closest one. I whirled my lash into my hand and cast it up high, aiming for the shoulder of Lionel Scipio. Once it hit, I pressed the controls in my hand, and the gyro began to pull the line in, yanking me off my feet. I leaned my weight into the line, throwing it off balance so that it swung wide around his side to his back, and then planted my second line on the back of the Founder's head and yanked, landing lightly with my legs spread wide, braced on his granite shoulder blades.

I stared down the rows of statues, following the line of their backs, and sure enough, I saw crimson-clad figures swooping toward us using their lashes, already halfway across the bridge and drawing rapidly closer. My mind raced, and I retracted the line even farther, climbing up onto his shoulders so I could look down at our defense. The hole that we had created was presided over by two statues on either side, for a total of four. The remaining bridge length that we had left in order to support the massive weight of the statues ranged between five to eight feet by the hole, and the gap between the statues was at least the same, if not more—plenty of room for them to land and create a foothold that would neatly cut our forces in half. The statues would give them reliable cover, and they could quickly become entrenched, which would be bad for us. If they became entrenched right there, then we'd have to *attack* them, which gave them an advantage and ruined our defense.

We needed to get the statues out of there. Now.

"We need cutters on the statues, there and there!" I bellowed, pointing out the statues. "Cut them down, now! Give me two from the forward team, and two from the rear!"

I leapt off the statue, using the still-connected line to slow my fall enough to keep me from breaking my ankle. I landed hard, the shock radiating up my legs, and nodded to Maddox as she raced toward the statue I had just been on, cutter in hand. I continued to scan the activity on the bridge as she passed me to make sure that my orders were being followed, noting that Leo, my mother, and Min-Ha were in fact rushing to the other statues.

"Cut at a downward angle!" my mother shouted, the cutter erupting into a five-foot-long length in her hand. "Start high on the inside, midway down from the knee, and cut at a downward angle, so that you end approximately three inches lower on the other end. That will tip them over the edge rather than to the inside!"

She started to cut below Rachel Pine's knees, just as she had described, the sickly orange color of the cutter glaring white as it bit into the metal, and within seconds it was a quarter of the way through, my mother's arms flexing as she pushed the cutter along. I watched for a second and then moved over to the edge of the hole, where I could now see Kellan hanging at the edge, looking around for me.

He spotted me, and his mouth opened in question, but I cut him off. "They're coming in from the back side of the statues. I need you and your team to go past the barricades, about a quarter of the way toward their side, wait for them to pass, and then follow a little bit behind them."

Kellan hesitated, and then nodded. "You're right—that's the only way to get any sort of advantage over them. Catch them between us in a classic pincer move."

He started to lash off, but paused when I said, "Watch out for anyone on lookout underneath. If they manage to sound the alarm, they can swing around on you and take you out. Don't get me wrong—it would buy us time to fix this statue problem—but you're more valuable the longer you stay in this fight."

Kellan gave a surprised laugh and flashed me a thumbs-up before moving away. I heard him barking orders to his team, and then turned away, confident that he would do the best he could. I looked around and saw that my mother was now two thirds of the way through her statue, but everyone else was moving more slowly.

"Maddox, get over there and help Min-Ha!" I called. I hated pulling Maddox off the statue she was currently working on, but Min-Ha's was the second one in, which meant it was the lynchpin statue for the other team's strategy. Without it, there would be a wide gap between the first and third statue that would leave them exposed and vulnerable, while giving us line of sight on them. We needed to remove it first to create a break in that cover, and then we could worry about the other one. "Dylan, Zale! Get up on the third statue in and report how close they are! They've got to be getting near."

Dylan, in an extremely gutsy move, immediately cast her lash onto the first statue—the one that Leo was currently cutting through. The statue creaked as she swung in a wide circle around it, causing Leo to retract the blade and stagger back, concern and fear that he had done something wrong crossing his face. I gritted my teeth together, angry that she would do something so dangerous, and motioned for Leo to keep going as Dylan tossed a lash toward the statue my mother was almost

CHAPTER 29

finished cutting through. The statue began to slide just before Dylan's weight hit it—and then sped up right after, beginning to tilt backward.

Leo watched for a second, and then turned back to cutting. I saw a grim yet satisfied look on Leo's face as he continued to slice through the statue, and the sight made me pause, until I realized which statue he was taking down: Ezekial Pine, the man who had murdered Leo's creator. No wonder he looked satisfied—he was exacting his metaphorical revenge on him. I absorbed that for a moment while I continued to track Dylan's movement.

Dylan threw another lash as she swung up and around Rachel Pine's falling form, connecting with the third statue and disconnecting her line just as the statue completely detached from the solid anchor its legs had provided. It landed headfirst in the water below with a splash. The legs, still visible over the banister, continued to swing over, until they landed with a second splash.

Dylan finished her belay-like climb up the statue's arm, and turned so that her back was facing us, leaning forward slightly so she could peek out past the statue for signs of our attackers. It was a good position, as it required very little movement on her part, while keeping her almost invisible to them.

And it would have to do. I needed to make sure that everyone else was in place and that the statues were well on their way down, because we didn't have a moment to waste. I leaned forward to check on the progress of Min-Ha's statue, and to see where Zale was.

Zale hadn't pulled off Dylan's theatrical stunt, and was now lashing his way up the front of a statue opposite Dylan. Frankly, I was little surprised to see him there—I hadn't expected him to follow my orders—and watched for a second as he climbed. Then a sharp grating sound caught my attention, and I turned in time to see the statue Min-Ha and Maddox had been working on break free. Only it didn't fall forward, so much as it slid. I watched, a knot forming in my stomach as the slanted edge of the statue's shins crashed into the handrails. They snapped free from where they were mounted, and the entire bridge shuddered as the statue scraped along the edge on its way down, kicking up sparks under the friction of the massive slab of metal sliding off the edge of the bridge. Min-Ha and Maddox danced back a few steps, their arms coming up to shield their eyes.

The sparks continued, an acrid smell of smoke filled the air, and then the statue finally hit the water with a splash, leaving only the face of Otto Klein—the first representative from the Mechanics Department and one of the Founders—resting against the outer edge of the bridge. For a second, his head teetered against the side, and then something gave and it dragged off to the left, disappearing with a shredding, metallic sound interrupted by the *snap snap snap* of the banister breaking.

For a second, I worried that the impact of the statue on the bridge might have tossed a few of our competitors free—but then realized that as long as no one got trapped underneath it, they'd be fine. If they did, they'd be dead.

I hoped for the former over the latter, but didn't dwell on it. There just wasn't any *time*.

Maddox and Min-Ha were racing toward the other statue, cutters in hand, when Zale whistled, and I looked up to see him making a hand signal at me—two open palms followed by two fingers. They were twelve statues away. I looked at Dylan, and she flashed eleven fingers.

"Zale! Min-Ha! Fill the void where the statue used to be. Dylan, you're with Holly, there, opposite of them!" I ordered, pointing at my mother. "Maddox, get that other statue down. Grey, how's it coming?"

"Almost got it!" he shouted back, and sure enough, seconds later, his statue came crashing down. Relief poured through me; we had limited their ability to enter on that side, somewhat. Now we just needed to make sure that Maddox got finished on the other side as well, and we could gain at least a level playing field.

"Great! Back up, Holly and Dylan. Maddox?"

"Give me a second," she grunted, and I glanced over to see her already about halfway through the statue.

Meanwhile, Zale and Dylan had clambered down their own statues to get into position, and I pulled my baton out, prepared to back up Min-Ha's side, while my father rushed over from his position in front of the hall, helping to fill the hole.

With him in place, and Leo backing up my mother and Dylan on the other side, I forced myself to stand still, needing to keep a clear picture of the battlefield as it unfurled. I saw Frederick racing back, almost to the forwardmost barricade, and realized that he had figured out that something was up. I was surprisingly glad to see him, his nebulous legacy status notwithstanding. We were going to need all the help we could get.

Seconds later, the first crimson-clad figure swung around the third statue on Min-Ha's side, and suddenly, both sides of the bridge were embroiled in battle. I checked on Maddox and saw that she was almost finished cutting through her statue, and then checked on the side of the battle that Zale was now leading. The first person through was already flying past him in an uncontrolled tumble that told me she'd been caught and thrown by the team there, but three more were swinging in behind her. Min-

Ha got hit in the chest with a brutal, two-legged kick, and went flying in the direction of the hole.

I snapped into action, throwing my lash end a few feet in front of her, anticipating her trajectory. It landed with a blue flash, and I immediately braced a leg against the barricade. She wasn't heavy, but she was falling, and the weight of her body hitting the end of the line was enough to make my bones rattle in my joints. As soon as she stopped bouncing, I began to reel in the line using my gyros. Then her weight suddenly disappeared, and seconds later, I saw her climbing over the edge of the hole under the power of her own lashes, and moving to rejoin the fight.

The bridge shuddered as the last statue dropped, and then Maddox was suddenly in the fray as well, her baton flying to push back three attackers. I watched them for a second, and then turned my attention to my mother's side of the bridge, checking to see how the battle was going.

The first thing I noticed was that Dylan was missing—and then I saw her clinging to the side of the third statue, lying in wait. Sure enough, a second person swung past her, and to my utmost surprise, she flexed her thighs and leapt off the side of the statue, aiming a kick for the attacker.

She caught him in the side, knocking him off course, and then swung back, narrowly avoiding a kick to her head as a third attacker swung by. My mother was in the process of electrocuting their first attacker when the guy who got past Dylan planted a foot into her shoulder, slamming her back several staggering steps, and right into Leo.

Leo caught her with a steadying grip, but then the man was on them, his baton whirling and swinging for my mom. I grabbed the edge of the barricade, preparing to vault over and intercede, but Leo, with one steadying arm still around my mother's shoulder, neatly deflected the blow with his own baton.

Something grabbed my wrist, and I looked down in time to see a baton aimed for my arm. I jerked my hand back, breaking the grip of the candidate who had somehow found a way to sneak up under the bridge, and stumbled back, still fumbling to understand how they could've gotten up here me without me noticing. Before I could figure it out, he swung up and charged.

I ducked down, avoiding the blow from the baton, but his knee caught me in the stomach, hard enough to knock the breath out of me and drop me to the ground. I curled up around myself as a deep, throbbing pain radiated from the impact site. I drew in a ragged, difficult breath, and then forced my body to roll, anticipating the next attack.

Sharp bursts of heat hit the back of my head as his baton came down in the place where it had just been, and panic suddenly gripped me. He had been aiming for my *head*! It could've been an accident, but my gut told me it wasn't. He was trying to kill me.

I scrambled to my hands and feet, a surge of adrenaline helping to neutralize the pain. Getting my feet under me, I tried to move away, but a hand grabbed my hair, yanking me back.

I slammed my foot back on instinct, and was rewarded with a deep crack and a sharp cry. I then twisted around and lashed out with an elbow, but my timing was off and I missed him as he fell to the ground. He retaliated by shoving a hand into my back, strongly enough that I fell forward onto my stomach.

My chin slammed into the metal ground, and then I felt a hand grabbing a fistful of my uniform on the back of my thigh, and an intense weight coming over my legs, and realized that he was climbing up the back of my body.

I heard the hum of the baton and began to struggle, but my

legs were weighed down by his torso. The hair on the back of my neck stood on end in anticipation of the blow he was about to plant there with his baton—but then there was a wet smacking sound, and suddenly his weight was gone.

I twisted around to see my mother standing over me, shaking out her fist, and my attacker on the ground, his right eye already beginning to swell. He groaned and started to push up off the ground, but my mother's foot snapped out and hit him square in the face, knocking him out.

"You okay?" she asked, offering me a hand up, her features lined with concern and fear. "Did he hurt you?"

"I'm fine, Mom," I said, suddenly self-conscious. I didn't want her or the rest of the Knights thinking I needed my mother to save me, but at the same time... I wanted to give her a hug for intervening. The guy had caught me off guard.

Instead, I settled for taking her hand, letting her help me up, and looking around. "Why are you here? What's going on?"

Frederick was down on the ground unconscious, but Zale, Norman, and Min-Ha were in the process of eliminating the last attacker on their side. Dylan was losing ground on hers, but she and Leo were being joined by Kellan and Sella, who were rushing in behind the two remaining attackers on that side, their batons already out.

"We took out three; Maddox's side took out four. Kellan's team got two on the statues, and with this guy here—"

My mother's voice was cut off as the final guy was pitched over the side by Leo and Kellan, and then a booming chime sounded. I looked around, stunned by how suddenly everything just stopped, and then the walls of the arena filled with Scipio's face.

"Congratulations, candidates," he announced in a booming voice that was encased in ice. I suddenly thought of Rose, and found myself wondering if she was the reason he sounded that way. Or rather... the lack of her. I made a mental note to ask Leo, and focused on what Scipio was saying, rather than how he was saying it. Now that the fight was over, all I wanted to do was go home and take a nap.

"—Under Liana Castell's leadership, you were able to repel the invaders. Now, normally, you would be given the rest of the day to rest and prepare for the next challenge, but due to heightened security concerns, we will be concluding the Tourney this evening. You are expected to report tonight at eight o'clock, and will be accompanied by officials for the remainder of the day. This change is top secret; only you, the council members, and the test designers are aware of this change, until it is announced to the rest of the Tower just before the challenge begins." I looked around and quickly saw that all the drones had left, leaving us alone in the still of the arena. It was disquieting. I knew they would be back—the Knights of the Tower would not uphold any Champion that won without being able to view their actions during the final challenge—but still it was eerie to realize that no one was watching this. "This secrecy is for your protection, so act accordingly. Please return to your starting elevators and proceed to the preparation rooms to have your equipment checked and exchanged for your own, as well as to meet your escorts. I will see you soon, candidates. Until then, rest, and prepare, for before the day is over, one of you will be named Champion."

The screen went dark, and I found the elation that had barely begun to form suddenly dashed under the realization that the Tourney would be finished. Tonight.

30

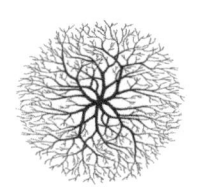

We walked back to the elevators that the officials had used to lead us into the arena, and I caught one last glimpse of my mother before we were lowered down into the starting rooms. The same officials who had overseen our preparation stripped us of everything, including our uniforms. My bracelet with Quess's shockers was left alone, thankfully, but all forms of jewelry were pretty much ignored, from the ring on Dylan's finger to the chain around Maddox's neck. We were issued new uniforms, our pads returned, and were then escorted from the room to our apartments.

Dylan insisted on going back to her own apartment instead of joining us in ours, and I didn't press her too hard about it. Now that the final challenge was upon us, we were back to being competitors again—not that we had ever really stopped. I knew she was worried about her standing after the stunt I had pulled on the bridge, and I felt a small pang of guilt that I had sabotaged her chances, though I didn't allow it to become remorse. I had done what I needed to at the time to ensure our victory and make it to the final challenge.

She and the official exited a few floors below us, and then we walked down the hall, escorted by three officials, right up to our door.

"You will remain here while the designers set up the arena," the lead official announced. "You are not permitted to exit the Citadel, as an additional security feature, so if you have need for any food, you will contact us, and we will have meals sent up to you. If any of you wish to drop out of the Tourney before the final challenge, you may do so from the Knights' server through your pad. Net permissions will not be restored until the end of the final challenge, to prevent any cheating, and you will have no visitors."

I blinked, growing alarmed by all the restrictions she was listing off. I wasn't completely sure about Tourney security protocols, but I was certain these were new, and meant to make us feel safe and secure. Still, all I heard was that we couldn't reach out to our friends, and they couldn't reach out to us. That we were potentially trapped, should anyone come after us. And that we would be susceptible to being poisoned or otherwise adversely affected, if we ordered our food from them.

Thank Scipio I had made us use our ration cards for the week to buy enough food to feed us all in our apartment, but that only addressed one of my concerns. I needed to figure out a way to get in touch with Zoe, Eric, and Quess, to let them know that the Tourney was ending today, but that we were fine, and still together. I didn't want to think about what they might do trying to find out what had happened to us, so keeping them informed was critical. Maybe I could try to net Alex. He frequently monitored my net, which meant there was every chance he would see that I was trying to reach out to him and override the block, right?

I honestly wasn't certain about that. I knew Alex could scramble the transmission and hide it from the logs, but overriding a block might be a bit more difficult. Even worse, it could put him at a higher risk of getting caught doing something he wasn't supposed to, and I knew for a fact that Sadie Monroe was gunning for him in an attempt to get to me.

Not to mention, Dinah might have already had him transferred into her department, and if that were the case, he might not even have access to net data yet.

But that made me consider Dinah as an alternative. Having her real name had its advantages... but what I didn't have was her identification number, and with the block in place, I couldn't access the history. On top of that, I was fairly certain she had gone in and erased that data to keep me from accessing it. Without that, I couldn't net her to ask her to tell Zoe, Eric, and Quess not to worry about our absence.

And I wouldn't be able to until the Tourney was finished.

I realized the Knight who had spoken was looking at me expectantly, waiting for me to respond. Unable to formulate anything past "Thank you," I forced a smile onto my lips and hit the door scanner, stepping through it as soon as the door was open.

We filed into our apartment, but the officials remained outside, and would remain there until it was time to go. None of us spoke until the door was closed, and I headed directly into the living room, eager to put some space between us and the officials. Even with walls between us, I felt exposed and vulnerable. People whose loyalty I couldn't count on were guarding the door. Who knew what was really happening on the other side of that wall?

Paranoia crept in, and I paused in the living room, and then turned and headed for the hallway, motioning for the others to follow. I opened the door to my room and stepped aside to let Maddox and Leo through first.

"Tian?" Maddox said as she entered, and Leo and I exchanged looks. He held back to let me push in before him, and sure enough, Tian was sitting up from where she had been reclining on the bed, half her shaggy, white-blond bob standing straight up on one side, and both eyes blinking heavily, as if she had been sleeping.

"What are you doing here?" I asked, alarmed by her presence.

"I'm—" She broke off, a yawn cracking her mouth open loudly, and then exhaled slowly. "—Here to warn you," she finished, smacking her lips together. She shook her head, her small hands running up to ruffle her hair and scrub her eyes, and then leapt out of the bed, landing lightly on her feet. "I can't find Jang-Mi."

My stomach dropped. "What do you mean?"

Tian gave me an exasperated look. "I mean she's gone, Liana! I woke up at one this morning, and I couldn't find her! I think whatever's happening is happening soon. She kept saying that she didn't want to leave me, but couldn't stop what was coming. She told me that if she left, I was supposed to wait for her, but when I saw she was gone... I came straight here to tell you. We have to find her. We have to stop her!"

I hesitated. On the one hand, she was absolutely right—we had to make sure the sentinel didn't follow through on whatever its programmers were forcing it to do. For all I knew, it was on an assassination mission to take out Lacey or Strum, or even another council member, to create a vacancy in case the Tourney didn't play out the way our enemies wanted it to. On

CHAPTER 30

the other, if we snuck out of the Citadel, and the officials found out—or worse, the final challenge started without us—we would end up forfeiting entirely.

Could I risk the final challenge of the Tourney to try to put a stop to whatever damage the sentinel was going to do? No. But I could do everything in my power to alert everyone who *could* put a stop to it.

"Tian, we can't leave," I told her. Her brows drew together and her mouth opened, ready to yell at me, but I cut her off. "We can't. We're under guard right now as a precautionary measure for the next challenge."

"The *challenge*!" she exclaimed. "Who cares? Jang-Mi is going to be forced to kill people again! It's *killing* her, Liana! Each time she kills someone, she gets farther and farther away, more and more broken! We need to help her!"

"It doesn't work like that, Tian," I said patiently, my heart aching the entire time. I wanted to move heaven and earth to help her. I wanted to take her in my arms and promise her that I would help save the thing that she had forged such a powerful bond with. But I had taken on a responsibility that was far greater in purpose than the problem of the sentinel. I had to make the responsible choice.

"Jang-Mi might kill a few people here or there, but if we don't win the Tourney, everyone in the Tower could *die*. But I'm not going to let that unfold, either. Do you still have your net?"

The girl gave me a confused look, her nose scrunching up, and then nodded. "Yeah, isn't that how you found me?"

I shook my head. "No, we couldn't find your signal. Could Jang-Mi be masking it, somehow?"

She shrugged, and I sighed. That mystery would have to be solved later. At least she had her net. Through it and her, we could reach Quess—and through him, everyone else. Which was good: I might not be able to leave, but now I could reach the others and get them to help track down the sentinel.

"Call Quess, and tell him that he needs to get in touch with Zoe. She needs to call Lacey and explain about the sentinel."

"Are you crazy?" Tian exclaimed, her eyes round. "Jang-Mi killed two of her people. Lacey will want to tear her apart."

"Not if she thinks keeping it intact could lead to Ambrose's killers," I replied. It was a guess, but I felt strongly in my gut that it was true.

Tian bit her lip, a reluctant look on her face. "All right," she said hesitantly. "I'll net them, but I get to go with them to find her! I know you'll tell me to stay, but I have to be sure she's safe! She's my friend, Liana, and she doesn't want to hurt anyone."

I exhaled slowly and touched her cheek, wiping away a tear as it started to drip down from one large, shimmering eye. "I believe you, Tian," I said. "And I think you're right. You should go."

"Liana!" Maddox said harshly, and I gave her an apologetic look.

"I'm sorry, Doxy, but she has to go." Tian had proven more than once that she could reach the sentinel—whether it was through her words or through appearing to be in imminent danger—and having her there could help tip things in our favor. She might even be able to get Jang-Mi to stand down without hurting anyone.

At least, I sincerely hoped she could.

"Liana's right," Leo added. "Tian managed to get Jang-Mi to stop before. Her presence could make a difference."

"And whatever this programming is that is compelling Jang-Mi to do this might be too strong for Tian's presence to help! She should stay here!"

"Doxy!" Tian said, putting her fists on her hips. "How can

CHAPTER 30

you say that? Jang-Mi thinks I'm her long-lost child! I can stop her."

Maddox gave her a tight-lipped expression and then sighed. "Okay, let me try it this way. What happens if you fail, and Jang-Mi comes back to herself, only to realize she's killed her little girl? What happens to your friend then?"

Tian's face grew horrified, and then sickened, and for a moment, I was appalled that Maddox would even go there.

And then I realized she had a point. The sentinel wasn't completely autonomous. There was someone forcing Jang-Mi to comply, and who knew what that entailed? If Jang-Mi wasn't able to resist the orders, then there was no guarantee she could stop herself, even for Tian.

Which was probably why she had been warning Tian that something was going on—she knew that she might not be able to stop herself while they were using her to do whatever it was they needed her to do. If Jang-Mi was self-aware enough to realize that she wasn't going to have any control over her actions, then that could explain why she had told Tian to wait for her. She knew Tian would try to intervene to stop her, and was afraid of her getting hurt!

"No," Tian said, and I realized that my reversal must've been showing on my face. At the very least, I was certain she could see the regret there, but she shook her head, as if refusing my unspoken apology. "No! I have to go, Liana! I can help. You won't be able to stop me after they come and get you for the Tourney!"

"But by then it will hopefully be too late for you to do anything," I replied. I couldn't be a hundred percent certain of that, but I hoped that Quess and the others could find the sentinel and stop her before the officials came for us. In which case Tian would be here—and safe. "Now call Quess."

She gave me an angry look, but stomped off to net Quess. I stood up slowly, still a little sore from the fight earlier, and Leo leaned close, pitching his voice low so as not to interrupt Tian's focus on giving Quess my orders.

"Are you sure about keeping her here? What if they don't find it before we have to go?"

"Then she'll run off to join them," I replied. "But at least we'll give them a little time to find it without her, first."

I hoped they would. Because I couldn't get rid of the heavy, sinking feeling that something was about to go terribly wrong.

31

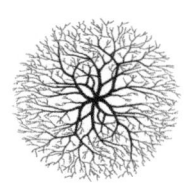

I checked my indicator. Four hours had gone by since Tian had netted Quess, and I was beginning to chafe under the fact that he hadn't netted back to let me know what was going on. After a modified conversation with him through her—one in which I thankfully remembered to ask him if he had working shockers with him, confirming that the ones on my wrist weren't the only ones available—I had anticipated a call back within an hour. But there had been no word.

I was anxious. Maddox was nervous. Tian was frantic, prowling around the inside of the walls as if the apartment were a cage keeping her in. Maddox and I had both sealed our bedrooms using the biometric locks we had available to us as a precaution to keep her from sneaking out that way, but we wouldn't be able to keep her in once the challenge started—she could just walk out the front door—and the knowledge made my stomach churn. I just prayed that Zoe and the others had managed to convince Lacey and Strum to help us, and that they were tracking the sentinel down right now.

That thought only made me feel more apprehensive, and I found myself looking at where Maddox and Leo were sitting, thinking. I didn't need them for the next part of the challenge—not really. I knew that they wanted to go to watch my back, but we still hadn't heard from Quess or Zoe, and I was really friggin' worried. If I could just get them to drop out of the Tourney, they would be free to net the others and find out what was going on.

I looked at Leo, the only one of us who had managed to remain calm—maddeningly so. He was currently flipping through a crimson manual for the Knight's Department at a rhythmic pace, the opaque plastic pages making a *fwip fwip fwip* sound.

"Leo?" I said, just as Tian swept from the living room to the kitchen, following her little path around the apartment.

"Hm?" he said, pausing mid-flip and looking up at me.

"What would you say if I told you and Maddox to drop out of the Tourney so that you could help the others?" I asked carefully.

His eyes widened for a moment in surprise, and then darkened, as if he had just pulled blinds across them. "No," he said flatly, turning back to his book.

"Absolutely not," Maddox added, looking over from where she was watching the final roster for the Tourney. "Several people have already dropped out: all of Frederick's team, including Kellan, in fact. But Zale's team is still intact, and Dylan hasn't dropped out yet, and neither has Frederick. You'll be outnumbered six to one."

"Five to two," I said, thinking of my mother. Maddox, however, seemed to miss the connection, and I added, "My mother?"

CHAPTER 31

"Do you think you can trust her?" she asked, giving me a searching look.

I bit my lip, considering her question and all the things my mother had revealed to me, and then nodded slowly. "Yeah," I said, sounding a little surprised even to myself. Maybe it was because I had never considered it possible that my mother would ever support me, or maybe there was still some small part of me that was a little doubtful, but it didn't matter—something had shifted inside of me, and I was making the choice to trust her.

I noticed Maddox giving me a doubtful look, and sucked in a deep breath, forcing more confidence into my voice. "Yeah, I really do. So I don't think that it would be that bad if you guys were to drop out and—"

"Well, I don't trust Dylan as far as I can throw the *Tower*," Maddox cut in smoothly. "As long as she's in the Tourney, you are not going in without backup."

"I honestly don't think she'll try to kill me, Maddox," I replied. "Drones will be everywhere, security is insane…"

"And if we dropped out, everyone would see and know that you were vulnerable," Leo said, filling the air after I slowly trailed off, trying to get them to see my point. He didn't even look up from the book he was reading, so he missed my frown and the flash of irritation that was undoubtedly shining in my eyes. Instead, he continued flipping through the book he was reading. "Not to mention, if we left to help Quess and the others, you'd be alone and exposed to a possible attack, whether it be before the Tourney or during. Especially without Quess there to keep the drones on you."

I bristled and narrowed my eyes at him. "You do realize that I'm in charge, right?" I asked him.

He and Maddox gave me identical looks that said "you're

not going to win this", and I sighed, rolled my eyes, and leaned back into the chair.

"Fine," I grumbled. I wasn't about to give up, but I needed to find the right argument to convince them. "Then distract me with something. What's going on with the standings? How is Dylan's approval rating?" I asked, dreading the answer. The server kept a real-time account of approval ratings as each Knight logged their preferences, and though they were free to change them until the end of the Tourney, they would give us an idea of who was currently favored by the Knights in the Citadel.

Maddox sighed. "You're in the lead with twenty-eight percent, but Zale has twenty-six, Dylan has twenty-five, and Frederick has twenty-one percent. It's anyone one's game, at this point."

And a pretty close one, at that. I sighed and began rubbing my eyes, my tension spiking. It was a close race, and one wrong move could get me eliminated. If I didn't win this next challenge, then there was every chance that the Tower would fall, and I couldn't let that happen. But at the same time, the danger with Jang-Mi and the sentinel, and the fact that I hadn't heard from anyone yet, was pressing. Four hours was a long time; they should've found the sentinel by now.

What if Lacey hadn't agreed to help them? What if they hadn't been able to stop it?

What if they were dead right now, while we were stuck up here waiting for this stupid Tourney to begin?

I went cold at the thought, and once again felt the need to try to convince Leo and Maddox to leave the Tourney and go help the others. It would go a long way toward reassuring me, knowing they were there, and then I could focus on the challenge.

Or at least, that was what I told myself as I opened my

mouth to once again encourage them to drop out. "Look, if you drop as soon as the officials come to collect us, then you can—"

"Liana, no," Leo said, closing the book with a snap. "Even without all the danger that it would cause to you, you forget one fundamental thing: you made a promise that you wouldn't go off on your own again, and if you order us to leave, you are breaking that promise."

"And Zoe will kill us and then you, in that order, if we let that happen," Maddox added.

"I'll do it right now," grumbled Tian as she stalked back in from the hallway, continuing her circuit of our small apartment.

"Knock it off, Tian," Maddox said, clearly tired of the young girl's grumblings. "You need to suck it up and accept that we're right about this. You don't need to be out there."

"I can help!" the young girl snapped sullenly for the umpteenth time. "Jang-Mi won't hurt me."

"Jang-Mi is not in control," Leo said flatly. "Or at least, not fully in control. Which is just as dangerous. You should trust Liana and Maddox on this, and stay once they come to collect us."

"Well, I won't," she said, coming to a stop and balling her hands into fists. "As soon as you're gone, I'm going to net Quess and find out where he is, and if he won't help me, then I'll call Alex and make *him* help me!"

I sighed and leaned back onto the couch I was sitting on. It seemed there was nothing any of us could say to change her mind about going, and trying to convince her that we were right was only a waste of breath. She was going to leave the first chance she got, and that was that. I just had to hope that Quess and the others keyed in to the fact that we'd kept her from joining them, and wouldn't tell her anything.

And that they were all right.

I sighed again and stood up, resolving to keep myself busy. All this sitting around and waiting for something to happen was driving me nuts—as was the communications lockdown, and the fact no one had netted Tian back.

"Anybody want anything?" I asked as I made my way to the kitchen.

"No, thanks," Leo said, opening his book back up.

"Nothing for me," Maddox added, turning the pad back on and accessing the server.

"Hot chocolate," Tian childishly demanded, and I rolled my eyes, but reached up into one of the overhead cabinets to fetch her a packet. I was in the process of pouring hot water into a mug when the doorbell sounded, and I froze.

"Candidates are ordered to the arena for the presentation of the final challenge," the automated voice announced.

I drew in a deep breath, blew it out, and set down the mug, which was now shaking in my hands. No, scratch that, my *hand* was shaking. I flexed it open and closed a few times, trying to calm the sudden apprehension that had surged.

I took a few moments to steel myself, and then turned, motioning for the others. They were already standing, and Tian was now leaning against the wall just outside of the hall, a pleased smile on her lips.

"Time to go," I said, softly, nodding toward the door. "Tian... I really hope you don't go, but if you do, please be careful, and don't do anything dangerous, okay?"

Tian stared at me for a long second, her features scrunched up into a scowl. "Can you promise that you won't do anything dangerous in the Tourney?"

I shook my head. "You know I can't."

"Then don't ask me to," she replied, holding my gaze with a blaze of determination.

"That's not the same, Tian," I said softly. "But... just try, okay?"

Her jaw held a stubborn set, but she nodded, just once, as the door buzzed again, repeating its demand.

"Go hide," I told her, and then turned to the door and squared my shoulders. It was time to finish this.

"Congratulations, candidate," Scipio said, his face glowing in the relative darkness of the room I had just been deposited into. I was alone now, having been separated from Leo and Maddox almost as soon as we entered the halls beneath the arena. I hadn't liked it, but there was nothing any of us could do as they guided us toward different paths. The official who had led me here had finally broken down enough to reveal that we would all be placed near each other, but that was all I got.

My equipment was assigned, and once again I did little to put it on myself, just nodding or shaking my head to answer the official's questions regarding my comfort. She dressed me, taking careful pains to make sure that everything worked the way it was supposed to.

Truthfully, her hands and presence had made me jumpier than a cat in a cucumber patch, and for half of it I was certain that I was going to pass out, I was so lightheaded.

Thank Scipio the officials either didn't notice or were too professional to comment. Maybe they'd been coached to be prepared for a candidate freak-out prior to the final challenge. I couldn't be the only one apprehensive about what was to come, could I?

Either way, I was relieved when I was deposited into the final room alone, and I carefully shook out my limbs and arms, trying to get the pins and needles to settle, while listening to Scipio's speech. My heart was pounding loudly in my ears, making it difficult for me to really focus on what he was saying, but I managed to catch most of it, using his words to help draw me back into the moment.

"—The challenges you face here will be like nothing you have faced before," he assured me solemnly, his dark blue eyes burning holes into mine. "The Battle for Six Bells will test your coordination, speed, and reactionary abilities. As you are well aware, not all of the candidates present in the challenge will be bidding for position; many of them will be trying to support their own candidates. The use of violence is authorized, but do not cause permanent harm to the other candidates, and keep a careful eye on your environment. The parameters are simple: the first to navigate the course and ring all six bells within three seconds will be the winner of the challenge, the Champion of the Tourney, and in all likelihood, the new head of the Knights Department, once the final votes from the Knights are taken into consideration. They will inherit the responsibilities that go along with that duty, including the obligation of the safety and well-being of the Tower. May honor, fortitude, and luck be with you, and may the best Knight win."

His image lingered for a second later, and then disappeared, leaving me in the dimly lit compartment, my stomach now twisted into knots. I had so many enemies going into this, and even with Maddox, Leo, and my mother backing me up, I couldn't be certain that I'd win.

Hell, I couldn't be certain I'd make it through the course. Dylan would be gunning for me, and so would Zale—and because of him, Min-Ha and my father, both of whom were formidable fighters. I wasn't a hundred percent sure that Min-Ha would actually target me specifically, given our interaction

CHAPTER 31

in the last challenge. I felt confident that I had earned her respect—but that didn't mean much in the grand scheme of things. Especially if she felt that Zale was better suited for the position.

Then there was Frederick. I hadn't had to fight him yet, but the vids taken of him during the Tourney revealed that he relied heavily on speed and agility. Agility I had, and speed as well, but not as much as him.

I would have to steer clear of them all, and try to get to the bells as soon as possible.

The screen glowed with the familiar instructions: *Stand in the center of the room.* I exhaled, and then moved over to the centermost part of the room, twisting my head around to try to relieve some of the tension. When the plate began to slide up, I was ready, and this time focused my gaze forward, not wanting to get overwhelmed by the view that looking up would bring, or the sickening, queasy sensation it produced.

I had placed myself in what I believed was a forward position, based on where the door had been in the other room, so I held perfectly still and waited, trying not to think about the door above me that still wasn't open, or the fact that if anyone had tampered with it, I'd be nothing but a splat against the ceiling.

My heart galloped in my chest, and my breath puffed in and out as the rapidly moving elevator continued to rise. Then light exploded from everywhere, temporarily blinding me and causing me to close my eyes.

When my eyes were opened, and focused again, I couldn't help but gape at the nightmare in front of me.

32

The elevator had deposited me on a long wall that was nearly fifty feet tall and ran in a circle around the edge of the arena. The top of the wall was flat, but not very wide; two feet in either direction would send me plummeting down. But that wasn't what held my attention or rapidly growing concern.

There were two concentric rings set into the ceiling, with enormous metal structures dangling from them, around a central free-hanging column in the center of the chaos, with six lonely silver bells at the bottom, waiting for someone to ring them. That was not going to be easy. The inner and outer rings were rotating, propelled in opposite directions like some sort of demented carousel—causing the giant metal structures to move, too. The inner ring was moving much faster than the outer, and in order to get to the column in the center, I would have to pass through both. Which meant lashing onto the dangling dark chunks of metal that were of all shapes and sizes—some as simple as a rectangular wall, but others far more complex and daunting.

One was shaped like the corkscrew of a pig's tail, another curved like an S. There were even more odd shapes behind those, all of them twisting and spinning together in a shifting obstacle course.

The closest thing I could compare the massive structures to were windchimes. And it was easy to see what the designers wanted—we had to navigate around each metal object using our lashes to get to the center, where that central column hung, a solid and still target that was a beacon of calm in the riot of motion.

I quickly recognized that the biggest problem would be balance: the structures had been designed to swing freely, so that any extra weight in the wrong place would cause it to swing out of place or spin faster. I had to be careful about which structure I chose, and where I landed. If I didn't, I could be thrown off—or collide with one of the other swinging structures, if any of their orbits overlapped.

I looked around the pathway I was on, suddenly recalling that others would be on it as well. I saw Leo already making his way toward me from the left, and then Maddox on my right. As I watched Maddox, she suddenly seemed to notice something behind her, and she whirled and began sprinting.

"Leo! Get Liana through that crap!" she shouted, her voice barely audible. "I'll handle Dylan!"

Confused, I looked past Maddox, momentarily losing her behind a new metal structure that was swinging into view—this one looked like a massive screwdriver or drill, poised to tear through the ground below. From just past it, I caught a quick glimpse of Dylan's familiar form racing away from Maddox—and realized that my teammate was angling to take on the competition early, in an effort to slow Dylan down and give me a chance to get to the column.

CHAPTER 32

Fear suddenly pounded in my heart, and I wanted to shout for Maddox to get back, but Leo reached me, grabbing me and spinning me around to face him. "I came up next to Frederick," he said, his eyes wide. "He's already made it to one of the structures. We have to move."

"But Maddox!" I said. "She just ran off without backup, against Dylan! We can't leave her alone!"

Leo hesitated, looking past my shoulder, and then shook his head. "No. My priority is getting you to that column. The faster we get there, the sooner you can ring those bells and end this."

I stared at him, and then clenched my teeth. He was right to a point, but he wasn't taking into account Maddox's recent trauma. She was trying to help me, she was doing it without backup, and I was worried that her recklessness would get her hurt or killed.

I opened my mouth to argue, but Leo's eyes suddenly widened, looking past my shoulder, and then he shoved me down, shouting, "Watch out!"

I tensed, my hands automatically coming up to protect my face while I bent forward, ducking. Leo's hands were firmly pressing against my shoulders, helping me get low, and then suddenly they slid off me. Leo gave a grunt, and I lowered my hands and arms enough to see him being dragged off the side of the wall, his arms stretching toward me.

I reached for him, trying to grab his arm to keep him from falling. Our fingertips brushed, briefly, and then he was too far away. I watched, horrified that he was falling, and then realized he wasn't. He was being dragged back and up, and as I followed his trajectory, I saw a figure in crimson standing atop a structure that had just swung by, long black hair streaming. I met Min-Ha's eyes from across the widening gap, and she gave me an apologetic smile before focusing on the task of reeling Leo in.

I realized that I had been her target, but Leo had gotten in the way, taking the hit from her lash. A flash of resentment went through me—slight betrayal by her actions after the earlier challenge—but it was followed closely by relief. Min-Ha was a lot of things, and at the top of that list of descriptors was the most important one: she was honorable. That meant that even though she had grabbed Leo, she wouldn't drop him; she'd make sure he was securely attached to the wall, even if she knocked him unconscious.

Not that she would, of course. Min-Ha was an excellent fighter, but Leo could hold his own and then some. I had no doubt he would overcome her easily.

But the fact remained that I was alone. Maddox was off chasing Dylan, and Leo had been grabbed. And I couldn't go after either of them, because that would only waste even more time.

Leo was right. I needed to get to the bells. Now.

I gritted my teeth and turned my back to Leo as he disappeared from view, dismissing the obstacle already passing me and focusing on the one that was swinging into view. My palms were sweating, and I wiped them against my thighs, studying the oncoming structure which reminded me of a massive chandelier.

I had to hurry. It was approaching quickly and would pass me completely if I didn't start running.

Immediately.

I turned and began to sprint, my arms and legs pumping. I became aware of a soft squeaking, and glanced over my shoulder at the oncoming chandelier, trying to gauge how close it was and where and when I would need to jump. As the edge of it began to swing past me, I realized that the entire structure was twisting.

That wasn't a good sign. As soon as I latched onto it, my

weight at the end of a long line would increase the speed of that spin, and if I didn't reel myself in fast enough, I could smack into one of the other obstacles, with such force that it would break every bone in my body.

But I couldn't wait for the next one. If I did that, it would give the other candidates more time to beat me to the bells. Hell, I'd given them too much time already.

I yanked a lash end from where it sat on the inside of my sleeve and pulled out a few feet so I could spin the short length in my hand, building up the static charge. Now that the chandelier was passing me, I faced forward and kept an eye on it, watching the gap between the structure and the wall grow narrower as it drew past. I waited for as long as I could, my heart pounding and my chest heaving, and then leapt out into the open space, my arms and legs still pumping even as I left the solid ground. My heart thudded once, twice, thrice, and then I cast my line just as gravity began to pull me down, using my hand controls to let the line fly free.

My throw was true, and a second later the lash end hit the structure with a blue flash. I instantly reversed the gyro at my back to pull in the line and reel me up, but the ring began to spin faster anyway, unbalanced by my weight. I flinched as a shadow caught the corner of my eye, revealing a beam swinging for me—I tucked my legs up to my chest and pulled myself up hand over hand, praying.

The other structure missed me by mere inches, coming close enough that a breeze formed against the back of my neck and sent chills down my spine. I stiffened, and then exhaled in relief as I realized it was gone.

The winch in my harness finished pulling me in, and I grabbed onto the base of the chandelier, hooking my arms over the metal frame and trying to squeeze as close to it as possible, in an attempt to slow the momentum I had generated with my landing.

The world spun as the ring continued to revolve, but after a few passes, it began to slow to a more reasonable rate, and I dared to look at my surroundings. The ring was carrying me back around, so that my back was facing the wall I had leapt off of moments before. I drew my gaze toward the central column and the inner row of dangling metal structures, trying to figure out my next move.

I quickly realized I would have to climb higher first. The inner obstacles were much shorter than the outer ones, making it impossible for me to lash onto one from where I was situated.

Letting go with one hand, I focused on a section of the chandelier a few feet above me, then threw my lash. It caught, and within seconds my gyros were whirring lightly against my back, reeling in the line. I flicked my other arm out, repeating the process to climb higher up the structure. The obstacle course swung on, but I did my best to ignore the motion, focusing completely on my task of getting up high enough to transition into the inner ring of obstacles.

After throwing my fourth lash, I paused for a moment to get my bearings, holding onto the edge with both hands, anchored by my lashes. My heart sank when the inner circle of obstacles came into view. The structure I was about to pass was a thin metal tube, and it carried a solitary crimson figure with light brown hair. He was climbing up it, using his lashes to ascend as it swung back and forth. It was Frederick, and even though he was just beginning his climb, it chilled me to see him so much closer to the bells than I was.

I was still too low to reach the tube, and I didn't like the idea of being underneath him—because he could easily drop down and knock me off.

I shifted my gaze past him, studying the next structure in the line, and saw that it was also a bit out of reach from my current position. Not only that; I saw not one, but *several* crimson figures clinging to that one. Like the one Frederick was on, it was too high for me to reach. I looked toward the top of the chandelier.

I had to get higher.

I breathed in, then slowly prepared to throw another lash. This throw would be trickier, as the higher I climbed up the chandelier, the thinner the frame became—which meant less space for my lash to stick.

I distributed my weight to one of my hands, pulled the line tight with my other, and then, taking a few more huffing breaths that only served to distract me from the fact that I was about to stand on a very thin strip of metal over a very long fall, stood up.

I wobbled, my heart dropping into the pit of my stomach, and then caught my balance, relying heavily on the connected line.

"Don't disconnect," I breathed to it, gingerly starting to look up. Vertigo assailed me as I caught view of one of the structures spinning past, and I continued to tilt my head toward the next section of the chandelier, adding a very stern, "And don't throw up," by way of a pep talk.

I swallowed the nausea the sight had stirred up in my stomach and sucked in a deep breath, focusing on the relative stillness of the metal above me. I gathered up the line in my hand, spun, and cast.

It hit dead center, and I reeled the line in tight, and began drawing myself in.

I was halfway up, when there was a loud, metallic clang, and the line suddenly jerked violently, tossing me around like a ragdoll. I was so shocked by the sudden movement that all I could do was hold on, shake with terror, and close my eyes, trying not to lose the contents of my stomach. It stopped suddenly, but the line was vibrating with such intensity that I could feel it where it ran through my suit and down my side. I immediately looked up, my heart in my throat, concerned about the lash-end connection.

It had shifted several inches down from where I had initially thrown it, and was now only a few short inches away from the bottom edge of the frame it was attached to.

I immediately threw my secondary line, my limbs quivering with fear that whatever had hit it would strike again, and I would be ripped free. It landed a few inches from the first lash, and I sagged into the harness, sweat pouring down from my hairline as I set both lines to reel me up.

As they worked, I started looking around, trying to figure out what had hit me. I assumed that it was another obstacle that had been offset by a candidate leaping onto it, and immediately searched for a telltale flash of crimson. Instead, as I swiveled my head around as far behind me as I could, I found a dark figure with a tattered cloak clinging to the opposite side of the chandelier's frame, its eyes twin red flames.

33

The sentinel wasn't looking at me. Instead, its head swiveled around as it scanned the arena, its lethal weapon gripped in one fist. I stared at it, dangling helplessly and perfectly exposed. If it saw me, then there was every chance it would shoot me. Hell, it was probably here for that reason!

I had to climb more quickly. Once I got higher up the chandelier, I'd be one step closer to making it to the inner ring, where I could figure out what I was going to do. I turned away from the sentinel, the muscles in my neck anticipating an attack, but focused on the metal frame above me.

As my lines drew me up, my mouth was dry, my heart pounding erratically in my chest. I rose up by inches which then became feet—all so painfully slowly, thanks to the murderous robot hanging opposite and above me.

As soon as the next section of metal was close enough, I grabbed it, hooking it with both hands and then a leg. The frame was so narrow here in general—less than an inch in width—but I spotted a metal strip that was just about broad enough to hide me. I quickly moved over to it, positioning myself out of view.

Only then could I check to see what was going on, and as I did, my muscles vibrated with tension and fear. The sentinel hadn't changed its position yet, and hadn't seemed to notice me, so I quickly pulled my lashes to reconnect them to a higher section of metal, trying not to let my hands shake too much.

I was in the process of fixing the last one when a shadow dropped down from the top of my vision. A second later, the chandelier shook violently, so much so that I threw my arms and one leg around its frame for fear that the lash ends wouldn't be enough to keep me on. My stomach lurched as the scaffolding continued to move, and I slammed my eyes shut and held on for dear life, convinced that the entire thing was already plummeting to the ground.

Several heartbeats of teeth-clenching agony later, the impact still hadn't come. I summoned up some courage and forced my eyes open, certain that I'd get a glimpse of the ground before impact.

But the chandelier was simply tilted to one side. And as I peered down across the ground, I saw why. The sentinel had jumped farther down the chandelier's frame, and was now level with my section of metal. It was clinging to it with one hand, peering over the edge. The cables connecting our section to the one above groaned, and suddenly I heard a sharp, high-pitched *twang twang twang* sound as strands of the metal rope began to snap under the extra weight.

Each sound made me flinch, but the sentinel merely glanced at them and then turned its attention back to the arena, clearly searching for its target.

And for a second, all I could do was gape at it, stunned by its presence and the implications of what its being here meant.

CHAPTER 33

There was only one reason that it could be here—the big mission that Jang-Mi had been talking about was the Tourney. Maybe she didn't know that, but I felt stupid for not putting her disappearance and the expedited challenge together. Whoever was controlling Jang-Mi meant to use her to try to kill off the competition.

Which meant that one of the candidates was supposed to win—and the sentinel was here to ensure that they did.

My heart skipped a beat as I thought about everyone I cared about in this arena: Maddox, Leo, Grey, my mother... hell, even my father! I might not miss him if he died, but Alex would be heartbroken, and besides, I couldn't let the sentinel do anything to hurt anyone, anyway. I had promised Tian that I would do everything I could to stop it without hurting it... and luckily, I still had the shockers on my wrist.

I just had to get to it.

The metal continued to quiver under my hands as more and more of the woven strands gave, and I realized that if the cables broke on the sentinel's side, those on my side would tear free immediately after, and the frame I was on would break off and fall. I needed to get off of this thing so I could find a way to get to the sentinel without killing it—before the sentinel took me down with the frame.

Tilting my head back, I looked for something—anything—close enough for me to latch onto.

I caught a fraction of movement on my left, saw the corner of an obstacle coming close—close enough that I was certain I could get to it with my lashes—and quickly pulled the lines back in. I was going to have to jump, and I needed as much power as possible.

I heard a feminine voice cry out, "Liana!", desperate fear clinging to it, but I ignored it as I exhaled sharply, tensing the muscles in my legs in preparation for the jump. It was now or never; if I stayed here, I risked being on the obstacle when it tore free. At least if I missed my target, the end result would remain unchanged: I'd fall down and die.

I inhaled deeply, set the lines to run free, and leapt out into the open space in front of me.

I shot forward, keeping my arms tight to my sides. My back was to the ground, but I didn't want to look—I was too busy looking for the obstacle that would save my life. I caught a glimpse of it, already moving away, and threw for it, my breath caught in my chest. The air started to whistle by as I began to fall, but my eyes remained on the lash end, transfixed as it flew away from me, dragging with it the line that would save my life as it streaked toward the dark, metallic structure.

The lash end hit the apex of its swing and began to fall—along with it my heart—closer and closer to the bottom edge of this new wall-like structure. I watched it, certain it was going to miss by inches.

Then it hit with a bright blue flash, just as the line reached its end. I jerked hard on the line, the shock rattling down my arm and making my elbow and shoulder feel like they were being pulled in two separate directions, but wrapped my hand around the line anyway, holding on for life itself while fumbling for the hand controls to reel me in. I went weightless for a second, and felt certain that the line would give, but it pulled with a snap, and suddenly I was twirling through the air in an uncontrolled spin.

I looked up, focusing on the line itself, and saw that it was dragging me closer to the edge of the hanging wall. It teetered for a second as I continued to spin around, and then I felt it give completely, throwing me free. There had been too much jerking on the line itself, and it had broken the connection of the bead. I

CHAPTER 33

cast my other line in a panic, but I was still spinning, and had no idea if I was even aiming in the right direction.

I shut my eyes and made my peace. *Dear God... Really? Really? This is how I'm going to die? I thought, at least, I'd figure out what the hell is going on here before the plug got pulled, but noooo... Also, can we discuss how not funny it is that I die from falling, given how much time I spent lashing in the first place? Yes, yes, irony, but screw you—this is just clichéd.*

And... since this is happening now... could you please see fit to strike that thing down and protect my friends and family for me, since I won't be able to anymore?

A second later, something struck my shoulder with enough force to make my flesh sting underneath. "Youch!" I shouted, reaching up to swat at the spot.

"It's me!" my mother called, and I stopped my hand just before I detached the lash line she had hit me with. I looked up and saw her, hanging from the bottom of the dangling wall I had just been attached to, one lash still connected. The gyros in her suit were already working, hauling me toward her—and her toward the obstacle. "I've got you," she said reassuringly, her eyes blazing with determination and concern.

I realized it had been her voice I'd heard screaming my name, and felt a moment of relief. She hadn't been about to let me fall. I let her reel me in, and threw a line of my own as soon as I was close enough, followed closely by a second one, just to be certain. My muscles remained tense until I had my boots on the flat surface of the wall, and I pressed close to it for a second, resting my sweaty face against the flat, cool metal in an effort to transfer some of the heat from my head and body into it.

"Liana!" my mother said, closing the distance between us, before reaching out to touch my face, her eyes scouring over me, looking for any injuries. She pulled me into a tight hug, and then let me go, her body radiating tension. "What was that thing?"

I twisted around as her question hit me, but I had lost track of the sentinel. I had to find it. Stop it before it hurt anyone.

"It's bad news," I replied. "C'mon, we have to stop it!"

"What?" My mother frowned and shook her head. "Sweetie, no. It's just a distraction, set up by the designers. We need to get you to the bells."

"Mom, no!" I said, grabbing her arm as she began to look around. "Listen to me! This thing, it's not under the test designers' control. It's... under the influence of someone else—likely the same people Devon was working with and who killed Ambrose. Someone who wants to kill all of the candidates here, except for the candidate they want to win."

My mother's brows drew together as she looked at me. She studied me for half a second, and then drew in a breath. "You're serious, aren't you? Scipio help us."

She looked around, and I followed her gaze, trying to figure out where exactly we were. I realized that the long, flat wall I was now riding was part of the rotating inner ring. My back was to the outer ring, and unlike many of the other obstacles, this wall structure didn't seem to spin. Being in the inner circle meant that the column was on the other side of this wall.

A column I wasn't going to get to: I was the only one here who had a weapon that could stop the sentinel.

"All right," my mother said a few seconds later. "We need to get up to the top of this wall if we're going to have any chance of spotting it."

I was already drawing back my arm, preparing to throw my line up the flat wall, when my mom reached out and stopped me. "We have to climb up the side of this one," she informed me, leaning back against her lashes and pointing. "This thing was built so that it'll flip as soon as any weight hits the top of it, but from the side, it'll stay still."

I glanced at my mother, grateful that she had seen and figured out this particular obstacle in the process of saving me. Then I thought about what she was saying, and saw that we also needed to separate, so that our weight wouldn't offset it. "You go up on the left, I go up the right?" I asked, and she gave me a proud smile.

"Absolutely."

I threw my line, this time toward the right edge of the wall, and swung onto it. I waited for my mother's "Okay," and then focused on the climb. I reached the top just as my mother did, and we made our way over to the central pole that connected the dangling wall to the ceiling.

As I moved, I searched for the sentinel. A flash of crimson caught my eye to the left, and I hurried to the pole, trying to see what it was through the twisting mass of the other obstacles. As soon as I reached the pole, another flash of crimson caught my eye.

Seconds later, I saw something small and dark—a chunk of one of the obstacles, perhaps—dropping from the air to the arena floor below, one edge glowing a molten red color that drew my eye like a beacon before it hit the ground. I looked back up and held still, watching the swinging mass of structures.

The sentinel slid into view, now attached to the corkscrew-like structure I had noticed earlier on the outer ring. Its arm was extended in a straight line, the crossbeam of its deadly bolt leveled at the structure swinging past it. At my father and Min-Ha, who were balancing on another wall-like structure which was spinning on the outer ring.

"We have to get to them," I said, but Min-Ha was already moving, racing toward the edge of their wall and leaping off in a swan dive, her lashes cutting through the air ahead of her, streaming toward the side of the corkscrew. "No!" I cried—but it was too late. She was already spinning through the air, shooting toward the sentinel, her long black hair waving like a flag of war.

The sentinel leveled its weapon at her, and I saw a fiery glint of crimson forming in the cross section of its jowls. Then it shot, a crimson beam cutting through the air, intersecting with Min-Ha's torso and tearing through it. The beam split into two around the bisected form of her body and continued on, stopping only when it hit the wall my father was on. The force of the blow shook the structure back and forth like a rag in the mouth of a dog playing tug-of-war.

My father stumbled forward, his arms wind milling as he tried to catch his balance, and then fell back, jerked off his feet. He fell, but was saved by the fact that he had attached a safety line to the wall itself. Min-Ha wasn't as lucky, and I looked away as the two pieces of her once-intact body hit the ground below, trying not to lose my stomach.

I looked around, waiting for some sort of alarm to go up to stop the Tourney, knowing that the Knights of the Citadel had just seen Min-Ha die, but nothing came. The drones were still there, watching, but there was no other sign of life, security, or even Scipio telling us to clear the field. Whoever was behind this had done something to stop us from getting help from the other Knights.

It was on me if I wanted to stop this.

My father hit the side of the wall... but then his line broke free, sending him plummeting down. I watched, helpless for a second, and then exhaled with relief when he threw his other lash, which connected. He hit the wall with a sharp cry of pain, and I saw him clutching the arm that he had used to throw the line. I was already moving, cognizant of the fact that my father

CHAPTER 33

was dangling free on a spinning structure easily thrown off balance, with a now-injured arm. My heart leapt into my throat as I realized it was swinging around, and that if he was carried forward, he would be in direct line with the sentinel again.

It would cut him in half like it had Min-Ha.

I watched the wall as it swung, studying it and the way it shifted back and forth while it was spinning, analyzing the distance. It was too far away to reach, and it didn't look like it would swing any closer before we slipped past. We needed to create at least ten more feet before we could jump it.

I looked down at the wall my mother and I were on. It was at least forty feet high, so if we could get it to start to spin, we'd have more than enough room to get there. There would be a point, toward the middle, where we would have twenty feet of extra room.

"Mom, help me," I said, pushing away from the pole and moving toward a point halfway between the center and the edge. "We're going to force this thing to flip so we can jump over to Dad together."

"On it," my mother replied, her voice tight with barely suppressed rage and sorrow at Min-Ha's death, and I felt the metal vibrating under my own feet as she moved into place, one equidistant from the middle and the edge, a mirror of my own position. I focused on my own task, knowing that we would only have one chance at this. If we failed, my father would be killed by the sentinel.

I threw my lash with a sharp pop against the wall, and then looked at my mom, watching as she threw down her own line on her side. She met my gaze and nodded, giving me the go-ahead to give the order. I looked back at the wall my dad was on, watching the spin, and then said, "Now."

My mother and I took a step forward into nothingness and

then spun, putting our backs to the outer ring to rappel down the wall. I landed a few feet from the top, my mother only a few feet below, and sure enough, the entire wall began to tip toward us and the outer ring. I rode it down, freeing one arm and turning around to lean outward, and watched the oncoming wall, gauging its approach versus the speed of our fall.

"Get ready," I shouted, spinning the free lash in my hand, winding it up. The wall swung even closer, and then seemed suspended in place for a moment. "NOW!" I shouted, throwing my lash. I caught a glimpse of my mother's line flying seconds behind mine, parallel with it, followed by two ghostly blue flashes where they connected to my father's wall.

Moments later we were swinging free across the gap, flying toward the wall. I bent my knees and landed hard on the surface, some thirty feet from the top, and looked down. My father had swapped out lines and was reeling himself up, but I could tell by the awkward angle of his arm that he had dislocated it on impact.

"Mom," I said, pointing him out, and my mother looked down and spotted him.

"I'll go get him," she said. "You just find that thing."

I nodded, and immediately began looking around. The corkscrew structure it had been on slid into view as the wall swung around, but as I scanned the curve of it, peering through the ladder that made up its internal structure, I realized it was gone.

My heart caught in my throat, and I carefully climbed up on my feet, throwing a lash down and connecting to the ledge I was perched on for more stability. I turned, my eyes scanning the moving structures and searching for any sign of the sentinel.

Instead, I noticed several crimson uniforms in the center of the arena, descending down the long, wide column at the center.

From this angle, I could see that the column ended in a flat surface with bells hanging at the edge, and realized that to reach them, they would have to swing in from underneath, and use their lashes to ring the bells.

I realized I would never get the chance. Dylan, Frederick, and Zale were already on the column, rappelling down. I wasn't sure if they were unaware that we were under attack by the sentinel—or if they were some of the ones secretly behind it. I just knew that in a minute or less, Zale would be at the bottom first, as he was the farthest down.

Not that it mattered. If I didn't stop the sentinel, more people than just Min-Ha would die. I had come here to win, but without the shockers on my wrist, the others would be defenseless. I was going to lose the Tourney, and everything was about to go to hell in a handbasket, but I couldn't let this thing kill everyone. Not when I had a way of stopping it.

I accepted this with a dull burn of anger, and continued to look around, searching for any sign of movement, and spotted Leo on the wall structure my mother and I had just come from, racing across the top of it toward me.

"Liana!" he shouted, pointing a finger down. I followed it, leaning into my line to hang over the edge, and saw the sentinel climbing like a cockroach up the side of the wall my mother, father, and I were on. It was nearly forty feet away from them, but as I watched, it paused and leveled the weapon at where my father was awkwardly trying to pull himself up. He hadn't even noticed the sentinel yet, and it was within fifty feet of him.

Neither had my mother—and she was still making her way down toward my father.

"Watch out!" I screamed, letting out the line and running along the wall, angling for the sentinel. I slapped my free lash end down just as a crimson blast cut beneath my feet, and tried not to think about what was happening with my parents. I had to pray that the blast missed. That my mother got there in time and got my father out of the way.

But most of all, I had to make sure that my aim was right. I couldn't let it take another blast at anyone.

I continued to race toward it, my toes barely touching the surface. At this point, I was falling more than running, but I needed as much momentum as possible. I threw my last line, my bead striking true a few feet ahead and above the sentinel's head, and then pushed off, surrendering my weight to the line. I extended my legs out and clenched my jaw tight, preparing for impact, as I dropped straight for the sentinel.

I braced, remembering what hitting it had felt like, and seconds later I struck, my knees and hips shaking from the force of the blow. I felt the sentinel break free, with a screech that kicked up sparks.

I didn't look down, but instead whirled around on my line, turning to face where I had last seen my parents, only to find an angry red slash where they had been hanging moments earlier. All that was left were two lines, cut clear in half, dangling where my parents had been.

34

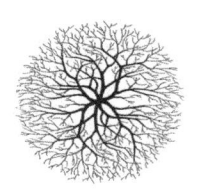

My panic at seeing them gone was quickly erased when I saw my mother dangling from a lash-line attached to the bottom of the wall, my father awkwardly holding her around her waist. They were doing their best to remain still, but their combined weight placed on that side was beginning to make the wall spin faster on its central axis.

My mother was fiddling with her hand control, and I realized that the strain of suddenly catching not only my father's weight but her own had damaged her gyro. It wasn't pulling them up. I quickly threw a lash down and jumped, angling for them. They only had two lines between them, the others cut in the sentinel's blast.

I had to help, or they would be sitting ducks.

"Liana, stop!" Leo shouted, and I jammed the hand controls, stopping myself with a jerk. I craned my neck up to see him swinging around the wall and lashing toward my parents. "The sentinel!"

I pushed a hand on the wall to spin around, and saw that the sentinel was in the process of climbing back up, its dark, metallic arms and legs somehow finding purchase on the wall's smooth surface. Its hood had fallen back, revealing the sharp lines of its angular, slightly humanoid face, and its eyes were glowing the same dark, angry red.

I quickly detached the line that I had thrown toward my parents and grabbed at one of the discs fixed around my wrist, clutching it between my finger and thumb, my heart pounding in my chest. If I could just get close enough to hit it directly...

Its head snapped up at me just as I wound back to throw, and its arm shot out, angling for me. My eyes widened, and I disconnected, lashing out with a leg and kicking off the wall. I tucked my legs to my chest as I pitched to the side, tumbling through the air, and caught a glimpse of a crimson line of fire passing just inches from where my legs had been before the world began to whirl on its axis.

I unlocked my legs, slowing my fall, and threw a line, aiming for where I sensed the wall was, relying on my intuition. It connected, and I let out some slack, not wanting to stop suddenly and present an easy target. I kept a tight grip on the disc pinched between my fingers and twisted my head up, searching.

The sentinel had resumed climbing, its focus now back on where Leo was currently reeling my father in. I watched as it leaned out, keeping one hand in a firm grip, and then leveled the weapon at them.

I threw, flicking my wrist and aiming for its outstretched arm. The disc was difficult to track in the air, though, and I clenched my teeth, watching as the sentinel began to tighten its hand.

CHAPTER 34

The disc hit the wall an inch below its arm, just as a crimson shot erupted from the end of its weapon.

I turned, a scream of warning in my throat, and saw the line cleave through the metal wall at an angle, carving a sharp line down that missed my father by mere inches.

And then my mother was falling, her arms and limbs flailing, and I realized that the beam had cut her line. I cried out, throwing my lash for her, but she was already beyond my reach. My breath caught in my throat as she fell through the air, plummeting down at terminal velocity, her hair flying free from her bun as the ground rushed up toward her.

A scream tore from my throat as I realized that there was nothing—no one—to stop her, and she kept falling, falling, falling...

I squeezed my eyes shut, incapable of watching her hit, but a soul-crushing grief crashed into my heart, and I felt it breaking, right inside my chest. Pain exploded into me as I realized that my mother was dead. She was dead. She was...

Murdered.

I screamed again. A deep-seated rage blossomed inside me as I thought of what the sentinel had just taken from me. There was no chance to tell her how I really felt, and I'd treated her so terribly after she'd shown me how much she cared! I'd spent so much time regarding her overtures with suspicion and disdain, and now I could never tell her how sorry I was for doing that.

My eyes snapped open, and I looked up, searching for the sentinel, only to find it inches from my face, its arm reaching out. I jerked back, dangling from my line, but it caught me around the throat and lifted me up, its red eyes glistening. Cold fingers tightened around my neck, and suddenly I grew lightheaded. It was cutting off the blood flow to my brain, trying to knock me out. Once it did that, it could just throw me off the side and be done with it. Then Leo and my dad would follow.

I couldn't let that happen, no matter what. I slid my eyes open, meeting its own in fiery defiance while I brought my hands together, grabbing for the bracelet. I tugged on the entire thing, ripping it off my wrist, and then slapped it down onto its face, bracing for death.

Seconds later, fire shot through my body as electricity arced off the bracelet, shooting tens of thousands of volts into the sentinel, and through it, me. My muscles locked up as a fine, high-pitched pain hit every nerve ending in my body at once, and my jaw clamped down. I barely registered the taste of blood in my mouth that signaled I had bitten my tongue, every organ in my body shocked into stillness.

Then the pain cut off suddenly, leaving me with only the sensation of falling, suddenly untethered from gravity as my consciousness slowly slipped away.

But not before I heard the sound of bells chiming in rapid succession, their beautiful song chasing me down into oblivion.

"Liana!" came a sharp voice, jolting me out of the darkness in which I had been encased. I drew back a fist before even opening my eyes, the memories of the sentinel rushing through me, but managed to restrain myself from lashing out when I saw Astrid kneeling over me, a concerned look in her eyes.

"Astrid," I said, and then swallowed, my voice coming out strangled and raw. My hands came up to touch my throat, and then flinched when I felt the bruises there. "What happened?"

"That's what I'd like to know," she said, standing up. I

winced as the light she had apparently been blocking appeared, and then looked around, trying to figure out where I was.

But moments later, Leo and Maddox were there, their eyes brimming with concern. "Are you sure you're okay?" Maddox asked, her green eyes raking me up and down.

"What happened?" I asked, not bothering to list the litany of complaints my body seemed to be experiencing. "Where are we?"

"Under the arena," Leo told me as he helped me sit up. I groaned as I moved, my muscles twitching violently under my skin. "You absorbed several thousand volts of electricity for one point eight seconds before I managed to yank you out of its grip. You should be in the Medica."

"Leo, my mother," I said, looking up at him, suddenly remembering watching her fall. "Is she—"

"I don't know," he replied honestly, his eyes brimming with remorse. "I'm so sorry, but I don't know what happened to her after she..."

He trailed off, and a shudder ran over me, sorrow stabbing deep. I drowned in it for several moments, feeling a hollow ache where my heart had once been. Something had reached in and scooped it out, and now there was nothing left but a raw, visceral pain that made it impossible to breathe.

Somehow, I managed to push past it, but it took me several shaky breaths, and Maddox and Leo felt compelled to hold my hands the entire time, as if trying to transfer some of their strength to me through the connection. I wasn't sure why, but it helped, and I swallowed back the tears and the searing agony, making my way to a place of clarity.

"The sentinel!" I said, looking at them. "Did I—"

"Kill it?" Maddox asked, and I nodded. "I don't know if you killed it. I didn't give it a chance to come back on. It was locked into place on the wall, and I managed to get to it and pulled the hard drive. The blast must've unlocked the cage on its neck, because I didn't have to do much to grab it. Nobody noticed, either; they were too busy trying to get you free from its grip."

Her eyes slid around the room as she spoke, but my gaze became riveted on her hand when it dipped into her pocket to reveal a clear plastic box filled with intricate crystalline features that had streams of lights pulsating through them. She only held it out for a second before hurriedly tucking it back into the pocket, which she zipped closed.

I watched her do it, and suddenly hated her for pulling the hard drive. I wanted the creature that had killed my mother dead and gone, not safe and sound and tucked away in her pocket. It took a moment, but I managed to remind myself that the code in there was important not only for finding the people behind the sentinel, but also because she was an AI essential to the Scipio creation process.

But Scipio help me, it was hard.

Beside me, Leo shifted and cleared his throat, and I looked at him. "The officials rounded us up right after Dylan rang the bells," he quietly informed me.

"*Dylan* rang the bells?" I asked, my brows drawing together into a tense line. "I thought Zale was closer."

"She caught up to him," Leo said.

"And beat the crap out of him and Frederick," Maddox added angrily. "But there seems to be—"

"Look, I didn't *see* it! I don't care that the drone saw me look over my shoulder!" Dylan's indignant screech cut Maddox off, and I pushed on my friends' shoulders, creating a gap that I could see through. It took a minute for my eyes to adjust—they were still sensitive from the electrocution—but when the blobs took form, I spotted Dylan standing with Astrid. She was gestic-

CHAPTER 34

ulating wildly, a wild and angry look on her face, while Astrid stood there calmly, her hands on her hips.

"Be that as it may, we need to show the vid to the Knights before the final vote is concluded," Astrid said. "Not to mention, I'm not sure the challenge results *should* hold up, considering the sentinel went ballistic on the course. Candidates are *dead*!"

Something sharp and hot stabbed into my heart, sending shockwaves of grief through me, but I summoned up a deep, ice-cold calm, trying not to get lost in the fact that my mother was one of those dead candidates.

Still, I wasn't exactly sure what they were arguing about. What didn't Dylan see? Why was Astrid insisting on uploading a vid capture to the server before the Knights had a chance to finish their voting?

Why was voting even happening? Why hadn't the whole thing been negated?

Anger burned in me as one more question hit me: why wasn't anyone telling me about my mother?

"That seems like the test designers' fault," Dylan snapped. "Not *mine*. I did what I was supposed to do. I completed the challenge. Just because I didn't see what was happening doesn't mean I wouldn't have stopped everything to help out! I would've! This is unfair!"

"When the results are in, you can lodge an official protest. Until then, sit down and shut up until it is your turn to make a statement. I want to get to the bottom of this."

Astrid's head turned to me as she said it, and I swallowed, realizing that everyone had seen me use that secret weapon on the sentinel, and were now wondering why I had brought an illegal weapon into the Tourney. I could feel Astrid's unspoken question pressing against my skin—had I known the sentinel was coming?

And for once, I wasn't sure how to answer her questions. All I knew was that Dylan had won the challenge, and with it, likely, the Tourney. She was popular with the Knights, even with me stealing command out from under her, and I doubted it would matter that I had stopped the sentinel. I had done so in a questionable way—one that put my integrity and honor into question.

My shoulders slumped as the realization came over me: I had lost the Tourney. And I hadn't died. Which meant Lacey would be gunning for me. I doubted I would make it back to the apartment before I found myself arrested, and with Dylan the soon-to-be Champion, I wasn't so sure she'd be understanding.

If she hadn't been behind the sentinel in the first place, that was. My stomach quivered with wonder, and I looked around the room, searching. My father was sitting in a chair, his gaze fixed on the floor, shoulders in a slouch. Grief and sorrow hung over him like a blanket, but all I felt was a deep anger at him for even daring to feel sorry for what had happened to my mother after the way he'd treated her. A part of me wanted to march over and scream at him for being so worthless, for not being there to catch her, to save her…

I blinked and looked away, not willing to give in to the urge. My father was a flawed man, that much was certain, but I couldn't blame him for what happened; I could only blame the people responsible.

Not that I'd ever get the chance to find out who they were. A deep resentment began to burn in my belly as everything that I had just lost set in—including any chance of getting my friends to safety, as well as the plan to save Scipio, or replace him with Leo. People were going to die as a result of my failure.

And there was nothing I could do about it.

I looked down at my hands, about to give in to my sorrow,

CHAPTER 34

when I heard a hushed, "I don't believe it," coming from a male voice to my right. I looked past Leo to see Zale sitting in a chair, gazing at the wall. I followed his eyeline, and stared blankly at a clock with the seconds counting backward from ten. Then my gaze dragged down to where my name and picture were sitting on top of the four-person list, with a 61% next to them.

Then I heard it, a deep, chanting sound that carried down through the layers of metal that separated us from the arena above, powered by multiple voices speaking as one.

"Honorbound! Honorbound! Honorbound!"

"Well how about that," Astrid said smugly. "Congratulations, Champion Castell."

READY FOR THE NEXT PART OF LIANA'S STORY?

Dear Reader,

Thank you for reading *The Girl Who Dared to Rise*. I hope it was as enjoyable to read as it was to write!

The next book in the series, Book 5, is called **The Girl Who Dared to Lead**, in which Liana has been named Champion, and her courage will be put to the test like never before... I'm extremely excited to continue this journey with you!

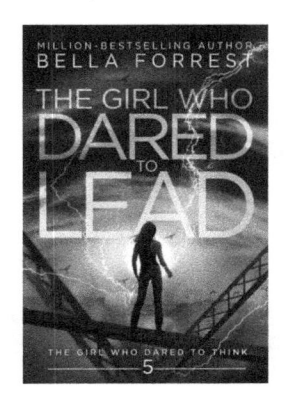

The Girl Who Dared to Lead releases **January 31st, 2018**. Visit: www.bellaforrest.net for details.

I'll see you there, back in the Tower...

Love,

Bella x

P.S. If you're new to my books or haven't yet read my **Gender Game** series, I suggest you check it out. It is where the Tower's story began and is set in the same world as *The Girl Who Dared* series—the two storylines complement each other.

P.P.S. Sign up to my VIP email list and I'll send you a personal heads up when my next book releases: **www.morebellaforrest.com**

(Your email will be kept 100% private and you can unsubscribe at any time.)

P.P.P.S. I'd also love to hear from you — come say hi on Twitter (@ashadeofvampire) or Facebook (facebook.com/BellaForrestAuthor). I do my best to respond :)

READ MORE BY BELLA FORREST

THE GIRL WHO DARED TO THINK
The Girl Who Dared to Think (Book 1)
The Girl Who Dared to Stand (Book 2)
The Girl Who Dared to Descend (Book 3)
The Girl Who Dared to Rise (Book 4)
The Girl Who Dared to Lead (Book 5)

THE GENDER GAME
(Completed series)
The Gender Game (Book 1)
The Gender Secret (Book 2)
The Gender Lie (Book 3)
The Gender War (Book 4)
The Gender Fall (Book 5)
The Gender Plan (Book 6)
The Gender End (Book 7)

HOTBLOODS
Hotbloods (Book 1)
Coldbloods (Book 2)

A SHADE OF VAMPIRE SERIES
Series 1: Derek & Sofia's story
A Shade of Vampire (Book 1)
A Shade of Blood (Book 2)

A Castle of Sand (Book 3)

A Shadow of Light (Book 4)

A Blaze of Sun (Book 5)

A Gate of Night (Book 6)

A Break of Day (Book 7)

Series 2: Rose & Caleb's story

A Shade of Novak (Book 8)

A Bond of Blood (Book 9)

A Spell of Time (Book 10)

A Chase of Prey (Book 11)

A Shade of Doubt (Book 12)

A Turn of Tides (Book 13)

A Dawn of Strength (Book 14)

A Fall of Secrets (Book 15)

An End of Night (Book 16)

Series 3: The Shade continues with a new hero…

A Wind of Change (Book 17)

A Trail of Echoes (Book 18)

A Soldier of Shadows (Book 19)

A Hero of Realms (Book 20)

A Vial of Life (Book 21)

A Fork of Paths (Book 22)

A Flight of Souls (Book 23)

A Bridge of Stars (Book 24)

Series 4: A Clan of Novaks

A Clan of Novaks (Book 25)

A World of New (Book 26)

A Web of Lies (Book 27)

A Touch of Truth (Book 28)

An Hour of Need (Book 29)

A Game of Risk (Book 30)

A Twist of Fates (Book 31)

A Day of Glory (Book 32)

Series 5: A Dawn of Guardians

A Dawn of Guardians (Book 33)

A Sword of Chance (Book 34)

A Race of Trials (Book 35)

A King of Shadow (Book 36)

An Empire of Stones (Book 37)

A Power of Old (Book 38)

A Rip of Realms (Book 39)

A Throne of Fire (Book 40)

A Tide of War (Book 41)

Series 6: A Gift of Three

A Gift of Three (Book 42)

A House of Mysteries (Book 43)

A Tangle of Hearts (Book 44)

A Meet of Tribes (Book 45)

A Ride of Peril (Book 46)

A Passage of Threats (Book 47)

A Tip of Balance (Book 48)

A Shield of Glass (Book 49)

A Clash of Storms (Book 50)

Series 7: A Call of Vampires

A Call of Vampires (Book 51)

A Valley of Darkness (Book 52)

A Hunt of Fiends (Book 53)

A Den of Tricks (Book 54)

A SHADE OF DRAGON TRILOGY

A Shade of Dragon 1

A Shade of Dragon 2

A Shade of Dragon 3

A SHADE OF KIEV TRILOGY

A Shade of Kiev 1

A Shade of Kiev 2

A Shade of Kiev 3

THE SECRET OF SPELLSHADOW MANOR

(Completed series)

The Secret of Spellshadow Manor (Book 1)

The Breaker (Book 2)

The Chain (Book 3)

The Keep (Book 4)

The Test (Book 5)

The Spell (Book 6)

BEAUTIFUL MONSTER DUOLOGY

Beautiful Monster 1

Beautiful Monster 2

DETECTIVE ERIN BOND (Adult thriller/mystery)

Lights, Camera, GONE

Write, Edit, KILL

For an updated list of Bella's books, please visit her website: www.bellaforrest.net

Join Bella's VIP email list and she'll send you an email reminder as soon as her next book is out. Visit: www.morebellaforrest.com

CPSIA information can be obtained
at www.ICGtesting.com
Printed in the USA
LVHW04s2316180618
581200LV00002B/207/P